The Riches of Mercy

C.E. Case

Supposed Crimes LLC • Falls Church, Virginia

Published in the United States.
Supposed Crimes LLC
Virginia

First Edition

ISBN: 978-0-9828989-2-5

www.supposedcrimes.com

This book is typeset in Goudy Old Style,
licensed by Ascender Corporation.

For Geonn

Prologue

Meredith was gazing at a picture of her kids when the call came. Forever afterward she would give the Lord credit for the connection between her sons' beaming faces, gazing up at her from the inside of her locker door, and all that followed.

The moment before, she had glanced at herself in the tiny mirror, making sure the nurse cap covered each of her brown locks, frowning at her ordinary face.

Then the voice came from behind her.

"Chopper en route," Colleen said, standing in the doorway.

A moment ago, Meredith made the whole hospital disappear, blocking everything out but her boys–no noise, no smell, no vision but them. With three words Colleen brought into her senses the green walls and antiseptic scents. Meredith checked her scrubs. Colleen held the door. They jogged together toward the emergency room.

Meredith was the lead nurse on duty, she had to be ready, though three more were on call. Being called.

"What's going on?"

"Car accident. Up on 40. They think she hit a deer."

Meredith hadn't realized she'd been fantasizing about alien crash landings or bank robberies gone bad until the phrase "car accident" dashed her hopes.

"She?"

Colleen shrugged. "One woman in the car. A civilian called 911, which put us on alert and sent out the highway patrol."

Meredith shook her head. Tarpley was a straight shot down I-40. "Must be bad if they're not using an ambulance."

"Guess so."

They reached the emergency room. A gurney was already in front of the glass doors. A policeman flanked it, listening to his walkie-talkie. Doctor

Wheeler, unshaven, with a polo shirt and slacks under his white coat, smiled when he saw Meredith.

"No aliens," he said.

"I heard."

"Just a lost little girl," the policeman said.

"Drunk?"

"It's always a possibility."

Meredith strained for the faint noise of the helicopter. Then she didn't have to strain. The roar became nearly deafening.

The parking lot had been cleared and was oddly desolate when the helicopter search light found it, and then there was a whirl of wind. Colleen and Wheeler pushed out the gurney. Meredith followed them, ready for whatever might come.

Six Months Earlier

Cold metal handcuffs pressed into Meredith's wrists. Standard procedure. She didn't think it was a particularly intelligent procedure. With her hands together in front of her like that, she could grab the gun off her escort. If she grabbed the gun, she could shoot herself.

The thought made her fingers itch.

She shook her head, trying to remind herself she wouldn't have worked so hard to keep her kids if she was just going to blow her brains out. All that effort, shame, and degradation had to be worth something—something more than her kids growing up in the shadow of murder-suicide. She wanted more for them, even if she suffered by continuing to live.

The bracelets still bothered her, even after all the hearings. She was captive. She was contained.

"You'll get to go home, Merry," the cop next to her said.

The cop she could shoot, if she wanted to, was being kind to her. He put his hand on her shoulder.

"Yeah," she said.

The judge, stern and tired, white and old, read with apathy the one paragraph decision. He wasn't the one who handled her criminal charges. They'd taken her all the way out to Goldsboro for the custody hearing. The trial would be even farther away. They were talking about moving to Charlotte for an unbiased jury. She doubted it would happen. Too expensive. Not for her.

She'd been so prepared for she barely heard the judge when he said, "I am loathe to take children away from their mother, especially when the record shows the children have thrived thus far. By all accounts, Meredith Jameison has done a fine job, and she is innocent until proven guilty of these charges.

The children have expressed a desire to stay with their mother, and while they're too young for that to be admissible, I see no reason not to honor their preferences. Full temporary custody is awarded, to be reviewed again in one year, or your trial date, whichever is sooner."

Meredith knew she should have cried when all eyes were on her, waiting to see her reaction as they had been for months now. She should be grateful. Relieved. But her heart was beating so hard in her chest it drowned out all emotion and robbed her of energy.

Her children's grandparents weren't crying, either. They were staring at her.

She'd taken their child away.

Now she was taking his children away, too. She glanced down at her hands, and then didn't move until the cop shook her shoulder and led her out.

"You looking forward to being back?" he asked.

He'd been best friends with her husband, Vincent, back in high school. Before the war.

Everyone had been best friends with Vincent. Not her.

Her eyes welled up. She rubbed at one, lifting her right hand, and dragging the left hand along with it.

"Yeah. Sure. Stay for supper?" she asked.

"Can't. Wouldn't be right, Merry. I just—I'd better not."

She nodded. No one liked to be seen with her. The implication an affair led her to this gave her a reputation. She could feel the red A burned into her forehead.

As if she would cheat on her husband. As if there was any opportunity in a town like this.

She hadn't seen the boys in four months. The grandparents took them, and hadn't paid her bail, and in a town where everyone knew what she did and judged her guilty, getting a loan for the bond took weeks. Once she started caring. She'd spent the first two months in the county jail not talking to anyone, just crying in fits and starts, wanting to die, wanting to explain.

Her lawyer did all the work on his own, but he'd done it, and when she saw what he'd prepared as her defense she wept again, because it was honest, and it was raw, and it might get her off.

But it wouldn't bring Vincent back.

"You think~" she started, coughed the sob out of her throat and started again. "You think they'll remember me?"

"Their momma? Of course. They've been crying for you every day, I hear."

She didn't ask her next question, though it came to her mind. "Do you think they'll remember their father?"

They took the exit off the highway for Tarpley. She impatiently wiped her face. Wouldn't do for the boys to see her upset. They'd think it was because of them. She had to be ready. She had to lie and tell them she was happy.

Chapter One

Meredith leaned her forehead against the glass. In the ICU chamber, a woman slept, her breathing even, watched over by the machine hissing every few seconds. The woman's eyelids weren't moving—no dreams at the moment for an induced coma. Her head needed to be examined every four hours. The gash across her forehead and cheek was swollen, squeezing one eye shut, making her mutant. Meredith glanced at the doctor beside her. He shared the same mousy brown hair she did, and the same lips. Sometimes gazing at him was comforting.

"What's the most dangerous injury in a car accident?" Wheeler quizzed, as if Meredith were going to be a doctor someday, in prison.

"Brain swelling."

"And the second?"

"Internal injuries can get overlooked."

"Yup."

"You're the one rooting around in her pelvis. See any swelling or bleeding?"

"Some. We put pins in her hip, and some stitches in her stomach. She's not going to be able to eat for a while."

Meredith regarded at the disfigured creature on the bed. "When can we wake her up?"

"Not until tomorrow, at least. Why, want to gaze into those beautiful brown eyes?"

"You already know they're beautiful?"

"Aren't they always?"

"You're too romantic for your own good."

"I'm trying to inspire you."

"I know where I'm going. There isn't any kinship in there. That's the whole point. Not watching my kids grow up. Not watching the seasons change. Not working."

"Merry," he said.

Her eyes stung. She pressed harder against the glass, to cool herself. She had a bad habit, everyone knew it, of caring too much about the trauma patients. Especially the ones from out of town, who were scared and out of place, who needed her the most. She gave her heart and her time and sometimes her money to them, but they always left and went back to where they came from. Just like this new Jane Doe. If she woke up at all.

Wheeler touched Meredith's back.

"There's circumstances," he said.

"There's facts."

"See, you're not a romantic." He pointed to the patient. "She could be a duchess. She could be a criminal. She could be Batgirl. We don't know."

"We don't even know her name."

Wheeler patted her back, and then walked down the hallway.

Meredith slipped into the room. She remembered the smell of blood~not alcohol, not burning flesh, only blood with an aftertaste of metal and gasoline~accompanying the woman into the emergency room. She'd been limp and lifeless, marred by the blood. Her leg~Meredith took a deep breath. Crush injuries were hard to think about.

She shouldn't, but no one was going to stop her, so she took the woman's hand in hers.

"Hey," she said.

The woman didn't move.

She breathed on her own, though, and if Meredith concentrated she could see a faint rise and fall of the chest. Surgery brought back a more lifelike tint to the woman's skin. Dark hair, thin, manicured nails, but beyond those features, Meredith could tell nothing about her. Duchess, maybe.

Meredith chafed the hand she held. She willed fingers to squeeze back. "There's something special about you. I just know it."

"Can you hear me?"

She could hear, but it took until the second reiteration for her to realize the voice was directed at her. The voice got louder and closer.

"Can you hear me?"

She wanted to tell the voices they were too loud. She tried to open her mouth. Her lips felt swollen. Twice their size. Hard. Like her face was made of bricks.

Something touched her hand. Cold fingers. She would have screamed in surprise, but her mouth continued to be uncooperative.

Stupid mouth.

"Squeeze if you can hear us," another voice said.

A woman's voice. A voice she thought she might have heard before. Okay, she was alive enough to be crazy. She focused all her brain power on her hand and flexed. Her hand, it seemed, was fine. Her fingers worked. She squeezed. Pain shot through her shoulder.

She needed to remember not to move the arm when flexing the fingers. Ouch.

The woman's voice again. "Move your index finger to the side twice."

Which finger was her index finger? She thought. She practiced.

"Good job," the woman said, and tweaked her finger.

She would have smiled, but her mouth was made of clay. This woman, whoever she or it was, some angel or future torturer, was her favorite creature in the whole world.

Her expression didn't change. Stupid mouth.

"Are you in any pain? Two for yes, four for no."

She inventoried. Except for her shoulder, she felt surprisingly good. Better than in her whole life. She focused. One, two, three, four.

"Are you tired?"

One, two.

"Do you see any light?"

Another realm entirely, past the clay mouth and the index finger. She investigated. Nothing, Darkness. They seemed to be closed. She tried opening them. No luck. The woman was certainly patient. She had no idea how long this inventory of senses was taking.

She focused. One, two, three, four.

"Thirsty?"

Reminded of the concept of thirst, her mouth screamed for relief. She moved her tongue. It resisted. Sandpaper and cotton and~blood?~filled her mouth, her throat, her stomach, all the way down to her toes, making them feel like dried paper.

One, two.

Metal touched her lips, and then ice chips touched her tongue, just enough to dampen. The taste of cold was as good. She crunched, barely moving her jaw. The best moment of her life. She swallowed. Pain seized her throat. She felt bruised, like someone had punched her in the face and neck repeatedly~oh god, had someone punched her? She seized.

"Hey, you're fine," the voice said, accompanied by a gentle squeeze against her fingers. "You're fine. Go to sleep. I'm praying for you."

She needed to be prayed for? Fighting terror, she managed two more twitches of her fingers before the darkness and silence took her back.

"Ma'am?"

The man's voice interrupted her sleep.

He was going to be a jerk. She knew already. There were little aches everywhere in her body. She twitched her fingers. Her hand was more uncooperative. Her shoulder hurt less.

There was light.

Blinding and white. She wanted to turn her face away, into the pillow underneath her head. She settled for making a face. Oh, how it hurt to make a face, but her lips moved. More water touched her lips. A sponge.

Maybe the woman was there. Her heart fluttered. The one who guessed her thoughts and prayed for her. She wanted so much to open her eyes, and see.

"Ma'am, can you hear me?"

If she never heard that question again, she'd live a happy life. The sponge pressed against her lips, and then retreated.

She rasped, "Yes."

Her lips cracked and it hurt.

"Can you open your eyes, please?" The woman's voice. If she could communicate, maybe she could have more of her voice, and less of the guy's.

She squeezed her eyes shut, and then let them open a slit. She winced against the light. The jerk waited. The woman waited. She tried again, and this time they opened enough to focus on the man with brown hair, wearing a lab coat.

A doctor? Why was~Oh. The pain~the aches~her shoulder~all became acute. She shuddered, which made her hurt more. Why hadn't she realized? How far gone~who was~

Her eyes must have widened, the woman spoke quickly. "It's okay. You're going to be all right. Breathe."

She breathed.

"You've been in a car accident. You're in a hospital in Tarpley, North Carolina," the man~the doctor~said.

She tried to remember. She only remembered a car in a carport, a sleek, black BMW. Warmth flooded her chest. She loved that car. She didn't remember buying it, or driving it. But she remembered she loved it.

"My car?" she asked.

"Can you tell me your name?"

She tried to stop thinking of the car and thought of herself. A dark-haired, tired young woman staring at a mirror flashed through her mind.

"Natalya," she said, sounding out each syllable.

The doctor seemed like a mirage in front of her, indistinct and waving. And frowning.

The image blurred, and then disappeared. That wasn't her name. Or even her accent. She turned away from the doctor and toward the woman's voice.

The woman stood there, also brown-haired, but shorter—had she been kidnapped by hospital pod people? The man she matched seemed indeterminately middle-aged, but the woman was young. Younger than her, if the gaunt vision in the mirror was to be believed. This brown-haired woman was too young to be another doctor. A nurse? A student intern? Brown hair swept into a bun at the nape of her neck, and eyes—Natalya wanted so much to see the woman's eyes.

The woman smiled.

Natalya smiled back. But Natalya wasn't her name. Drat. What was her name?

The pod people probably weren't going to be helpful or they would have told her her name, but she worked up all her energy and asked.

"Don't you have—driver's license?"

"It burned up in the fire," the doctor said.

She turned her neck so fast the tendons would never forgive her. Pain shot through her spine. She cried out. The woman cupped her neck and supported it, massaging the muscles. She moved close enough Natalya could really see her eyes—blue, crystal blue, open and giving.

The pain eased.

"You're not burned," the doctor said. "You had some smoke inhalation, but a Good Samaritan got you out before the EMTs arrived. Your engine was on fire. And then he just didn't get to it—there's bad cell reception out there so he flagged down a motorist to drive a few miles until they could place a call."

The man's accent was thick—not fake Charlotte politician thick, but honestly rich—farm boy thick—She must be in Eastern Carolina somewhere. She could sense the coastal plain in his words. What was she doing there? She'd been going~where had she been going?

"Where did you go to medical school?" she asked.

"UNC."

Definitely a jerk.

She tried to nod, but couldn't. She scrunched her face into an expression of condemnation.

"Very funny. Do you know where you came from? What you were doing?" he asked.

The woman's hands left her neck, but smoothed her cheeks before retreating.

Natalya tried to remember who she was. And what her name was. Flashes~Colonial pillars, fireflies, the Charlotte skyline, the Biltmore estate~a class trip to Washington, D.C. where she'd gotten in trouble for drinking with the boys in their hotel room~A man, wearing a suit, grinning like a slick good old boy.

Not John Ashcroft~who?

The doctor frowned.

"I think I'm an attorney," she said.

The man nodded.

The other woman gasped, then shook her head to dispel the glances Natalya and the doctor gave her.

"Is my car okay?" Natalya asked.

The man took her hand gently and sat next to her. "I'm afraid not."

She closed her eyes.

Chapter Two

"Her reflexes are good. She isn't paralyzed," Meredith said, watching Natalya through the glass.

"And I'll bet she has health insurance," Wheeler said.

Meredith rolled her eyes.

"If she's really a lawyer."

"She is. She seemed so certain. And I know~"

"A hope is forming. Not good. Do you recognize her, Merry? Is she your lawyer?"

She sighed and pushed away from the glass. "You old fox. Don't you ever watch the news?"

"Too depressing. I'd rather be out with my dogs."

She dragged Wheeler out of intensive care and through the general ward. Sick people in the waiting room turned to them hopefully, and then ignored them when Meredith pointed at the TV.

News 14 showed the weather.

Wheeler glanced at Meredith. "So, it's sunny. It's nearly summer, Merry."

"The crawler, Hank."

He squinted, and read, mumbling, "...for Natalie Ivans enters its fourth day. Police are dragging Lake Wylie for a possible body. She's the state's lead attorney for the prosecution against Mike Roland..."

"Natalie. Natalya," Meredith said.

"And Roland? The guy who drowned his wife?" Wheeler asked.

"Allegedly."

"And they think he knocked off the prosecution? That's. Wow. That's almost like alien abduction."

"More than a car crash. They don't know, I guess," Meredith said.

"She was just on her way to the beach in her fancy BMW that she's obsessed with and hit a goddamn deer."

Meredith raised her eyebrows.

"Sorry. Jesus." He took out his wallet and handed her a dollar bill.

She tilted her head.

"Christ." He took out two more dollars. She put them in her pocket.

"You know I have to request dollar bills at the bank now? My banker thinks I'm seeing a stripper."

Meredith winked.

The weather segment ended.

Natalie Ivans' visage filled the screen as the lead story began.

With Natalya's face bruised from the steering wheel and her body made into a pretzel from the car flipping, she looked nothing like her picture. They'd shaved most of her hair. They'd barely seen her eyes.

The television showed a city I.D. badge picture--an angry-looking woman with black hair loose and past her shoulders, and then rotated to a DMV photo with the same expression, and then a candid shot from some sort of party. Natalie was smiling in the photo, leaning on the arm of someone just out of frame.

A sheriff's face replaced the images and reported Natalie's description. Her age--33--jolted Meredith, who thought the woman in the hospital bed was much younger, and the woman in the photographs seemed older.

The sheriff explained after 48 hours, hope was unrealistic. Natalie Ivans never checked into her rented beach house. Her car was missing. Her cell phone was off. Her cat was being taken care of by a friend.

"Well, I'll be," Wheeler said.

"We should probably call the police."

"Yeah. And then see if we can get in contact with her family." Wheeler ducked back into the hallway.

Meredith stayed to watch the end of the news report. The on-scene reporter mentioned Natalie's background. There were no parents to contact, no boyfriend or spouse, no leads in her townhouse in downtown Charlotte. Nobody cried on television for Natalie's tearful return. If Roland hadn't been on the front page of the Charlotte paper every day for a year and a half, no one would have even noticed Natalie was gone.

So nice a murderer could be so helpful.

Alleged murderer, Meredith corrected herself, her chest constricting.

Despite being a suspect in a prosecutor's disappearance, Mike Roland was a free man. Meredith hadn't followed the case beyond the nurses' gossip in the locker room, but seeing him in handcuffs from stock footage from his original arrest filled her with dread. She glanced away.

The conversation of the waiting room seeped through her—worried voices, sad voices, deflecting away from whatever brought them individually to the intensive care ward. Together, they could hate Mike Roland.

"You think he did that lawyer?"

"He ain't got the guts. She probably just went nuts. You know, like Anne Heche."

"Or maybe she's a runaway bride, on up from Georgia."

"I think she just realized she couldn't win against a man like Roland and ran with her tail between her legs. Arf!"

"Nah, I think he drowned her, just like the other bitch. They should dredge Lake Norman next."

Meredith shook her head. She left them to the conversation and the blaring television and pushed through the door.

Natalya stared at the Jell-O on the tray in front of her. She shook the tray. The Jell-O jiggled. They wanted her to eat it? She felt like throwing up. Stupid pod people.

"Your name is Natalie Ivans. The district attorney is coming to see you," Wheeler said.

"Harry?"

She could remember Harry. She could remember she was Natalie Ivans, assistant state prosecutor working out of the Charlotte regional office. She could remember her apartment and her car and what her computer background at work showed. She remembered she was dull. She sighed.

"Yes. Harold Taylor. Do you remember what happened?"

She shook her head.

"Do you remember heading down to the beach?"

"Yes. It was just for the weekend. Two days, before I had to go back and the defense case would start."

"They've postponed while they searched for you."

"Searched for me? Why?"

"You were found Saturday morning."

"Worked late Friday night," she said.

Wheeler nodded, and said, a little too carefully, "It's Wednesday."

"What? Jesus Christ."

He hesitated. "You weren't in a coma. You were just—out. We kept you lightly sedated to encourage you to stay unconscious, so you'd heal. It's working."

"It's working."

"Your shoulder is broken, two ribs are cracked, and we removed~well, we'll get to that later. But you're going to be all right. Sturdy little car."

"I owed a fortune on it. And it was used. You wouldn't believe what I paid."

"You seem to be fixated on the car."

Natalie shook her head. "I don't know why. It was just~there with me, at the accident. I don't remember. But it was there. I was there. My purse was there. My cat—Oh, my cat. I just left her with some food and~"

"They're taking care of her," Wheeler said.

"Who is?"

"I don't know. But she was on the news."

"My cat was on the news?"

A few days ago~no, a whole week ago—she'd been an entirely different person. One not confined to a hospital bed in the middle of nowhere. Making it to the beach would have been preferable, she decided. She'd already be back in court.

"The whole state's been searching for you," he said.

"Everyone wants to be famous. What about the trial?"

"Postponed. But picks up tomorrow now since we've called Charlotte. It'll continue without you, I guess."

"With Rich instead. He'll bore them to tears. And he under-objects."

"How do you feel, Natalie?"

She assessed, and then met his gaze. "I guess I feel...kind of awful. I feel guilty making everyone worry. I feel bad missing work. I'm angry I'm stuck here, and that this happened, and it's really inconvenient."

"Natalie, Natalie. How do you really feel?" he asked.

She snorted.

"Eat your Jell-O. It'll help. Really." He got up.

"Hey, doc? When you said I wasn't in a coma. You were going to say something else. What?"

"Oh, just~We don't think much of cursing around here."

Her eyes widened.

"Think nothing of it. It's just the nurses." He left, closing the door behind him.

"This place is damn creepy, pod person!" she shouted at the door.

Lightning didn't strike her.

The Jell-O, though, watched her every move.

Chapter Three

Sedation made Natalie's head heavy. She couldn't think clearly. She wanted to oppose the drugs, just long enough to think about something, but she was afraid of pain. She stayed awake long enough to eat or answer questions when they made her but she didn't have the strength or the focus to observe her surroundings.

The generic nature of the hospital room didn't help. The interesting things were at the edges.

Her eyes hurt.

She noticed the closer things they tried to hide–her leg under the blanket, framed in metal, like she'd caught it in a bear trap. Her hip and belly had surgical lines that were to be bandaged every four hours.

They told her what her name was. Scary more than embarrassing. But now she could remember everything except the accident–she could even remember driving down the highway with the BMW's convertible top down, her hair wrapped in a scarf to keep it from blowing in her eyes. Her eyes stinging anyway. Her mouth watering for the first scent of salt in the air.

But she remembered nothing else until the darkness and the voices in the hospital. The doctor–Doctor Wheeler?–told her there'd been a deer.

She couldn't see a deer. But she remembered Roland's face.

The bastard.

She hadn't been seeking any spotlight. She'd just wanted a steady job that didn't require eighty hours of work for twenty years to get anywhere. The state prosecutor's office had been fine, even at a post outside of Raleigh, which meant no upward mobility. Still, she had a steady job, and overworked meant fifty to sixty hours a week, when there was a big case.

There wasn't often a big case. She was just doing her time in the trenches right after law school, prosecuting drug felon after drug felon, before moving onto domestic violence, and then onto sex crimes. High profile murder was not her job. At least putting rapists away gave her some feminist satisfaction. And the cases were complex and involved enough she felt person-ally involved. Something to live for.

"You're taking the Roland case," Patrick said, coming into her office and announcing it without preamble.

"I don't want the Roland case. I've got an FBI thing. Can you believe they're actually questioning the bust?"

"They're defense attorneys. That's what they do. But someone else can do it. An intern~"

"You think an intern can do my job?"

"Paralegal?"

She shot him an annoyed look.

"Nat," he said, sitting down across from her desk.

She raised her eyebrows.

He sighed.

She put her pencil down. "This is the case of the year. And it doesn't involve Duke. Thank God. You've got to be shitting yourself for this."

"I have to recuse myself, Natalie."

"What? Why?"

He studied her pencil.

She ran her fingers through her hair and frowned at him. He looked sad, and tired, and she wondered for the first time just how close to retire-ment he was.

"Roland~he's a friend of mine, Nat. Not just a guy I know at parties, I schmooze money from, I see at the golf club. An actual, real friend. Our kids play together. We're from the same alma mater. Roland~he's a good guy."

A sickening, twisting feeling came in Natalie's stomach. She picked up her pencil. "You don't think he did it?"

"I don't know." Patrick turned away, and his eyes were watery. He folded his hands. "I guess he did. I guess~we arrested him. But Jesus, Nat. I can't do this."

"Okay. Okay, I get it. Why me?"

"You do your job, but you're not an asshole about it. I can't stand to see anyone out for blood. Rodriguez~" He sighed.

"Can be a prick on high-profile cases," Natalie said.

"And you're qualified. It's out of your zone, but not out of your rank."

"Thanks. I guess. I'm sorry, Patrick."

Patrick leaned across the desk and said, "Make sure he pays for what he did." He squeezed her hand.

She covered his with hers. "Okay. Don't worry about it."

But when he got up and walked away, his posture showed he'd be worrying about it for the rest of his life. And she had another reason to hate Roland.

Meredith leaned her forehead against the glass. This would be the last night she'd see Natalie from this particular angle. Natalie was healing her way out of the ICU. She was talking. The color in her was getting brighter. Meredith was relieved she wouldn't die, but relief hadn't eased any of her apprehension. She didn't think it was a coincidence such a powerful attorney ended up in Tarpley. Meredith wouldn't have expected a woman~not this broken, not this seemingly bitter~but she had been searching for a sign.

Praying so hard.

Whenever Natalie caught her passing by the window, Natalie offered up a radiant smile that only twisted the knots tighter inside Meredith's stomach.

This gift from God. She wasn't sure what to do with it besides heal it and look after it. She knew not to try anything more, or hope for anything more, than having this one person in all of Tarpley that looked at her with warmth, not pity and studied her with curiosity, not condemnation.

She wasn't ready for this test. Not yet. Not so soon. But God brought this creature via helicopter right to her and Meredith couldn't deny that kind of sign.

Not anymore.

"You awake?" A nurse asked Natalie, coming into the room. She carried pills. Sedatives, Natalie hoped. And a glass of water and a newspaper.

"Thank God."

"Are you in pain?" The nurse came closer. Her badge read Teresa.

"No, I was just thinking. And~You're the first person who isn't white with brown hair. I thought I'd been abducted by very bland clones."

Teresa chuckled. "Wheeler and Merry are cousins. Distant cousins. Not in the Southern sense. Well, maybe a little. You probably understand."

"Everyone knows each other around here?"

"Of course. Merry sat two seats down from me in elementary school. I tutored her in math."

"Charlotte isn't like that."

"You grew up there?"

"My parents were from Pittsburgh, but you know, the economy."

"Yeah, Charlotte is full of transplants. The bases down here bring in all kinds of foreigners, too~" Teresa stopped herself. "Sorry."

Natalie grinned.

Teresa put the pills on the tray. "Let me tell you why you need to take these, girl."

"You could tell?"

"I can always tell. Confusion lies close to the surface."

Natalie sighed.

"You're tired, right?"

"Yes."

"And don't feel much like moving."

"Yes."

"And you want to think about everything. How you got here, where you're going, what the hell is up with your leg."

"And my hip."

"You've got to sleep. You're a big-time lawyer. You're going to keep yourself up all night. You're going to seek all the angles. So. This is the off-switch."

"For how long?"

"We have you scheduled for three more nights, but if you're good, we might make it two."

"And then~" Natalie's eyes filled with tears, unbidden. Teresa was right~she felt chaotic, emotional, terrified. She didn't want to feel like this all night, for hours in the darkness. "And then will they tell me what's wrong with me?"

Teresa put her hand on Natalie's shoulder. "First thing in the morning."

Natalie took her pills.

"Good, good. Now, as your reward, I brought you the paper. You're on the front page."

"Oh, come on."

"And so's your car."

Natalie grabbed the paper.

Teresa laughed. "They said you'd like that."

Natalie's fingers traced the image of her crumpled BMW. Her grief overwhelmed the shame she knew she was supposed to be feeling. She'd been inside. Maybe thrown out. She felt nauseous. The destroyed machine was like an extension of herself~a visualization of her insides. Not pretty.

"You going to be all right with your paper?" Teresa asked.

"Yes. Thank you. Hey," Natalie said, glancing up, forcing herself to put the paper down. "When is Merry scheduled?"

"She'll be here in the morning. Everybody loves Merry."

"I love you, too, Teresa."

"Everyone loves the Candyman. And hey," Teresa said, going to the door. "Merry needs a good lawyer."

Natalie raised her eyebrows, but Teresa waved and left, leaving Natalie to wonder why a nurse she'd known for two days needed a lawyer. And why, after such a short period of time, Natalie wanted to help her.

Must be the drugs.

She studied the front page. She started to read the article on herself, but by the second paragraph her eyes were too heavy to hold open and her head threatened to give her a headache if she tried anymore. The great thing about hospital beds, they were always ready to let her sleep. She didn't even have to lie back down.

Chapter Four

"Ready to see your favorite patient, Merry?" Wheeler asked.

Meredith's face grew hot. "She's not my~I treat all my patients equally."

"How noble."

She frowned.

"We're delivering the bad news. She may need you to make her feel like your favorite patient."

"I know the drill." Needed in a crisis and then forgotten afterward. Caring wasn't lying, even if it was brief. She'd wanted to do this. She made it her life's work. And caring for the boys. Those two tasks gave her life balance.

Wheeler put his hand on her shoulder.

Meredith glanced at the door.

A tall, dark, and handsome stranger literally dropped from the sky. Different, somehow, than the other patients coming and going. The ones focused on their own lives. Natalie was present. Meredith wanted to tell Vincent how weird it all was. She sent him a prayer. Then she took a deep breath and nodded at Wheeler. They went into Natalie's room.

The breakfast tray lay across Natalie's lap. Dry toast with marmalade and ice water. The marmalade came from Colleen's aunt's farm. Meredith felt like sharing the fact with Natalie, but didn't, and just trailed after Wheeler to the bed.

"How many patients are at this hospital?" Natalie asked Wheeler.

"About thirty. We have fifty beds."

"Wow," Natalie said.

"Wow." Wheeler answered.

A pang went through Meredith's heart as Natalie struggled to get her bearings. Meredith wanted to take her hand and explain everything. But she couldn't. This was Wheeler's burden.

He sat down beside Natalie and put papers on her bed.

Natalie raised her eyebrows. She let Meredith take the breakfast tray and set it on a side table.

"We talked to your insurance folks this morning, everything's going to be all right," Wheeler said.

Natalie's eyes flickered toward Meredith's. Meredith met her gaze and smiled. Natalie gave her a faint smile back.

Meredith pulled a second chair up to Natalie's bed, sitting beside Wheeler, down near Natalie's knees. Natalie wouldn't have to turn her head much to see either of them. They'd done this a hundred times.

Meredith looked at her hands.

"How was breakfast, Natalie?" Wheeler asked.

"Was it real?"

"It wasn't a figment of your imagination. Call me Hank if you want. Do you think you imagined it?"

"I'm not calling my doctor, Hank, and I'm not having hallucinations." Natalie said.

Meredith nearly laughed.

"Dr. Henry?" Wheeler asked.

Natalie picked up the top paper.

"It's time to give you a full assessment of your injuries and your recovery time," Wheeler said.

Natalie's face grew pale. She blinked rapidly. Merry leaned forward. She knew nausea when she saw it. She knew pain.

Wheeler waited.

"Okay," Natalie finally said.

"You were out for four days, you know that. I'm glad to see you've recovered so well from the anesthetic."

Natalie nodded.

"During that time, you had two surgeries. The first after you were medevaced in—"

"You have a helicopter?"

"The state does. They took care of it. We put you down in the parking lot. People are still talking," he said.

Meredith was still thinking about it; how the first spotlight shined on the pavement; how small and still and bloodied Natalie had been.

Natalie didn't respond.

Wheeler's expression sobered. "The first surgery was part of your triage. We put the pins in your hip to keep your midsection from collapsing. We took out your appendix, part of your spleen, and assessed your intestines. And we tried to stabilize your crushed leg. But we couldn't devote much time to it, because we were focused on making sure you didn't have any head or neck trauma."

"My neck hurts. A good sign, right?"

Meredith nodded.

"You pulled just about every muscle in your body, and it's going to be a couple of weeks until we can see if there's any real lasting trauma on your spine. But you're mostly okay," Wheeler said.

Natalie nodded again. She swallowed.

Meredith took Natalie's hand.

Natalie exhaled, and then as the silence gathered in the room, tensed, her fingers tightening on Meredith's. "There's more?" she asked.

Wheeler took a deep breath and said, "We did a second surgery on your leg to repair tendons and make sure the blood could flow properly. The swelling was more than we would have liked. I don't know if we're going to have to do more~I'll talk to you about that in a moment. But Natalie, even though you aren't paralyzed, I don't know when you'll be able to walk again."

Natalie glanced away.

Meredith squeezed her hand.

Wheeler said, "Or how things will go. It'll be rough, whether you get full mobility back or not. We're also looking at only sixty to eighty percent recovery of motion in your right shoulder. You should still be able to write. Continue as an attorney."

"But my leg," Natalie said, in a small voice, gazing down. Meredith's heart broke. Natalie held her fingers.

Wheeler said, "Only time will tell. Beyond that, there's going to be a pain issue."

Pain was such an ugly, four-letter word.

Wheeler said, "We can't keep you on these kinds of drugs forever. There are other kinds of drugs, though, and we may be looking at lifetime treatment for chronic pain. We won't know until you start healing. It's going to hurt."

Natalie's eyes filled with tears. She blinked them away, and turned to the wall opposite them, at a poster of a cat hanging from a tree.

Already, nurses and therapists moved Natalie's limbs, re-bandaged her, changed her clothes, and washed her and shuffled around her. Contact would only increase in Natalie's near future. By exponential factor, when they started teaching her to put weight on her legs again. Lying for nearly a week in a hospital bed hadn't done her body any good, even as broken as it was.

"What kind of pain have you been in before, in your life? Can you recall any instances?" Wheeler asked.

Natalie exhaled. She slowly turned her head back to meet Wheeler's gaze, her hand slack in Meredith's. She said, "I broke my arm one summer, when I was ten."

"Tell me about it," Wheeler said.

Natalie swallowed. "I remember--Really?"

"Yes."

Natalie said, "I remember lying in the grass, smelling the fresh summer clippings around me. I was trying to breathe--it was hard--hard to breathe through the pain. I remember my friends screaming out for my mother, and trying to breathe."

"What happened next?" Wheeler asked.

"I guess after a minute or two in the grass it got easier. My mother drove to the emergency room and they numbed the arm. I don't remember the recovery, the cast, or anything else. I'm sorry. Just the long, aching moments in the grass."

"All right. By the way, your insurance wants to transfer you up to Duke Medical Center." Wheeler said.

"I'd rather stay here," Natalie said.

Meredith's hand involuntarily tightened on Natalie's. She glanced down, her relief unprofessional, shame burning her cheeks. Her heart pounded in her ears. She prayed Natalie wouldn't notice her reaction. She prayed Natalie, too, saw some cosmic reason she'd been sent to Tarpley.

"It's just as well that you do. Transport would be painful. We're going to have one of their specialists come down and examine at your leg and your neck for you," Wheeler said.

"Thanks--Doctor Henry."

He nodded. "Sign these?"

Natalie reached for the papers, and grunted when her shoulder wouldn't let her cover the distance. Wheeler moved them closer, and then took her elbow to cushion her weight.

Meredith let go of her hand.

Natalie signed her life away to Blue Cross Blue Shield. She rubbed at her eyes.

"Are you all right?" Meredith asked.

"Just thinking about my cat. One of the maintenance workers found her in a city sewer and brought her to the government building. She was just a kitten then. Muddy and beautiful."

"She's fine," Meredith said. "I talked to~Susana?"

"My next door neighbor," Natalie said.

Wheeler took the papers. "See? Just fine. I'll come by tonight, when you've processed this all. Write down your questions as they come to you. We'll go over them."

Natalie nodded.

Wheeler patted Meredith's back and left.

Meredith sat on the edge of the bed and wiped Natalie's face with a cool cloth. "You all right? That's a lot to take in."

"I don't know."

Meredith tapped her cheek with the cloth to get her attention. Natalie met her eyes.

"We'll get through this," Meredith said.

"We will?"

"Stick with me."

She said the words the same way to Natalie as she would to a geriatric man facing a liver transplant or a little boy with a pencil up his nose, and the words had the same effect. Natalie relaxed.

Merry sat back. "You've eaten your breakfast and heard the talk. It's nap-time. When you wake up, everything will be different."

"Promise?"

"I promise."

Chapter Five

An attorney called ahead to the hospital to see what was to be done about the cat. He got a hold of Wheeler, who passed him to Meredith. Meredith listened abstractly to his tale of woe about his children's allergies and Natalie's strange and distant neighbors. Susana had stopped answering her door. The rest might be cat-murderers for all he knew. It was this or the kennel. He pleaded, but his voice also held authority. He brought the cat carrier with him as he drove down to see Natalie.

Meredith met him in the lobby and received the cat, unable to make it anyone else's problem. The cat's name was Hollingsworth. The attorney, twice her age, took her hand and introduced himself as Patrick. Natalie's boss. Meredith tried to picture Natalie with him at some bland office in the city. She took the cat home and let Patrick go on his way.

She only had a cat once before. An outside cat that strayed too close to her family home. She'd fed it. She'd bought cat food with her own money for weeks until her father caught her. He told her they were a sign of the devil. The cat was trying to seduce her—already she kept secrets for it

She'd been so ashamed she never thought about cats. A dog, maybe. But Vincent was afraid of dogs. Now, God sent her a second cat, by way of a Charlotte attorney.

And a horrific accident.

She didn't know if it was good or bad, temporary or permanent, or if it would change her. She told herself she was just babysitting for a stranger. But when she knelt next to the cat and gazed into its wide, blinking blue eyes, and felt its purr under her fingers when she stroked the long, grey hairs, she figured He had a hand in it somewhere.

If the cat needed her, well, she had love to give. Her neighbors didn't much talk to her. Instead she got hard stares if anyone happened to be out in the neighborhood when she drove through. Sometimes her boys waved at the people they saw. No one waved back.

Even Mrs. Cranston, her babysitter, didn't speak to her. Though she took Meredith's money. At least she was kind to the children.

At work no one seemed to know her anymore. There were moments with Colleen where everything felt like it was before, when Vincent was still alive, when the boys were just infants, and everything at work felt right. But Colleen would back off of those moments before Meredith would.

Aside from her children and a stranger who didn't yet condemn her, Meredith had nothing. So when the cat rubbed against her hand, seeking more, she didn't have the strength to resist.

"Where did you come from?" she asked.

The cat merely circled her ankles and stretched out for another touch.

She wished she had more faith.

Natalie missed her life. She missed her city. With each long, slow, pain-filled day passing, the accident felt less like a horrible inconvenience and more like her whole life was altering.

She only talked to doctors and nurses. The reality of her empty life was sinking in, and it made her feel terribly cold. She trembled and reached for nurses with icy fingers. She slept endlessly.

Since Wheeler told her about her leg, she preferred to sleep. She would float, at ease and dreamless, for hours. No pain, no past, no future. And then she would wake up, and the panic would set in~always within the first minute. She'd burned through a week of sick leave. She only had two more left.

Roland's trial restarted. The newspapers reported the defense team's argument was making inroads now that Natalie Ivans' steely, cold gaze wasn't there to thwart it.

That was how they thought of her. She wanted to dwell on it, but her head still hurt most of the time and all she could really to do was sleep again.

In this early afternoon, for the first time since waking up in her new life, she had a visitor. Theresa brought Patrick into her room. He'd driven down from Charlotte.

"How's the case?" she asked. She let him kiss her forehead, unable to reciprocate. She felt limp and useless in the hospital bed. Not even her brain worked, and she was starting to get tired again.

"Screw the case," he said.

"Give me a dollar."

"What?"

"They don't like you to cuss around here." She lowered her voice. "I think it's a like, Christian hospital."

Patrick glanced around furtively. "Eastern Carolina. Jesus. A good reason I didn't go to school down here."

"Oh, that's why?" she asked.

"And I thought Atlanta would be really exciting."

Natalie'd worried about what he'd say when he saw her like this, but he was just himself, reminding her of home. She could be herself, too. She could slip into the patterns of her life for the past year, and feel like everything was normal.

"Was it?" she asked.

"Hot."

"Patrick, tell me about the trial. I'm going crazy. I'm atrophying."

"We're hoping you'll be back before closing. It'll have an impact on the jury, to see you strong and~well, vengeful."

"I~I can't, Patrick. My recovery is going to take months."

"Months?" He paled.

She clenched her hands together. "I don't know what I'm going to do."

"It was just a car accident, Natalie. It's not the end of the world. We'll take Casey's car and let you use it as a loaner until you get all this sorted out."

"I'm not taking your kid's car."

"Nat~"

"Please. I'm not ready for much."

"Can I get you a computer?"

"Maybe soon."

"How are you?"

His be-okay tone persisted.

"They don't think I'm going to walk again." She felt like she was going to throw up.

"Oh, God. I didn't~I'm sorry, Nat."

She glanced back.

He tried not to look at her, tried to be brave and see her at the same time. If she ended up disfigured, or limping, or worse, everyone would be seeing her the same way for the rest of her life.

"Most of me will heal. They scooped out some of my insides," she said.

Patrick coughed. He'd always been too sensitive for bravado. He was a nice guy. He didn't cope well with hard edges. Even his job made him nauseous.

She changed the subject. "How's Nancy?"

"Oh." He leaned over and opened his bag, and pulled out a teddy bear wearing a beret and handed it over. "Nancy got you this."

She accepted the bear.

He pulled out a bag of M&Ms. "And the kids got you these. Not sure what you're eating."

"They cook for me."

His eyes widened.

She nodded. "Really. Homemade."

"Wow."

He glanced around, politely. She followed his gaze. No flowers, no cards, no books.

"Natalie, you know you're family." He took her hand. "You are. I just wish you had more. We're taking up a collection at the office, but I'm supposed to, uh, report back on how you're doing and tell them what you need. Everyone asks me every day. God, Natalie."

She didn't say anything, just kept staring at the bear, until her face stopped hurting, and the tears retreated.

He left her with case files, a Blackberry to replace her burned cell phone, and a promise to come back in a week. The Blackberry didn't get reception. She read the cover page of the first document, and then fell asleep.

Meredith opened the front door. She heard thuds–an avalanche rumbling down the hallway toward her–before she saw the boys, who yelped and then skidded to a stop. They stared at what she carried.

She shut the door behind her. "Boys, I brought something home."

"But we made lunch," Merritt said.

"I know. I can't wait to eat it."

Every day she worked, she came home for lunch. Ms. Cranston saw to it the boys prepared something for her. Ten minute drive, ten minutes to eat, ten minutes back.

"Is it a cat?" Beau asked.

"Yes. It belongs to a patient. It's not ours. We're going to take care of it for her, okay?"

Beau frowned.

Meredith sat the carrying case on the floor.

"Be gentle," she said.

Merritt nodded.

She opened the cage.

The cat stayed inside.

Merritt knelt, and then stretched out on his stomach, peering into the cage.

Beau gave the case a little kick.

"Beau."

Merritt grinned.

The cat cautiously stepped out and sniffed at Merritt.

Beau stood perfectly still.

Meredith enjoyed the moment of silence. The cat was already a blessing.

Beau lunged.

The cat took off for the kitchen.

Merritt howled.

Meredith shook her head and went in to lunch.

Meredith took Natalie dinner. Natalie smiled wanly at her and the mild anxiety Meredith felt whenever she was around Natalie intensified. Natalie didn't look good. Meredith settled the tray and then at Natalie's encouragement, sat on the edge of the bed.

"Thanks." Natalie picked up her fork and then set it down again, sighing.

"You all right?"

"I'm worried."

"About your leg?"

"Not really. Wheeler explained it all. I understand. Stupid leg. I'm worried about what I'm going to do."

Meredith glanced at the briefcase next to the bed. "Seems like you got plenty to do."

"Yeah. But~I don't have the energy. I read a few pages and then have to stop. My head hurts. I'm tired all the time. Oh, hell, do I sound like a four year old?"

"I have four year olds. Twins. You sure don't sound like them. The headache'll go away in a few days. I promise."

"You promise?"

"I do."

"All right then." Natalie leaned back. "I can bear it."

"Those papers look like pretty heavy stuff. Do you want any magazines? Books?"

"I, er. Are you going to bring me Christian literature?" Natalie asked.

"What?"

"I don't~nevermind~It's something I've been wanting to ask and it just came out. No one will tell me anything about this place. I don't know where I am," Natalie said.

Meredith's eyes widened. Natalie was either reaching out or warding her off. But her eyes didn't reveal which way she meant it. Natalie hadn't come into the emergency room wearing a cross or a star. She hadn't asked about Sunday services. She didn't want a chaplain. But outward signs were not always the way to tell something about a person.

Meredith was afraid of answering wrong, and hurting this fragile connection they'd forged. "I~I suppose I could bring you whatever you want. Are you a Christian, Natalie?"

"Are you?"

"I am." She asked, just as carefully, "Have you been depressed?"

"Yes." Natalie glanced away, at a stuffed bear.

Meredith reached out for Natalie's hand, but stopped herself, settling her fingers nervously on the edge of the dinner tray. She said, "You're tapering off some of your post-surgery meds. I can ask Wheeler to give you something mild. Help with the anxiety. The worry. I know it's rough. Believe me, I know."

"Sure. Like it's easy. My car~my life~my leg. Merry, you've seen this before, what~" she hesitated. "What happens?" She studied Meredith's fingers.

"Natalie. I've been praying for you. Rest assured. But God doesn't really say how he's going to heal someone. I just get the feeling He will."

"Thanks. For the praying. Though I don't know what good it will do me."

"Other things will help you heal, too. It's a multi-faceted system here at the hospital." Meredith tried to sound jovial. "You should eat."

"I'm not really hungry." Natalie held her gaze, but silence grew between them.

Meredith didn't know what to say. She slid off the bed, to add more stature to her words.

"Just one bite."

"Yes, mom," Natalie said. She picked up her fork.

"It always works."

"I bet it does. You're hard to refuse."

"I'll remind you of that."

Then Natalie grinned, open and genuine and Meredith grinned back, gazing right into those wide, dark eyes.

Chapter Six

The East Carolina Pirates were losing and they were losing by a lot; on national TV, too. Meredith wished she lived in the blackout zone. The carnage was almost too much to bear.

Angelo cursed. Then scowled and glanced at Meredith.

"Don't you make me think my swear jar is working. You'll only encourage me."

"You promised pizza for the shelter, right?"

"If the patronage doesn't dwindle. Blessed is the day."

"Yeah. I don't think we'll ever get there."

"Not with how East Carolina's playing."

"Right. How can we do good works if the world is so bleak?"

"Is it really bleak, Angelo?"

"Don't look so sympathetic, *chica*. It's only bleak because I clean the bathrooms." He glanced at the television. "I'll clean with a vengeance, today."

"We've got the cleanest bathrooms between Wrightsville and Raleigh, for sure."

"What did you do before the Latinos moved into N.C?"

"Went to Baptist church, instead of Catholic."

"We don't deal with any snakes."

"Nope. In your church, the snakes have to talk to the Pope before they can get involved in church affairs."

"Don't think they don't, either. Snakes everywhere. How's your patient?"

"Which patient? I've got twelve on my rounds."

"Oh, come on. You know the one."

Under Angelo's interested gaze she faltered. "She just looks so lost."

"They all look lost, Merry. And none of them can be saved. You tried on every damn one. No one listens."

She frowned at him.

He got out his wallet, but said, "I'm doing this for emphasis. Her looking lost doesn't make her a little lamb, wandered off from the flock. You're no shepherd. She's a lawyer. You know what a lawyer is? A snake. A rat."

"She hasn't asked for anything yet."

Angelo whistled. "A new record. Not a phone call, not food she can't get here, not morphine, not the Good Book?"

"I don't think she has much to ask for."

"If she latches on, she'll suck you dry. Just like everyone else. Just like~"

Meredith glanced away, flinching when she should have been angry, but it stopped Angelo all the same.

"Merry, got enough problems of your own. Think hers are going to distract you for long?"

"Everyone tells me I need a good lawyer. One just appeared out of the blue."

"It's not a sign from God. Especially if she's on the other team." He sighed and put a hand on her shoulder.

Meredith wiped at her cheeks. "Well, I guess I should have been more specific."

"He knows what you meant, Mer."

"And He knows what He's doing. Give Him a little more credit."

"*Si, chica.* But don't get hurt, okay? Give yourself a little credit, too." Angelo patted the top of her head, and then left her alone in the break room.

East Carolina turned over possession and took off running, trying to stop the avalanche of players crushing down on them. Meredith understood the futility. But she couldn't tear her eyes away. Having someone new, someone innocent, to talk to~a foreigner, practically~made life feel a little less stagnant.

Angelo singled her out for nothing. Roland had been on the news every day for over a year. Natalie was a local celebrity. Everyone talked about her.

Meredith knew tourists only ever stopped in town for gas. No one ever stayed. But someone had to save her from all this, and it wasn't going to be anyone around here.

The cat cried half the night in its carrying case, so Meredith let it sleep on her bed instead. She'd nearly wept herself at its purr~another heartbeat, another life beyond her children and her own.

She had the late shift the next day so Mrs. Cranston came at lunch to watch the boys, annoyed about the cat.

Meredith chided herself for looking forward to work. Throughout her ordeal~and for a long time before, if she were being honest, work was her salvation. Despite the cold stares she got, she had the work.

But work wasn't the reason she was looking so forward to the hospital tonight.

"Knock, knock," Meredith said, tapping on the hospital room door.

"Come in," Natalie said. "Since when do you knock?" She ran her fingers across her short hair self-consciously.

"I'm not here on official business." Meredith brought in an old brown shopping bag and closed the door.

"Social call?" Natalie asked.

"If you're up for visitors."

"I am so up for visitors."

"I thought you might be asleep."

"I'm tired of sleeping. It's six o'clock in the evening, shouldn't I be awake?"

"Are you in any pain?"

Natalie glanced away.

"Natalie."

"Yeah. But it's not too bad. Just~mostly sore. And then throbbing when it's close to medication time. And then back down to sore. There's an ache."

"Must be depressing," Meredith said.

"Yes. Yes it is. And I'm awake to go through it." Natalie studied at the ceiling. "Whee."

"Do you miss the sedatives?"

"I'm tired of being tired."

Meredith glanced at all the papers strewn across the bed. "And you're thinking straight."

Meredith's voice held a lilt that took the 'g' off thinking, making her sound soft and sweet, like Dolly Parton really was the angel she seemed like on TV, and manifested in Podunk, N.C., not quite having made it to the beach. Natalie found it comforting. Meredith talking was so far the most soothing curative she'd experienced. She had a sense telling Meredith would make everything awkward. Meredith talked like everyone else. Even Wheeler had a voice that sounded like butter.

Natalie didn't want Wheeler to talk to her.

"Well, I'm back to usual," she said. Her mind did seem to wander more, following tangents, analyzing new stimuli. The last week and a half she'd lived mostly in her half-formed memories~still images floating in front of her eyes. Scents. Feelings. Her brain, done being tormented, was back to tormenting her.

"It's good you have a job where you can still~I mean~"

Natalie couldn't imagine making a career for herself in a wheelchair. Second-chair A.D.A., maybe. All paperwork and witness interviews and nothing interesting. She wouldn't be able to run for office~not as the chick who flipped her car on the way to the beach. She might, though, make judge. There was a thought. Her gaze strayed back to the paper bag. "So, this is a social call?" she asked.

"Right." Meredith opened the bag, and then pulled Natalie's tray over her lap. On the tray, she laid out a chess board~old and worn wood with black paint, and pieces, some painted with the same black lacquer, some plain wood. Natalie helped her with the pieces. She made herself, by default of the piles, the white player, and lined up the black along Meredith's side.

"We're going to play chess?"

"I saw on *The West Wing* it helps with mental acuity," Meredith said. She pulled up a chair and settled into it.

"So it's therapeutic?"

"Unless you get all enraged and throw the board across the room."

"It might feel good to throw something."

Meredith touched a rook, thoughtfully running her fingers over the battlements. "Wouldn't want you to pull out any stitches, though. I mean, if you want to, we'd have to start stretching every day."

"Yeah. There's a thought." Natalie felt her face grow hot.

"There's just one problem."

"What?" Natalie was thinking too much. Her body was far too awake. She wasn't ready. She wasn't healed.

Meredith grinned. "Can I go first?"

Natalie turned the board around so the white pieces faced Meredith's chair.

"See, I read all the instructions last night~just a refresher, I'd like to teach my boys to play when they're old enough. But I memorized how to start."

Natalie grinned. "So, start."

Meredith moved a white pawn forward two spaces, and then folded her hands in her lap and smiled at Natalie.

Natalie considered, and then moved a pawn out to meet it.

"So, you're a lawyer. Are you like some chess grandmaster?"

"I was on the chess team in high school. For like, a week. I thought it would be cool, you know? I was bookish. But I was awful at chess."

"What did you do instead?"

"I volunteered for the teen hotline. Far less stressful."

Meredith studied the board, and then moved another piece.

Natalie moved one out to match it. "You're right. This is engaging."

"Don't think too hard. I don't want to lose by an embarrassing margin."

"Will all the other nurses find out?"

"Yup, and then I'll never be able to face playing you again. Or anyone. Can you imagine what Wheeler'll say? He'll want to play you himself. And then you'll just cause a general disruption of hospital operations while the pecking order gets established."

"Well, wouldn't want that. I'll just let you win."

"That'd be really nice of you," Meredith said.

Natalie decided to start moving pieces at random. The last time she'd played chess was in college. Not counting the time she played it on the first computer she bought for herself, just to see if it worked. It worked. She'd closed the program and never opened it again.

Meredith thought carefully over each piece, taking long minutes to decide. Natalie would spend a few seconds on her move, and then spend the rest of the time gazing at Meredith.

"I'm spending too much time thinking," Meredith said.

"But you're winning."

"Are you letting me win?"

"Well, I'm not trying very hard."

"Natalie!"

Natalie froze in mid-movement. A pawn dangled from her fingertips. She had been about to move it into Meredith's kill-zone. Really, thinking up ways to die, to catch Meredith's attention for moves, coaxing Meredith into taking advantage had all been rather fun. She grinned, but Meredith's eyes were filling with tears.

"No one's ever let me win before," Meredith said.

"Will you let your boys win at chess?" Natalie asked. Her throat constricted around the words. Foolish of her to picture Meredith single and alone, an angel waiting for her and having nothing else to do. Meredith had a whole life.

"I'm just glad they're past the age where they'll eat the pieces. They're good at checkers, though. I don't let them cheat. Their dad~he would have let them cheat," Meredith said.

The blood drained from Natalie's face.

Meredith met Natalie's eyes. "They're four. Merritt and Beau."

"Merritt. Like Merry?"

"It's what we call him. He gets a kick out of having a name like his mommy. It makes Beau jealous."

"Is Beau~" Natalie couldn't get the words out. She set down the piece, in a defensive spot, unwilling to open her side up to attacks when she was feeling so vulnerable, and then tried again. "Is Beau named after his daddy?"

"Nah, his daddy's Vince. He didn't want a kid named after him, so we went with Grandfather Beauregard." Meredith sobered up and glanced down at the board. "Can we change the subject, please?"

"Yeah. Um, sure." Natalie felt heat returning to her cheeks. She was as happy to change the subject as Meredith. She was happy, though not by honest means, Meredith wasn't still married after all~no ring, no visits, and no mentions of going home to her husband. It was nearly seven. Natalie wanted to ask where the boys might be, if not at home, but the topic was now forbidden.

She shrugged and asked, "What's the weather like?"

Meredith chuckled. "We don't have to talk about the weather."

"I haven't been outside in a week. I know it's almost summer. Perfect beach weather. I would have loved to have seen the beach," Natalie said.

"You will." Meredith leaned forward and took her hand.

"Maybe. I don't know if I'll ever swim in it."

Meredith squeezed her fingers. "It's nice outside. Sunny every day. It's almost hurricane season."

"Hurricane?"

"Well, not yet."

"Let's change the subject," Natalie said. Being near the eastern shore of hurricane territory was unsettling. She remembered the devastation Fran wrought, and Floyd, and Hugo~this was not a good place to be. Not when the seasons changed.

"Want to talk about politics?" Meredith asked.

"Oh, sure. Or how about God?"

She meant it flippantly, but Meredith put her other hand over Natalie's, clasping Natalie's hand in both of hers. Her thumbs rubbed Natalie's wrist. "We can talk about God anytime you want."

Natalie managed not to flinch. She turned her head to the side. "Not tonight."

Meredith gave her another squeeze and let her go. "Not tonight. Is it my turn?"

"Yup."

Meredith moved. "Check, I think."

Natalie studied the board. She moved her king out of harm's way.

Meredith moved again. "Check."

"Oh, come on." Natalie shoved a bishop in front of her king.

Meredith circumvented it. "Check-mate?"

Natalie flicked her king over.

Meredith grinned. She offered her hand to Natalie. Natalie shook it, and then fell back on the bed while Meredith scooped the pieces and the board back into her bag.

"When are we doing that again?" Natalie asked.

"If you're good, I'll swing by after lunch tomorrow."

"I have to be good?"

"Teresa tells me everything."

Natalie closed her eyes. She felt a warm pressure on her shoulder.

"I'm going to get you something mild to help you sleep." Meredith said.

"Thanks," Natalie said. Her back and leg were sore, and her head hurt from paying so much attention to something for so long. She hadn't been ready for fun, probably. Was she going to feel like this from now on, every time she wanted to play a game with a nurse?

Meredith ruffled Natalie's hair. "It'll get better."

"Yeah?"

" I know what I'm doing."

And even though there was a note of false bravado in Meredith's voice, Natalie decided to believe her. She exhaled slowly. "Bring me the good drugs."

She heard the door shut. She lay in pain until the door opened again, and someone pressed pills and a paper cup into her hand. She took the pills without opening her eyes and she waited for the pain to ebb so she could sleep.

Chapter Seven

Natalie woke to pain. Worse than before. Light shone against her eyes. Morning. She was afraid the pain was so bad she couldn't breathe. But, she reminded herself, she'd been breathing before she woke up. She could do so now.

Shooting pain ran through her leg and hip and shoulder and neck. Tears came to her eyes, but it hurt to cry--it hurt to be tense with the need to sob. She tried to breathe more slowly. In and out. If Meredith were here, Meredith would be telling her to breathe. Even though she was already breathing and it wasn't helping.

The room stayed filled with light. Natalie sank into it, and closed her eyes and let the light glow on the backs of her eyelids. The room was so empty and so quiet she couldn't tell if it was early morning light, pure and cold, before everyone woke up, or afternoon light, warm and beating down on everyone who was too busy to interrupt a sleeping woman in a hospital bed.

The pain came in waves. After one subsided, she breathed deeply--into soreness in her chest that was pleasant, after the sharper pains, and turned her head to see the clock. 6:36 in the morning.

She was clear-headed.

The button to call the nurses was by her side. But she'd never called them. She would wait. They'd be in around 7:30, she supposed.

Whatever Meredith had given her last night hadn't lasted, and they'd taken off her IV bag. Nothing dripped through her veins since they established her stomach, kidneys, and intestines, though enveloped by bruised skin, were functioning adequately. Mostly adequately. One of her kidneys, she'd learned when Teresa let her read her chart, frightened Wheeler enough he'd considered scooping it out. But it was still there.

Her back hurt. She shifted, prodding her abdomen, wondering if she was bleeding internally.

At 6:42 she reached for the button, crying before her fingers even brushed the knob. She'd never felt this helpless. She'd never wanted to ask for help this badly in her life.

The doctors and nurses earned her trust in the last two weeks. They took care of her and saved her and cleaned her and put her back together, she should trust them now--maybe the pain was normal.

Maybe she was just being a baby about how much she hurt. Maybe she should pray. Find a way to be stronger.

She clutched the call-button remote in her hand and closed her eyes and tried to open herself up to the universe. The pain ebbed and flowed through her. The light in the room stayed constant. Everything around her was ordinary hospital furniture, and she felt ordinary, too.

God would probably tell her to push the damn button and stop being so full of herself. He was busy and had doctors for that sort of thing.

She squeezed, just as the door slid open.

Colleen, the nurses' aide, came in carrying breakfast and a newspaper.

"Oh, thank God," Natalie said.

Colleen rushed to her side, and put her hand on Natalie's forehead. "Where does it hurt?"

"Everywhere."

Colleen studied Natalie's chart, and then picked up the phone by Natalie's bed and called someone. When she hung up, she sat on the edge of the bed. Natalie sniffled.

Colleen gently pried the remote control out of Natalie's fingers and placed it by her side. "Good morning. The P.A. is on her way."

"Is it going to be like this every morning?"

"They took you off the codeine. I don't know what they'll give you for the long-term pain management." Colleen looked over her shoulder, and then lowered her voice. "Your doctor should tell you this, but yes You're going to be in some discomfort for a very long time."

"Okay."

Wheeler came in, carrying a syringe case and some medication. "I ran into the P.A. when I was coming in this morning. You're doing badly?"

"Worse than ever."

Natalie's tears stopped and her face, she hoped, was less puffy. She could even move around a little.

"We're going to put you on Percocet, since the stuff you were on before hasn't made you nauseous. Same family, different branch. You're going to feel great."

"I don't want~" she started, but Wheeler cut her off.

"You can have the addiction discussion with your pain therapist, okay? I already signed three sheets of paper just to get this out of the cabinet. You might as well try it."

She held out her arm.

Colleen got alcohol and a cotton ball from the cabinet. Natalie felt about two years old, but she let Wheeler give her the shot without complaint, even though it stung.

"Give it about twenty minutes. I'll be back. Try and have some breakfast when you can, but don't worry too much if you can't."

"I never worry," Natalie said.

He closed the door behind him.

Colleen laid out her breakfast tray and stuck the newspaper next to it.

"I'm sorry to cause so much trouble."

"You're not." Colleen put a hand on her shoulder. "Try harder. I mean it. Give us something to do around here."

"I will." The pain in her hip started to ease and her head was floating. Food? She didn't care about food. Anxiety? She'd call the nurses a thousand times. She grinned goofily at Colleen.

Colleen grinned back, and then left her in peace with her breakfast.

The county school board met last night, she read in the headlines.

Drama ensued.

Natalie decided to nap instead.

The drugs had mostly worn off and the pain and soreness returned. Back to normal. Natalie's head still felt heavy when Meredith came in with the chess board and dinner. Natalie was relieved to see her. Meredith's brow furrowed in concern.

"Were you bored today?" Meredith asked.

Natalie shook her head. "It was a bad day."

Without the IV drugs, it was a lot harder to explain herself. She missed feeling invulnerable and not caring. Especially in front of Meredith, who crept over, trying to see her face.

"Don't worry, Wheeler hooked me up."

"Are you ready for this? We could just watch TV."

The thought of television had never been more appealing in her life, which scared her. Maybe it was a sign of healing, to want to lie in bed and watch sitcoms, like she'd done at home, between work and late night prep.

They were her friends. She might be ready for the outside world again.

She sighed. "What did you bring to eat?"

"Chinese. I thought about Greek, but the aides would kill me if I gave you that much fatty meat."

Natalie laughed. "You should only feed me asparagus and carrots."

Meredith grinned and pulled out small white cardboard boxes.

"Are there many Chinese? I mean, around here?"

"There are mostly Laotians. And Koreans? There are Koreans with the boys in day care when they go. And a great barbeque place. I'll take you when you can~Though, I think it's mostly, uh," she faltered, contemplating the boxes.

"Branding?"

Meredith snapped her fingers. "Bingo. Most of the Chinese places are run by Hispanics." She pulled out chopsticks.

"Is there a fork?"

Meredith blinked. She searched the bag, and sheepishly said, "No."

Natalie took the chopsticks and examined the instructions on the wrapper.

"They're not hard," Meredith said.

"I'm Eastern European," Natalie said. "If I ever ate out, I'd have learned, but... I mostly ate at home. And my mother used forks." She stopped explaining and pulled apart the chopsticks and held one in each hand, pointing them at Meredith. "Is stabbing an option?"

The blood drained from Meredith's face so fast Natalie yanked her hands down.

"I'll teach you. I tried teaching the boys, but their motor skills aren't quite up to it. Maybe next year. They like to eat the little corns with their hands, though, like it's real corn."

Natalie kept her hands in her lap until Meredith clasped one and took the sticks from her, positioning them in her fingers. Meredith's hands were cold, and slightly scented. Natalie inhaled.

Meredith pulled back. "Sorry. Lotion."

"It's fine. It's nice."

Meredith lifted Natalie's hand by the wrist. "Now. Like they're scissors."

Natalie scissored. A chopstick fell to the bed.

Meredith laughed. "Try again."

Natalie tried. The scissors ended up perpendicular. She frowned.

Meredith giggled. "I'm sorry. I'm being so impolite. You're doing great."

"Let me practice."

Meredith gestured to the box of food.

Natalie inhaled the steam and the scent of brown sauce and the chicken and broccoli and water chestnuts soaking in it. Hunger gnawed at her. Pain left her. She carefully closed her chopsticks on a piece of chicken and squeezed as hard as she could. The chicken lifted out of the box, and then fell back with a splat. She stuck the sticks in the box, feeling chagrined.

"Here." Meredith scooped up a piece of broccoli and waved it at Natalie.

Natalie opened her mouth and Meredith dropped the broccoli inside.

"Impressive coordination," Natalie said.

"You're easier to feed than a four year old." She tilted her head and frowned at Natalie. "A little."

Natalie snorted.

"Watch me do rice." Meredith opened the smaller box of rice and scooped some up on her chopsticks.

"Wow."

Meredith popped the rice into her own mouth, and then scooped more out for Natalie. She paused. "This is unsanitary."

"I don't care."

"I could have mono."

"You're already my nurse."

"Good point."

Natalie opened wide.

Meredith couldn't quite get the rice close enough because she'd doubled over in laughter.

Natalie tried to look hurt.

"Sorry, sorry. I'll get you a fork."

"You don't have to~" Natalie started, but Meredith was out of the room before she finished. Natalie scooped some rice out with her fingers.

When Meredith came back, Natalie asked, "What did you give me last night?"

"What?"

"I mean, the medication."

"Oh. Tylenol, did it help?"

Natalie nodded. "Yup."

"I'm glad."

"Me too. Real glad."

Meredith chopped her chopsticks. "You're making fun of me."

"Just joining in."

"Welcome, then. In a week or two you'll be up to barbeque and lemonade."

"You keep promising me food. Is this some sort of ritual?"

"Just hearth and home and family. I guess so." Meredith glanced down, and plucked out a baby corn. She offered it to Natalie, like a peace offering, and said, "You look like you're not eating enough vegetables."

"I've been eating Jell-O with the fruit in it. Doesn't that count for anything?"

"Sure it does. Why do you think we put the fruit in it?"

Natalie grasped Meredith's wrist and steadied it while she took the corn between her teeth. Sweet and crunchy and a little cold. Meredith stayed still, letting Natalie hold her hand. Natalie met her eyes.

Meredith grinned. "You're feeling better."

"Think they'll let me out of here?"

"You?"

Natalie took another piece of chicken with her fork and chewed thoughtfully and thinking things over. The food was warm and fortifying, and gave some steadying weight to the nervousness in her stomach.

"Wheeler's specialist is coming tomorrow afternoon. He might want to operate, or move me up to Duke, or—I don't know." Natalie the contents of her box. Chicken and broccoli lay limply together. "I don't know."

"I don't, either."

Natalie nodded.

"If I did, I'd tell you."

"You'd reveal all the secrets in the universe?"

Meredith shrugged. "Tell me about your case. Papers say the jury has it."

"I don't want to talk about the case." The case felt far removed from this little hospital in this little town.

"You're not on the news anymore."

"Good." Natalie ran her hand through her hair. She closed her container and put it on the table, away from Meredith's reach. "I'm done for now. That's for later."

"Don't tell Teresa where you got it, okay?"

"I won't. Your secret is safe with me."

"One at a time, then," Meredith said. She put away the rest of the food.

"Here's your chance to redeem yourself at chess."

"I didn't lose so badly."

"Oh, Natalie."

"I let you win!"

"Oh, I know you did," Meredith said, in the most condescending tone she could manage while grinning.

Natalie hadn't known she could be provoked into seeking revenge in a chess match, but energy came through her to wake up her brain and make her fingers tingle. The pieces waited.

She lost anyway.

A hand on Natalie's shoulder shook her awake. She grunted, groggy and sore. Slowly she opened her eyes. Teresa stood by her bed. Her hand touched Natalie's cheek.

"Ungh?"

"Take these," Teresa said, helping Natalie sit up and pressing two pills into her hand.

Natalie oriented and wet her lips, and then took the cup of water Teresa offered. She took the pills, then the water, and then handed everything back so she could lie down and gaze out the window. No stars were out. The only light came from the half-open door leading into the hallway.

"I'm going off shift, but Merrybelle wanted me to give you these on my way," Teresa said.

"What are they?"

"Just Tylenol."

"Make a note in my chart." Natalie yawned.

"Already taken care of. Go back to sleep."

Chapter Eight

The specialist from Duke arrived a half hour early and he and Wheeler came in to see Natalie during her lunch break with Colleen. *All My Children* was on, but Colleen turned it off and guiltily scrambled off the side of the bed.

"Doctor Wheeler," Colleen said.

"Colleen. Mind giving us some privacy?"

"Sure." She slipped past them and through the door.

The doctor, a short man with graying hair and clay-colored skin offered his hand. He said, "I'm Doctor Bhatti." His accent was a blend of foreign and Southern. The result was a melodic lilt.

Natalie shook his hand. Dry and leathery, but steady.

He set his coffee down on her table. "Mind if I have a look at your leg?"

"Only if you buy me dinner first," she said.

"I brought barbeque down from our church fundraiser. It's in the staff fridge for you."

"Really?"

He nodded. "Best barbeque in North Carolina."

Wheeler grunted.

Bhatti winked.

Natalie drew back the blanket over her leg. Colleen had helped her shave, not over the damaged flesh, but her calves and the other leg, so at least she looked presentable. The doctor didn't care about the dark hairs her ancestors brought over for her DNA strands, but she cared.

Colleen offered to shave the rest of her, too, but Natalie was too nervous about the appointment to even think about her armpits. Maybe if Bhatti wanted to prod her lymph nodes, she'd regret it.

"How are you feeling today?" Bhatti pulled up a chair and leaned against the arm.

"Okay," Natalie said.

The midnight feeding of Tylenol helped--it was true what they said about hospitals and Tylenol--but the soreness was never-ending, and every so often a sharp pain would overtake her. If she moved too quickly, or if something on the television made her excited or sad, or even for no reason, sharp pain would rush through her and leave her breathless.

"Sprains?" Bhatti asked.

Natalie opened her mouth but Wheeler fielded the question. "Shoulder, knee, ankle. We were afraid of an ACL tear but it's just dislocation."

"But you think the tissue damage is severe," Bhatti said.

"We're afraid the major arteries were crushed and have lost integrity. Internal bleeding in her leg is a concern."

"May I see your abdomen?" Bhatti asked.

She hadn't been able to do anything about the standard-issue cotton panties she wore, or the tattoo of Pravda written in Cyrillic, the result of a drunken all night study session before her Criminal Justice final at law school, which she was far too proud of as long as no one but her saw it.

Now Bhatti did, gently opening her gown. He didn't comment on the ink, but instead asked, "What are you eating these days?"

"They won't let me have steak."

"But almost everything else. No complaints of stomach aches or intestinal distress," Wheeler said.

"Soreness?"

"When I eat?"

"Yes?"

"No. But I thought that might be because of the medication."

Bhatti nodded. "It might be." He stood back and Natalie closed her gown.

"I'm going to examine at the scans and x-rays of your leg, all right? I've seen them up at Duke, but I want to get Doctor Wheeler's perspective."

"Okay," she said.

"Move your toes for me?" he asked.

She wiggled her foot. It hurt, but she grimaced and said nothing.

He patted her foot, through the blanket, and then he and Wheeler left.

Natalie turned the television back on and tried not to cry. Doctors frightened her. Nausea gurgled in her stomach. Maybe the food she ate was secretly damaging her.

Colleen slipped back in. "What'd they say?"

"Nothing. Not yet."

Colleen settled into the chair. "There's pork for you in the fridge. God, I hate you."

"You hate God, or is that an inflective?" Natalie asked.

"I hate everything," Colleen said, and rolled her eyes. "God, lawyers."

Natalie smirked.

Colleen put her feet up on the edge of Natalie's bed. She said, "You know, when a patient becomes ornery, you know they're getting better."

"It takes spare energy to be ornery?"

"Yup. Soon you'll even be wanting to use the bathroom in something other than a tin."

Natalie didn't even try to hide her blush. Colleen winked, and together they laughed and watched TV and pretended Natalie was in the hospital to have a hangnail removed.

As usual, an hour later, she was sound asleep.

Wheeler sat on Meredith's couch. "Chutes and ladders is kind of a creepy game," he said.

"I know. But it's action-packed."

"We used to play it with daddy," Merritt said. He stood, holding onto Meredith's shoulder.

Meredith rubbed a player piece idly.

"Did you?" Wheeler asked.

Meredith nodded.

"I won!" Beau shouted. He dug his fingers into Wheeler's leg.

Wheeler winced.

"Boys, get ready for bed, and I'll let Hank tell you a story."

They leapt up.

Merritt lingered. "What about the board?"

"I'll clean it up."

He beamed, and set off down the hall.

Meredith gathered pieces.

"Merry~"

"You're the only one I ever see," Meredith said.

"Not true. You've got friends."

"People who tolerate me aren't friends."

The bitterness in her voice made Wheeler pause.

She met his eyes. "Even you're not here for a social visit."

"Well, I am. Just not in the usual way."

She raised her eyebrows.

"It's about Natalie Ivans. We can't keep her in the hospital, Merry. It's costing a fortune."

"I know."

"She's healthy enough to go somewhere."

"To go home?"

"Maybe not. She can't do it on her own, Meredith. She can't even stand yet."

Meredith settled the board into a box.

"I was thinking here."

Meredith sat up. "Here? No."

"You got anything else going on?"

"Do I have anything else going on? You can't bring her here. The boys—"

"Her cat's already here. This is not the toxic place you think it is, Merry. It's just lonely."

"What does that have to do with patient care?"

"Hear me out. Please."

Meredith came to play chess with Natalie and tease her that she had a secret waiting at home, watched over by the boys. Natalie spent a good hour trying to figure out what it was, to no avail.

Wheeler came by after morning rounds after Natalie ate breakfast. Real scrambled eggs and hash browns, slightly burnt, and a slab of ham Colleen informed her was from Virginia.

Natalie debated between Tyra Banks or reading about the new cases Patrick wanted her to review; the eternal question, leisure or work. She had no other options, really, which meant life was returning to normal.

The idea depressed her. Shouldn't the accident be a more life-changing event? She wanted her life changed. She wanted a portal into another world, like those guys on TV who got hit on the head and woke up somewhere else. Though, technically, she woke up somewhere else–Tarpley was not a place she ever expected to be. But she still felt the same. Awake, she just had her old life, waiting impatiently for her. And Wheeler.

Wheeler asked, "Mind if I sit?

"Sure, Hank."

"I'd tip my hat if it were on."

"I suppose I should close my robe with a man in the room."

"It's the new century. But that's what brought me, actually."

"Oh?"

He began to take off his lab coat.

"Hank." She reached for the call button. "I may not be able to move, but I can scream."

"Oh, no, Natalie." He put his coat on the chair, and rolled up the sleeve of his tee shirt.

Wheeler was the only doctor on staff who wore tee shirts~this one was of a rock band she'd never heard of, black and stretched tight across his chest~ ~but she assumed from too much television Greg House made sloppy dressing acceptable for doctors who had the skill to back it up. Wheeler qualified in her mind.

Under his sleeve was a tattoo of a red heart with an arrow through it, and the word, "Dawn."

"Who's Dawn?" she asked.

"Ex-girlfriend. I think of her every time I look in the mirror. Keeps me humble. I could have it removed, but then I'd just look at the absence and think of her."

"Do you still love her?"

"No. But I did."

She nodded. The tattoo had stretched and faded with time and did no favors to the age of his skin.

He rolled his sleeve back down and asked, "What about you? Any exes tattooed on your heart?"

"No." She shifted away and gazed out the window.

"Natalie."

"Huh?" Her voice sounded hoarse. She swallowed.

"You haven't had any visitors, except your boss and the district attorney. Isn't there someone?"

"No. Mom died, no siblings, no~relations. Friends to have a drink with or see a movie with, friends to email once in a while but not to schlep all the way down the coast for me. They're concerned, but they have lives."

He touched her arm. "I thought it was something else."

"Nothing else."

"Natalie, no one's going to lynch you for who you love. Not down here."

Her whole body felt hot. She breathed slowly. "There's no reason to have this conversation. But it's nice you said that."

"We're all Christian here. We try. Not everyone is as obnoxious about it as Merry. She has her reasons. But we try not to judge."

"She's not obnoxious."

"She's got a good heart. You getting along with her?"

"Yes. I guess. Sure." She tried to shrug nonchalantly without hurting her shoulder or her stomach too much, and mostly succeeded.

"That's good, because~Look, Doctor Bhatti's going to come operate on your leg next week, but until then we'd like to discharge you."

Panic made bile rise up in her throat. "Back to Charlotte?"

"We wouldn't want you to travel far. You could get a hotel, but the ones with the internet you'd probably need for your job are pretty far away. Merry lives just down the road. She'd be able to provide nursing care. She'd take you in."

"Why can't I stay here?"

"You know how much it costs? Your health insurance is getting harder to authorize already."

"It's always about money."

"Yes. Besides, you're getting back some mobility. The stitches on your insides are holding just fine. This hospital isn't doing any good for you. I mean, you're only taking Tylenol. Merry's able to give you Percocet in an emergency. I know you think you're in a lot of pain, but the change we've seen in you is remarkable."

Natalie put her hands on her forehead, and thought. "Why are you telling me this, and not Merry?"

"Thought it would sound more official this way. Doctor's orders. And I talked to your insurance company about nursing care. Besides, you'd refuse any hospitality offered by a friend."

"I've got manners. The decency not to put people out."

"Not always in your best interest. Take advantage."

That's what Colleen said to do. It was the hardest thing anyone asked her. The thought made her sick. She liked Meredith too much to be resented underfoot. She really had no idea how it would turn out. It was terrifying to be so helpless.

Wheeler squeezed her shoulder. "Think about it. I'll be on my rounds."

"Later, gator," she said.

When he left, she turned on the television. Tyra over work, definitely, just to get her emotions steady. And Tyra would have good advice, though Natalie didn't need to hear it.

Live a little, make a friend. Love was important.

She turned off the television and tried to sleep. She couldn't.

Chapter Nine

"I am your physical therapist extraordinaire," Jake said.

He had a gentle, quiet accent to match his round, kind eyes. He was of indeterminate Asian origin and Natalie didn't want to ask, because it was rude, and because her years in court gave her a pretty good handle on the basics. She enjoyed the guessing game. Though usually she could read the docket in front of her.

He was rotating her ankle in a most pleasant way, and asking her how she liked North Carolina, when she finally said, "Jake Syha. Nice name. Where's it from?"

"My grandparents came from Laos. You know, after the war. And my parents had a farm out by Fayetteville. Growing tobacco, until the government told them to grow soy. So they grow soy."

"Fayetteville's where the big base is?"

Jake nodded. He lowered her ankle and started massaging her calf. "I went into the Army, got some medic training. Paramedic, combat stuff. Got out and here I am."

"Wouldn't have thought the Army would have taught you to be so tender."

"Farm taught me. I'm still in the reserves, though. Keeps my hand in. I have a little girl now."

"What's her name?"

"Sunisa. Sunisa Syha-Jackson. My parents wanted to kill me for going back to the traditional ways, but I feel the same way about them changing everything, you know?"

Jake had silver studs in each earlobe, black hair brushing his neck, and a leather bracelet on one arm. He didn't look traditional. But he was as friendly as everyone else she'd met.

"Why'd you come back to North Carolina, after the army?"

"Wanted to live at the beach. But the hospital's better here. Still, I go surfing every other weekend if I can."

"Sounds great," she said, closing her eyes.

"You surf?"

"Never have."

"I'll teach you. I give classes to all the Yankees who come for vacation."

"All right."

He moved on to her good leg, and lifted it. "Rotate your ankle."

She did. "This is my good leg."

"Sure, but it's just lyin' around. You don't want it not to remember how to move, once you're ready to stand on it. You'll flop right onto the floor."

"Ugh."

"How soon will it be?"

She sighed. "Today's the big day." She glanced at the bathroom. "There and back."

He squeezed her foot. "You'll do it."

"I don't know."

The thought exhausted her. Having an assigned physical therapist, long-term, instead of just the guys who did shifts at the hospital, exhausted her. Jake would be coming to Meredith's house. Nearly every day. She'd have to get him something for Christmas if this kept up. Him and Sunisa.

"You celebrate Christmas, Jake?"

He began working on her arms. "Yeah. But we're Buddhist. Gotta go down to Cape Fear for the big celebrations. Yet another reason to live at the beach. Sit up?"

She tried to sit up. "Stomach hurts."

He put his arms around her waist, supporting her back. She found she didn't mind being touched by him, being near him, even though he smelled like cheap cologne and she was only in a flimsy hospital gown.

"Put your hands on my shoulders and try again."

She pulled herself up, and it hurt, but nothing pulled. "Okay."

"And you're not even breathing hard."

"Will it get easier?"

"Of course it will. Faster than you think. You'll forget all this."

"Never."

He grinned and patted her hand. "I'll be back on Tuesday. Don't slip on the way to the bathroom. There are parts of you I don't want to massage."

"You haven't even seen my tattoo."

He wolf-whistled, and left her alone to contemplate lunch and her great adventure of the afternoon. By the time she saw Meredith, she might have something to brag about.

Meredith could tell from the tension in Natalie's expression she was in some pain. Meredith brought dinner from the cafeteria~French toast with fresh fruit and bacon. She brought it in, feeling apprehensive in the face of Natalie's mood change.

"For dinner?" Natalie asked.

"It's Breakfast Tuesday," Meredith said.

"I never noticed." Natalie picked up her fork, but just sat glumly staring at the toast.

"Television?" Meredith asked. The natural desensitizer when people didn't want to feel anymore.

Natalie nodded.

Meredith turned on the television and found the six o'clock sitcoms on. Natalie nibbled on bacon. Beyond the grayness of her complexion, Natalie's hair was washed and her hospital gown was crisp. The bruises were faded from her face and arms. Except for the shaved part of her head, she looked halfway to healthy.

Meredith kept quiet until the first commercial break, and then asked, "You smell like~strawberries?"

"Yeah. Colleen brought it for me, now that I can do my own sponge baths. Well, I helped. I was sweaty this afternoon. Can you believe it? Sweaty. From lying in bed."

"Well, that's not all you did today, is it? You exerted yourself."

"Barely," Natalie said. She sighed.

Meredith reached for a raspberry on Natalie's plate.

Natalie said, "I just can't believe I can't walk across a room without my entire body hurting. I want to lie in bed for a week. And with enough drugs in my leg to put down a rhinoceros."

"Two weeks ago you were in a coma, you know. You've come pretty far."

"Yes, but three weeks ago," Natalie said.

"What is it?"

"I was just trying to picture where I was three weeks ago. There'd been the beach trip, all planned. All by myself. Solitary. But here I am, with you." Natalie said. She turned and met Meredith's eyes and gave her a genuine smile.

Meredith smiled back. Sharp relief struck her heart at the shedding of

Natalie's despair. With it her own despair rose up in her chest. She bit her lip until it hurt. Her thoughts turned inward, to Vincent, and she forgot Natalie was still gazing at her.

"You don't look very good, Merry," Natalie said.

"I just got some bad news, is all. I don't mean for it to affect you."

"It does. I mean, it should. I mean~" Natalie put her hand on her forehead.

Meredith, her thoughts still half-distracted by the morning call from her lawyer, said, "You have enough on your plate without me adding mine."

"I could say the same thing. I've been taking advantage of your kindness for too long. I've been selfish. You probably have bigger problems than being able to walk across to the bathroom or not."

"It's just about my husband, is all." Even saying that made her feel better.

Natalie hesitated, and then reached over and brushed Meredith's arm. "What about him?"

Meredith said, having to clear her throat and restart. "Well, you know he passed away."

"Okay. I didn't know~Okay." Natalie slid her hand down Meredith's arm, past her elbow, and tugged, until Meredith willingly clasped her hand with one of her own. Meredith squeezed. Natalie winced.

"Sorry," Meredith said, letting go.

"No, it's okay." Natalie took her hand again. "I was just~I was surprised. I haven't been held on to so tightly in a long time."

A tear rolled down Meredith's cheek. She impatiently brushed it away. She wasn't even thinking of Vincent at all, not since Natalie took her hand. The despair, though, remained, coiled up and heavy in her chest, and somehow Natalie's presence made her feel even more lonely.

"I'm sorry. Whatever it is, I'm so sorry, Merry."

Meredith half-bent and half-raised Natalie's hand so that she could press her forehead against the clasped fingers. She inhaled deeply, fighting back the crying. Natalie's grip was strong. Meredith let herself draw on the strength. She got control of herself and lifted her chin to give Natalie a watery smile.

Natalie smiled back, meeting her eyes with a solid, compassionate gaze.

"I think I'm in the wrong room," Meredith said, drawling for effect. "I heard you was a lawyer."

Chapter Ten

Natalie woke up to her own pain and the memory of the previous night, and Meredith's tears.

Her mother had never clung, wanting instead to spare her from the pain of her death. Everyone spared Natalie. Patrick, her closest ally, never revealed much--he'd only told her about Roland under great duress. She'd seen it bother him to have to burden her.

She'd been left with people's petty complaints. Co-workers hoping for sympathy because a boyfriend hadn't called or the traffic was bad. She became bitter because people didn't connect with her. So long as she could connect with the jury, she felt alive.

She didn't offer much of herself. She just channeled victims through her own emptiness. It worked.

Jake came with the wheelchair. "Big day."

"They're all big days here."

Jake nodded.

Natalie couldn't get herself into her own wheelchair, even though she'd become quite adept at sliding herself inches side to side or front to back on the bed. She put her arms around his strong shoulders and let herself be lifted. Once in the chair, she felt better, though it hurt to hold her neck up. Two weeks in bed made her muscles lose all purpose.

"Is it normal to lose so much mobility, even with a fabulous physical therapist?"

"Yes ma'am. It's completely typical to be pathetic."

Natalie let her head loll to the side. So this is why people sagged in wheelchairs. She blushed. Her hand twitched. The instinct to cross herself ran through her, but the strength wasn't there.

She gripped the wheelchair arms.

Jake parked her out on the sidewalk under the awning. She got her first view of Tarpley.

The world in front of her wasn't remarkable~a parking lot, a ring of trees beyond it. Pavement. Sidewalks. The awning itself was dark green. The hospital signs were grim.

She breathed deeply. Her chest burned in protest.

She'd never been a fan of the outdoors. She'd only been camping once in Girl Scouts and she'd gone home crying in the middle of the night.

Here she was in the wilderness.

"How far is the beach?" she asked.

Jake stood beside her. He had one hand on the handlebar, just behind her shoulder, and he was slouching companionably. She was glad he was there. Even having met him only a few times, he'd healed her~she could feel herself healing in his presence~and now she looked forward to his easy, friendly smile as if he were a drug.

"It's about an hour by car that way." He pointed in a direction she assumed was east. "But by wheels..." He looked her up and down. "Better start rolling."

"Maybe I could hitchhike."

Jake giggled. "I just pictured you, chair and all, strapped into the back of a pick-up truck, like some old rocking chair."

She rolled her eyes.

"Want me to do your makeup?"

"Makeup?"

"It's just~This is your first big day out. You're a little pale. And blotchy. I don't know if you've looked at yourself recently."

"Recently. You mean since~"

"I mean since," he said.

She'd seen in the mirror in the bathroom. She'd looked sixty years old, stooped, and feeble.

"Do I look haggard?" she asked.

"Sort of like a zombie. But~You're clean, your clothes look okay. Sometimes women like to 'put their face on.'" He made air quotes. "A right of passage. Makes them feel whole again. I'm speaking as a therapist here, not as Mr. Black."

She glanced down at her leg.

"Forget I said anything."

"Jake, I didn't mean it like~" From emotional leech to depressed drama queen already. This was a slippery slope.

A horn honked.

A van with a handicap access symbol painted on its side rolled up. A driver got out. He yanked open the bay doors, and began to lower the ramp.

"Only one in the county," Jake said. "Cost your insurance $200 every time you use it. Though I don't expect you will much, except for coming back for your surgery. Be right back." Jake darted inside.

Natalie glanced at the driver. He unlocked the brake on her wheelchair and pushed her onto the ramp.

"Is this safe?" she asked.

He snorted and pushed her in. The tilt of her chair made her wince, but she managed not to yelp. Once inside the van, he locked her wheels.

"Over here," Jake said.

Natalie glanced back toward the van door. The hospital entrance lay before her. Demure concrete and brick with a red cross on a white background near the sliding glass doors. Her home for two weeks. And in front of her home stood Jake, who was holding a gift basket.

Natalie raised her eyebrows.

"For you, my dear," Jake said.

He stood at chest-height. So the terrifying ramp hadn't taken her as high as she thought. She snorted and took the basket. There was soap and body oil and chocolate and Tylenol-3.

"The chocolate's for Merry, for putting up with your white ass."

"What do I get?" The driver asked.

Jake stepped out of Natalie's line of sight. She cautiously leaned forward to see around the van door just in time to see Jake tuck a ten dollar bill into the driver's shirt pocket.

"Drive slowly," Jake said. "She's never been to Tarpley."

"Absolutely true," Natalie said.

The driver frowned at Jake. "What's with the accent?"

"She's from Charlotte."

The driver looked askance at her. Natalie retreated back into the van. Jake appeared in the doorway again. He leaned in and took her hands. "See you soon, Nat."

"Thank you, Jake." His name caught in her throat. Tears stung her eyes. Jake winked.

The driver got into his seat. "What was that? You two going to the big Pride rally? Tweedledee and Tweedledum?"

Natalie rubbed her cheek and didn't meet his eyes in the rearview mirror.

The driver started the van. "I'm Harold. You thirsty? I got coffee."

"No, thank you. How long of a drive is it?"

Harold grunted. "Ten minutes."

"I'll just stare out the window, then."

The van pulled out of the parking lot. Harold turned on the radio, and then turned down the volume, so the country-western music became a faint background sound.

"Get lost on your way to the beach?"

"I guess. Yeah. That's what happened."

"So did I. Hell, I should've stayed in Rocky Mount."

"What's in Rocky Mount?" Natalie asked.

"They got a Starbucks."

Natalie nearly threw herself out of the van. "Tarpley doesn't have a Starbucks?"

"Welcome to Tarpley, ma'am. We got a nice Hardees."

The urge to cross herself returned; the urge to ward all of this off and beg for forgiveness. She'd survived the accident and survived surviving the accident so far. Outside the van windows cars and trucks rushed by. Beyond them she saw empty, flat land. She was descending into Hell.

The van slowed to a stop. A train whistle blew.

Harold sighed and put the van in park. Past the front windshield, a freight train rumbled by, impossibly slow, right there in the middle of the road.

"You golf?" Harold asked, distracting her from her horror. "I mean, when you were better?"

"No."

"A shame. Not much else to do around here."

"Would you drive me all the way to the beach?"

Harold glanced over his shoulder and smiled. "Not today. But Wilmington's closer than you think. You'll see it before you know it. Smells like the sea. That's all you need."

"And a job."

"Good point, there. What do you do?"

The van finally began to move again. Natalie glanced around furtively for the train. "I'm an attorney."

He whistled. "Not many of those around here. Not even in Rocky Mount. You go up to UNC?"

She shook her head.

"Oh, Lord. Not Duke?"

"Wake."

"Fair enough."

"Have you always been in North Carolina?" Natalie asked.

"I was born in Rocky Mount. My parents came from Ecuador. A long journey," he said.

"Have you ever been there?"

"Ecuador?"

"Yes."

He shook his head. "No. Don't think I ever will."

The van turned into a neighborhood. He slowed his driving, and asked, "Your people come over on the Mayflower?"

She shook her head. "During the war."

"You Jewish?"

"No, just~" She paused, trying to think of what she was.

"Just screwed. I got it."

"Everywhere you turn."

"Yup. World's a shitty place."

He stopped the van in front of a two-story cottage. Toys were strewn over the front lawn.

The house needed new paint and a good window-washing, but there were flowers planted around the mailbox and the porch had a swing.

Harold pulled open the van door and carefully wheeled her down to Earth.

"Home sweet home," he said.

Meredith came onto the porch.

"I could probably do worse," she said.

He snorted.

Meredith stepped onto the front stoop. Two little boys rushed past her. They stopped halfway up the gravel driveway and stared at Natalie.

Natalie felt her blood drain from her face.

"Better get used to it," Harold said.

"I have to get used to it?"

He didn't say anything more as he pushed her up the driveway. The wheels moved easily over the thin gravel~more like gray and silver packed dirt. The boys scooted backward as she approached.

"You better say something," Harold said.

"Um. Shit."

"Maybe not that."

She glared at him and then tried to smile at the boys. If she thought of them as the check-forgers and wife-beaters she used to deal with, maybe it would work. She could fake-polite if it was her job. Winning over Meredith's children was her new job.

"All right," she said. "Which one of you is Beau and which one is Merry?"

One of the boys giggled.

"Aren't you Russian?" the other boy asked.

"Not exactly."

"Little Merry, why don't you help her carry her basket?" Meredith said from the steps.

Natalie held out her gift basket.

The bashful boy~slightly leaner than his brother~giggled. He took the basket carefully from her and clutched the handle with both hands. He wobbled carrying it to the stoop.

"Do you like dogs?" Beau asked, trying not to stare at her legs.

She kicked at him with her bad leg. He leapt away. She grinned. He grinned back, showing his teeth. The spell of her appearance seemed broken. She wondered if it would be so easy with everyone else. She would just have to kick them, too.

"I like dogs," she said.

"Good. I want a dog, but Mommy won't let me. See, Mommy? She says we can have a dog!"

Natalie blushed and glanced helplessly at Meredith. She tried to remember how she'd gotten herself into this situation. She'd been driving east. She'd been driving, and it was dark~

Meredith waved her off. "You know why we can't have a dog, Beau."

Merritt stopped in the front door and put down his basket.

"In the corner, Merry," Meredith said.

Merritt picked up the basket again.

"Because you're going away." Beau said. He stomped inside the house.

"You're going away?" Natalie asked.

Meredith frowned and shook her head.

The wheelchair's front wheels bumped against the stoop.

"Here we are," Harold said.

"And now what?" Natalie asked. Surely he didn't expect her to get up and stroll over the threshold.

"Watch," Meredith said. "Well, I guess you won't be able to watch, per se, but observe."

Harold headed back down the driveway. Natalie watched over her shoulder. He got in his van. She waved. He didn't wave back. He just drove away, like she'd never see him again.

Meredith took the wheelchair handles.

Natalie started. "Merry, you're not strong enough~Please don't hurt yourself."

"Hush, I know what I'm doing." Meredith pulled her back and tilted the smaller front wheels over the stoop. Then she rolled forward, and with a heave, the chair rolled up onto the stoop.

"Holy crap," Natalie said.

Meredith smacked the back of Natalie's head.

Natalie ducked her head.

"Sorry. That's what I do with the boys when they use bad language." She pushed Natalie into the foyer.

"Your boys use bad language?"

"You wouldn't imagine what they learn from the neighborhood. Anyway. The boys'll want to push you around some, but you're going to learn to do all that on your own." She let go of the wheels, and Natalie rolled to a stop.

"Do what?"

"Up the curb, down the curb. Easier than you think."

"And then what, enroll me in the basketball league?"

Meredith frowned.

"I'm sorry."

"You've got a right to be bitter, I guess. Let me show you around." She walked in front of Natalie and into a room on her right.

Natalie rubbed her hands together and then pushed the wheels. The wheels moved. "Hey, cool."

Meredith chuckled.

Natalie, emboldened by being able to roll herself, tried intermediate wheelchair maneuvering. She held one wheel still and rolled the other to turn. Physics 101. She spun around and ended up facing Meredith.

"We converted the dining room into a guest room. Vince put in the doors himself."

"It's nice," Natalie said.

The front windows let in light. Through the glass she saw the road she'd come from and other houses along the street. The room was filled completely by one hospital bed, metal arms and all.

"I'll have to help you in and out for a couple days, probably. I couldn't get one of those bars installed, since you're here temporarily. But the rest is from your insurance company."

"Amazing."

"Sure is. Now, there's a full bathroom down here, so you won't have to worry about the stairs. Unfortunately, the kids use it too. They sleep in the den a lot. The kitchen's in the back. There's a porch out there, too. Not too big, but we've got a grill."

Natalie settled her arms on the armrests and tried to get comfortable. She wasn't. The room was nicer than the hospital's~richly polished hardwood floor, a dresser with a mirror and candles and figurines~A Jesus, a Mary, a clown with balloons, a horse rearing. The windows had lace curtains. Compared to the hospital room, this one was about the same size with the same bed.

A nicer prison.

"So. This is my life," she said. Something caught in her throat.

"There's one more thing. Wait here." Meredith disappeared.

Natalie heard her running up the stairs.

When she came back, she had Hollingsworth in her arms.

"My cat!" She was too shocked to cry, but her chest burned.

Meredith piled Hollingsworth onto Natalie's lap.

Hollingsworth crawled up her chest and licked at her face and began to purr.

"Oh my God. You~"

"Shssh. It's a big adjustment." Meredith squeezed Natalie's shoulders. "I'll call you for dinner, all right? Let me know if you need anything beforehand. I'll keep the boys out. I won't always be able to, but this afternoon is yours."

Natalie sucked in a breath. She wanted to thank Meredith but a sob in her throat escaped first, drowning out whatever she'd wanted to say, taking over her facial muscles so they contorted in an anguished grimace. She fought as hard as she could against the tears.

Meredith, still rubbing tense shoulders, leaned over and kissed the top of her head, and said, "It's going to be all right."

Then she left, shutting the door behind her. Shutting Natalie in.

Natalie put her face against fur and cried. And then she cried harder, because it hurt so much to cry.

Chapter Eleven

The diet of a four-year-old boy was the same diet as an invalid with intestinal trauma. They were having cinnamon toast at 5:30 in the afternoon. Even at the hospital, Natalie ate later. The afternoon sunlight was turning from orange to dark gray outside the French doors. Natalie contemplated verandas and ate what she could, not hungry and uninterested.

For the blessing, Natalie felt awkward with Meredith's cold fingers in one hand and Merritt's hot paw in the other. Beau led the prayer, thanking God they got to eat one of his favorite foods when so many other people had to go without or eat gross things. He wasn't sure which was worse, but he thanked God he didn't have to find out. When he started in on how he felt about his glass of apple juice, Meredith finally interjected with, "Darling, He can hear your thoughts, you know."

"Like Daddy?"

"Yup. Just like Daddy. They're up there together, hoping you'll eat your dinner and become a big, strong man."

Natalie squeezed Meredith's hand.

Meredith squeezed back and gave her a smile.

After the blessing, Beau ate four pieces of cinnamon toast, but only drank half of his apple juice.

Merritt ate one piece but drank two glasses of juice, and gazed hopefully at Meredith, and then Natalie.

"Why is he looking at me like that?" Natalie asked.

"He wants more juice."

"But why would–Does he want mine?"

"How it works."

"Should I give it to him?"

"Only if you want to train him like a dog and say it's okay to beg for food from your elders at the table."

Merritt made a face.

Natalie picked up her glass, drank it down, and smiled at Merritt.

He scowled, but he didn't cry or bang the table, which surpassed Natalie's expectations enough she felt guilty.

"He's good with adversity," Meredith said.

"I'll say."

"Merry, go get some juice from the fridge. It's all right."

He slid off his stool and backed into the kitchen, keeping his eyes on Natalie.

"Should I make a scary face?" Natalie asked.

"No."

Natalie shrugged and went back to picking at her toast.

"Not hungry?" Meredith asked.

"Not really. I mean, it's really good~"

"Please. It's cinnamon toast. There's dessert later, good to save room for it."

"What is it?" Beau and Natalie asked simultaneously.

Meredith rolled her eyes. "You'll see. After your bath."

Beau grumbled.

"Bath?" Natalie asked.

"Off with you," Meredith said.

Beau took his plate into the kitchen. Natalie craned her neck and could see around the door. Beau put his scraps into the trash can, and then put the plate in the dishwasher.

"How'd you get him to do that? Even I don't do that," Natalie asked.

"If he completes all his chores before bed, he gets a nickel and a strawberry. We have a checklist."

Natalie gasped.

Meredith grinned. "What's that look on your face for?"

"You bribe your children?"

"It's positive reinforcement and providing structure and personal motivation."

"Merry," Natalie said.

"It was recommended by Focus on the Family. And it works. For Beau. Merritt just wants kisses and hugs."

Natalie wrinkled her nose.

Merritt came back and gave the apple juice bottle to Meredith, who poured him half a glass. "You can drink this, and then it's bath time."

"But Natalie's here," Merritt said.

"And she likes little boys better when they're clean."

"She does?"

"Yes," Meredith said.

Natalie nodded.

Merritt took his glass and drank it all down. Then he set it on his plate and carefully walked with it into the kitchen.

"Hey. Usually in an hour or so you bring me dinner. What do the boys do?" Natalie asked.

"I give them their bath and read them a story, and then my next door neighbor comes over and reads them another story and puts them to sleep. Then she hangs out in the living room and does paper work for her business until I get back. She's self-employed."

"Do you have to pay her?"

"Natalie, stop looking so guilty. What I do with my home life is none of your concern."

Natalie glanced away.

"Though, actually~"

Natalie froze.

"I've got to run to the hospital for about two hours tonight, to get all my hours in this week. Once the boys are asleep."

"Is~Is your neighbor coming over?"

"Nope. I thought I'd leave them with you."

"Merry! I can barely move."

"If there's a fire or a flood, just yell really loud and get them to haul you out. But you'll be fine."

"Merry, please don't leave me here with your kids."

"You won't notice a thing."

Upstairs, a faucet turned on. Beau yelled, "Mommy."

"Time to get the little rascals clean and sleepy," Meredith said.

"Should I do something in the kitchen?"

"No, no. You can watch TV if you want, though it's probably better to start after the boys are asleep."

"Mommy!" Beau yelled again.

"Go. I can fend for myself," Natalie said.

"More than you think," Merry said, patting her shoulder before jogging upstairs.

Natalie rolled herself back to her room, listening to the laughing and splashing above her. More civilization and home than she'd experienced in years. Perhaps ever, beyond what the television offered.

Being around people wasn't so bad.

She prayed she wasn't going to cry again.

The house was so blissfully quiet after sunset Natalie couldn't be sure there were kids around. The peace wasn't what she'd expected, having not grown up with brothers or sisters or nieces and nephews. She'd been a hellion as a teenager, so she assumed all children terrorized their parents.

She hoped she wouldn't be there long enough to corrupt Beau and Merritt.

She dozed, finding sleeping in a bed in a home so comforting she wanted to stay in it forever. Her world in Charlotte evaporated. Patrick and Roland were gone, along with her coworkers and her friends and the memories of her mother. Instead she dreamed about the sidewalk outside and the gravel driveway and the awning of the hospital. She found it hard to believe she had seen it for the first time that morning.

Her laptop was on the dresser, beckoning to her. She had emails to read and her internal clock was pointing out it was only nine at night. At home, she'd be in the thick of her case files, with dinner packed away and the late night shows far off.

She tried reminding her body sleep came much earlier every night for the last two weeks. But she wasn't in the hospital any longer, she was in a home. Someone else's home.

The last time she'd been in someone else's home was a trip out to Utah. Her friend had a ranch. She hadn't talked to her friend in a while. Maybe an email was warranted.

She scowled at the laptop.

Trickery!

Meredith hesitated outside of Natalie's door. She'd gotten home and gotten dessert, but Natalie might be asleep. Natalie might want to be alone. Coming home to someone was harder than Meredith remembered.

She knocked.

"Yeah?" Natalie said.

Meredith poked her head in. "You awake?"

Natalie smoothed her blanket over her legs. "I was contemplating doing some work."

"At this hour?" Meredith asked. She ran her fingers through her hair.

Natalie was settled in bed, looking sleepy and tousled, and it all suggested to Meredith she could be asleep, too. She yawned.

"You were working at this hour, weren't you?" Natalie asked.

"Last hour. Makes all the difference." Meredith came into the room, holding a bowl of strawberries. "Up for dessert?"

"Absolutely. But I didn't clean my plate or brush my teeth."

"Or take a bath." The banter removed her apprehension; her friendship with Natalie happened too easily and too quickly to be understandable, but she was glad nothing changed.

"Hey, I spent nearly an hour in the bathroom. I'm somewhat clean."

"Then you deserve a strawberry." Meredith plucked one out of the bowl and offered it.

The strawberry was sprinkled with powdered sugar. Natalie bit into the sweetness and nearly convulsed. Her expression of delighted surprise warmed Meredith. Juice dripped on her lips. She wiped her mouth with her hand.

Meredith chuckled.

"Geez, why don't I eat strawberries more?"

Meredith produced another.

"Thank you."

Natalie studied Meredith and then patted the bed.

"Thanks," Meredith said, sitting down with a sigh.

"How was work?"

Meredith shrugged. "You know what my day is like. People are nice."

"Really nice." She took another berry from Meredith's bowl.

Meredith smiled.

"You seem happy. Explain yourself."

"Having another adult in the house who doesn't~it's just amazing."

"Who doesn't what?"

"Never mind."

Natalie frowned, but leaned over for another strawberry.

Chapter Twelve

In the morning, Meredith lingered upstairs. She should wake up the boys for preschool. She strained but could not hear them waking up on their own. In the room under her feet, Natalie slept.

Meredith didn't really believe in feng shui, but she knew she felt a different energy in the house and didn't know what else to call it. Natalie brought an aura with her. Meredith was still too nervous about having Natalie around to discern if the changed reality was pleasant or unpleasant. She needed to get used to everything, which meant going downstairs.

She slung her pocketbook over her shoulder. When the boys were distracted by cereal and only calling for her every 30 seconds, she ducked into Natalie's room.

Natalie slept, oblivious to the play of morning sunlight over her features. The hospital bed loomed scarily and out-of-place in such a light-filled room. Meredith was glad at least there were no machines. Natalie's wrist still had blotches from the IV needle. Her face was mottled green and yellow from the fading bruises. Asleep, she was perhaps the most beautiful person Meredith had ever seen.

Meredith moved closer to the bed. She didn't know quite what to make of Natalie's appearance in her life--here, in her home now when she was about to lose everything. Natalie couldn't have come at a worse time. Meredith didn't think she was up to helping anyone else, with her own life the way it was. But she would try. She resisted the temptation to sit on the bed and smooth hair away from Natalie's face. Her slumber was relaxed and pain-free.

Meredith envied her.

"Natalya," Natalie's mother would say, "If you're going to just sit there and drink coffee, study. Read."

"I know it all, Mom," Natalie would set down her coffee mug and toss her mother a textbook. "Quiz me."

Her mother would glance at the book and frown and shake her head. On good days she would express a desire to beat her daughter with the book, like in the old country.

On bad days she would just say, "Drink your coffee," and leave the room.

Natalya didn't make her own coffee often. Starbucks was enough. The office always had coffee. The courts always had coffee. She bought expensive beans over the internet from far off places and~on rare, quiet Saturday mornings~she'd grind them up and make pancakes and drink pretentious coffee that never quite tasted as good as it should.

Meredith's kitchen was stocked with pre-ground bags and a percolator. Natalie sat in her wheelchair and watched it brew for nearly a half hour. What else did she have to do? She took the coffee into the living room and turned on the television. Proud of those accomplishments, cursing her mother's voice in her head telling her to do more, she slept.

A talk show was on television when she woke up. She squinted and Ellen DeGeneres came into focus; too bright and sunny and cheerful and Californian to take when she was groggy and full of despair. Natalie turned the television off. Silence descended. Her coffee was cold. She turned the television back on and put it on mute. Just enough light to live by.

Wheeling herself back to the microwave to heat up her coffee seemed like too much, so she settled for drinking it cold and cringing and drinking some more. She had papers to sign, things to do. Patrick priority-mailed her paperwork to go from her sick leave to short-term disability.

She had to eat through her vacation days first. Watching her time slip away depressed her. Those days had been for a vacation. This was not a vacation, even if she was an hour from the beach.

The boys had gone off to preschool and Meredith was at work.

Natalie missed them.

They'd been noisy and happy at breakfast. And she missed the hospital~Teresa and Colleen and Wheeler and everyone she'd been friends with, or at least, those who were pleasant to her and kept her from being alone.

She was alone and hurting, too far from her medicine or hot coffee, across an abyss of living room carpet, with nothing to do but contemplate her sorry life. The one she'd lived before the accident. She gazed at the television, waiting for distraction. Knowing not to hope for salvation.

The choice between sleeping and pain continued. Natalie dozed all day in front of the television and, stiff and achy, did her stretches over the course of a half hour, and tried to choose whether or not to bathe off the sickly sweat gathered on her skin or call Meredith and offer to start dinner.

In the end, she ordered pizza and then finagled herself into the bathroom. She was exhausted by the time she'd combed her hair and contemplated another nap. The soreness in her abdomen made her want to curl into a ball and whimper. The doorbell rang.

"Come in. Door's open." She backed out of the bathroom and into the hallway that opened onto the foyer.

A young man stood just inside the door, holding a black bag. "Ms. Ivans?" he asked.

"That's me. Take those into the kitchen, would you? The money's on the table."

He scooted past her, trying not to see her wheelchair or her face and trying not to look away. She sighed, deciding she'd prefer one or the other to the tip-toeing.

He scooped up the money and asked, his voice cracking, "Need any change?"

"Nope."

"Thanks, ma'am." He backed toward the door. "Uh~thanks."

She waved.

He left and closed the door.

She texted Meredith, "Be warned. Got pizza."

Even with pizza on the table, there was nothing else to do but wait. She wheeled herself into her bedroom and took Tylenol. Her doctor told her if she was to take pain medication, she should take the maximum dose they'd worked out and not to cut it in half in order to tackle half the pain. It didn't work like that, he said.

Her instincts told her otherwise, but she followed orders.

He'd also told her to be light with the Tylenol, because a shot liver did no one any good. Contradictory advice. He was appealing to her lawyer's nature, and figuring out the puzzle of dosage and balance each day so far kept her goal-oriented. And in pain.

Stupid stomach. Stupid steering wheel. Stupid glass.

She set out her antibiotics to eat with dinner. Shifting herself back into bed tempted her. Meredith could bring her pizza. Or not. It didn't matter. She rubbed her stomach. The pain didn't go away.

Her eyes itched. She blinked rapidly, but tears still formed at the corners of her eyes, and then fell on her cheeks. She tried to read the book by her bed, but was too distracted by aches. She rolled herself back into the living room, slowly. She banged her hand on the doorway past the kitchen, and cursed as loud as she could, yelling at the empty house.

The new pain stung worse than the old pain. She angrily managed to get herself all the way into the living room. She turned on the television.

"The Roland case's local angle has~"

The front door swung open. Children's voices filled the space, drowning out the newscaster.

And Meredith's, louder, calling, "We're home."

Natalie bit her lip. She wiped at her cheeks.

"Pizza," Merritt said.

Beau screamed and ran to the kitchen.

Natalie turned off the television. She wheeled in a backwards circle until she faced Meredith.

"Natalie got the pizza. You'd better thank her," Meredith said.

"Thank you, Natalie!" Merritt flung himself at her, landing against her good leg, thankfully, and not against her stomach or her other leg.

She oofed anyway, but when Merritt hugged her she awkwardly hugged him back. No one hugged complete strangers with such affection over pizza. She didn't think she'd ever been as naive and open-hearted as Merritt.

Beau just leaned against Meredith's side and said, "This is awesome."

Meredith grinned. "Thank you."

"I was too lazy to cook."

Meredith shook her head. She walked into the living room and shooed away the boys, telling them they could start eating as long as they used plates and napkins. Over the clamor of cupboards opening and plates hitting the counter, Meredith took Natalie's hands.

"Any little thing that brightens their day~I'm grateful. It doesn't matter how small. It's a positive contribution to the universe."

"Gluttony, laziness, and junk foods are positive contributions to the uni~verse?"

"If you do it every day, now, it won't be special."

"Good point."

Natalie studied their intertwined fingers. Her skin tingled, like Meredith was infusing her with the very graciousness she was talking about. The touch made her feel better.

"Can you afford it?" Meredith asked.

"I can afford it right now. Who knows if I can afford it in a week. But everything can change. I'm not going to worry about next week until next week."

Meredith chewed on her lower lip. Then she shrugged and said, "I guess you've got enough to worry about."

"All kinds of things."

"Then come have pizza. You don't have to worry about where you're getting your next meal. That's a blessing." Meredith tugged on Natalie's hands.

Natalie grunted. "You could push me, instead."

"I guess you've been wheeling yourself around all day."

"More or less."

"Think of how buff you'll get." Meredith let go of Natalie's fingers and went around to the handles.

Natalie leaned her head back. "Just what I always wanted."

Meredith squeezed her shoulder and then pushed her to the kitchen table.

"Your turn to say the blessing, Merritt."

"What about Natalie?" Merritt asked.

Meredith glanced at Natalie, and then said, "It's your turn tonight, Merritt. Come on."

Merritt shifted in his seat, curling his legs under him so he could more easily reach the table. "Thank you for pizza, Jesus and Natalie." Then he gazed expectantly at his mother.

"Amen," Meredith said.

Beau reached for his slice.

Natalie picked up one from the box, and turned her eyes heavenward. "Thank God for pizza."

Meredith elbowed her.

Natalie took a bite and chewed smugly.

"You are a terrible influence," Meredith said.

"I knew I would be."

Meredith held her gaze, and then reached over and rubbed her arm.

Merritt burped. Beau spilled his milk.

Natalie ate her pizza. She wondered if Meredith had bigger troubles than her influence on four-year-olds. It felt good to put food on the table for people she cared about. Totally different than doing it for herself.

Meredith nudged her shoulder. Natalie swallowed.

"You're staring at the French doors. Thinking of bolting?" Meredith asked.

"No." Natalie sat back and ran her hands through her hair. "Just thanking God for pizza. Really."

"Tomorrow you can thank Him for tilapia. Friday night is grill night."

Merritt giggled. "Mommy lets us play with the charcoal."

"I figure they're past the point where they're going to eat it."

"Smart."

"They just draw all over the porch with it. Come winter I'm going to start having to worry about my walls again."

Natalie snorted.

Merritt slid off his seat and took his plate into the kitchen.

Beau started picking the pepperoni off the pizza still in the box.

"You're not going to make me babysit again, are you?" Natalie asked.

Chapter Thirteen

Natalie spent Friday in bed imagining her leg was getting worse. The laptop was by her side and she typed half-heartedly with one hand. She felt far-removed from the day-to-day drama of the Charlotte courts. She didn't miss it. The criminals, the petty bickering, and often the stench of the jail. The judges who didn't like her, or the judges who liked her too much.

She checked her work email, but it mostly pertained to other cases. Patrick had re-assigned them and turned over her notes. He even hired a temporary clerk to sort through everything. Today, she told herself, she could just stay in bed and have fish later and worry about tomorrow, tomorrow.

She didn't like fish.

Refreshing her email box produced an email reply from Patrick in reference to a query she'd sent about Roland.

The letter read only, "You shouldn't be reading your email anymore while on official leave."

"Well, all right then," she said. She turned the computer off and then dozed.

Only after she woke up did she realize it was the first nap she'd taken without painkillers.

She smiled.

Her leg throbbed.

Natalie wheeled herself out onto the front porch. She checked herself. Not tired. No pain. Well, some, if she reached for it. A lingering feeling like her abdomen was bruised. If she lifted her shirt up, there was the yellow and purple skin and the angry pink rash of zipper-like stitches.

Her leg gave her the most trouble. The drugs she took to keep the blood flowing through its pinched, rerouted veins gave her the most anxiety. Her foot was white. She couldn't move her ankle or her toes very easily. It hurt to try. If she lost the leg–well, it might be better than this. But her life would be over.

Except for the leg, she was stronger. Her wheelchair moved easily under her fingers. She'd learned the tricks and corners of the house. So she made it to the porch and gazed out at the other little porches and two-story bungalows.

The neighborhood had been developed only ten years ago, when golf moved inland and Wilmington real estate shot sky-high. The city seemed suspended between cute and depressingly generic, but none of the grit of Charlotte was there, and none of the crime.

Natalie inhaled deeply. When she felt better, Jake was going to take her on a tour. The water tower, the railroad depot, the farmer's market, the library.

For the first time in weeks, she was energetic enough to be bored. She dug her cell phone out of her bag and called Patrick.

He was at his desk. "Uh, hi, Nat."

"Uh, hi, Pat," she said, trying to be jovial, but miffed at the hesitation. He was her only lifeline, didn't he know?

"I've been meaning to call you. I thought maybe I'd come down and see you on the weekend. When's your surgery scheduled?"

"Patrick, is something wrong at the office?"

"Tell me how you are first."

"No."

He paused, breathing evenly against the phone, and then coughed, and asked, "Have you seen the news?"

"Not really. I mean, sometimes the local stuff here, or CNN on the computer, but I haven't really been up to it."

"Oh, okay."

She was purposely avoiding Roland like a spoiled child. But she assumed everything went on as normal in her absence. Life usually did.

"Roland's lawyers have started these rumors, and you know the blogosphere, and it's just you've been so under the radar--in the hospital, I know--"

"Patrick!"

"Maybe you should talk to the District Attorney directly."

She was so infuriated by his babbling, she wanted to throw the phone on the ground and roll over it with her wheel. She trembled, and whispered into the phone, hoping calmness would bring clarity.

"Patrick. What the heck is going on?"

"They're saying you were drunk."

"What?"

"You were drunk and distraught over having no case and framing poor, innocent Roland you took off for the weekend to drown your sorrows."

She made some sort of squeaking sound.

"We're placing you on administrative leave," he said.

"Agh? What about my vacation leave?"

"It's a good thing. More money than short-term disability, so you can ride this out longer. Once the trial is over--" He paused again.

"Once the trial is over what?" she asked.

"You can come back to your job."

"Not until then?"

"It's only until the verdict comes back and everything's straightened out. A week, maybe two. Nat," he asked. "Were you drunk?"

"No!"

"Can you prove it? The Tarpley police have been very uncooperative with the press."

"Do you want the damn police report? I'll fax it directly to the Observer."

"Have you seen it?"

"Not yet. But I will." She seethed, but at least he was giving her a plan. She could clear her name. Once she stopped being brutally offended she needed to clear her name.

"Nat," he asked, his voice quiet. "Were you speeding?"

"I don't know. I don't remember anything."

"The police report will say."

"I could have been. It was night, and the highway was wide open, and God, I was so angry about the case--"

"I don't want to hear anymore," Patrick said.

"So basically my career is ruined."

"Come on, Nat. Don't be dramatic."

"The case is tainted, the jury will think the city is either laughable or corrupt, and Roland seems like a victim."

"Those are issues we're dealing with. You need to heal," he said.

"He drowned his wife. He drowned her."

"I know."

"I didn't drown anyone."

"Natalie--"

"I didn't drink. I didn't hurt anyone. Just myself."

"It's politics," he said.

"I thought I worked for justice."

He didn't say anything.

She relented, still angry but not at him. "How're the girls?"

"Great." He launched into a story of their fall break, and Natalie listened, red with rage, breathing hard. She listened quietly and wished she could scream, instead.

On Saturday, Natalie made dinner, even though it was hard to deal with the stove when she sat underneath it. Macaroni and cheese from a box. On Meredith's instructions she added a vegetable mix from the freezer and set out ketchup on the table. She didn't know if she could watch them eat it.

Hollingsworth followed her around, wary of the metal contraption housing her. Only when she was in bed or on the couch would he leap up to join her. Sometimes when the chair was otherwise unoccupied, she would find him curled up and asleep. Hollingsworth dozing in the wheelchair miffed the boys because they liked to roll the wheelchair through the house. Which miffed Meredith. One big happy family.

She'd timed dinner so she was stirring the butter into the noodles when the door flew open and Merritt and Beau bounded through.

"Natty!" they called.

Her name sounded so much better on their lips than Patrick's. The bastard. She shouldn't think about that when the kids were home, hugging her. She pulled Merritt onto her lap so Beau could crowd her good leg without touching her bad one.

Meredith followed more sedately. She held Natalie's gaze, smiling, until Natalie's face ached from smiling back. She wanted to hug Meredith, too, but her arms were full, and Meredith finally reached over and tousled her hair, smoothing locks in front of her eyes.

Natalie blew the hair back. "Thanks," she said.

"Hey, anytime I can beautify you, you just let me know."

"Mommy, you made Natalie ugly." Beau said.

Meredith cringed, but Natalie laughed. "What am I, Clark Kent?" she asked.

"What's your superpower?"

"Making dinner?" Natalie said.

"Right. Good one. All right boys, set the table."

Beau and Merritt climbed off of Natalie and slunk toward the silverware.

Natalie patted her lap. "Space free."

Meredith blushed.

"I got fired today," Natalie said.

"What?"

"That was just for dramatic effect. Kind of. Placed on 'administrative leave.' They said I was drunk when I had the accident."

"You weren't drunk. I saw the toxicology report myself. I just violated HIPAA. I'm sorry."

"It's all right. I mean, you're telling the patient."

"Sure, but~Natalie, I'm so sorry." Meredith took Natalie's hand, and Natalie squeezed it, drawing it against her arm.

They stood together until Beau banged his fork on the table, and said, "Hungry!"

"You're raising monsters," Natalie said.

Meredith let her hand go. "Wolves, disguised as sheep."

"We're going to be soldiers, like daddy," Beau said.

Natalie glanced at Meredith, who went to kiss the top of Beau's head. "Yes, you will. And what else did daddy tell you to do?"

"Go to college," Beau said.

Merritt picked up macaroni and cheese with his fingers and put it on his plate.

"Guess he's ready for Stanford," Natalie said.

"I told them they weren't allowed to leave the state for college unless they were real smart and wanted to go to Emory. They had no idea what I was talking about. They're four, you know."

"I finally found the audience for my cooking," Natalie said.

"Aw, honey, if you read the directions on the box, cooking's real easy."

"Don't you think I've tried?" Natalie asked.

Meredith grinned.

Natalie freed the pot of macaroni and cheese from the boys long enough to get some only lightly spittle-covered noodles for herself.

"Hold hands," Meredith said. And then when she saw Merritt's orange-stained hands, she mouthed "Sorry" to Natalie.

Natalie shrugged. Three days with children in the house and she'd already acclimated to parts of her feeling gross. She clasped the slippery, warm hand. Merritt giggled.

Meredith bowed her head. "Dear Heavenly Father, bless this food we are about to eat. We pray it may be good for our body and soul. If there be any poor creature hungry or thirsty walking along the road, send them in to us that we can share the food with them, just as You share your gifts with all of us. Amen."

"Amen," Beau said. Then he got out of his chair and ran to the door.

Natalie blinked.

"Every time I say that he goes to the door to let in the hungry and the thirsty."

"Have any come?"

Meredith called out, "Beau, come back. She's already here."

Beau skittered back. He frowned but climbed back into his chair.

Natalie picked up her fork but waited until the lump in her throat subsided so she could eat.

Natalie hadn't talked to her law school friends in nearly a year. They'd all once been close, spending at least two hours a night studying together in the law library. Quizzing each other, memorizing words, eating bad pizza and good Chinese food. After every semester they'd go out for beer, and the second time Natalie puked it all up, she decided after every semester she'd have ginger ale.

Thinking about drinking made her slightly nauseous. But it always made her think of her friends. She'd been a blip on their social networking for a while, and commented on baby pictures or a good book, but she hadn't paid much attention. So it took her a good ten minutes to figure out her blog's password. Then she composed the note. "You'll never guess where I am..."

Meredith knocked on Natalie's door.

"Come in."

Meredith opened the door. "Heard you typing. Thought you might want breakfast."

"I do want breakfast." Natalie put the laptop aside.

Meredith chuckled and maneuvered in a tray. Natalie was small under her quilt~tired, still. And yet, something about the way her dark hair shined in the lamplight made Meredith's breath catch. She settled the tray over Natalie's lap, just like at the hospital, except this one was made of wood and the dishes on top were ceramic, not plastic.

The pancakes were homemade, but not as good as Colleen's.

Natalie raised an eyebrow at the water glass with dandelions and clover blossoms.

"Boys picked those for you. But I made them promise not to come in."

"Where are they?"

"In the living room, petting your cat," Meredith said.

"Is my cat all right?"

"When I left he was."

Natalie bit her lip, but gazed at the plate.

"Do you want syrup?"

"Yes."

Meredith tapped the little polished silver vessel.

"What's that?" Natalie asked, tapping a glass.

"Iced tea."

Natalie took the glass and carefully took a sip.

"Unsweetened," Meredith said.

"I see."

"Gotta start you slow."

"We do have tea in Charlotte, you know," Natalie said.

"Is it Lipton?"

Natalie shook her head. She put the glass down and poured syrup on her pancakes.

"Ain't tea," Meredith said.

Natalie snorted.

Meredith eased off the side of the bed.

"Going to work?"

"Day off. We get those sometime. I was thinking of going to Wal-Mart and getting a few things. It's a couple of towns over."

"Want me to watch the boys?"

"They can get pretty wild on you. How about you take one, I'll take one."

"I think I can handle that. Maybe after breakfast."

"Got a preference?" Meredith asked.

Natalie took another bite of pancake, chewed, swallowed, and said, lifting her tea to toast Meredith, "I love them both the same."

Meredith's chest constricted. "Good answer. I'll leave you to your breakfast."

"I really do," Natalie called, as she went through the door.

Chapter Fourteen

Natalie got up early Sunday morning and carefully made her way out of her bedroom. The boys were already awake. Merritt colored in the kitchen. Beau played with blocks. What he was building, Natalie couldn't guess.

"What're you doing?" Natalie asked as she wheeled herself into the kitchen. Her legs itched. Her hips were sore. She wanted out of the chair, but she was pretty sure she'd forgotten how to walk.

Merritt came over and crawled onto her lap. He'd gotten good at avoiding her broken leg by wedging himself against the arm of the chair and her shoulder.

Beau said, "We can't watch TV without mommy. And we have to be quiet. She's asleep."

"What time does she usually wake up?"

Beau glanced at the clock. "Um. Nine."

Merritt began combing his fingers through Natalie's hair. Natalie hoped they weren't sticky.

The kitchen clock read 8:15.

"Should we make Merr--Mommy breakfast?"

"Okay," Merritt said.

Beau put down his blocks.

"What's her favorite food?" Natalie asked.

"She likes eggs," Beau said.

Merritt pushed his face into Natalie's shoulder and giggled. "With hot sauce."

"It burns," Beau said. He wore a dismayed expression.

"Hot!" Merritt shouted.

"Shssh," Natalie said.

Merritt grunted.

"Beau, see if we have any eggs," Natalie said.

Beau scampered to the refrigerator.

"Merry, do we get the paper?" Natalie asked Merritt.

Merritt nodded. "On Sundays."

"Go get it," she said.

Merritt slipped off her lap and wandered in the general direction of the door.

Beau carefully set the hot sauce and the eggs on the kitchen counter and then frowned.

Natalie wheeled over.

Beau said, "We can't reach the stove."

"Good point. Maybe mommy will make everyone breakfast."

Beau nodded. He looked determined and marched back over to the refrigerator, and pulled out the milk.

"We can have cereal," he said.

"Where are the bowls?"

He opened the bottom cabinet and pulled out a bowl, and then more carefully stretched to pull a spoon from the silverware drawer. His triumphant grin faltered when Natalie narrowed her eyes at him. She waited. He gazed down at his bowl.

Merritt scrambled in with the paper, which he dumped on Natalie's lap. "I want cereal," he said.

"Me too," Natalie said.

"Oh," Beau said. He got out two more bowls and two more spoons. Natalie took it upon herself to open the Corn Flakes box. Meredith had picked up a boggling assortment of bulk cereals at the Wal-Mart.

"I want Froot Loops," Merritt said.

Beau and Natalie turned on him, growling.

"Or Corn Flakes," he said.

Meredith studied herself in the bathroom mirror. Her face was pale and splotchy. She prodded her puffy skin. Noises came from downstairs—the occasional giggle, rustling around, but the happy family below couldn't block out the memory. The blood. Vincent's anger. Heat rising inside her to match it.

The memory was so incongruous with what awaited her downstairs she didn't know which one was real. Death was forever. The rest was transitory. She didn't know how she could face her children.

But Natalie was downstairs. She wanted to see Natalie. Every time she did, she felt lighter. Almost happy. Just from being in the same room.

To be in the same room, she'd have to go downstairs, and face her children, too.

Her eyes stung with fresh tears. She tightened her bathrobe and went downstairs. They were piled onto the couch, reading the comics page. Dirty bowls were stacked in the sink. A cereal box was open and out on the counter, along with eggs and hot sauce.

"We made breakfast!" Merritt said when he saw her.

"I made breakfast. You ate it," Beau said.

"I helped."

"Did not."

"Did too. I brought the paper." Merritt said.

"Boys. Merritt did bring the paper. Beau got the bowls," Natalie said.

Beau and Merritt both looked smug.

Meredith put the eggs and the hot sauce away and poured herself a bowl of cereal.

"Natty's reading us *Garfield*," Beau said.

Natalie cringed.

"Is it funny?" Meredith asked.

"There's lasagna," Merritt said. He began laughing so hard he rolled off the couch and onto the floor. He writhed until Beau kicked him.

"Ow," he said.

Beau laughed.

Hollingsworth shot across the living room, headed toward the French doors.

Beau took off in pursuit.

"Kitty!" Merritt said, joining the chase.

"Cats are evil after all," Meredith said.

Natalie gave her a lazy grin and then flipped the page to *Dear Abby*.

"Sleep well?" Meredith asked, bringing her cereal into the living room.

"Yes, actually. You?"

Meredith shrugged.

"It's Sunday," Natalie said. "Do you go to church?"

Meredith shook her head. "Not anymore."

Natalie nodded. She read the paper.

"Oh, no. Did you want to go? There's a Catholic Church right here in Tarpley. Or, if you're Orthodox or something, I don't know if you are. I think the church is all the way down in Wilmington. We should have left hours ago~"

"And yesterday. Orthodox, and I haven't been to church since I was confirmed."

"It's just–most guests want to go and be a part of their spiritual community, you know? It's like being homesick. Makes people feel grounded."

"I don't know what would make me feel grounded. Why don't you go to church?"

Meredith fiddled with her spoon.

"Sorry, it's none of my business. Forget I–"

Merritt and Beau came back, holding Hollingsworth between them. "We watch church on TV," Beau said.

"We do. We're starting a little late. That's all right." She turned on the TV.

Natalie put down her paper.

"You don't have to–" Meredith started.

Natalie waved her off. "Have to set a good example for the children."

"By watching television on a Sunday morning," Meredith said.

Natalie grinned.

"Ready for bed?" Meredith asked, coming into Natalie's sunroom.

Natalie sat on the bed.

"It's only eight."

"It's Sunday night. The boys are tucked in. Something else in mind?" Meredith asked.

"I'm just thinking about my week. Therapy. The hospital. It seems overwhelming, even though I'm not actually doing anything. I would give anything for a shower."

"Anything?"

Natalie closed her eyes. "I can't take a shower."

"It would be difficult."

"Yeah."

"But not impossible."

Natalie opened her eyes and met Meredith's.

"Can't get your leg wet," Meredith said. "The cast."

Natalie nodded.

"We'll use plastic."

"What about–"

But Meredith was out the door before Natalie finished. She heard the water come on in the bathroom with the tiny bathtub across the hall. If she'd needed to use the stairs, her shower would have become impossible. She didn't know what to do. Undress, perhaps. Or start hobbling. Or go get the plastic.

"Don't move," Meredith said from down the hall.

Natalie sighed and gazed at the ceiling.

Meredith came back with a kitchen trash bag, which she split into sheets, and then, with duct tape in her hand, considered Natalie.

Natalie raised her eyebrows.

"Do you mind? Me, uh, seeing you."

"You have before, I guess."

Meredith nodded, not quite looking at her.

Natalie could undress herself. She'd gotten almost okay at it since coming from the hospital. Meredith unbuttoning her shirt made her feel like a child. She swatted. Meredith hesitated.

"Why don't you get things ready in there," Natalie said. Maybe this was a bad idea. "I'll call you."

Meredith nodded and slipped out of the room.

Natalie exhaled and finished unbuttoning her shirt, leaving it and her bra on the bed. She stood, leaning heavily on the wheelchair's arm, and managed to get her pants to drop. Taking off her underwear required sitting back down, butt to leather seat rest, and slowly, inch by inch, pushing and leaning. She considered kicking them under the bed, but instead managed, with her good leg, to get them into the hamper.

Her robe was at the end of the bed. She debated attempting to put it on, but decided the struggle wasn't worth it. The boys were asleep, anyway. She covered her lap with her hands, leaving her arms strategically stretched over her breasts.

"I'm ready," she said.

Meredith opened the door. The water was running. Meredith chuckled at her pose. She took up the plastic and wrapped Natalie's leg, and examined at the bandage on her side.

"What do you think?"

"It'd probably be good to wash your side. As gently as you can, then I'll rebandage it."

"I didn't contemplate how much this was all going to hurt."

Meredith went to the bedside table and tapped two pills out of her bottle.

"I never take that much anymore."

"And you never take a shower anymore, either," Meredith said, wrin-kling her nose.

"I'm pretty good at the self-sponge baths."

Meredith grinned and handed the pills and water to Natalie.

"All right, all right." Natalie took them and let herself be wheeled into the bathroom. The humidity greeted her and she nearly purred. The vinyl shower curtain was pushed aside, and inside a folding chair sat.

"Your chair's getting all wet."

"You wanna stand in there?"

"Well, no."

Meredith stroked her hair, and then unbandaged her side, examining the stitches. "Time to get up. I'll close my eyes if you want."

"Then we'll both fall over and crack our heads."

Meredith winced.

Natalie latched onto Meredith's arm and pulled herself up, grateful when Meredith hugged her waist and helped lift her. She stepped safely into the tub and sat down on the chair. Meredith handed her a loofah.

"Soap?"

Meredith handed her soap.

"Take your time. When the hot water runs out, call. I'll clean the kitchen."

"You're not going to help?"

Meredith closed the curtain. "I'm going to leave you alone."

Natalie closed her eyes and bowed her head. The spray hit her hair and ran in rivulets down her back and sides. The water hitting plastic made an obnoxious crinkling sound. She felt better immediately, despite the pain, de-spite being in a strange house, with a family. She'd never known a family. Growing up she'd only had her mother, nervous and foreign and ultimately defeated by cancer, sick where Meredith was healthy, scared where Meredith was smart. The boys—Natalie did love them already—made her feel like she fit in.

It scared her. This outpouring of domestication, of waking up and ex-periencing Meredith. She wanted to stay, and learn more about Meredith, the better to laugh with her, to play, to raise the children. She'd never before been so drawn.

Her life was reduced to sitting naked in someone else's shower. Nothing was hers anymore.

Meredith never would be.

She was just being nice. She was nice to everyone. Natalie certainly wasn't anything besides bedraggled, taking advantage of some gentle Southern woman's hospitality. Just a thing, not a person. Nothing Meredith could really love.

The feeling was supposed to go away. Meredith assured her. Patients got better. Patients grew less attached. The feeling she'd first felt in Meredith's presence, pulling, hadn't faded. Each smile Meredith granted her, each touch, made it stronger instead.

Natalie bowed her head and cried.

She could cry without pain now, and the tears came quickly, and then the heaving sobs, as she tried to contain herself, tried to reach for the soap. She shook until her side began to hurt in earnest, until the loneliness hollowed her out. She was sitting in a folding chair in a shower. Absurd. She steadied, and managed to soap herself, and let the spray fall on her chest, on her legs. With cleanliness came a sense of newness, and peace.

She filled her hand with shampoo, and then reached up. Pain jolted her arm. She lowered it again. She'd never have full motion of the arm, they'd told her. Trying to wash her hair with one hand sent fresh tears to her eyes.

"Merry?" she called. Then coughed, and said louder, "Merry?"

Footsteps, and then Meredith cracked open the door. "Nat?"

"Can you come in?"

Meredith slipped in, shutting the door behind her.

Natalie gave her a wobbly smile, tears now dripping down her cheeks at the sight of Meredith, whole and beautiful and standing so close.

"Can you wash my hair?"

"Sure. Just let me..." She glanced around, and then before Natalie could protest, pulled off her shirt and draped it over the sink, leaving herself in a bra and jeans. She pulled the shower curtain to the side.

"Thank you." Natalie closed her eyes. Then the tears might stop.

"I figured you'd want your hair washed. Water's still warm, even."

Natalie would have preferred nettles stinging her skin. When Meredith touched her scalp, Natalie began to sob. She endured Meredith's hands in her hair, and the smell of conditioner, and the massaging motions should have soothed her, but made her feel wild and exposed.

"Why are you crying?" Meredith asked, her voice quiet, barely audible under the spray.

"I like it here."

Meredith traced her neck. "Don't you miss your home?"

"No."

Meredith didn't say anything, just slipped down to hug her. The water turned cool. Natalie patted Meredith's hands.

"It's okay. We like you here."

Natalie felt Meredith tremble against her. She planned to cry again, becoming a habit, but a laugh came out instead.

"Nat?"

"I think I'm out of tears."

"And out of hot water." Meredith turned off the water and pulled away to get a towel.

"Taking a shower was a bad idea."

"You think?"

Natalie felt cool but limber, no longer in much pain, drained but brave enough to attempt getting back into her wheelchair, naked. To stand, even. She met Meredith's gaze, finding it tremulous. She reached and Meredith took her arm, helping her up. Then she was eye-to-eye with Meredith.

"I think it was a good idea," Meredith said.

"Maybe. But I don't want to do it again for a while."

Meredith gave her a smile. "Maybe not. Maybe just some sleep."

Chapter Fifteen

Harold came to take Natalie back to the hospital, where there was a therapy room and a gym. Merritt and Beau watched in awe from the safety of the front porch.

"How's living with that woman?" Harold asked her.

'Just wonderful' was on the tip of Natalie's tongue, but something in his tone made her hesitate. She said, instead, in measured, lawyerly tones, "Fine. I'm lucky to have nursing care."

Nursing care consisted of fresh flowers in her room and breakfast in bed in exchange for dinner and babysitting. Natalie wasn't even sure it was a fair trade, much less worth what her insurance was paying Meredith. Not that she'd tell the driver. Or the insurance company. She was happy about the arrangements.

"Sure. Just like living with Kathy Bates," Harold said.

Natalie rubbed her nose. She didn't see the resemblance.

Harold didn't elucidate.

Natalie focused on the scenery outside her window. She was sorry when the van pulled up to the hospital entrance. Numbly, she let herself be lowered and then pushed inside.

Jake came out to greet her. He kissed her cheeks and said, "Mon cherie! You have color! You have tone!"

Natalie blushed.

He pushed her wheelchair and leaned over to smell her hair. "Your hair is so clean and shiny. Are they feeding you new oats?"

"Corn Flakes."

"Oh, honey. At least in the hospital we cook for you."

"You came to this job for the food, didn't you? This physical therapy thing is merely incidental."

"Merely incidental." He giggled. "You're such a lawyer."

Natalie lifted her chin.

"I'll put you in your place. Today you're going to walk. Not step from the chair to the bed. Not stand up. Walk."

"What? No. I'm not ready to walk."

He parked her wheelchair next to the parallel bars, and produced crutches. He sprawled on them, swinging one foot forward.

"Jake, I'm still in pain every day. I can't~"

"Look," he said, pointing two fingers at her, and then at his eyes, and then back at her again.

She folded her arms.

"You've gotten downright comfortable, haven't you? You can get to the bathroom. You can bathe, obviously. Your leg hurts like hell, and isn't it great you don't have to worry about it so much? You can feed yourself, probably, and watch TV, and probably even work. Are you working?"

"Sort of."

"Plenty of people are in wheelchairs and do just fine. And besides, it's only temporary, right?"

"Right." Her face felt hot.

"Do you have Tivo?" he asked.

"Sure, back at my condo."

"You have a condo."

She stuck her tongue out.

"Girl, I have a house here and a condo by the beach. There ain't no cute little apartments in Tarpley. Or Warsaw. Or~"

"There's some in Wilmington," she said.

He tossed his head. "Let's walk."

"You're good at this," Natalie said, falling with relief into her chair. Jake held her, making sure her hips didn't slam into the sides and her back didn't bunch up.

"I was trained well. I went to school, you know."

"After the army? And you found it worthwhile?"

"Oh, yeah. They taught us things I never would have thought of on my own. How to keep you happy." He winked.

"Just smile," she said.

He blushed. "It's all about total health. And preventative. Weird to say after trauma, but true."

"Is this your, uh, calling?"

"Oh, no." He laughed, sprawling on the mat in front of her, gazing up with his wide, friendly brown eyes. "I wanted to be a soldier. I enlisted the second I graduated high school."

"But you didn't stay?"

He shrugged. "I did my four years. Stayed in the reserves for a while, but they stopped calling. Isn't it obvious?"

She raised her eyebrows.

"Right. You ain't from around here. Everything must seem a little off."

"It does. I've gone, what, a hundred miles? And it's like visiting a foreign country. All the signs have English on them and the people are dressed the same as me, but I'm worried using the wrong fork could land me in an underground prison."

"Right, well, my dad. He tried to forbid it."

"Doesn't like soldiers?"

"Well, he listens to what the Quakers say when they come to do their outreach. He thinks they're misguided Buddhists. But no, he's an American, he believes in the costs. You'd think he'd be proud to have a son go into the army."

Natalie nodded.

Jake glanced away and ran his fingers through his shaggy hair. "But Dad said, 'They'll kill you. They'll beat you. I don't want my boy to get hurt. You just aren't man enough.' Well, he didn't say the last bit, but that's what he meant. And he was serious. I never want to see that reflected in his eyes again~an old man imagining his son's death. But I went anyway. My best friend and I, we did it together. That's what we wanted."

"But now you teach people how to walk again."

"Yeah. It's a living."

"You don't seem resentful. You're too good at what you do."

"Around here, I'm lucky to have a trade."

"Ever thought about upgrading? Becoming a nurse?"

"Thought about it. But it's a different job. I don't think I could be like Merry. I'm more physical. Maybe when I grow up I'll transfer to sports medicine, though. Follow the Panthers around."

"Merry. Did you know her husband?"

"Yeah." A shadow fell across Jake's face. "He's the buddy I enlisted with. Even though he ended up infantry and I got my ass stuck in a chopper."

"You were friends?"

"Oh, yeah. Since grade school. Hard to see someone who wet his pants in third grade and who set a frog free in middle school as a soldier. But there he was."

"What happened?"

She didn't know precisely what she was asking, but Jake had a far-off look in his eyes, and wherever he would go, she would follow. Guiltily, she wanted to learn more about Merry. Sinfully, she hoped for clues to Merry's heart.

"How'd he end up playing army man? 9-11. We were seventeen and he wanted to enlist the next day. He was so~I mean, all of us were terrified. We were just kids. We didn't watch the news much. We didn't read *The New York Times*. So this happened in a vacuum and just filled all the space. Everyone talked about it and nothing else. And everyone was afraid. Even around here. It was totally shocking. And Vincey got so angry~So angry. He just never stopped. He was never truly happy again. Not even at prom. When the boys were born, he wept. Right here at the hospital. But he wasn't happy."

"Was he violent?"

"No~Hell no. Not before the war. He brooded like crazy, sure, but he was the sweetest guy. My dad didn't think I could be in the army? I was always the one getting in fights to defend Vince's sissy ass. He liked furry animals and stuff. There was a reason he and I were—Anyway."

Natalie swallowed.

Jake sighed. "He was a good guy."

"No wonder Merry married him."

Jake rolled onto his feet and frowned. "When you've got a life plan from kindergarten, it's kind of hard to deviate. They found more reasons as they got older. They were a team. Inseparable. And they kept planning. She did the nursing school fast track on his combat pay, and they got the boys and the house~they had everything worked out. And now she has~"

Natalie put her hand on his arm as he hung his head.

Jake rallied himself. She just let him push her toward a low table.

"Massage time," he said.

"Really?"

"Oh, yes. You've earned it. You've walked. I can't send you home to Merry all stiff and sore and expended. She'd whup me. Now, the trick is to get onto this on your stomach, so you don't have to roll over."

She gamely planted her hands on the edge of the table and strained forward. Jake was there, wrapping his arms around her waist and leveraging her. She felt lighter than air and toppled easily onto the table, face-first. She spread her arms and her good leg and sighed. The scent of lavender tickled her nose. She turned her head. Jake lit a candle and placed it in front of her on the floor.

"I'm going to take off your shirt, okay?"

"Okay," she mumbled. The obvious joke came to her--dinner and a movie, first--but she didn't make it. She was used to Jake's hands.

Jake worked her shirt up over her head. "Once you're walking again like you've done it all your life, I'll come to your place more often. After the surgery. But we've got all the good equipment here, and you need it."

"So there's a plan."

"There's always a plan, girl. And there's a plan for if you don't follow the plan, or if there's a flaw to the plan, or if we all get nuked from orbit."

Natalie breathed in the lavender air and then breathed it out again. "Thanks for telling me the plan."

"You're welcome. I don't tell everyone. It's nice, having a lawyer around. You understand things."

She blinked. Her back must have tensed, because his hands settled onto her shoulders and he pushed her gently back down.

"I mean, you're smart. You see things. Some people--lovely people, just differently lovely--it's a one day at a time thing. Goals are vague, or short-term. Their recovery seems miraculous to them, to their friends."

"I won't be miraculous?" Natalie asked.

"Oh, you will. In my hands? But you'll feel better if you see the future."

"I hate that you know that."

"Don't like being obvious?"

"I thought I had it all figured out."

"Until splat," he said.

"Yeah."

"So, are you going to get back on course with your fancy lawyer life story, after we patch you up?"

She shook her head. "I hope not."

"No?"

"I pray I don't go back there."

"What are you going to do?"

Natalie closed her eyes. "I'm going to start having physical therapy at the place I'm staying next week. Short term. Different. I like the sound of that."

Jake rubbed her back. Sorrow was in her bones and he comforted her, as gently as he could, using his hands and his knowledge to try to keep every part of her from hurting.

The van took Natalie home. The neighbor brought the boys over. She cooked them dinner and read to them and made them brush their teeth. Constant, cloying demand for attention from the boys made them just another obstacle to conquer. Merritt, in particular, would not move away from her even when she wheeled around the kitchen cutting up hot dogs, and Beau terrorized her cat.

She couldn't quite match up their faces--though mischievous--with the tormentors of her childhood, who called her Polack and beat her up and made fun of her left-handedness. She swore she would correct Merritt and Beau if they taunted their friends.

As if she'd have a say in it.

She'd expected her monumental accomplishment to exact a monumental price, but her hips and leg, while sore, felt loose.

No headache plagued her.

She put the boys to bed in the living room and stayed with them until they were asleep, reassuring them their mother would come home soon. They were past true separation anxiety, but they looked at her with worried eyes until she promised them she'd wake them up when their mother got home.

A promise she intended to break. She cleaned the kitchen and let her mind wander. Her early evenings in Charlotte never felt this fulfilled, doing paperwork alone. Here, she was doing domestic work and she was actually happy.

She checked on the boys one more time before bed, choosing to stand and pant and hold onto the wall. She took the step to peer around the door rather than squeak through with the wheelchair and risk banging into something. Exhausted, aching, and proud, she crawled into bed and fell asleep. She trusted the night would continue as planned and Meredith would come home.

In sleeping, free of drugs, exhausted by the day, she dreamed.

She saw the deer for the first time. A fragmented, still photograph of a deer. The deer was caught in motion--leaping like a gazelle but impossibly small--She'd imagined deer as moose, large, black shadows across the night road.

This doe had white spots on the flank and a watery, gentle look in her eyes.

No terror. There wasn't enough time to be terrified. To turn the wheel. To scream.

Natalie and the deer were powerless, both of them, against physics and atoms spinning in the universe to bring them right to that collision. She didn't take a breath. She didn't yank the wheel. The deer was still and moving, from right to left across her vision, and she was still and moving.

Heisenberg, damn him. She could see where she was and how fast she was going.

She could see the future.

Everything went black.

"Natalya, Natalya, get up."

Natalie's eyes fluttered open. Her mother stood over her bed, shaking her shoulder.

"You're going to be late for school."

"I don't want to go. They make fun of me," she said. If she'd been clearer in the head, she never would have confessed.

"Screw them," her mother said. "You're there for an education. A free, good, American education."

Natalie groaned and tried to roll over, but her mother's grip on her shoulder tightened, pinning her down.

"You will go."

Natalie turned, ready to stare her mother down. The nails hurting her shoulder made her set her jaw. Her mother had no idea what she was going through.

Her words failed.

Her mother grew older, frailer, and smaller in front of her eyes. Natalie blinked. Held in the grip of the dream, she couldn't move, couldn't turn away. Her mother turned into the deer—not a metamorphosis, but just instead of her mother's face, there was the deer, the deer from the picture, twisting Natalie's stomach with a sense of déjà vu. The deer was her mother, and everything was perfectly still and yet rushing past.

She gathered up all her strength, terrified, and thrashed. Her arms landed against the pillows. Her back sank. Her eyes flew open and she heard herself yelping.

The lamp beside her bed came on, and then hands were on her shoulders, pushing her down, but tenderly. Not her mother.

"Natalie," Meredith said, sounding far away but feeling close.

"Wha~" Natalie tried to speak. Her eyes were wide. She blinked, feeling foolish for having dreamed about deer and her mother and yet being scared.

"You had a bad dream."

"No kidding. What are you doing here?" Natalie asked.

"I couldn't sleep, so I decided to check on the boys. And then I decided to check on you," Meredith said.

"Oh. Good timing."

"Are you all right?"

"I think so."

"Didn't pull any stitches?" Meredith dropped a hand to Natalie's leg, pressing through the blankets.

Natalie tensed. "No pain."

"Good."

Natalie exhaled slowly.

"Your heart is pounding. You're sweating." Meredith put her hand on Natalie's forehead.

Natalie closed her eyes. "You put the heat on."

"No, I didn't."

Natalie frowned.

"It's the humidity."

"Oh, crap."

"Yes." Meredith soothed her, stroking her cheek.

"All year round?"

"Except for winter," Meredith said.

Natalie made a face.

Meredith laughed. "Sorry. What was the dream about?" She dropped her hands to her lap.

Natalie wanted to reach for them. She hooked one hand around Meredith's forearm, trying to put on a brave face to answer.

"My mother. And~the accident, I think. Or, my idea of the accident. Or my idea of my mother."

"Is she~"

"When I was sixteen. Cancer."

Meredith covered Natalie's hand on her arm and squeezed her fingers. "I'm sorry."

"It's all right. I mean, we weren't close. That makes it sound worse, doesn't it? I just mean, I turned out okay."

"Yes, you did."

Natalie made a wry face. "I lived with a friend until I graduated high school, and then as a poor, smart orphan, made a life for myself through student loans and on-campus housing."

"Huh."

"What?"

"Nothing."

"Tell me?" Natalie wanted the conversation to continue, to go in unexpected, sharp directions, to shatter the image of the deer's eyeball, staring at her, impossibly vivid. Weren't dreams supposed to fade? She felt like she was still trapped in this one, only Meredith appeared and was warm and tactile.

Meredith blushed. "I just~it's wrong of me, I guess, but I thought lawyers were just born rich. And~born lawyers."

Natalie chuckled. "I was just like everyone else."

"And your father? Oh, geez. Stop me. I don't mean to ask such personal questions. I~"

"It's okay."

Meredith swallowed.

"Mother always says he died in the war~I'm not sure what war. Just combat. I mean, the Iron Curtain. Everything. We fled. I know that. But I think-~I've always thought he just abandoned her."

"Oh, Natalie." Meredith leaned forward, hugging her shoulders. "I'm so sorry."

"What about your parents?"

"We'll talk about that later. You need to relax."

Even with Meredith closer so her hair tickled Natalie's ear, Natalie could still only see the deer. She blinked and cursed to herself, but it wouldn't go away.

"I don't want to go back to sleep," Natalie said.

"You don't have to. We'll~"

"Stay?" Natalie asked.

"Sure, I can stay." Meredith let Natalie go, and then walked around the bed and crawled onto the free side. Sitting against the headboard, companionably next to Natalie, she put one hand on her arm.

Natalie closed her eyes.

Chapter Sixteen

Meredith blew a kiss to the picture of her boys and closed her locker. She'd changed into clean scrubs, brushed out her hair and put it back up, and had twenty-five minutes left for lunch.

Natalie packed cold pizza and an apple. She could eat it in the locker room and not have to worry about the break room at all. Before everything she would have eaten whatever the patients were eating, but now the cook stared at her as if she was taking the food of orphans right out of their mouths.

She'd retreated to the vending machines, but even there she got stares and whispers. Natalie had no idea. Natalie liked packing her lunch.

Working was okay in the eyes of her peers. Penance. But eating was a luxury reserved for non-criminals. Better she do the world a favor and waste away.

She settled onto the bench and pulled out the foil-wrapped pizza.

Angelo came in, half-way to pulling off his shirt before he noticed Meredith.

She waved.

"Oh, hey. I'm hitting the shower. You're not eating the crackers that come in packs?"

"Not today. Natalie packed my lunch."

"You have your patient doing your chores?" He whistled.

"It's not like that."

He yanked off his shirt and straddled the bench. "What's it like, Merry?"

"It's~nice. She's nice. It's nice having someone around who's~"

"Nice? Who doesn't know?"

She unwrapped the slice of pizza.

Angelo leaned forward. "How nice, Merry?"

She glanced away.

"Look, I never met Mr. Jameison. Everyone around here knew him~I never met the man."

She didn't move when he put his hand on hers.

"But I met the Russian~" he started.

"She's not Russian."

"Whatever. I've seen you with her. It's~" He grinned. "Nice. You should be hanging out with her, not with us clowns."

"Gotta pay the bills."

"Lawyer bills, right. You know I'm praying for you, right, girl?"

She swallowed.

"I should shower." He started to get up.

She put her hand over his, clasping his wrist. "Angelo, talk to me. No one ever talks to me."

"Merry."

"I'd rather be offended than ignored. Please. My few remaining friends walk around like they're on eggshells and everyone else~"

"Pretends you don't exist. I've seen it. Even some of the patients. I want to punch them in the face. You're healing them and it's like they want to scrape you off their shoe."

"Angelo."

"Sorry." He squeezed her hand. "Merry, I've been wanting to tell you. We have your name on our prayer roster. You and the boys."

"Thank you."

"You could come by sometime. If you're not doing anything on Sundays. We don't even do the Inquisition thing anymore."

She laughed. "I'm not ready." The idea of walking into a church put fear in her heart. Even the conversation made her skin prickle.

"Sure. When you're ready. God's with you, Merry," he said.

"You too." She didn't meet his gaze.

"Been talking to God much, Mer?"

Meredith shook her head. "Are you witnessing to me, Angelo?"

"I'm on a roll. Aren't I? I'm never eating in the break room again."

"You should still shower."

He stuck out his tongue. "Come on. Remember when the beach house caught fire and they brought those kids to us?"

She remembered. The man and the woman who couldn't be stabilized in Wilmington. He had died of smoke inhalation. She lost an arm to the burns. They'd been able to save her shoulder. Her grief at the death of her friend had been untreatable. Even the smell came back to her~backyard smoke, charred skin, salt and sweat and fear.

"I remember," she said.

"I didn't know you then, but I was running back and forth for you and the doctors, and--You had peace itself in your hands. Every time you touched those kids, something happened. It was like a miracle. I'll back you anytime, Meredith."

"I'm not anything special. I never felt I was."

"But you're a nurse. You have a calling."

"I just it happened. By default."

"And you're afraid to ask God?"

"No. I'm--it's fine."

"What are you--" He stopped.

"I just don't know what He expects of me, sending Natalie into my care. I'm trying to help her--heal her--but it doesn't feel exactly right. Not enough. I can't figure out what He wants. Maybe he's just testing me, or--"

She said those words, and would say no more, she decided. That was already too much voice to give to what made her heart ache, but voicing it brought her relief, and if not to Angelo, then to no one. She seized what opportunity she could, and let it be enough.

"I don't speak for Him, Merry. I don't mean to. And I sure know you shouldn't be like, psychoanalyzing Him. But He's not screwing with you, Merry."

She took a bite of pizza, purposely filling her mouth. Silencing her tongue.

"He loves you."

She swallowed, and felt a hollowness in her chest. She knew God loved her. She could feel warmth when she reached out, whenever she was alone, or in a crowd--it was as real to her as the boys. But--

"And there ain't nothing you can hide from Him."

"I know."

"He knows every part of you, Merry. He knows the thoughts you're afraid to think. So what's the point in being afraid to think what He already knows? And He sure as heck knows what He's doing."

She glanced up as he stood and put his shirt in his locker, and then flung a towel over his shoulder. He flexed.

"Like what you see?" he asked.

She looked away.

"I know I already said all the things you're not supposed to say to another person. Not in a 'work environment.'" He made quotes with his fingers. "So I'm going to say one more thing. Because God commands me to help. I'm not very good at helping. Just talking too much."

She crumpled aluminum foil in her fist.

"You may think there are worse things than killing a man. Or not honoring your father and mother. Or gossiping. You may think those worse things are inside you--deep inside you where you put them, so no one can see them. You may think it's worse than all the abortions and rapes and assaults and poisonings and sheer stupidity we see every day. The one line you cannot cross."

"I do think that," she said.

He touched her arm. "It's not true, Merry. Those things inside you, you're pushing down--God wants you to raise them up. He wants to shine a light on them. He wants you to sing."

"You're in the wrong line of work, Angelo."

He grinned. "I was an altar boy."

She chuckled.

"Don't believe me? Ask Him." He pointed at the ceiling.

She inhaled deeply, and then made a face.

"I get it, I get it. I'm going." He went around the corner and turned on the shower. "Ask Him!" he shouted.

Meredith put her chin on her hand and contemplated her apple.

Maybe it was the lack of sleep after her nightmares, but the children seemed more manic, less tolerable. Natalie eased herself onto the back steps and forced them to play outside. They begged to watch television. Overruling their desires was difficult. Morally, she knew what she was doing was right. But it would be so easy to make them happy. She wanted them to be happy. She loved them.

She wanted them to shut up, more than anything. More than good parenting. And now they were crying and sitting in the grass.

She hung her head. She hadn't thought to bring a magazine or her laptop out with her, and the journey inside would be arduous. She couldn't leave the boys out there, not with the street a few feet away. They were fast. So she watched them, and the afternoon sunlight, and the trees. The boys wrestled. She threatened to turn the hose on them. They all laughed together, the television argument forgotten. Forgiven.

A hand dropped on her shoulder. Natalie glanced up. Meredith smiled. Before the boys even saw her, Natalie reached up to her shoulder and clasped Meredith's hand and said, "Wait."

Meredith wrinkled her nose.

Slowly, because her muscles stiffened on the uncomfortable concrete seat she'd made, and because her bad leg was still mostly bad and her hips felt too fragile for this~though Jake assured her they were not~she held onto the stoop and held onto Meredith and stood.

She stood up all the way, with Meredith watching her, holding onto her with nurse strength and not saying a word.

Merritt and Beau ran up. They were proud.

"Look what she can do!" Beau said.

Natalie stood and faced Meredith and loosened her grip on Meredith's hand, to balance herself. She could stand on her own. "Hey, Merry. Jake says the chair's just for show now."

"Hay is for horses," Meredith said, and hugged her.

Natalie sank into the embrace, wrapping her arms around Meredith and hugging her closer. She felt Meredith's hand against her back. Meredith's cheek went against Natalie's ear. Natalie inhaled deeply. She felt ten times more alive than she had all afternoon. Her last hug, her last friendship, had been so long ago she couldn't remember it. Someone was happy enough to hold her.

"Merry."

Meredith pulled back. Her eyes widened as she searched Natalie's face. "Sorry."

"No, don't be sorry."

"I see."

Merritt and Beau grabbed a leg each, and Natalie wobbled. She put her hand on Merritt's head.

"We helped. Do we get ice cream?"

"Yes," Meredith said.

"Yes?"

"Ice cream for dinner," Meredith said.

Natalie blinked at sharp, sudden tears. She swayed.

Meredith reached for her elbow. "Are you all right?"

"Yes. I think so. I just~"

"Inside, woman," Meredith said.

Natalie shook her head. "I just~Is this what having a family is like? Really?"

Meredith sent the boys inside to set the table and wrapped one arm around Natalie's waist to help her.

Natalie met her eyes~the sad, worried eyes—trying to send strength.

"I wish," Meredith said. "Oh, I wish."

Chapter Seventeen

Natalie stretched and glanced around the van's interior. She sat in her wheelchair but could move around more easily. Both in bonding with the chair, and in getting stronger, she felt rather unstoppable.

Jake was right, darn him..

Harold grunted. Natalie turned away from the parade of trees and strip malls. He'd grunted three times. She met his eyes in the rearview mirror.

Her lawyer senses tingled for the first time since the accident. They must have healed, too. She sensed something brewing.

"You think next week's going to go well?" he asked.

"Next week?"

He shrugged.

"I guess, if all goes well, I could go home."

"Charlotte."

She nodded. "You?"

"Honeymooned on the Outer Banks. Wife wanted to go to the mountains. We go there now. Get a cabin. Sometimes on a lake. Not the same."

"I haven't seen many mountains."

"But you've seen the ocean. Wilmington?"

"No, not yet."

He looked annoyed.

"Maybe someday," she said.

"You should go before you go back to Charlotte."

She shrugged. "You going to drive me?"

"You don't need me anymore. You could drive yourself."

"My car is in little pieces."

"You could get a new one. You're a rich lawyer."

She frowned and glanced away, back to the window.

She tried not to think of her car.

Being in the hospital without being sick was surreal. Natalie's skin itched. She was afraid of getting something. Flesh-eating disease. Pneumonia. She'd felt immortal in the van. She didn't belong here.

Teresa and Colleen were happy to see her, but to be treated like a patient and an invalid offended her. Before she had been too weak to protest. Now she could be belligerent, and she had to fight her impulses. She'd be going under the knife. She'd better be nice to everyone.

She fasted throughout the night and in the morning. They were going to continue rebuilding her leg, they told her, and it was going to hurt like hell. Morphine and rods and pins and necrosis and bone growth and muscle atrophy—every word made her want to throw up.

Only she couldn't throw up, because they wouldn't let her have any food or water.

She sat in her hospital room and flipped through *Highlights for Children*. Teresa promised her ice cream after the surgery. She wanted to cry. She turned on the television. She turned off the television. She couldn't concentrate. Every sound touched her ears. Scrapes on the floor and the buzzing of machinery tortured her nerves.

When she recognized Wheeler's voice, somewhere out in the hallway, it was a blessing. She listened. She tried to go outside herself and into the hallway, where he would be, comforting and serene.

Meredith's cousin.

Except he was angry.

"Go back to Rocky Mount," he said.

Natalie leaned forward. She considered getting out of bed.

"Don't you think it's bad for the hospital to have a murderer working here?" A woman's voice.

"Alleged," Wheeler said.

"She confessed. Come on, you know. All of North Carolina knows."

"What's going on in her personal life has no bearing on her position here. She's an excellent nurse."

"Her personal life? Justice affects the whole society, Dr. Wheeler. Do your patients know? How would they feel?"

Natalie certainly didn't know. She slipped off the bed, grabbed a walker, and hobbled, one-footed, toward the door. She reached it just in time to see Wheeler storming past. He didn't glance in her direction.

She peered into the hallway.

A young woman stood, polished and citified, overwhelming Natalie with a sense of nostalgia. The woman wasn't even wearing sneakers. She carried a briefcase. Her long dark hair was pulled back into a bun, and she was short and slender and pale. She noticed Natalie noticing her.

"Are you a patient of Meredith Jameison?" the woman asked.

"Who are you?" Natalie asked.

"Oh, sorry, most folks around here already know me. I'm Erica Mendes, reporter for the *Rocky Mount Telegram*. Merry's hearing is tomorrow, so we're doing a follow-up piece."

"Hearing?"

Erica frowned as if Natalie were wasting her time. "Do you know Nurse Jameison?"

Meredith hadn't told her what the appointment tomorrow was for, and Natalie has assumed, selfishly, it would result in some sort of surprise for her. Like cake.

Was Meredith suing someone? Why wouldn't she say? Why hadn't she asked Natalie for help?

The reporter staring at her hadn't stormed off yet. "Hey, haven't I seen you before?" Erica asked.

"In the news, maybe," Natalie said. Her stomach was starting to hurt. She leaned more heavily on the walker. She should have stayed in bed. Wheeler was going to be angry.

The reporter looked her up and down, the leg, the walker, the fading welt on her face. "You're her. The state prosecutor. You hit a deer."

"No comment."

Erica grinned. "I called your office in Charlotte. I tried to get your contact for an interview. I didn't know you were here in Tarpley. I knew you were nearby."

"Here I am."

"Are you still involved in the Roland case?"

Natalie knew she should keep her mouth shut, but she was far away from any recrimination, and she hadn't eaten and she was worried about Meredith. "Administrative leave," she said.

"Why?"

Natalie shrugged.

"So you don't have any active cases?"

"Not at the moment. They've been reassigned while I do my rehabilitation here. My injuries were too extensive, initially, to transfer me back to a Charlotte hospital."

"They've got good facilities down here."

"Yes, ma'am. You can quote me."

Erica grinned. "How are you liking Eastern Carolina?"

"It's wonderful. Very peaceful."

"Remind you of home?"

"No."

"Been to Wilmington yet?"

Natalie shook her head.

"Outer Banks?"

"No."

"Cape Hatteras? The Wright Brothers? Cape Fear?"

"Isn't Cape Fear on the other side?"

Erica chuckled. "Sure, but still. Myrtle Beach? Have you just been sitting here?"

"Massive injuries resulting from deer," Natalie said.

"Right. But if you ever want anyone to show you around~" Erica took out her wallet and pulled out a business card. "In return for some inside scoop on the Roland case, of course. No one around here cares, but I bet I could make the AP wire."

"I'll keep that in mind."

"You didn't curse me out. Surprising."

"I'm used to reporters."

"I guess you are."

"And Rocky Mount's the big city?"

Erica laughed. "Oh, no. It's just got a supermarket and a couple of Wal-Marts, you know. I'd love to be working in Wilmington or Charlotte."

"Ambitious."

"Just want to get out of Nowheresville. The small towns~you can't imagine."

"I'm learning."

"This hospital is kind of an oasis. For employment and otherwise."

Natalie felt kinship with her. She wanted to pursue the conversation. "Where'd you go to school?"

"Wilmington. Party school. My parents are first generation, they moved from Texas to here to work in the factory. Why, I don't know. They could have made it to middle class by now if they'd stayed in the *maquiladoras*. They tell me they like the climate better."

Natalie nodded. "My mother, too. From the old country."

"The eastern part of the old country?"

"Yeah." Natalie never said much to a reporter, but Erica's clothes, Erica's accent~Midwestern trim, without a trace of drawl, despite her upbringing~lulled her into trust. She wanted to talk to an old friend. She didn't have many. But here was Erica, smiling, still standing in front of her, just like a work colleague. And Natalie had her number.

"How's your leg?" Erica asked.

"It'll be all right. It's better than they expected. They thought they were going to have to saw it off. But I'm even walking." Natalie shook her walker. "Except, I'm exhausted. Mind coming in?"

"Sure. Can I help?"

"I'll be all right." Natalie limped back to the bed. Erica stayed silent as Natalie sat down and exhaled.

"Not walking much?"

"I actually prefer the wheelchair. At least my leg doesn't hurt."

Erica nodded.

Natalie asked, with a lump in her throat, "You were talking about Merry?"

"You do know her."

"She's been my nurse. Off and on. When it's her shift."

"You must know everyone in a small place like this."

"Pretty much."

"But you don't know what she did?"

"What did she do?"

"It's just like the Roland case," Erica said.

Natalie's blood ran cold. Her world went gray. She didn't need to hear Erica's next words, but they rang in her ears, above the ping ringing in them.

"She killed her husband. Vincent Jameison. She pled not guilty. Self-defense. There's an evidentiary hearing tomorrow. We're running something tonight."

Spots swam in front of Natalie's eyes. She rubbed them, and then could only see black. Like before she'd seen Meredith's face for the first time. She rubbed harder. Haze and light re-entered her vision.

She'd been in worse spots than this; received worse news. Her principal at school telling her her mother was dead. Defendants lying on the stand. Rape victims telling the truth. The expression in Patrick's eyes, handing her the Roland case.

The expression she probably wore now. Seven years at her job gave her the conditioning to ask, if not the strength. "What happened?"

"He was in Iraq. A war hero."

"I know. I know."

"You do?"

Natalie thought of Jake. "It's a small town, remember."

"Right. Well, things were different when he came back. Her story is he was ill. PTSD. His parents claim she was cheating on him."

"With who?"

Erica shrugged. "No one knows."

"But she's working."

"She did about six months before she finally got bail lowered. Hardship case. Parent. His parents have been trying to get the kids away from her, but at the moment, they don't even have visitation. The police are too afraid of a kidnapping incident."

"That seems so-different from how it would play out in Charlotte."

Not totally different. She thought of all the poor mothers that had come through her doors. She'd never associated Meredith with them. Or with Roland. Another shuddering chill went through her. Roland was an evil, sick bastard.

"Small town," Erica said. "Her husband had friends on the force. They're sticking by Meredith. Guess they noticed a change, too."

"Seems that would taint the jury pool."

"Sure." Erica leaned forward over the chair, dangling her briefcase. "They want to move it down to Charlotte. I'm in favor. More sensational, I think. And I'll definitely get a travel budget."

Natalie felt sick. She closed her eyes.

"Are you all right?"

"Feeling a little weak. Would you mind? I've got your number."

"Sure," Erica's footsteps retreated. "Give me a call. Even if you just want to go to dinner or something. It's nice to see a kindred spirit."

Natalie waved but kept her eyes closed, willing her heartbeat to slow. She wasn't sure how many minutes passed with just her quiet, slow breathing and the sense of dread infusing her, but there came a knock on the open door. She didn't open her eyes, but she rolled her head vaguely in the direction of the sound.

"Nat? You ready?" Wheeler asked.

She opened her eyes and sat up.

He met her eyes with a friendly smile and came into the room.

"Is it true?" she asked.

"Is what true?" He sat down on the edge of the bed, still gazing into her face. Concerned. Doctorly.

"About Merry. I talked to Erica."

"The bitch," Wheeler said.

Natalie recoiled.

He took her hands. "I'm sorry. She isn't. I just~Yes, it's true. Everything she told you is probably true."

"Oh. Oh, Jesus." Natalie couldn't breathe. Wheeler held her hands, watched her, until she sank into the bed.

"It's bad. If you care about her~"

"I do," Natalie said. She wanted Merediths' arms around her. She wanted Meredith laughing with her at dinner. Her chest hurt. She couldn't see again. The black spots were back.

"I don't know why she didn't tell you."

"Seems obvious to me."

He squeezed her hands. "Maybe so."

She turned her head away. Her eyes stung with tears. Wheeler scooted closer so he could put one hand on her shoulder.

"It's okay, Natalie."

"It's not. How can you say that?"

He rubbed her shoulder with his thumb in slow, soothing circles. Contact with another human being~not Meredith, but someone connected to her, and to Natalie, and to the whole human race~comforted her.

"It's horrible and sad, but we'll get through it," he said.

"Tell me everything."

"After your surgery. Your health is more important."

"It's not important at all."

"It is to me."

"Well, screw you."

"Just for that, I'm bringing a mirror to the surgery so you can see everything."

"You wouldn't," she said.

"Oh, I'm devious."

"Just like everyone else around here."

"Nat~You can only trust yourself. You've got to get stronger."

"I'm an attorney, maybe I could~" she searched for the words. "Help. Maybe I could help."

"After your surgery," he said.

She scowled.

"I promise."

He stood, and after pausing, leaned forward and kissed the top of her head. "It's time. I'll go get Colleen."

She closed her eyes and waited for the doctors to come to her and change everything.

Chapter Eighteen

"We'll be going in with laser scalpels," Bhatti said. "You won't feel a thing after."

"We just got the equipment installed a couple of months ago," Wheeler said.

Those tools had been available for years–perhaps longer than a decade––in Charlotte. If she'd been transferred, if she'd been injured there, she would have had top surgery at Presbyterian instead of emergency hacking. They wouldn't call a doctor down from Duke Medical.

Wheeler settled into the chair and the anesthesiologist came in.

"Usually I'd do this myself, but since he was on site–" Wheeler said.

"Better for your liability, though it costs more," the anesthesiologist said. "Gotta love insurance, right?"

Her insurance company told her this would be the last surgery they would pay for, and at the end of the week, she was out the nursing service, too. She'd be on her own.

"Nat?" Wheeler asked.

She glanced up, meeting his eyes.

"You looked pale for a second. You'll be all right."

"I have good hands," Bhatti said, and wiggled his fingers.

"I'm ready," Natalie said.

The anesthesiologist pushed a long, thin needle into her leg, hurting her, but the numbness came after, flooding through her leg, warmth and then incredible lightness. Wheeler poked her leg for her, since she couldn't reach, and there was only the sensation her leg had turned into a giant pillow.

The anesthesiologist stabbed her several more times, some she felt, and some she didn't, and she began to worry something feeling this incredibly good must be wrong, somehow.

Wheeler's face was filled with concern.

"Am I all right?" she asked.

"We're waiting to see if you're going to swell up like a balloon and stop breathing," Wheeler said.

The anesthesiologist glanced at his watch.

"What happens if I do?" Natalie asked.

"Epi pen, right into the heart," Wheeler said. "You'll be fine."

"Fabulous."

The anesthesiologist took her pulse. "She's doing well," he said.

"We're ready," Wheeler said.

Bhatti rubbed his hands together. "Let the games begin."

Wheeler and Bhatti cracked jokes with her throughout the surgery, poking her leg with small metal tongs, going into the side of her abdomen with a tube and a camera, testing stitches. She'd have known earlier if the internal wounds had not healed, if her intestines leaked and poisoned her~as it was, she was eating hot dogs and macaroni with impunity. But now they were medically sure, and they smiled when they told her.

With her leg numb she was brave enough to glance at the surgical monitor three times. So gross.

"Take your medicine exactly as instructed. Do not be brave. Do not be bold. Do not be ambitious," Bhatti said. "Then, you won't feel any pain."

"He's serious. And so am I," Wheeler said.

"Stay drugged out of my mind. Got it," Natalie said.

Wheeler patted her good leg. "It'll be a different experience than before. I promise."

Lighter, then. The light she felt inside her, especially inside her leg and her side, would continue.

"There's my angel," Bhatti said.

She smiled, her cheeks warming under his words.

Then it was all over with her still floating and numb. Colleen took her back to her room and kissed her cheek and pointed to the flowers sitting on the table.

Natalie took the card. "Way to go, champ. Love, Merry."

Colleen grinned and folded her arms.

"Champ?" Natalie asked.

"Want me to scruff your hair?"

Natalie's hair had grown out some since they'd shaved it the first night~ ~the last night~and it was of scruffable length. She made a face.

Colleen winked and went to the door. "I'll bring you lunch. Well, a liquid lunch. You'll love it."

"Hey, Colleen?"

Colleen turned around in the doorway.

"When will the numbness wear off?"

"Oh, about four hours. But you'll be on the painkillers. Don't worry."

"Oh, I'm not worried," Natalie said.

Colleen grinned back and gave her a little wave, and then left her alone with her absence of pain and the card from Meredith. She traced the writing. Champ. She'd have to get Meredith back. She'd have to~

The memory of her conversation with Erica came back to her, filling her mind and pushing out the happiness. Her heart sank. Her hand, holding the card, trembled.

The idea of Meredith being a different person than she'd thought~an evil person~warred with the thought that Meredith might go to prison and Natalie would lose her. She tucked the card back into the flowers. She felt ill. She wanted to go home. She wanted to see the boys~to see they were safe, that everyone was safe~that there was no deer, no Roland.

She rubbed her wrists. Maybe this is what it was supposed to feel like, to be healthy in a hospital. She felt ready to go back to her old life, the one in the sick, sick world. The world Meredith was of. She was just like everyone else.

So Meredith was a murderer.

She turned her head. The flowers were daisies and lilies, arranged in earthy combination. Their scent tickled Natalie's nose. She sighed. She could walk. She could run all the way back to Charlotte. Roland was free of her, and she of him, but Patrick could quietly slip her back into a caseload.

She could take a demotion. She could transfer to Washington, D.C., or Delaware, or Pittsburgh. She could enter private practice. She could run for office. She would never have to see Meredith again.

Meredith played cards with Terrance, who was in for his regular dialysis.

"Gin," he said, spreading his cards on the hospital tray.

"I wasn't even close."

"You shouldn't let an old man beat you at cards."

"'Let' had nothing to do with it."

Terrance grinned.

Meredith reshuffled the cards.

Wheeler knocked on the open door. "Nurse?" he said.

'Nurse.' Used in the hospital, it was code for, 'keep cool, keep professional, because something's about to go down.' Or 'Don't scare the patients, but~."

White-faced, she smiled at Terrance and got up. "Next week. I'm going to read some strategy books. You won't know what hit you."

"I'd at least like a challenge."

She winked and went into the hallway with Wheeler.

Wheeler ran his hand over his head. "Merry. I don't know how to tell you this."

Dread washed over her, icy cold, robbing her of senses. Her boys~It could only be~

"It's Natalie," he said.

Relief brought with it confusion. "I heard the surgery went fine. You asked~" He'd asked that she avoid Natalie when she came in for her shift. The memo seemed ominous at the time, but since she never saw Natalie at work these days anyway, she slipped into her routine, comforted when she'd heard Natalie was fine.

"She knows. She knows everything, Merry. Everything about you."

Her mind filled with the things Natalie could possibly know, that she'd kept secret from her without even realizing, Meredith sagged against the wall. Wheeler tried to put his hands on her shoulders. She shook him off.

"What am I going to do?" she asked.

"You're going to go home and talk to her."

"I can't. I can't." Her home hadn't been a home since she'd lost Vincent. Since before ~Since he'd come back from the desert. Natalie's coming made it feel like it once had, safe and loving and full of light. She'd known it was just a mirage, but in just days, she had gotten used to it. The absence of pain. The joy that filled her whenever she thought of Natalie.

"I can't go home," she said, knowing she wouldn't be able to make Wheeler understand there would be no home left anymore.

"Take some time. You're off-shift, but take some time. Think. Pray. We're keeping her here for a day or two, but you've got to go home." he said.

Then he left her, going on to do his rounds, and for long minutes she leaned against the wall, too stunned to cry, too empty to be ashamed.

When she regained her senses, she asked God what to do. Then she asked Vincent. Then she asked her heart. All were agreed on the course of action~the one she didn't want, the one that would be the hardest to face.

Sooner or later, she had to look Natalie in the eye.

Natalie stayed in the hospital two days. The first day she slept sedated in between bouts of pain. She didn't really miss the Vicodin, but she welcomed the new doses. She was familiar with the high.

The second day, of course, the nurses gave her Tylenol instead. She tried not to think about Merry. She tried not to think about anything.

At three p.m. on the third afternoon, Wheeler appeared.

"We're releasing you. The van'll be here to pick you up in about a half hour."

"Am I healed?"

"As long as you take it easy at home, especially tonight, I think you'll be fine. Your leg is happy with what we did, even if you can't tell. Have you been taking it easy?"

She blushed. She rubbed her cheek and frowned at him.

"Well? How's the home front?" he asked.

"Come on, Hank. I take it easy. I mean, as well as I can with two boys. But they've been really great~fetching things, being quiet, pushing me around. They feed the cat every morning. I mean, I have to remind them. But we make it a little game. 'Okay, you get to feed the cat now!' They have no idea they're doing chores."

Wheeler stared at her.

"What?"

"You just didn't strike me as a cat and kids kind of person when you rolled up in here."

"I was heavily medicated and you sawed me open. Pissed me off."

He shrugged. "I get that a lot. No one ever likes my technique."

"I'm grateful, you know. You saved my life. Thank you."

"Come on, Nat. Just doing my job."

"When I do my job, people go to jail."

He winced.

"Sorry," she said.

He shook his head. "People like Merry?"

"No, not people like~" She stopped herself. It wasn't fair to say they weren't like Meredith. Maybe Meredith was just poor and desperate and raised wrong and addicted and trapped like the rest of them. Even Roland thought he had no way out. No easy way.

"People just don't seem willing to do what's hard," she said.

"Even you?"

"Especially me. I just wanted not to feel too much. I was just going to get hurt, anyway."

Wheeler sat on the bed.

"Oh, Hank. Not one of the talks."

"Yes, Nat. All part of the service here."

She narrowed her eyes.

He grinned and then turned slightly to gaze out the window. It was only mid-day. Natalie was healed enough to think lying in a bed in the middle of the day was a crime. She stretched. Pain traveled through her leg and up to her abdomen and her chest. She settled back into the bed and frowned.

Wheeler turned back and asked, "You going to be able to go back?"

"To Merry's?"

He nodded.

"Yeah. I want~I want to talk with her. I want to know."

"And if she doesn't want to talk?"

"I guess, then, I guess I'll just sleep and eat there. I'm not afraid, if that's what you mean."

"I didn't think so. And what about the boys?"

"I think~I love those boys. And they had nothing to do with it. Right?"

"No, they didn't."

She squared her shoulders. "Hank, what'd you come here to say?"

"I was thinking about the conversation we had a few weeks ago. About your visitors."

"And the lack thereof."

"Then you remember."

"Yes. You accused me of being~" her words stuttered. She made no second attempt, and only stared at him.

"I didn't~I'm sorry. About making you uncomfortable."

"You were doing something good. I mean, I don't hold it against you. You were being kind."

He nodded.

She reached out and put her hand on his arm.

He covered her hand with his. "I have a favor to ask."

"All right."

"It's a big favor, and I have no right to ask it."

"All right."

"You're being brave," he said.

She shrugged.

He squeezed her hand. "If you can find it in your heart to be Meredith's friend~with all you know~then do it. Try. I could tell before it revolted you. As it does all of us. But please, try."

"Okay."

"It'll be hard. I know you want to leave."

"Of course I do," she said, and tears spilled down her cheeks.

"You can't believe she was who she is. You can't help but see a different person."

She nodded, then shook her head, and squeezed her eyes shut to stop the tears.

He didn't say anything more, just sat with her until she could breathe evenly. She let go of his hand and hugged her shoulders. He didn't say anything. She cleared her throat and then found the strength to look him in the face.

He was the same calm, kind man.

"Any more advice, before you send me back into the den of lions?"

"Have faith in your own abilities. I know you feel you can't do this. I can see it. You're just not that kind of person. Who is? We're only human."

"I only have faith in your abilities, Doctor Hank."

"I'm only good with my hands. Merry needs you."

"I'm just a stranger."

"I know." He took her hands in both of his. "Love bears all things, believes all things, hopes all things, and endures all things."

She squeezed his hands. She met his eyes.

"Don't worry," she said.

"I'm not." He got up and smoothed down his coat and went to the door.

"Hank?" she asked.

He leaned against the door and gazed back at her.

"Tell me where that was from. I think I'm ready to hear it."

He grinned. "First Corinthians 13:7." Then he shut the door, leaving her in contemplation.

"Great," she said. She stared up at the ceiling. "I heard you. Bastard. There's no way I can do this."

Chapter Nineteen

Natalie crawled into the van, with Harold helping, treating her like Queen Elizabeth. They'd wheeled her to the exit, hospital policy. Fair enough, she wouldn't have wanted to make the walk herself. The walker and the walking cast were coming home with her. Five steps. She could do five steps.

Halfway to Meredith's house, the van always passed a stoplight with a gas station and a strip mall, an area Natalie could squeeze out cell phone reception. She dialed.

Patrick answered. "Hey! I have good news."

"I do, too." She gazed through the window. People were shopping at the Dollar Store across the street. A woman walked two big dogs right past the van. Life continued in the early afternoon, and she was a part of it. She grinned and pressed her cheek to the glass.

"You first," Patrick said. "I want to hear how you are."

"I had surgery a few days ago and I'm doing better than they expected. I can go home this weekend. Be at work Monday."

"Great! We can accommodate you, you know. What do you need? We can move your desk so--"

"Pattypat," she said.

He grunted.

"I can walk."

The words carried as much dramatic weight as when she'd told him she might never again, but these words were joyous, and she told him because she wanted him to be as happy as she was.

He cheered. "Natalie, that's so great! I'm so glad."

"Me too," she said. "What's your news?"

"Oh. I'm glad you're doing better. I didn't want to bother you, you know? When you're trying to heal. I guess you haven't been reading the papers, either. You don't need this shit."

"Pat."

"What?"

"Oh, nothing. I just haven't heard bad language in a while. I was surprised."

"Fuck it, Natalie. The city needs you."

"Tarpley?"

Harold glanced over his shoulder.

"Charlotte, honey. I'll email you some links. Or you could just do a Google search for your name. Nothing ever comes up under my name, unless it's like, paperwork related."

"Uh huh."

"You've been cleared. The police released your report, and they said alcohol and speed were not factors in the crash."

"I wasn't even speeding?"

"Well, maybe you have friends on the force? But no. They said it was a freak accident. Could have happened to anyone. Deer with their timing. And they said you reacted and left a skid ten feet long on the road."

"Woo."

"Right, girlfriend." Static came through the line.

"You're breaking up, Patrick."

"I'll email you. I can't wait to see you!" he called through the phone, and then the line went dead.

She snapped the phone shut. Harold glanced at her.

"What?" she asked.

"You're very professional. With the cell phone and all. I guess you're back to normal?"

She frowned and glanced out the window. Trees, now. Power lines. Nothing else. The van was between civilizations.

"I guess so."

He nodded. "It's nice."

"I guess so."

"Your fellow?" Harold asked.

"What? No. My boss."

"Sounds like he's a fan of yours."

"I guess so," she said.

Patrick had always been nice to her. Friendly. Invited her over for Thanksgiving and Christmas and always brought her a card on her birthday. He'd never made any moves on her.

Maybe he just liked her.

Maybe they were actually friends.

She glanced at the phone, wanting to call him back. But the reception was too weak, and anyway, she didn't know what to ask. She didn't even know how to tell who her true friends were.

"I'm an idiot," she told Harold.

"At least you're a healthy idiot," he said, as he pulled the van into Meredith's driveway. "God bless."

He got out and opened the sliding door and helped her down carefully. She patted his hand when she steadied. "You, too."

Natalie called the neighbor and said the boys could come home. Apparently they were swimming in one of those big plastic pools in the backyard, so it would be a while. She planned dinner. She tidied. She convinced herself Meredith's personal life was none of her business. She was just a patient, after all. One who would be going home in a few days. She didn't want to be impolite to someone who'd been kind to her.

She passed the staircase leading to Meredith's room. The stairs were insurmountable. She took her laptop to the front porch, where she could watch the boys come home, and Meredith, and took Patrick's advice. She Googled herself.

"Prosecutor Cleared in Probe" was the headline in the local section of *The Charlotte Observer*. There was a picture of her. She wore a cocktail gown and her dark hair was swept up on top of her head. She'd paid a hundred bucks to her hairdresser an hour before the picture was taken. She wore diamond earrings and she didn't, thankfully, appear drunk.

In the picture she wasn't smiling.

She glanced down the street. No diamond earrings here. No BMW. No mansions housing state attorneys. Maybe before she left—

"Natty!" Beau's voice, as he rounded the corner. His shirt was off, but his shorts were dry. He carried a toweled bundle. He ran straight toward her. She closed the laptop.

Merritt followed with the neighbor, holding tightly onto her hand. He grinned shyly when he saw Natalie, and then narrowed his eyes when Beau climbed into her lap. Natalie reached out her hand to Merritt, around a squirming Beau. He took it.

She locked eyes with the neighbor, Mrs. Cranston. "Thank you for watching them."

"They going to be all right with you?" Mrs. Cranston regarded her suspiciously.

"Sure. I'm used to watching them now."

"You don't have your wheelchair."

"Don't need it as much anymore," Natalie said.

Mrs. Cranston's face softened. "Glad to hear it."

"Me, too. Oh, me, too." She squeezed Merritt's hand. "Merr, go set the table."

Merritt slipped in the door.

Beau climbed off. "What about me?"

"You've got some wet things to hang up in the bathroom. Over the tub. Okay?"

"I don't know how," he said.

"Well, give it a shot, and I'll come help you in a bit."

He frowned, but padded off in bare feet.

"Wipe your feet on the mat."

"Then Merry has to, too," Beau said.

"I'll tell him. You get into the bathroom." Natalie turned up at Mrs. Cranston. "A fight waiting to happen."

"They've been pretty good all day. They know something's up this week."

"And you~" Natalie paused, regarding her. "Know?"

"Whole town does. Some're even going to the hearing." The woman helped herself to the rocker opposite Natalie. Natalie turned to face her, pasting on her best, non-offensive, 'confess everything to the nice prosecutor' face.

"We got one of the most mixed places in 'Carolina, you know. Blacks, whites, Latinos, Laotians, Indians~both kinds. And we're all united around one thing."

"Then why do you take care of the kids?"

"Them boys ain't never harmed anyone," she said.

Natalie nodded.

"And Merry ain't harmed anyone before or since. She's a nurse, you know. Do no harm. I figure it was a crime of passion. Won't happen again. Unless she gets herself another man." The woman made a face.

"Until then?" Natalie asked.

"She'll get hers before God and man. But the boys deserve a normal life. I don't know what they'll do when they take her away."

Natalie's stomach twisted. She felt faint and hot. She kept her expression neutral. Friendly.

"And you?"

"I'm going home next week," Natalie said, and then clarified, "to Charlotte."

"Been nice having you around. For the boys. They were getting kind of isolated."

"Wonder why," Natalie said.

Mrs. Cranston's expression hardened.

Meredith's van pulled into the driveway. Mrs. Cranston got up. "See you later, you hear?"

"I hear."

Mrs. Cranston stepped lightly off the porch and was around the corner before Meredith got out of her car. She locked the door. Natalie stood up. Her leg ached. She cursed it, inwardly, and waited, a smile still plastered on her face. She'd faced bad news before.

And bad people.

Meredith came apprehensively onto the porch. "Wheeler called me."

"Yeah."

"I~" Meredith met her eyes briefly, and then turned away. "You~"

"I'll start dinner," Natalie said.

"Okay." Meredith went through the front door.

Natalie lingered on the porch and then gathered up her laptop and hobbled inside, one step at a time. She wanted to scream at Meredith, to ask how could she have done it, how could anyone so good have done something so awful.

She wanted to demand to know if it was really true. She wanted to know every detail. She wanted to figure out a solution. She wanted to see the guilt on Meredith's face.

She wanted to run away so much her feet itched.

She went through the front door. Nausea overcame her as she passed the threshold. She swayed into the side bedroom and put her laptop on the bed and sat, breathing in and out, until the energy normalized and her head felt clear.

Merritt peeked around the corner. "I'm hungry."

"Okay," Natalie said.

"Mommy's upstairs."

"I know."

"She's crying," Merritt said. He looked worried.

Natalie pulled herself up off the couch and leaned heavily on her walker. "You know what will make her feel better? Dinner."

"What are you making?" He watched her carefully, like a guard dog, as she made her way out into the hallway.

"Pancakes."

"For dinner?"

"It'll be a surprise."

He cackled.

She was probably not a good influence on the kids.

In the kitchen she found the pan and put it on the stove, heat on low. "Where's the Bisquick?" she asked.

Merritt opened the pantry and pointed upward. She grabbed the box.

"And where's your brother?"

Merritt shrugged.

"Beau!" she shouted.

Beau popped his head up from the arm of the couch. He slid off and came into the kitchen, holding Hollingsworth in his arms. Hollingsworth's feet dangled down to the floor

"Bravo. Could you get the milk?"

Beau dropped the cat. Hollingsworth and Natalie winced. Hollingsworth darted into the hall, toward Natalie's room. Beau got the milk from the refrigerator.

Natalie winked at Merritt.

He scratched himself and frowned at her.

Beau carried the milk over to the table.

"What do you like in your pancakes?" Natalie asked. She got a bowl from the cupboard for the batter and began mixing.

"Syrup!" Beau said.

Merritt made a face. "You're gross."

"You are," Beau said.

"What do you like, Merry?" Natalie asked. She was getting a headache. She sprayed oil in the pan--Meredith had the canola-in-aerosol that was fun to use, but clearly didn't come from Whole Foods. Of course, neither did the Bisquick. She grinned.

Merritt said, "I want mouse pancakes."

"What?"

"Shaped like a Mickey Mouse face," Meredith said. She'd come to the doorway of the kitchen, wearing a bathrobe and smiling wanly at them. Her face was pink and scrubbed but the skin under her eyes was puffy. Natalie's heart ached.

"Mice all around," Natalie said.

"I want syrup." Beau said.

"The boy wants syrup," Natalie said.

Meredith slid past her to the pan. "You know, we have a griddle. But this'll be fine."

"Next time," Natalie said.

Meredith glanced up and met her eyes.

Beau jostled her. "Can we really have pancakes for dinner, Mommy?"

"Yes," Meredith said.

"Every night?"

"Maybe. We'll see if we feel like pancakes tomorrow night."

"Pizza?" Beau asked.

"I like pancakes better than pizza," Natalie said.

"Oh, me too," Beau said.

Merritt climbed onto his seat and leaned on the kitchen island.

Natalie poured the first batter into the pan.

"Can I help?" Meredith asked.

"No. Shush," Natalie said.

Meredith grinned and settled down next to Merritt, wrapping her arm around his waist.

Beau disappeared.

Keeping busy kept Natalie pretending everything was happy. Everything was fine. Still, she turned around and caught Meredith's eye. "Do you have any wine?"

"Mommy doesn't drink," Merritt said.

"No, but our guest might, and we should respect her," Meredith said.

Merritt looked down.

Meredith kissed the top of his head. "You know where the wine is. Why don't you go get it?"

"Okay." Merritt slid off the seat and went to a bottom cupboard.

Meredith got two wine glasses. She glanced questioningly at Natalie.

Natalie mouthed, "I'd like to talk." She'd almost said "know."

Meredith nodded at her, almost imperceptibly.

Natalie put the first pancakes onto a plate. Meredith poured the wine. The kids squirmed around them like eager, honking seals, reaching for the food before it was cool enough to handle. Beau attacked with the syrup, making a mess. Natalie took an offered wine glass gratefully and drank, the cool liquid tasting shockingly exotic and sinful after a month without alcohol.

Her stomach warmed. Her skin flushed. She set the glass down and poured the next few pancakes. Her back turned, liquor in her, she could safely let her eyes water with how much she loved this family, and how fake and fragile and hopeless the idyllic setting really was. She should have stayed in Charlotte. Being happy was worse than anything she'd experienced before.

She took the spatula, and with blurry eyes, dug at the patties.

"Hurry up," Beau said. His words were garbled. His mouth was probably full of dough, and maple syrup probably stained his face.

She'd be glad to leave, she told herself. Her apathy was helped by the wine and the smell of food and the ability to stand up without crying out in pain. She could turn inward now, and it wouldn't matter what Meredith said to her tonight.

Chapter Twenty

They'd let the boys stay up and watch *The Lion King*. The boys fell asleep on the couch with the movie still flickering in front of them.

Meredith did the dishes. Natalie worked her way from the couch to sit at the kitchen table. She poured a second glass of wine. Meredith settled into the stool opposite hers. She looked tired and for the first time Natalie noticed lines around her eyes and the blotchy, imperfect texture of her skin.

"It's none of my business," Natalie said. She took a sip of wine and found it hard to look at Meredith. But Meredith watched her.

"It's okay. I guess I misrepresented myself. It was just~you were the first friend I had since it all happened. And the first one who didn't know. So I guess I didn't want you to know." Meredith inhaled.

Natalie studied her glass.

"He drank a lot, after he came back. That's why the boys were worried. Soon they won't remember their daddy's bad habits. When they're older, they won't really remember him at all." Meredith's eyes filled with tears.

Natalie wanted to reach out to her, but she didn't know what she should say. She swallowed hard, and kept listening.

"We didn't even keep alcohol in the house before the war. Baptists, you know. And such a church wedding. Punch and pretzels." She chuckled. "It was great."

"But after?" It pained her to hear about Meredith's happy times with Vincent. Maybe that idyllic time was just as fake as dinner had been.

"He'd been sending me letters. He'd met someone~he wanted me to meet them. And the boys, too. He sounded so happy. For the first time in his life~you don't know, but it was hard. I mean, he had Jake, but around here, it wasn't always easy to make friends. Real friends. Not just the people you grew up with. The people you'd resented your whole life. He said the military was different. For the first time, he could see what the world was like, and it wasn't like it was back here."

Meredith smiled sadly at Natalie and took another sip of wine. "He wanted to take us there. Be a part of that life. But his friend was shot. Friendly fire. And Vince felt, I guess, like that was his last chance. He just gave up. Didn't think he could do it again. Handle all the pain. That and the war and being away from the boys, it all messed with his head so bad. And the drinking helped, but it made him weak. He tried to hurt himself so he could come home. Home to this place he hated.

"And once he was home, he kept trying and trying. It just got worse."

Natalie put her hand on Meredith's arm. Meredith cried, turning away from her. Her voice was shaky, and there was hesitation between her words.

"What happened?" Natalie asked.

"We were arguing~shouting. We did that a lot. It scared Beau and Merritt. And the neighbors. Heck, they called the cops on us a couple of times. It wasn't any different that night. But the way Vince was talking~I was afraid he'd hurt the boys. He wanted to go away~He wanted to go back~but it was gone. It was all gone." Meredith patted Natalie's hand with her free one, and then wiped at her cheeks.

Natalie nodded. A lump rose in her throat.

"He hit me and it wasn't~It wasn't the first time. I didn't hate him. He was in agony, and he trusted me~me and no one else, anymore. But~it hurt."

Natalie imagined the bruises on Meredith's cheeks~now faded, but shadowed there, in her past.

"Lots of men do it to control. You know, they get so frustrated their world isn't in the order they'd like it to be~we see it at the hospital all the time. And it was the same with Vince, in a way, but he just wanted it to stop. He wanted it all to stop. I think he hated me for being alive when his true love wasn't. And I was in Hell. I shouldn't have loved him so much, but I did."

"So," Natalie said, her voice hoarse, "You stopped it."

"He was screaming. He had so much anguish in him, he just couldn't let it all out fast enough, he wanted to rip off his own skin to let it out, I could tell, and he came at me, and I thought he was going to make me hurt the way he did, with his bare hands, and I~I grabbed the knife."

The last word was choked, and after she said it, Meredith kind of deflated. Her shoulders slumped. She stroked Natalie's fingers idly, worrying them. "I wish I could say it was purely self-defense, but a part of me was just~ ~so tired. So tired of it all. So tired of him. He wanted out. I wanted out."

"I'm sorry," Natalie said. And she was. All the fear left her. She reached across the island and cupped Meredith's face, first in her free hand, and then in both. Meredith's cheeks were hot, and tears dripped onto her fingers.

Meredith squeezed her eyes shut. She took Natalie's wrists, to hold her hands against her face, but she didn't say anything and she made no movement until her breathing slowed and she didn't have to clench so hard to keep the pain from showing. She smiled weakly and squeezed Natalie's wrists.

Natalie dropped her hands, self-conscious. "Who was this person he met? In the war?"

Meredith exhaled. She stared at the wine instead of Natalie, and said, "That's the other half of it. I've never told anyone. Not my lawyer. Not my family. Only Jake knows, and I—I didn't tell him."

"I'll go away, and you'll never have to worry." Natalie meant it jovially, but Meredith winced.

Natalie got up from her stool and walked around the island, glancing once at the sleeping boys before putting one arm around Meredith's shoulders. Meredith shuddered and went on staring at the wine glass.

"Tell me," Natalie said. She knew when people were at their breaking point. She used her free hand to stroke Meredith's hair.

"They were in love. I was okay with that. Because Vince and I never were. Not passionate. We were best friends. All through grade school and high school and prom and I never had a friend like Vince. He protected me and took care of me and—but he'd found someone, finally. I was so happy. Jealous, too. The way he talked. I never knew that kind of happiness, the kind that would make him think he could take the boys and live and his friend would care for me, too, and it would all be okay.

"Have you felt love like that? The kind that makes you think paradise is possible?" Meredith asked.

"No."

"Me either. But Vince found it. And then they took it away from him."

"Who was his friend?" Natalie asked.

"Tommy. Tommy Birch. From Georgia. I have his picture somewhere. His parents wouldn't let Vince go to his funeral. They knew who Vince was, and they wouldn't—It killed him. Not as much as I did, but it killed him all the same."

Natalie hugged Meredith, standing by the stool. Meredith began to sob against her chest. Natalie didn't know what to do, what to say. She smoothed Meredith's hair and stayed silent, wanting to cry too but processing too much to let her emotions overtake her thoughts, at least for the time Meredith cried in her arms.

"I'm sorry," Meredith said, her breathing ragged. She held onto Natalie tightly. "I'm sorry. I've never had a friend to tell that to. Not with Vince gone."

"And his family?" Natalie asked.

"They loved the old Vince as much as I did. Loved him so much they wouldn't believe in the new one. They blamed me. They never wanted me to marry him. They knew, somehow, we weren't in love. That there was something...wrong. But they thought it was my fault. I was tricking him. If I hadn't tied him down, he could find someone. He wouldn't have to~"

Meredith stopped, and Natalie rubbed her back, still full of questions about the boys, and about why Meredith would marry a man who didn't love her and didn't want her, but for now she could see Meredith was spent. She was exhausted and drank too much wine. Natalie eased back, keeping one hand on her shoulder.

"Mom," Beau called from the couch, "Why aren't you watching the movie with us?"

Natalie glanced at Meredith and shrugged.

Meredith took Natalie's elbow and walked with her slowly across the living room carpet, where they crowded onto the old, lumpy couch with Beau. Merritt slept sprawled on his back on the floor, his mouth wide open, snoring.

Natalie felt awkward, sitting next to Meredith, their shoulders pressed together, pretending to be normal. So she shifted and put one arm around Meredith's shoulders instead. Meredith gave her a grateful smile, and reached across and took her free hand and pulled it into her lap. They stayed together, reading the subtitles, with Beau curled against Natalie's back like a heating pad.

Meredith fell asleep in her arms. Merritt woke up enough to crawl off to his own bed. Natalie knew her body would hurt all over tomorrow morning.

Meredith woke in Natalie's embrace. She snuggled closer, wrapping herself against warm curves. Her cheek pressed a breast, and she~Her eyes flew open. Everything twisted inside her. She wanted to get away. Confessing everything to Natalie should have resulted in recrimination, not comfort, and if she even deserved comfort, exploiting it was~She shook herself, suppressing the thoughts, wishing away the heat from her body, and stood up.

Beau squirmed. She scooped him into her arms and took him upstairs to bed. The boys slept on as if nothing had happened.

She went back to wake Natalie.

"Mugh?" Natalie said.

"Come on. I put Beau to bed. You're going to be in a lot of pain tomorrow if you stay on the couch."

Natalie yawned. "I don't feel any pain now."

"You will. Come on." Meredith tugged on her hand.

"It's hard to walk."

"Big baby." Meredith squeezed her fingers.

Natalie sighed.

"Come on."

Natalie put her arms on Meredith's shoulders and together they stood. "Ow."

"See?"

"Ow. I had surgery!"

Meredith ignored her and helped her hobble to the bedroom. She made Natalie stand while she turned down the sheets and then tucked her arms under Natalie's again, pulling up her hem.

"Um," Natalie said.

Meredith's hands froze on her abdomen, with her shirt halfway to her breasts. "Fine, change clothes yourself." She ducked out of the room, blushing at what she had almost seen.

"That isn't what I meant," Natalie called.

Meredith went upstairs to the medicine cabinet. When she went back to Natalie's bedroom, she handed Natalie a pill and a glass of water.

"I've been drinking."

"Hours ago, and not very much."

Natalie frowned at the pill in her hand.

"Please. I'm your nurse."

Natalie swallowed the pill and then finished off the water.

"Goodnight." Meredith's thoughts turned to leaving and going upstairs, to re-living their conversation over and over.

"Stay."

Natalie gazed at Meredith as if Meredith weren't some kind of monster, but just a woman and a friend.

The tenderness of the gaze made Meredith feel worse. "I can't stay."

"It's been a shitty day."

"Nat."

"Well, it has."

"Are you trying to reason me out of my emotional state? Not going to work."

Natalie patted the bed.

Meredith sighed and sat down.

Natalie reached out, her hand landing on Meredith's thigh. "I know you."

The words sent chills through Meredith, even as the touch brought heat. She had no idea how to feel.

"If you go upstairs, you'll just cry all over again."

"If you're going to let me take advantage of your kindness~"

"I am."

"Then at least let me change."

Natalie nodded rolled over, into her pillow. Meredith went upstairs. Her bedroom felt empty and she was glad, pulling on a nightgown and a robe, glad she didn't have to stay. There were places to go. She went back downstairs with a pillow, apprehensive as she slipped into Natalie's bedroom.

Natalie grinned and yawned.

"Thank you," Meredith said.

"I owe you."

Meredith started to say something, but Natalie lifted her hand. Meredith sat on the bed.

"Life will probably be awful all over again tomorrow," Natalie said.

"But not until then?"

"Not until then."

"I brought my own pillow."

Meredith laid it by Natalie's head, and then slid up to get under the sheets. The hospital bed was not quite a double. There was barely room for both of them without touching. Meredith settled cautiously onto her back.

"Good idea," Natalie said.

"I haven't slept with anyone since my husband died."

"You two slept in the same bed?"

"Almost every night he was home. I felt so protected. We tried sleeping with the kids. Very New Age. Merry didn't take to it. He liked his own space. If he was in our room he slept on the floor. But Beau would wriggle in between us, and it was almost perfect."

"I can't promise that."

"No. This is something entirely different."

Silence descended, and after a while Natalie spoke. "I'm glad you told me, Merry. You didn't have to."

"I've wanted to. Thank you for listening."

"Anytime."

"Do you believe me? How I saw it?"

"Yes."

"Other people might have seen it differently."

"I know."

"'Course you do. You're a lawyer."

"I've heard it all before."

"Have you?"

"Yes."

"Did you ever believe them?"

"No. But I believe you."

Meredith closed her eyes. "Night, Nat."

She stopped with those words even though there was more on the tip of her tongue. She figured she'd said enough for one day.

Chapter Twenty-One

Natalie woke up inside a fog. Her back and legs ached. The worst of both worlds, she thought. She tried to stretch her calf and winced. Every morning was going to be like this, probably for the rest of her life. She closed her eyes against the sunlight and tried to sleep until the pain went away.

Of course, she was starving and had to go to the bathroom. A lack of movement was in no way going to help.

Merritt pushed open the door. "Natalie."

"Mare, get out of there," Meredith's voice, louder down the hallway.

Merritt slipped in and closed the door. To buy himself more time, Natalie decided, peering at him under the lids of her eyes. Clever boy.

He bounded onto the bed. No need to slink since he was caught. "Natalie!"

The bed shifting and bending to him sent waves of pain through Natalie. She seized and let out a whimper, and then covered it by gritting her teeth at him.

He grinned. "Get up."

"Don't wanna."

He leaned forward and shook her shoulder. "Get up, get up, get up."

This would be endless, she thought, until she got up. She didn't have the determination and time-management skills of a child.

Meredith burst through the door.

Natalie smirked.

"Merry, you're going to get a whuppin'," Meredith said.

Merritt squirmed off the bed and darted underneath it. "Have to catch me first." He hit upward, against the bed frame.

Natalie grunted.

"I'm so, so sorry," Meredith said, coming to sit on the bed.

Thump.

"Don't be. I have to get up, anyway."

"I was going bring you breakfast."

"I can bring myself to breakfast."

"If you want. How do you feel?"

"Awful."

"Jake's coming by today. He'll make you feel real good."

"Oh, sure." Natalie rolled her eyes. "Hasn't happened yet."

Meredith got up. "We're having eggs. How do you like yours?"

"Poached."

Meredith folded her arms.

Natalie batted her eyelashes.

Meredith went to the door and said in a sing-song voice, "I'm going to make Natalie's eggs all by myself, and she'll love me best, and she'll forget anyone else is in the house."

"No she won't!" Merritt hollered, and scooted out from under the bed and was through the door just as Meredith opened it.

"Well done," Natalie said.

"A mother's gift." Meredith tossed her hair and then went out, shutting the door and leaving Natalie in peace.

Natalie groaned and very slowly and very carefully swung her legs over the side of the bed, and braced herself for standing up. If not for the children, she might not get out of bed at all. Not this morning, not any of the others.

"Let me go with you," Natalie said, hobbling into the kitchen. With her walker, which she was not ashamed of, which was her new best friend, it took five minutes to go from the bedroom to the kitchen. Her back was stooped—too cramped to straighten. But her head was clearing, and breakfast would help, and she didn't want any more drugs. She hated the haze they brought. The idea of being mentally useless made her nauseous.

"No," Meredith said.

"I would be useful."

"You'd take over my case?"

Natalie glanced away.

"I'll be all right."

Natalie wanted to say, "Like hell you will," but she bit her tongue and hobbled toward the table.

Meredith lowered her voice even more and said, "It's just an evidentiary hearing. One of the neighbors making a fuss about what he heard, the 911 call, things like that."

"You called 911?"

"Of course."

Natalie should have stayed in bed after all. Might as well go for broke, then. "When's the trial?" she asked.

"Month after next," Meredith said.

A chill went through Natalie. It had seemed so far in the past—Meredith recovered, adjusted. The fact that she was still in her own home, working her own job, raising her children—Natalie hadn't worried.

"Two months?" That felt like nothing. That felt like tomorrow.

"It'll probably be up in Oxford. They wanted to move it. Less prejudicial, I guess. I don't think it matters."

"Merry~"

"Eat your eggs, Nat."

But Natalie didn't want them. They'd be as cold as she was, as unappetizing as the churning in her stomach. She gazed at the boys. Beau was drinking the last of the sugary milk from his bowl. Merritt was concentrating, brow furrowed, as he fished one marshmallow out at a time.

"I can't move," Natalie said.

"What hurts?" Meredith came closer.

"My back," Natalie said. "I think it's done."

Meredith laid her hand on Natalie's back. "Hardly."

"It is. Something got weakened by the accident, and now it's shifted and I shall be a hunchback, all the days of my life."

"Feeling poetic, are we?"

"Impressive education at one of the finest law schools in the country. I wish you'd let me help."

"You are helping," Meredith said. She stood behind Natalie and wrapped her arms around Natalie's waist, so she was pressed up against Natalie's back.

Her body heat radiated through Natalie, and turned her to liquid, and without the walker, Natalie would have toppled to the floor, boneless, robbed of her senses.

"Relax," Meredith said.

"Oh, sure."

"I mean it. I know it sounds illogical, but lean forward. Let go." Her hand moved to Natalie's shoulder, crossing her front like a seatbelt, and Natalie didn't need much encouragement to go limp.

Meredith squeezed, giving her back the support to stretch and bring Natalie upright, with her knees bent and her arms braced on the handles.

"Now, stand."

She straightened. Her grip lessened on the handles, and then she let go completely, raising her arms out to her sides. About forty-five degrees Her shoulder wouldn't allow any more.

Meredith stepped away and rubbed Natalie's back.

"Thanks."

"I knew you had it in you."

"I'm glad someone did." Natalie turned and hugged Meredith, as hard as she could, which was not very hard, but enough Meredith pressed against her, and kept smoothing her back.

"Thank you," Natalie said.

"Any time. You're welcome."

She didn't move back from the hug, so Natalie let it linger, pressing her cheek against Meredith's hair. It felt good to move her arms and her shoulders like this, to be in this position, to feel limber and encompassing.

"Hey. I'm taller than you."

"Sure are, tiger," Meredith said. She laughed and stepped back, moving her hands to Natalie's shoulders to steady her.

"I guess I didn't notice."

"This is the first time you've stood tall. You looked so small in that hospital bed. You should've seen yourself."

Natalie snorted.

Meredith glanced at the clock. "I've got to go. My lawyer's picking me up. My other lawyer."

"We'll be fine."

Meredith glanced at the boys. "I'll try to slip out. I'll be back before you know it."

"Don't worry," Natalie said.

Meredith met her eyes, and there was tension in her face, and her hands moved awkwardly against Natalie's arms. Natalie made a guess, and gave in a little to her own self-interest, and hugged Meredith again, burying Meredith against her.

She did feel tall.

"Don't worry. When you come back, we'll fix everything."

"Just like this," Meredith said, in a small, muffled voice against Natalie's shoulder.

"What?"

"Nothing." Meredith stepped back and gave Natalie a watery smile. "Say hi to Jake."

"He's going to break me in half."

"Good. Then I'll be taller than you, and the boys will each have their own Natalie."

"Oh, God," Natalie said.

Meredith gave her a stern look, and then as a horn honked, headed toward the front door.

Natalie gazed at the ceiling. "These people are going to tear me apart."

Nothing on the ceiling answered her, but a warmth tingled at the back of her neck and down to the base of her spine, and while she was standing there, contemplating it and the possibilities of some sort of sunlight angling into the kitchen, Merritt came and tugged at her hand, sending a sharp pain through her hip and nearly toppling her to the floor.

"Merry?" she asked.

"Read to us!"

"All right. Go get a book. But it'll have to be one you can read to me. I've still got to eat my eggs."

"They're cold."

"All the better to distract me."

He frowned, but went to his room.

"Merry reads better than me," Beau said, coming up to sit next to her and contemplate her eggs with a studious expression.

"That's okay."

"Why?"

"It just is."

Beau frowned.

Natalie put one arm around his shoulders and picked up her fork with her free hand. She wanted to tell him she didn't love him any less for being less eloquent than his brother. He was too young to understand. But she made a mental note. When he got older—

Maybe she'd write him a letter. And in ten years, when he read it, Meredith would have to explain who the hell this crazy woman was, writing to him from the past.

Natalie grinned.

Merritt came back and spread his book on the kitchen table.

Beau dug his fingers into her eggs.

"Mom's coming home soon. What's her favorite meal?" Natalie asked.

"She likes fried chicken," Merritt said.

"Are you only saying that because you like fried chicken?"

Beau giggled. "Merry hates fried chicken. Crunch. Crunch!" He waved his arms at Merritt.

Merritt screamed.

Natalie wrapped her arms around Beau and held him off. "I still need your advice, boys. I can't make fried chicken."

Merritt pulled up his chair to the counter and climbed first onto the chair, and then onto the counter, and stood, carefully opening the pantry. Natalie winced, imagining him falling. She wanted to warn him, and all the recriminations were on the tip of her tongue, but she held it. He seemed to know what he was doing.

He pulled out a box of Shake 'N Bake and then climbed down. The chair squeaked under his weight.

Beau sighed and gave up resisting against her grip. He leaned in. "There's chicken in the freezer. We're not allowed to touch the freezer."

Merritt smirked.

"Bring me the box, Mare," she said.

Merritt looked sullen. He'd brought it this far.

"Please?"

He grinned and brought her the box. She read the instructions. Seemed doable. "Are you boys allowed to touch the stove?"

Beau's eyes widened.

Merritt shook his head rapidly.

Natalie opened the box. "Is there no Popeyes around here? No KFC?" She'd never had to work for fried chicken before. She wasn't even sure how it was really made.

Beau ignored her in favor of getting milk out of the fridge and then getting a bowl.

"There's a KFC at the beach, but mommy never takes us." Merritt said.

"She takes us to McDonalds, though. Can we go to McDonalds?"

"Tonight we're making a special dinner for your mom," Natalie said.

Beau sulked.

Natalie pre-set the oven, thinking about small towns and having to cook all the time. At least pizza delivered, and Chinese, but she hadn't been to a restaurant since she got here, and Meredith was a good-enough cook she hadn't noticed.

Now she noticed.

"Mommy, Mommy!"

Beau and Merritt tore out of the living room as Meredith made it into the foyer. She took off her coat and set down her briefcase. The kids hugged her. She knelt to hug them back. Strands fell around her face and against her neck. She was so relieved to see them. She wanted to see~

Natalie hobbled into view and Meredith smiled. "What's the smell?"

"Fried chicken!" Merritt exclaimed.

"Nat wanted to make something special for you. So we made her make chicken," Beau said.

His words made Meredith want to cry. The day had been awful, away from her family, back out into the world. Even the mood of it, full of dread with an underlying current of hate, coming from everyone in the courtroom except for her lawyer, drained her spiritually and physically.

Coming home washed everything away.

Meredith straightened up and hugged Natalie. "Thank you."

Natalie put her hand on the back of Meredith's head, tightening the embrace. "How did it go?"

Meredith squeezed her before pulling back and said, "We'll talk about it after dinner."

Natalie nodded.

"I can't believe you got Merritt to eat fried chicken."

"Well, he hasn't eaten it yet."

"All right, since you all cooked, I'll set the table."

Natalie limped over to the kitchen.

"Is there just chicken?"

"There's peas in the microwave, ready to be heated, and I made a pot of rice. It's still warm."

"You made rice?"

More and more the day at the courthouse felt like she'd visited another world. She didn't understand how badness and goodness could co-exist in one life.

"There're instructions on the bag. I can cook."

"I just assumed you'd have a rice cooker."

"I do have a rice cooker. But I can improvise."

"Thank you."

Natalie settled in at the table. "Would you mind getting everything? I think I've been standing too long."

"It's my pleasure."

"I was hoping you'd say that."

Chapter Twenty-Two

Meredith put the kids to bed. Natalie put herself to bed, which took nearly as long as making sure two four year olds washed and brushed their teeth, got read a few stories, and whined about glasses of water and more television.

Similarly sponged, minty, and reading, Natalie was engrossed in First Corinthians. She'd remembered what Wheeler said, and found the passage, the words elegant and beautiful in Meredith's New King James, but the rest of the chapter at parts enthralled and irritated her. She hissed in frustration, and would have thrown the Bible across the room if it wasn't Meredith's.

Meredith knocked on the door.

"Come in," Natalie said. She closed the Book.

Meredith came in wearing a nightgown and robe that nearly touched the floor and it took Natalie's breath away. The fabric was satin the color of corn silk, pale and flowing, and Meredith, like the rest of them, had washed her face, so she looked young and sweet and pure with her hair falling against her shoulders.

"May I?" Meredith asked, and Natalie patted the bed. She'd moved over to the other side, to make space, the anticipation buzzing through her so much she'd been driven to pick up the Book, to remind herself just exactly what was going on here~healing.

"How's the Good Book?" Meredith asked.

"Um."

"Not so great? Are you so pagan it burns your flesh?" Meredith grinned.

"It's just~Oh, it really doesn't matter."

"Come. Tell me." Meredith put her hand on Natalie's shoulder. "I don't really get to have adult conversations that don't revolve around basketball. I promise I won't judge."

Natalie considered, biting her lip. Aristotle, she could quote. Machiavelli. Augustine. Solon.

This wasn't even an Orthodox Bible. She shouldn't even care.

Meredith cared.

"Corinthians. The stuff about love is beautiful, right? I mean, it sucks you in. I heard it at a wedding once, when I was a kid. My mother cried~but~"

She took the book back from Meredith and opened it, searching for the passage that had inflamed her. She flipped through several pages and scanned, and Meredith was quiet, still rubbing her shoulder.

Natalie said, "Now I have written to you not to keep company with any-one named a brother, who is sexually immoral, or covetous, or an idolater, or a reviler, or a drunkard, or an extortioner~not even to eat with such a per-son." She scowled. "You can't even eat with them?"

Meredith moved closer, to see the page. Her shoulder brushed against Natalie's as she pointed. "It does point out the whole world is full of those people, and you'd basically have to die to get away from them."

"How often do I feel like that," Natalie said.

Meredith grinned. She stroked the words with her fingers. "It's really only the good Christians you have to worry about. The ones in your temple, or in your home, who are close enough to poison you."

Natalie shivered at the word 'poison.'

The passage made her burn with something she couldn't express to Meredith, not without confession~not quite shame, but revulsion. "I deal with those immoral perverts every day. They're not bad people. And even if they were, they need help. Compassion. Not to be flicked off like some flea. I mean~" she stopped.

"You mean, if you followed Paul's tenets, you couldn't live in my home. A lot of people around here believe that. Casting out the sick among us so we ourselves are not blighted is a common instinct. Self-protection."

Natalie didn't say anything.

"There are any numbers of ways you could look at it. Paul is merely a servant of God, and not Jesus, and he doesn't even really say he's speaking for Jesus or God here. Or he's just a man, and he's fallible. Or he's frustrated with the founding of the first church."

"But those are cop-outs."

"Maybe. But I'm not trying to give you an excuse. I'm saying what you'd hear in Bible study somewhere. I'm speaking as a Christian. This stuff is com-plicated, and to be honest, not all of it requires understanding to live."

"Oh, I understand," Natalie said.

Meredith took the Bible from her hands and flipped the pages. She said, "Here. 'Was anyone called to God while circumcised? Let him not become uncircumcised. Was anyone called while uncircumcised? Let him not be circumcised. Circumcision is nothing and uncircumcision is nothing, but keeping the commandments of God is what matters.'"

"The ten commandments?"

"Or the ones Jesus set down~love God and your neighbor."

"And you're illustrating this with circumcision? Ew?"

"Let me read on, lawyer." Meredith read, "Let each one remain in the same calling in which he was called. Were you called while a slave?"

Natalie folded her arms.

"So, if God speaks to you, listen. If you're a slave and he speaks to you, it doesn't matter. If you're a homosexual, or an alcoholic, or in prison, or a jerk~it doesn't matter. You are what you are. So reconcile that with what Paul said about who to eat with."

"I can't," Natalie said.

"Then don't. It's all academics, as long as you understand God loves you."

"Well, I don't understand that either."

"Do you understand that I~" Meredith stopped.

Natalie leaned over to see the page. "What's this about virgins?"

Meredith elbowed her.

"Volatile stuff."

"It can be." Meredith turned on her side, to regard Natalie. "What words do you live by?"

"Whereas the law is passionless, passion must ever sway the heart of man."

Meredith smiled.

"And yours? Surely not Corinthians," Natalie said.

"Faith, hope, and love. But I've always preferred the Book of Job. More so when it was less prescient, I suppose. Losing everything."

Natalie shifted, facing Meredith as best she could, lacking the strength to lie on her side. She winced as her shoulder throbbed.

"Are you all right?"

"Just being smote."

"As if."

"I'm no saint."

"Why?" Meredith asked.

Natalie froze. She swallowed hard and considered her words carefully.

"I am unkind to orphans."

"You are not."

"I have road rage."

"The deer started it."

Natalie chuckled. "How was court?"

A cloud passed through Meredith's expression. "Fine. I mean~fine. They provided me a bill for my court-appointed lawyer. Apparently I make too much money to qualify, even under North Carolina guidelines."

Natalie frowned.

"I should have taken my kids, right? Pleaded single mother. Shown them my grocery bills."

"Merry~"

Meredith shook her head. "Vince's parents showed up. They always do. For the smallest thing. They stare at me with such hate~"

"Merry, hey." Natalie pushed herself up on one arm, though her shoulder threatened to collapse out from under her, and found the strength to cup Meredith's cheek.

"Don't worry yourself. It'll sort itself out. Somehow."

Natalie brushed away tears with her thumb.

"God," Meredith said, and then, perhaps since the curse had already escaped her lips, closed her eyes tightly and said, "God. How did I have no one to talk to for months? How did I survive?"

Natalie's shoulder gave way and she sprawled against Meredith's side, still holding her cheek, forcing Meredith to see her. Their eyes were only inches apart, and Meredith blinked, holding her gaze. Neither of them moved.

"Because you're stronger than you think."

Meredith broke into a sob. She covered her face with her hands.

Natalie pulled her close, slipping her arm under Meredith's neck and holding her, as best she could with her leg still useless. How she cursed the uselessness. How she hated the weakness.

Meredith curled into her, burying her face against Natalie's chest. She adjusted to Natalie's posture, and Natalie offered what comfort she could. Meredith's sobs turned to sniffles, and then sobs seized her again, making her shake with the energy she was trying to scream out of her system.

"It's okay. It's okay. I'm here." Natalie whispered over and over. She moved her fingers in Meredith's hair and let Meredith's tears fall against her throat.

Meredith rolled onto her back, onto Natalie's arm. Natalie could see the dark circles of her eyes as Meredith gazed at the ceiling.

"Stay," she said, before Meredith could say goodnight.

Meredith closed her eyes. Natalie reached out and brushed a final stray tear from Meredith's jaw.

"We're going to the beach tomorrow," Meredith said. "Our last weekend."

"Finally."

"We'll see the ocean. It'll be nice."

Natalie put her hand on Meredith's arm. "Our problems will seem small in front of the ocean."

Chapter Twenty-Three

Natalie woke up before Meredith. The sunlight, blinding and orange, shone on them. Natalie slept on her back, with Meredith still curled up on her side. The stiffness in her body brought agony, but Natalie knew how to work through it.

Slowly.

She rotated her ankles and then rubbed her shoulder with her good hand. Turning her neck to gaze at Meredith resulted in satisfying cracks. The sunlight, too, made her limber.

Meredith stirred.

Natalie held her breath and settled down against her pillow. She thought about pretending to be asleep, but she kept her eyes open, staring at the yellow ceiling as Meredith sat up.

"Did I wake you?" Meredith asked.

"No. I was awake."

"Just lying there?"

"Trying to move."

"Are you all right?"

Meredith's face appeared above her, concerned. Natalie laughed. "It's fine. It just takes a while to stretch out the muscles again."

"Right. You should have a nurse or something."

Natalie tried to protest, but Meredith, nimble and healthy, cupped Natalie's neck in both of her hands. She massaged, lifting Natalie's head enough to roll back, and there were more painful crunches traveling down her vertebrae. Natalie sank back and rubbed her shoulders, working the muscles.

"Lift your arms," Meredith said.

"Oh, come on."

Meredith took Natalie's wrists and raised them upward. Natalie grunted. Meredith pulled, stretching her, and when she let go, Natalie felt looser.

"Thank you. Are you always this chipper in the morning?"

"I think it's kind of an anticipatory energy to deal with the boys. Wait until I have to send them to school~" she paused, and sadness went through her, making her whole form shrink.

Natalie, with newly invigorated limbs, reached for Meredith. "You will."

"Maybe," Meredith studied Natalie's face with a serious expression. "At least I want to, now."

Natalie nodded.

Meredith touched Natalie's cheek and leaned down, pressing her lips to Natalie's forehead. Natalie tilted her head back, trying to see Meredith, and Meredith took that as an invitation. She kissed Natalie's lips, briefly. Then straightened.

"I'm going to need your help at the beach," Meredith said.

"Do I have to carry chairs and coolers? Frisbees?"

Meredith slid off the bed and walked around to the foot. Her robe, though wrinkled, flowed with her steps. She looked radiant in the morning, and Natalie's own self-image~sweaty, broken, slug-like, and immobile, diminished. She scoffed. Undaunted, Meredith took Natalie's left calf in both hands.

"No," Natalie said.

"Hush. It'll help." Meredith slid one hand up to cup her knee.

"It'll hurt."

"Big baby."

Meredith lifted until Natalie's leg bent, guided by gravity and professional skill. Natalie groaned with pain. Meredith straightened out her leg. Natalie exhaled.

"Again," Meredith said.

Whatever Paul of Tarsus had to say about spending too much time with the wrong people, there was absolutely nothing sexy about physical therapy, even in a bed lit by the morning sunlight. Even with Meredith in a robe like that.

Bundling two boys into the car took a long time, even when they were eager to get to the beach. Forgetfulness plagued them, and laziness, so Meredith carried everything for four people. They'd intended to pack sandwiches, but Natalie suggested KFC. The boys dissolved into giggles.

Meredith just shook her head.

They finally left. Meredith drove and Natalie sat beside her, leaning against the window, trying to ignore the boys as they wrestled and shouted in the back of the station wagon.

"Isn't it unsafe?" she asked.

"There are degrees of unsafe. They're four. And they're boys. As long as they aren't poking at us we can consider ourselves blessed."

"Okay. I consider myself blessed."

Meredith grinned, the corner of her mouth twitching upward. She turned back to the road.

Natalie, too, watched the expanse of highway open up in front of them. On either side of the road were only wetlands and farmland, low and flat and a verdant, invigorating green. Scrub brush joined the landscape as they got closer. The car traveled easily on the open road. Here in the daylight, Natalie's accident seemed silly. How, on such a benign highway, had she nearly died?

Around a bend, and nearly immediately, the traffic pattern changed from heavy highway travel to a full stop. Meredith slowed deftly while Natalie was still recoiling from the vision of hundreds of cars, red brake lights blinding, winding through the lowlands.

"Did you know to expect that?" Natalie asked.

Meredith grinned. "Tourists."

"From where? There aren't this many people in Tarpley, are there?"

Meredith shrugged. "From Charlotte, mostly. Columbia. Greensboro. Raleigh. People coming down for the weekend. They won't all be at the beach. There's fishing, and golf, and the boardwalk. And I guarantee they'll all be gone by noon when the tide comes in. Isn't much beach left."

"Erosion," Merritt said.

Natalie nodded. They crept along. Meredith turned on the radio to listen to the traffic report, but all she found was country and beach music. She settled on the beach music, and that was the setting for Natalie when the car rounded another curve, and behind a grove of ordinary trees growing out of the grassland, she saw a palm tree.

"Oh, wow," she said.

"What?" Meredith glanced at her, and then stomped on the brakes as the car in front of her stopped unexpectedly. She narrowed her eyes.

"The beach. It's close."

"It's close enough to feel," Meredith said.

Natalie tried not to sniffle at the stupid tree and started to wonder how well her walker was going to work in the sand. She should have switched to crutches.

Beau climbed toward the front seat. He poked Natalie.

"Ow. Stop."

He poked her again.

She hissed.

"And so it begins," Meredith said. "Who wants to play the license plate game?"

"Me!" Merritt said.

Beau scowled.

A month ago, Natalie, upon witnessing these boys in the grocery store or on the sidewalk, cavorting as they were, loud and obnoxious and motivated by absurdist self-involvement, would have dark thoughts. Though she would not have acted on any desires of violence, she would have gone out of her way to avoid children. She would have crossed the street, turned around and driven home, maybe even stopped shopping at that store.

Whatever it took.

Her senses must have dulled because she barely noticed they had increased their racket, and they were so cute, the way Merritt squeaked at cars and Beau kicked the side of the door whenever he got beaten, that she could only smile.

The first thing Natalie saw upon closing the car door and convincing Meredith she could, in fact, handle a walker, a backpack, and a chair, as long as she moved along at a slow pace, was the giant sand dune. The ocean roared from somewhere nearby, unrelenting. The smell of salt had been with her since the highway.

Meredith had rolled down the windows as soon as they'd gotten close to Wilmington, before she'd veered south and took them down the coastal highway, past tiny hamlets and big billboards proclaiming beach after beach. She'd only seen trees and stoplights and more billboards until they'd turned left, across traffic, and then it was over a bridge and to this tiny strip of brush and sand and houses on stilts.

And the dunes. Seaweed grew like cattails, and there were picket fences and barbed wire around each dune, and a staircase, wooden and weathered, in the middle of it all, the boys bounded up, and Natalie inched toward.

"Is this *China Beach*?" she asked Meredith.

"What?"

"The dunes."

"It's for erosion. The barbed wire is there to protect the sea turtles."

"There are sea turtles?"

"Welcome to the wild coast."

Natalie crept forward.

"Boys. I want you to stay at the bottom of the stairs. If you go near the ocean, I'll drag you back into the car and we'll go home," Meredith said.

A chorus of giggles came from the other side of the dune. Natalie reached the steps. She wanted to be with them. She wanted to see the delight on their faces. She hadn't dealt with stairs since the accident. They were like a wall in front of her, and the walkway, precarious and holed, started above her head. She felt dizzy.

Meredith appeared and trotted down the stairs. Like a mountain goat, Natalie thought. She squelched the jealousy and the fear when Meredith touched her arm and studied her with concern.

"You can do this," Meredith said.

"There's so many of them."

"Eight."

"You counted? There has to be more than eight."

"I counted. Give me the chair."

Natalie handed it over.

"And the walker."

"Merry, I can't walk."

"There's a railing."

"I'll get a splinter."

"Hush. Now let go."

Natalie raised her hands and gave Meredith a dirty look. "You'll feel guilty when I fall over."

"Sure I will." Meredith hefted the walker over her shoulder and went back up the stairs, shouting, "Boys, what did I tell you?"

"We didn't do anything," Beau shouted. "Where's Nat?"

She took a deep breath and put her foot attached to her good leg on the first step. Her bad leg, holding more of her weight, protested, and she leaned forward, squatting, and clung to the railing. She pushed with her foot. She rose up, precariously balanced, more used to pulling than to standing with one foot, but her shoulder hurt too much to take more on.

Maybe Meredith would give her some Percocet, just to get up the stairs.

Meredith re-appeared, with Beau and Merritt lingering on the walkway. She came down and put her arm around Natalie's waist.

"Come on, hurry," Beau said.

"Cute kid," Natalie said.

"Darling, isn't he. Put your arm around me." Natalie put her free arm around Meredith's back, unable to quite reach her shoulders, and clung to the railing with her other hand.

"Okay, you're not going to like this, but lean on me when you take your next step."

"Merry, I can't~"

"I told you. Now try."

Natalie put her foot on the next step, and leaned into Meredith, who balanced her and held her up.

Merritt giggled.

Meredith kept a death grip on her own railing. "On the count of three. One, two, three." They heaved, and Natalie toppled onto the next step.

She was embarrassed. Her face was hot, and she was starting to sweat from the exertion and the heat.

"Again," Meredith said.

By the eighth step, they were getting the hang of it. On the walkway, Natalie leaned over the railing and panted with relief. Meredith kept her hand on Natalie's back.

Merritt and Beau ran past them and back down to the beach.

"No throwing sand in anyone's eyes. Especially people you don't know," Meredith said.

"This might have been more trouble than it was worth."

"That's what the ocean's all about, isn't it? Come on. We get to go down now."

"Oh, no."

"Come on." Meredith took her elbow.

Natalie let herself be dragged along. The ocean lay before her, greenish and calm, with a hazy horizon and a paler, golden sky above. She grinned, moving forward with greater ease until the tide itself came into view, rolling onto the sand, leaving its wet imprint, trying again. Higher and higher.

People bobbed in the surf, specks even at this proximity. The beach was sparsely populated with families and umbrellas and kids. There was a volley-ball net down the beach and farther the curve of the land, jutting out to sea, creating a destination.

Down the beach the other way was the pier, which went a long way out into the water, farther than anyone could swim. In the haze, it seemed to shimmer.

"Smells like fish at the end," Meredith said.

"It seems so romantic from here."

"So does the water, until it gets up your nose and stings your eyes and your bathing suit is soaked with sand and you get stung by a jellyfish."

"Were you always like this?"

"I'm a nurse. It's all about applying pragmatism to foolish notions."

"Did you bring me here just to force me to exercise?"

"That's why I brought your physical therapist."

"I don't care what you say, it's beautiful. I wonder~" Her throat got choked up, and she swallowed hard to regain her voice. "I wonder if it would have been this beautiful, six weeks ago."

"Of course it would have," Meredith said. She put her hand on Natalie's back. "You would have seen it at night, with the moon and the stars reflecting on the water, and the lights of the pier, and the comforting darkness and the deafening sound of the waves that could almost swallow you up, but the hotel lights in the distance remind you that at the long, invisible cord connects you to the world, there are still other people."

"Now who's romantic," Natalie said. A tear escaped her eye and rolled down her nose. She turned to Meredith.

Meredith met her eyes, and they gazed at each other rather than the ocean until Beau yelled.

"One step at a time," Meredith said.

Natalie turned back to the descending staircase. She gripped the railing with her hand, and leaned forward bravely. Then she paused. "Which foot do I start on?"

"Reach out your good leg." Meredith went down two steps, and then said, "Put your hand on my shoulder."

Natalie did so, and took the first step. She nearly toppled over, but Meredith caught her by the waist and held her until she regained her balance.

"Good," Meredith said, looking flushed and a little frightened. "Maybe we could~"

"Excuse me ladies."

At the bottom of a staircase was a tall, dark man wearing only swim trunks. "I mean no offense, but I would be happy to help~if I can," he said.

Natalie opened her mouth, but Meredith shushed her.

"Would you mind carrying her down the stairs? She's a bit heavy for me."

Natalie opened her mouth again.

"I'd be happy to." He trotted up the stairs and before Natalie could protest, he'd stopped at roughly chest level, and wrapped one arm around her legs, propelling him against her shoulder. She hung down his back.

"Really, this isn't necessary," she said.

He was already backing down the stairs, very carefully, and holding on only to her good leg, letting the other dangle as it would. Her shoulder strained, but the trip was short, and he planted her on the sand easily.

"Um. Thank you," she said.

Meredith offered him a drink. He declined and jogged off down the beach.

"Nice guy," Meredith said.

Natalie looked agape at her.

"Take off your shoes," Meredith said.

Too in shock to argue, Natalie numbly kicked off her flip-flops. The sand under bare feet sent warmth from her toes to her ankles. She wriggled her toes and sank down into the sand.

Meredith bent easily and picked up her flip-flops. Natalie took them.

"Want your walker?" Meredith asked.

The boys parked it about fifty feet down the beach, along with a blanket and cooler and chairs they abandoned in favor of chasing a seagull.

"Hope they don't catch the poor bird," Meredith said.

"I think I can manage. Natalie straightened up. "If you'll~"

Meredith glanced away from the boys and back at her.

"Help?" Natalie asked.

Meredith slipped her arm around Natalie's waist. "Of course."

"This was a good idea."

A breeze blew across them, bringing with it salt and a faintly fishy smell.

"Wait until you see it at night."

Chapter Twenty-Four

For lunch, they went into town. Natalie was getting better at climbing up the walkway from the sheer panic she'd be stranded. The boys had played in the surf and with strangers' dogs and with the Frisbee and then made it through lunch. Now they were asleep in the back of the station wagon. The dash clock read one o'clock, but sun-stroked and exhausted, Natalie felt like she'd been at the beach all week.

"What's next?" Natalie asked. "Are we going home?"

"We're staying at a condo overnight. It's a surprise. It's near the beach, but not 'on' the beach. Still, it's near the coastal waterway. The boys will love it."

They'd gone over the bridge and back to the mainland where the restaurants were and weren't going back the way they came. Natalie furrowed her brow.

"Trust me," Meredith said.

"Oh, I trust you." She glanced out the window. Another bridge, another neighborhood of stilt-houses and palm trees and scrub grass, and then they were pulling into a concrete driveway and pulling up under the stilts.

"Is this safe?" Natalie asked.

"Well, if the flood comes it'll wash away the car. But we'll be fine."

Natalie got out of the car and glanced at the house. It seemed grand and looming. Then the side door opened and Jake came running down to see them.

"Hey!"

"This is Jake's place?"

"It is," Jake said. "My partner's a banker, you know. Investment. Though with the ocean washing away, I think he's cra-zy. And the mortgage is killing us. You wouldn't believe. So! Happy homecoming."

Natalie accepted his hug, and then he went to scoop up a sleeping Beau while Meredith grabbed Merritt. Merritt protested and dug his fingers into Meredith's shoulder.

"Can I help?" Natalie asked.

"I think your job is to get up the stairs."

"Geez. I'm calling the ADA about this whole place."

"I'll come get you in a sec," Jake said. He bounded upstairs with Beau. Meredith grinned and followed him more slowly.

Natalie glared and inwardly cursed at the stairs, but they remained stalwart. She took the railing.

Jake came back with a crutch. "How come you don't have a crutch?"

"Because my shoulder's doing all it can to hold onto my arm."

Meredith disappeared inside.

"Take the railing with your bad arm."

"Jake."

"It's just for balance. Come on."

Natalie switched sides, and then let Jake foist the crutch under her undamaged armpit. He adjusted the height, and then adjusted again.

"It's on the wrong side, really. But you'll have to adjust. Now lean your weight on the crutch and put your good foot on the step."

She did so as carefully as she could, but she still swayed to the side. Jake caught her. "Balance, see? Good. Now, up."

She pushed herself up using her crutch, and forward, putting her weight on her good leg. The technique was, she admitted, sturdier than what she'd been doing. With practice, it could probably be faster. If she didn't topple backwards down the stairs. When she reached the top step and opened the door, a blast of cold air greeted her. She closed her eyes and offered her face to the breeze.

"Daniel's out buying steaks," Jake said.

The living room was decorated in wicker, and the furnishings and walls were white with grey tile.

"There's four bedrooms. One has bunk beds, that's where the boys will be. You two get the one on the far end, I hope you don't mind sharing, but it's the nicest room. There's a television. Oh, and we have wireless."

"I have truly returned to civilization," Natalie said.

"I have wireless," Meredith called from the kitchen.

"But you don't have a beach."

Jake grinned.

Meredith brought Natalie iced tea and complimented her crutch. "I bet I can read your mind."

"Oh?"

"You," Meredith said, taking her free hand. "Want to take a nap."

"I do. More than anything, I do. I'll pay you."

Jake giggled.

Meredith tugged her hand. "Come on. Sorry, Jake. We'll visit later."

"Girl, I see you at work."

"Thanks, Jake."

He went to the kitchen for a beer. "I'll be on the porch. I'll distract the boys when they wake up."

"Should be in about a half hour, when all the chicken wears off." Meredith glared at Natalie.

"Chicken's healthy."

"Bless your heart," Meredith said.

Natalie chuckled.

The bedroom held a queen-sized bed taking up nearly the entire room. An alcove at the far end contained a large mirror and two doorways on either side.

"We get our own bathroom, at least. Is this all right?"

"Seems like my room. I thought you didn't have any friends."

"This is for you, Natalie. Jake likes you."

"Merry."

"I don't want to talk about it."

"Or think about it?"

"Either way. Nat, please."

"Okay."

"Anyway." Meredith went to study herself in the mirror. "We probably shouldn't be doing that so much, you know. The boys might get confused."

"Merry~" Natalie hobbled over with her crutch and stood behind Meredith. "It's fine. It doesn't bother me."

"Me either. That's what bothers me."

Natalie frowned.

"It's not you. I like your company." Meredith patted her side.

"A little too much?"

Meredith's expression softened. She put her hands on the edge of the counter. "A little too much."

Natalie nodded. She hobbled to the bed and sat down, carefully leaning her crutch against it. "No one's ever cared about me before."

"I find that hard to believe, Natalya Ivans."

They had just had this exchange about Jake. "You're probably right. I~I haven't really been paying attention."

Meredith came to the bed and put her hands on Natalie's shoulders. "You've healed. I'm glad. You're going to be okay. And you're going to love being back home."

Natalie didn't say anything. She thought of the woman in front of her, and the boys and the sleeping girl and her friend outside the door, and how much she wanted to pretend she was a guest, just someone to show the sights, she didn't actually belong.

Natalie put her arms around Meredith's waist and rested her forehead against Meredith's torso, and prayed, 'Please, God, don't let her pull away.'

Meredith hugged her back. She settled her chin onto the top of Natalie's head.

"I'm not leaving," Natalie said.

Meredith pulled away and sat next to her. "I've got a lot of problems."

"Don't we all?"

Meredith grinned.

Natalie held her gaze and reached up to touch her chin. Meredith took Natalie's hand. She pressed it to her cheek.

Natalie swallowed. She broke the gaze and scooted back on the bed until she could lie flat on her back. She reached for Meredith's hand, and Meredith gave it, moving up to sit against the headboard.

"Aren't you tired?" Natalie asked.

Meredith shook her head. "I'll watch you sleep."

"Okay."

Natalie closed her eyes.

Natalie woke up alone. And stiff.

The clock on the VCR read 4:30 but the afternoon sun made it seem like noon. She heard voices. She spent the next five minutes getting up and then hobbled out into the living room. The voices came from the deck, so she went out there, and saw a tall, tanned man in shorts and a Bermuda shirt standing over a grill.

The smell of steak made her mouth water.

"I'm Daniel. I hope you like steak," he said.

"I do when it smells like that. I'm Natalie."

"Heard all about you. How are you feeling?"

She hobbled closer. "I feel great. Fantastic."

"Glad to hear it."

She nodded. "Nice place you have here."

"I like it. Course, I'm from Waxhaw. Jake thinks it's nothing special."

"Not true," Jake said from a lounge chair. He lifted his head. "You want a drink, Natalie?"

"I'm good. Where's Merry?"

"She's down with the kids, fishing. Lean over the railing and you can see her."

Natalie crept to the railing and peered down at the muddy creek making up an inlet. The boys each held long reeds in their hands, and they were giggling and pushing each other. Meredith sat on the bank, watching them and a little girl, who was digging a hole in the bank.

"Have a seat," Jake said.

Natalie sat in the nearest deck chair and blinked against the angle of the sun.

"Jake says you're a lawyer," Daniel said.

"I am."

"Here to help Merry?"

"I'd like to. Working on how."

Daniel nodded.

"He's so happy he has another smart person to talk to," Jake said.

"I ain't that bright," Daniel said. "Just ask Jake. But at least I vote Republican."

"He does. He doesn't ever want us to get married," Jake said.

"'Course not. Republicans need mistresses. So much more fun. Don't I buy you pretty things?"

Jake sighed and gazed in the direction of the ocean. "You sure do."

Natalie glanced in Meredith's direction.

"Oh, just try it with her. I dare you," Jake said. "The woman has a mind of her own."

"Does she?" Natalie asked.

"She put you together, didn't she? If I recall, you weren't initially all that interested."

"It was the drugs. I wasn't interested in anything."

"Oh, that's a mess. I have a steel rod in my leg. I wouldn't wish the process on anyone," Daniel said.

Natalie nodded.

Daniel leaned over the railing. "15 minutes, everyone."

"Rest, relax, Natalie. You're on vacation."

Natalie tilted her head up and closed her eyes.

Chapter Twenty-Five

"Ready to go?" Meredith asked.

Natalie listened to the crashing waves, low and steady. The plate beside her held only juices. The rest of the steak was in her stomach. Conquered. She'd been dozing. The breeze off the water was cool and the sky turned grey, and then charcoal, without the benefit of a sunset. The sun was behind her head, all the way to California where the other ocean was.

Meredith promised to wake her up for the sunrise.

"I'm ready," she said, and thinking about it, she was. Excitement grew within her, taking over the lethargy and the desire for sleep. She wanted to be out there in the night. Jake went to one side, and Meredith to the other, and they lifted her up. She groaned. The chair had been perfect and her body resented moving.

"I'll stretch her out," Jake said.

"You'll what?"

"Trust me."

So Jake took her into the bedroom and stretched her out while Meredith kissed the boys goodnight, and it was humiliating and painful and left her in tears, and after it she felt like jelly and like she could fly.

Jake and Daniel carried her down stairs, and then she walked with Meredith the block to the beach.

Jake's beach was different than the public access she'd seen in the morning-rockier and thinner. The tide was just starting to go out again and the sand underfoot was wet. They walked toward the point, where it was only rocks, and some seaweed and some scrub, where the houses ended and they could see more of the ocean. There were stars, and except for the waves everything was quiet.

"Are you all right?" Meredith asked.

Natalie leaned heavily on her, holding her arm. She'd left her crutch at the bottom of the infernal staircase. She felt weak and more broken than she had in days, and she would pay tomorrow.

She grinned. "I'm good."

Meredith patted her arm.

"I was a trial lawyer, you know~Am. I mean, it's nothing like on *Law &* *Order*. Oh, how I wanted it to be. But it's mostly procedural items and long dockets read aloud and witnesses who are reluctant and afraid and who lie and who smell. And the jury, seeking blood. Bored. Salivating. If they have to miss work, or miss their children, then they want something.

"All they get is tedium. Endless tedium. But I didn't care. I would go there. I'd say, 'Look, look at that killer,' or, 'We're going to tell you what he allegedly did. But you know he did.' I took risks."

"But you weren't good with people."

Natalie shook her head. "I never felt like I was a nice enough person. So I worked harder."

Meredith nodded.

"You're not going to tell me I'm crazy?"

"I'm not a psychologist. You seem all right to me. A little testy."

"I was in a car accident!"

"Mmhm."

Natalie snorted.

At the point of the beach where rocks made a natural barrier and waves splashed unevenly, there was a bench. An ordinary park bench, sitting there in the middle of the flatness.

"Kind of incongruous, don't you think?" Natalie asked.

"I prefer to think of it as found art. The tourists complain, but they sit."

"Like we're about to do."

"Why, yes. Smartiepants."

"I made it weeks in Tarpley without hearing that."

"Well, to your face," Meredith said.

Natalie gasped. Meredith sat on the bench and Natalie sat next to her. "I take it back. I would have never been able to get up from the ground."

"Nope."

Natalie sighed.

"You're getting stronger every day. Soon you'll forget all this."

"Not all of this."

"The bad parts."

"Not all the bad parts."

"You should."

Natalie gazed at Meredith and not the ocean, crashing, demanding attention, offering moonlight dancing on water and fish leaping up like black spots and ships in the distance with pretty lights.

"Tell me about the case," Natalie said.

"You know~"

"I mean, the details. The procedures. What they said. What you said. What you've filed. What evidence has been presented~"

"Whoa, hold on."

"I want to help you."

"You can't help me, Nat."

"I know what I'm doing. I'm good. I win. I know it's none of my business~"

"It's not."

Natalie held Meredith's gaze. She licked her lips and noticed how the moonlight reflected in Meredith's eyes. Little flecks of white moving along a glossy black surface.

"I want~" Natalie started, and then rethought her words. She said, deliberately, "I want to be the one that saves you."

"You know, for a long time," Meredith said, with equal slowness and precision, as if the words were warding off crying~Natalie could hear tears in her voice, the sob underneath, and the way she blinked more. "I didn't want to be saved."

"I know," Natalie said.

"But now."

"Let me help," Natalie said. She put her hand over Meredith's.

"There's nothing you can do."

Natalie swallowed.

"I'm sure you're a good lawyer and all, but you're not a part of it. I don't want you to be."

"Listen."

"Oh, you've convinced me," Meredith said.

"That's not what I meant," Natalie said. She put her free hand on Meredith's shoulder and leaned in and kissed her.

Meredith squeaked. Her mouth opened slightly as she gasped, but she didn't move. Natalie pressed against the warmth of her lips long enough to make a memory, and then pulled back. Meredith breathed. Natalie felt the breath against her face. She let go of Meredith's shoulder.

"Sorry," she said.

"It doesn't change anything," Meredith said. She gazed at Natalie evenly; their heads still close together, their breaths mingling.

"Why not?"

"I'll be convicted, Vince's parents will get the boys, and you'll be back in Charlotte seeing it all on the evening news."

"I could~"

"You're not my attorney."

"I want to help you," Natalie said.

"Help me do what?"

"Stay out of jail?"

"It's my fault I'm going. My decision. I made it. It wasn't in a vacuum~. It was every decision I've ever made, since childhood. And Vince~Do you think you can irrevocably change the course of my life? It's going to keep going, just the way it is."

Natalie was silent. Her eyes stung with tears. She moved her hand from Meredith's shoulder to her neck, cupping it gently. The skin was smooth and warm under her fingers. She wanted to stroke it, to see where it led. She wanted the family, and the woman with it.

"You saved me," Natalie said.

Meredith turned away. "Not in the strict definition."

Natalie dropped her hand. She felt something closing in on her. Walls. Pain. Darkness. Convincing by argument is all she had ever done. She knew the right words to get someone to convict someone else; to get them to push someone else off a cliff. But she could no more get defendants to confess than she could get Meredith to fight.

Meredith was right~she didn't change lives, she just got people to where they were going. Commit a crime and get caught, and the rest was inevitable. With enough poverty or enough oppression or enough torment, even com~ mitting a crime was inevitable.

"Fine. Fine. But can't I do something while I'm here? Tell me. Let me."

"I don't~"

"Come on."

"Natalie Ivans, are you whining?"

Natalie dropped her head.

Meredith touched her shoulder. "You're serious."

"I will grant one wish in return for being able to walk again."

"Okay," Meredith said. The word was so small the ocean almost deaf~ ened it. Meredith wouldn't meet her eyes. She studied the horizon instead, and said, "Then hold me."

Meredith didn't move until Natalie took her in her arms. Stiffly, she leaned. Natalie put one arm around her shoulders and the other against her head, stroking her hair. Meredith relaxed. They stayed close and at the ocean together until the moon rose and Natalie started to get cold.

Natalie tilted her head, preparing to ask if Meredith was ready to limp back inside, or fetch a sedan chair for her. Meredith had been completely still for minutes, but at Natalie's shift, lifted her head. Her cheeks glistened with spilled tears. She cupped the back of Natalie's neck and pulled her down.

Their lips met solidly.

A thrill went through Natalie as they kissed, as the touch lingered past doubts and hesitations, as Meredith's lips parted and there was heat. Natalie felt supple and eager and powerful. She cupped the side of Meredith's face and returned each kiss.

Meredith moaned. The sound escaped her throat and found Natalie's ears. Natalie kissed the corner of Meredith's mouth. Meredith panted against her lips, and then kissed her cheek, then the side of her face, then her hair.

Meredith clutched her so tightly Natalie felt strong for being able to withstand it.

"Oh, God," Meredith said.

Natalie chuckled. She cupped Meredith's face and said, "Did you just take the Lord's name in vain?"

Meredith closed her eyes and said, "No. I really, really meant it. You have no idea."

"I have some idea."

Meredith's eyelids fluttered open. "You do?"

"Yes." Natalie, still cupping her face, leaned in and kissed her, trying to share all the things that the hurried, passionate kisses hadn't.

Meredith kissed her back, tipping her face, smiling through the kisses until Natalie broke off, laughing. Then she brought Meredith back against her. They watched the water, and Natalie's heart quieted in her chest, though Meredith's hand was on her leg, and the breeze blew Meredith's hair across her neck.

"I don't know what's going to happen," Meredith said. "What I deserve, I suppose. But this will help. I promise. I'll think of this. Can you stand?"

"I don't know," Natalie said.

Meredith stood up and offered her hands. "Come on."

Natalie took her hands. She tried to pull herself up. Pain shot through her shoulder. She fell back onto the bench, wincing.

"Breathe," Meredith said, moving back to her side.

"Hard to breathe."

Meredith wrapped her arms around Natalie's waist. "Try again."

"Let me just stay here forever."

"Forever?"

"Sure. Reliving the best night of my life."

Meredith chuckled. She heaved, and Natalie put all her weight on her good leg and let Meredith guide her into a balanced standing position. She teetered, but her legs held under her. Neither turned to twigs. She turned carefully and hugged Meredith.

Meredith held her~not just up, but close~and the embrace was warm and strong. Meredith ran her hands down Natalie's back. Natalie nearly fell to the sand. The current going through her was far more than friendly. She bit her lip and stepped back from the torture of Meredith's hug. She took Meredith's arm instead.

"I can stand," she said.

Meredith stepped back so they could walk back toward the house.

Pier lights glittered in the distance. Natalie hobbled toward them, toward the sounds of civilization and the nightlife of the beach. The dunes were empty of other people, but full of crabs hidden somewhere in the sand, and seaweed and shells and rocks.

The houses along the beach were mostly dark and even in the moonlight the darkness was deep enough Natalie missed the wooden staircase. Meredith tugged her to get her to stop plodding forward.

"Here," Meredith said.

"How could you tell?"

Meredith pointed to where Natalie's crutch stood against the railing.

Natalie went toward the stairs, aching, wanting to lie down in the sand and rest her muscles. Sharp pains started in her leg. She clutched the railing, and panted. Then Meredith's hand was on her back, friendly again.

"Help me with these?" Natalie asked.

Meredith got her propped up, and then walked behind her as she ascended, touching her hips and making sure she didn't topple backwards. Going back down the stairs was more terrifying. She mostly let gravity pull her, using Meredith to hold her up while she lowered herself to the next step, rather than the crutches. Then up again at Jake's.

"I'm so becoming an ADA enforcement attorney," Natalie said.

"You'd be good at it."

"I'm a good criminal attorney."

"Nat~"

"Sorry. We won't talk about it again."

"Good."

"At least not tonight."

Meredith snorted.

Jake was asleep on the couch when they got in. He woke up, rubbing his eyes. "I stayed up to help Nat up the stairs."

"I can see that," Meredith said.

"Sorry, Nat. You guys hungry?"

Natalie shook her head.

"No, Jake. Go on to bed," Meredith said.

He went, leaving them in the living room.

Meredith said, "Take a shower. Hot. Trust me, you'll feel better in the morning."

"I have to keep standing?"

"Just a little while longer."

Natalie swallowed hard. She put her hands on Meredith's shoulders. Meredith pushed forward and stretched up to kiss her. Natalie felt Meredith's warm lips against hers and the kiss held and lingered until Meredith was in her arms again and Meredith's fingers were dancing up and down her back. Natalie tingled.

Then, from somewhere, a kid coughed. They broke apart. Meredith bit her lip. Natalie wanted to wipe the expression away with kisses, or logic, but Meredith smiled on her own and mouthed the word, "Shower."

The thoughts of hot water pouring down Natalie's back and steam rising to her face were enchanting temptations. She limped to the bathroom. Meredith went to check on the boys. Natalie managed to get the water on, but her clothes presented a problem. Her shoulder was done for the night. Or at least, until the shower was done.

Meredith knocked on the door. "I've got pajamas and towels."

Natalie opened the door.

Meredith put the bundle on the closed toilet lid.

"I can't get undressed," Natalie said.

"Why not?"

Natalie frowned at her.

"Oh. All right." Meredith put her hands on Natalie's waist, under her shirt. "Lift your arms."

"It'll hurt."

"As far as you can."

Natalie lifted one arm haphazardly above her head and the other arm out in front of her. Meredith maneuvered the shirt up, over her head, then over the arm Natalie brought down at her bidding to tuck through the shirt, and then over the bad arm. Meredith so perfunctorily set down the shirt and turned Natalie around to get at her bra clasp that Natalie didn't have time to be embarrassed, or turned on, or embarrassed about being turned on.

"I think you're fine from here. But holler if you need me." Meredith slipped through the door and closed it behind her.

Natalie nodded. She kicked off her sandals and pushed down her pants. She put up her hair and then tucked it into a shower cap. Already from the salt it felt gross in her hands, but going to bed with wet hair seemed worse. The shower left her skin red and searing and drained her last vestiges of energy. She stepped out thirsty, but warm and limber, and managed to get on the sweatpants and tee shirt Meredith left before she padded back into the bedroom.

She wasn't sure what she expected as she pushed open the door.

Meredith was asleep. She'd pushed down the blankets and was lying on the sheets, as if she'd conked out mid-plan. Natalie chuckled, and got into bed beside her, and turned out the lamp.

"Goodnight, Merry," she said.

She was sorry she was at the beach because the roar of the waves outside, crashing against the sand, drowned out the sound of Meredith's breathing.

Chapter Twenty-Six

Natalie woke easily to sunlight, and though she was stiff, she still felt miraculously warm from the night before.

Meredith was gone. The imprint of where she slept remained. Natalie sat up and ran her hand over the sheets. Two capsules of Tylenol and a glass of water were on the nightstand and Natalie took them and then considered the empty bedroom.

Sleep beckoned. She was tempted, but there was also the smell of coffee and syrup from somewhere beyond the door. Merritt shouted something. The ocean crashed. She wanted to see the water.

She wondered if she knew Daniel and Jake well enough to stumble out there with sleep-straggly hair and pajamas. A robe hung behind the door, though, so she took that as a compromise, patted her hair, and went into the living room.

Meredith sat at the kitchen table with the boys. She glanced up when she heard the door and met Natalie's eyes. Natalie's cheeks flushed with warmth. So there was no shame about the night before. She went to the table, where the boys were eating cereal.

"Mommy says we're going to the airport later," Beau said.

Natalie nodded.

"Are you leaving?" Merritt asked.

"Only for a little while. I have a job in Charlotte, remember?"

Daniel, at the stove, narrowed his eyes. She wondered if he thought she was lying. She sat down at the table and Daniel asked what she wanted on her omelette.

"There are omelettes?"

Meredith nodded. She stabbed some egg off her own plate with her fork and waved it at Natalie.

"We have ham, cheese, spinach, pickles, relish, Tabasco, cheese, ketchup—"

"Just cheese and spinach, please."

"Ewwww," Merritt said.

"Gross," Beau said.

"Daddy didn't like spinach, either," Merritt said.

Natalie glanced at Meredith.

Meredith shrugged. "Must be genetic."

Jake came out of his bedroom, wearing swim trunks and carrying a big inner tube. A sling was tied around his chest, carrying Sunisa, who slept. "Ya'll boys ready for the beach?"

Merritt got out of his chair so fast he tripped, fell flat on his face on the floor, and started crying.

Beau, witnessing this, carefully got out of his chair and poked at his brother's back.

Merritt whimpered.

Jake went to the door and opened it, and Beau darted past him and down the staircase.

"Don't get too far from Jake, Beau," Meredith said.

"He won't drown," Natalie said.

"He doesn't have the sense God gave a rock."

Daniel slid an omelette onto Natalie's plate.

"You're a prince, Daniel," she said.

He grinned.

"Thank you."

"My pleasure. And now Merry gets to clean the kitchen." He scooped Merritt off the floor and threw him over his shoulder. "Later, ladies."

Meredith laughed.

Natalie ate while Meredith cleaned, and they talked some, not about the night before or the trial or Charlotte, but about the weather and the boys. Natalie thought about asking Meredith what her favorite color was, or her sign, but she realized she knew all that already and she didn't need to tease. So she ate until Meredith took her plate away, and then went into the bathroom. The Tylenol had done its job to take the pain from her body and she moved easily to wash her face, to comb her hair, to brush her teeth.

"Are we going to the beach?" she asked.

"Do you want to?"

Natalie came out of the bathroom. Meredith was leaning against the edge of the couch, waiting for her.

"Sure, I guess. If we have time."

"I sure think so. Why?"

"I'll shower after, so I won't smell like salt and sweat on the plane." Natalie self-consciously ran her fingers through her hair.

"I don't think you'd smell as bad as all that."

"No?" Natalie's heart felt like it was going to stop beating at any moment, but she took a deep breath and walked toward Meredith anyway. Meredith wasn't crying, wasn't angry~maybe she didn't need Natalie for what she needed her for last night. Natalie leaned in and Meredith rose off the couch to meet her. Their lips touched, and then their hands. Natalie linked her fingers with Meredith's and they stood together, kissing. Meredith lifted their linked hands and kissed Natalie's knuckles.

"We don't have to go to the beach. It's my last morning."

Meredith, heart pounding enough to make her feel foolish, took Natalie to the balcony, where they could see the ocean and the sky and the children. Past the front row of houses, past the dunes, the ocean glittered and shifted, the water catching the light. They heard shouts of joy.

"There they are," Meredith said, pointing to where two men and three smaller people swarmed around each other on the sand. "I think they're playing hacky sack."

"That does sound fun," Natalie said. "But~"

"But," Meredith said. She turned into Natalie's shoulder.

Natalie smelled so good. Meredith buried her nose against her and breathed. Natalie's heart beat under her cheek. Natalie's trembling told her for once~only this once, this day before Natalie left her~she wasn't alone in what she felt.

"Back inside?" Meredith asked.

Natalie moved faster than Meredith had ever seen, and they were barely back in the air-conditioned shade of the living room when Natalie kissed her. Her hands found Meredith's cheeks. Meredith gave in and hungry kisses consumed her lips. She tugged on Natalie's shoulders, pulling her down.

Meredith sat on the couch. Natalie's hands stroked her shoulders with quick, fluttering rubs, as if she didn't know what to do with her hands. Meredith opened her mouth to Natalie's kisses, her tongue equally eager, and bunched the fabric of Natalie's shirt at her waist. She slipped her hands under Natalie's shirt. The smooth skin under her fingers was pleasure enough, but the resulting groan from Natalie made the decision irrevocable.

Just when Meredith wanted to kiss Natalie until her mouth hurt, Natalie pulled back, gazing at her with dark, hesitant eyes.

Meredith took a deep breath. She freed her hands and Natalie took them.

"We shouldn't~" Natalie started.

"I need~I need to. Please. I don't know what's going to happen tomorrow. But if I don't~" She squeezed Natalie's hands. "I'll regret it for the rest of my life. Will you?"

She took Natalie's hands and brought them to her breasts, pressing them there, open and flat against her. Unmistakable, and if Natalie called her indecent or worse, there would only be the morning to get through.

The pressure of Natalie's hands warmed her. She held her breath. Her body acted of its own accord. Her nipples tightened. She longed for Natalie to press just a little bit harder. Her mouth was dry with anticipation.

Natalie swallowed. Her jaw worked, her throat moved, as if she wanted to say something, but it was her glance over her shoulder at the bedroom that answered the question. She glanced back at Meredith, and Meredith found her mouth for a kiss.

Natalie squeezed gently, perfectly. Meredith closed her eyes.

"I want." Natalie said against her ear, and then hesitated.

"What? Tell me."

With her eyes closed, all that existed was the heat of Natalie's hands and the touch of Natalie's breath. She inhaled. She couldn't hear the ocean as she strained for Natalie's next words.

"I want you to touch me. Please, Merry."

"Then the bedroom," Meredith said.

Natalie took a step back. Meredith stood and led her to the bedroom. Once across the threshold, she pulled off her shirt. Before she could lower her arms, Natalie encircled her waist from behind. Meredith leaned back. A sound escaped her lips.

Natalie held her strongly and she felt secure, even with Natalie's lips brushing her shoulder, her neck, her ear.

Heat pooled in her stomach. Lower. Her legs turned to liquid even as cold air chilled her chest. She arched back, resting the back of her head on Natalie's shoulder, curving into Natalie's hips.

"Natalie."

Natalie held her stomach with one hand. The other she slid down Meredith's thigh. Meredith reached up and pulled down her bra straps and freed her arms, and then reached behind her to bury her fingers in Natalie's hair. She wanted to keep her close.

Natalie kissed the side of Meredith's face.

Meredith let go and turned around. Natalie, face to face, smiled and kissed her. Her hands splayed across Meredith's back and unclasped her bra. Meredith kissed her mouth, her chin, her neck. She couldn't get close enough.

Natalie's mouth fell to her shoulder.

Meredith arched, offering more, whispering, "Please."

"Anything you want."

"Make love to me, Natalie."

Natalie eased her back onto the bed, leaning over her, and unzipped her jeans. Natalie's hand rested on her abdomen, just above where Meredith needed her touch. Any feeling this was too soon after their first kiss, she was loose for considering it, it was wrong, God hadn't sent Natalie to her to be corrupted and she was failing—all the negative energy left her as soon as Natalie's head lowered toward hers and their lips met. Natalie's weight settled against her side and on her chest. Meredith wanted to cry.

Natalie's head rested on Meredith's shoulder. She stroked Meredith's stomach, and then her breasts, avoiding her nipples, which strained upward, pining for her touch.

"You're injured," Meredith said. Her voice came out hoarse. She cleared her throat, and nearly yelped when Natalie brushed her nipple. She captured Natalie's hand and held it to her breast so her nipple pressed against Natalie's palm.

Natalie cupped her, applying pressure, and then drew back so her fingertips grazed and then tugged the nipple.

Meredith hissed.

Natalie cupped her breast again, easing the ache by offering her whole hand, massaging, and then tantalized her again with her fingers.

"So what?"

"I don't want you to hurt yourself." Meredith rolled onto her side, facing Natalie, and replaced her shoulder with a pillow, so Natalie's eyes were even with hers, her lips only inches away.

Natalie moved in and kissed her. "I'm fine."

Meredith shook her head.

Natalie carefully, slowly, sat up, propping herself up on her good arm. She tickled Meredith's abdomen with her weaker arm. "See? Very mobile." She twisted and leaned down to kiss the hollow of Meredith's shoulder. "Nimble."

Her mouth moved lower.

Meredith could not protest. She was too weak and too aroused to stop. She could only clutch Natalie's head and encourage her as Natalie kissed her chest, and then the slope of her breast, and then~

"Yes." Meredith said.

Natalie's mouth settled onto her nipple and sucked. Meredith arched her back, pressing more of herself against Natalie's lips. Natalie's tongue flicked. Meredith lost her breath. She squeezed her eyes shut, and wondered if she could die from having her nipples kissed. No wonder this was considered so dangerous.

Natalie lifted her head. "Doctor Wheeler said I could start having sex once he saw there were no complications from the surgery."

Meredith laughed. "Did he say with who?"

"No." Natalie kissed Meredith's stomach. "But I'm sure he had some idea."

"Too smart for his britches, he is."

"Good old Hank," Natalie said.

Natalie sat up and traced with her fingers the places her mouth had been, where Meredith's skin wore a sheen left by kisses. She strayed, more boldly this time, into Meredith's jeans, over her panties. Meredith squeezed her thighs together and moaned.

"You're so beautiful," Natalie said.

Meredith blushed. Natalie cupped her where she was all liquid and heat, her fingers hard. Meredith's toes curled.

"Natalie."

"Take off your clothes," Natalie said. "I can't~I can't quite manage."

"Only if you take off yours," Meredith said. Her threat was empty. She was already pushing down her jeans and her panties.

Natalie worked up her shirt. Meredith pulled down the covers, bunching them around Natalie. She wanted to feel the cool sheets on her naked body.

Natalie carefully drew her shirt off her shoulders.

"Better," Meredith said.

"You picked out the pajamas."

Meredith wanted to touch Natalie where she'd been touched~to feel the heat through the fabric, to see Natalie arch and twist and breathe hard~but she was not bold enough. She sat on the bed, her arms around her bent knees, while Natalie worked the pajama bottoms off her hips and kicked them to the floor.

Then she was naked.

Meredith, overwhelmed to have a woman in her bed, drank in the sight of Natalie's flushed skin, the freckles on her back and arms, the dark curls arrowing between her legs matching her dark hair.

She had been afraid of facing this for so long~in her own heart, and in the world~and here was Natalie, just sitting next to her, accessible. Touchable. Almost ordinary. The obviousness of it made her laugh, made her heart leap. Her soul and her body and her mind were all aligned, all singing, "Yes." From somewhere deeper, someone was whispering, "Finally."

Natalie moved to the headboard where she could lean back, sitting against the pillows, and beckoned. Meredith knelt and kissed her. While they kissed they touched, hands on breasts, knees and legs bumping. Meredith took in her fill of curves and angles and slopes giving way to softness. She ended up straddled on top of Natalie, her curls brushing against Natalie's stomach, one hand on Natalie's breast and the other against the headboard, to hold her up so she could kiss Natalie's lips. She felt open and swollen and ready, and accepted Natalie's tongue, thrusting and firm, into her mouth.

"Please," she said between kisses. She knew it would be quick and she didn't care. They didn't have time. She didn't have the strength. She searched for Natalie's hand and tugged.

Natalie touched her.

"Natalie." Her eyes closed.

Natalie's fingers laid her bare, opened her up, filled her.

"There?"

Meredith crumpled into Natalie's shoulder. "There."

Natalie was touching her more deeply than she'd ever felt, and stroking gloriously, not just inside her but against her, with polished motions and knobby fingers. Excitement rose in Meredith, making her tremble. She strained to hold herself up. Her hips moved against Natalie. Her thighs ached.

She could hear Natalie whispering to her. She tried to listen.

"Shssh," Natalie said. "Look at me."

Moving with Natalie's eager, gentle thrusts, Meredith pushed back from Natalie's shoulder far enough to meet her eyes. Natalie held her gaze. Without breaking the rhythm of her hand, already knowing Meredith so well, exposing every desire, Natalie said, "Kiss me."

Meredith moved forward to Natalie's mouth. Natalie pushed apart her lips with her tongue and deepened the kiss.

The orgasm shook Meredith. She was breathless and powerless against the penetrating kiss. She sought Natalie's hand to sooth the lingering tingles, and then retreated, her whole body searingly sensitive and raw.

She kissed Natalie one more time and then twisted onto her back, panting. She pulled the sheet to her waist, and then, after considering, over her breasts, and slowly became aware of the sweat on her back, sticking to the pillow, and the scent of herself.

"Natalie," she said.

"I'm here."

Meredith shifted closer to lean her head on Natalie's shoulder. Natalie put an arm around her. Meredith put her hand on Natalie's bare thigh, and laughed. "Natalie."

Natalie kissed her hair.

"I've always heard there was something depraved about the homosexual act," Meredith said. Natalie tensed against her, but she went on. "Not in the moral sense~in the physical sense. Like, the Freudian sense. Something half-formed. Like, men settled for other men when they feared women. Stunted. And vice versa. We should feel sad for homosexuals, because they couldn't experience a wholeness."

"Uh huh?" Natalie asked.

"Not going to believe anymore. That was everything I thought it was supposed to be." Meredith swallowed hard.

"Maybe it's too potent, and thus, not fit for anyone stained with original sin."

Meredith snorted.

"This~" Natalie's fingers traced her jaw and said, "Is the beginning of wisdom."

"Oh, shut up."

Meredith turned against Natalie's shoulder. Her hand traveled, in darting finger dances, up Natalie's side and over the slope of her breast, and across her collarbone. Natalie shifted, unsettled. Meredith knew the feeling. Her hand moved down Natalie's chest, over her heart, between her breasts. Natalie trembled.

"Your turn," Meredith said.

"It's all right if you're not~"

Meredith put her fingers on Natalie's lips. "I am."

Natalie exhaled slowly.

Meredith kissed her shoulder and then slid around to kiss her neck, her jaw, her ear.

"Please kiss me," Natalie said.

Meredith kissed her. She ran her hands down Natalie's side, enjoying how Natalie squirmed when tickled and shuddered when stroked. Sated, she could take her time.

She kissed and nipped at Natalie's mouth. Natalie growled.

Meredith pulled away, moving back on the bed.

"Merry," Natalie said.

Meredith stroked the sole of Natalie's foot. "Ticklish?"

"Not there."

Natalie's sole was smooth, without calluses. Meredith knelt, feeling naughtily powerful she could move around, she could bend and dip and twist, and Natalie couldn't. She kissed the pad of Natalie's big toe.

Natalie shivered.

Meredith took the toe into her mouth and sucked.

"Oh, Merry." Natalie closed her eyes.

"How are your feet so soft?"

"I haven't really been on them in six weeks."

"There's more to it." Meredith moved up Natalie's legs, crouching, bracing herself on one arm while she stroked Natalie's leg.

"Fine. Peppermint foot scrub."

"Pedicure?"

"Once a month, at *Le Nail*." Natalie said.

"I had no idea," Meredith said. She kissed the side of Natalie's knee.

Natalie convulsed. "No kids, no partner, cheap real estate in Charlotte--I spent for myself."

"Oh. It paid off."

Natalie grinned.

Meredith met her eyes and said "I~" Then she hesitated.

Natalie pursed her lips.

"I need you to scoot down," she said.

"Why?"

Meredith kissed her belly, and then her thigh.

"Lawyers," Natalie said, carefully pushing off to shift down the bed, "Ask dumb questions."

Meredith settled onto her stomach, sliding her arms under Natalie's legs. Natalie obliged by bending. Her breathing was short and rapid. Her mouth was slightly open. Meredith wanted to kiss her.

She lowered her head.

"Merry?" Natalie asked.

Meredith glanced up. Natalie touched her jaw, cupped her face, and met her eyes. "This is the best morning of my life. I'm serious. It's everything to me."

"Me too," Meredith said.

"Hey, if I pass out, will you give me mouth to mouth?"

Meredith lowered her head and kissed tight, trimmed, damp curls. Natalie gasped. She held herself still, trembling. Meredith took a deep breath, trying to gather courage. Natalie's musky scent came with each intake of air.

"God, please. Merry, please."

Meredith took another deep breath, nosing into Natalie's curls. She opened her mouth and pressed. Slick heat met her lips. Natalie filled her senses. She took a quick, tentative lick.

Natalie groaned.

"Does that feel good?"

"Do it again."

Meredith kissed. Her tongue explored, finding places that made Natalie gasp and moan.

"Yes, it feels good, don't stop," Natalie said, and then, "Merry. Merry."

Then she found a spot to make Natalie whisper her name instead of call it. Natalie trembled against her shoulders. She knew what Natalie was feeling—what she felt with Natalie against her. She used her lips and prayed she was good enough to bring Natalie pleasure, to make nothing but this moment matter. She bowed her head.

"Merry."

Natalie strained, stilling, and then arched against Meredith's mouth. Meredith held her. Natalie shuddered. Meredith felt each tremble and pulse against her lips like kisses.

A hand touched Meredith's hair. "Stop."

Meredith worked her way up into a crouching position, her shoulders aching, her lips numb. Natalie's stomach quivered under her. She licked her lips and glanced up. Natalie was crying. Meredith took Natalie in her arms. Natalie stayed silent, breathing hard with tears rolling down her cheeks. Meredith kissed her hair. She tightened her arms.

"I'm sorry," Natalie said.

"Don't be."

"That was--I didn't expect--"

"Me either," Meredith said. She held Natalie close. "Me either."

"But you're not crying."

"Too excited," Meredith said.

Natalie turned her head to wink at Meredith.

Meredith said, "I'll cry later."

"Then I'll hold you."

"You'll be gone."

"Doesn't matter."

Meredith kissed her over and over until Natalie's breath was even and her tears had gone away.

Chapter Twenty-Seven

"Mommy, I'm hungry." Beau ran into the living room in dripping-wet swim trunks, sunburned. Meredith pointed to the kitchen table, where sandwiches and milk sat. Beau dutifully climbed into a chair.

Daniel came through the door, carrying Merritt. Merritt giggled.

"Ready to get down?" Daniel asked.

"No!"

Daniel spun him around. Merritt screamed.

Beau rolled his eyes and kept eating.

"You're going to strain your back," Jake said, following them in, putting his daughter on the floor so she could run to Daniel and clutch at his leg.

"Lucky I know a physical therapist," Daniel said. But he put Merritt down.

Merritt whimpered and ran to Natalie.

"Hi, Merry," Natalie said as he climbed onto a chair and then wedged himself onto her lap, between her and the table.

"I got bit by a crab," he said.

Meredith gasped.

Daniel shook his head at Meredith.

Merritt held out his arm. "See?"

"I see. Does it hurt?" Natalie rubbed his arm.

Merritt nodded.

"Why are you with Natalie, Merritt?" Meredith asked.

"She's hurt, like me."

Natalie grinned.

"Well, you'd both better eat something if you want to get well."

Merritt grinned. Natalie hugged him and turned him around. He faced the sandwiches.

"I see everyone's dressed." Jake said.

Meredith shot Jake a look.

"And ready to go," Natalie said.

"What about Hollingsworth?" Merritt asked around a mouthful of sandwich.

"Chew, swallow, then speak," Natalie said.

Merritt chewed and swallowed. Everyone waited. He asked, "Where's Natalie's cat?"

"He'll stay with you guys until I come back. If you promise to take care of him."

Merritt cheered.

Natalie jerked her head back from the sound.

"I'll brush him," Beau said.

Meredith put her hands on Natalie's shoulders, needing to touch her. Natalie leaned her head back and smiled. Meredith puckered her lips.

Merritt, in his attempt to get his milk, elbowed Natalie in the chest. She grunted.

Meredith patted her head. "Okay, boys, go get changed. Let the men eat."

"Then we have to leave?" Beau asked.

"Then there's popsicles. But only when you're dressed and have your shoes on."

Another elbow as Merritt bounded off Natalie's lap and into the bedroom.

"You shouldn't bribe your children," Daniel said.

"I'll remind you of what you said when your girl learns four."

The ride to the airport was noisy as the boys talked about their morning on the beach in grand, rambling detail. Every time their attention would stray Meredith would prompt them with pointed questions to keep talking.

"We built sand castles right in the wet sand so the waves would come up and get them," Beau said.

"It was awesome," Merritt said.

"Boys and violence," Meredith said and shook her head.

She pulled up to the curb and made the boys sit in the car while she got Natalie up on her crutches, with her carry-on over her shoulder and chest.

"I'll be fine," Natalie said.

"We could wait with you," Meredith said. She let the boys out of the cage and they ran toward Natalie.

"Wait with me? What kind of airport is this?"

"One on the beach of North Carolina," Meredith said.

Natalie shook her head. "I'll be all right. I'll go face the music."

"All right boys, say goodbye," Meredith said.

Natalie handed her one crutch so she could give each of them a one-armed squeeze.

Merritt burst into tears, startling the three of them and the baggage handler and the family getting out of the car a few feet away.

"I don't want you to go," Merritt said.

"I don't want to go either," Natalie said.

"Then don't."

"I have to. Remember Patrick? He brought the cat?"

Merritt shook his head and then asked, "Is he your husband?"

"No, honey. He's just going to help me."

Merritt sniffled. Natalie held him, and Beau did too, until a security guard at a station down the sidewalk coughed at them.

Meredith pried Merritt off. "She'll call you tonight, okay?"

"Okay," Natalie said.

Meredith blushed.

Merritt got in the car and slammed the door. He glared at them through the window.

Beau gave Natalie a more solemn hug. "He'll be all right. He's just a baby."

Natalie ruffled his hair.

Meredith shooed him into the car. Then she turned to Natalie, but it was Natalie who hobbled toward her and caught her in a tight embrace.

"Oh, no," Meredith said.

She buried her face in Natalie's neck and prayed tears wouldn't come. Natalie held her, rubbing her back.

"It'll be okay," Natalie said against her hair.

Meredith inhaled. A sob was in her throat. She breathed sharply and tried to swallow it, and pulled back from Natalie to see her face.

Natalie grinned. "I'll call Merritt tonight. Maybe I'll even talk to you."

Meredith brought Natalie's head down for a brief, tender kiss. Then she let go, turning back to the car. Her lips tingled. The boys sniffled and rolled around and watched Natalie.

Natalie's hand touched her back. "I love you."

Meredith cried. Crutches thudded against the sidewalk, and receded, and Meredith wiped at her cheeks and went around to get into the car.

The family passed by on their way to the door, and a woman asked, her tone somewhere between curious and accusatory~right on the point of nosy, "How sweet. Your sister?"

"Yes," Meredith answered, almost without even thinking. The woman gave her a sympathetic glance. Meredith got into the car and slammed the door.

"No," she said, but the woman was already gone.

Her first test.

She started the car. The boys buckled themselves in.

They'd fall asleep. She'd wake them up when they got out of Wilmington. Maybe she'd take them to McDonalds, and then home, where she'd try to pretend six weeks couldn't change her life. She'd switch out the rumpled sheets in the bedroom, feed the cat, and try and put everything back to normal.

Chapter Twenty-Eight

Patrick met Natalie at the airport. He'd pulled rank to meet her at the gate rather than at baggage claim. With his presence came a price. The photographer next to him took pictures of a smiling, tired, triumphant city prosecutor on crutches.

"I'll take that," Patrick said to the flight attendant who'd carried her carry-on up the ramp and kept her from falling.

Not, "Can I help?" or "Let me take the bags," but "I'll take that." Natalie wondered how long Patrick had been getting his way. But when he shooed the photographer away and helped her into the handicapped golf cart, she was grateful. The cart beeped and rolled. Natalie laughed at the people scattering in front of its progress. She should have felt guilty. She'd always been annoyed by those cars and the passengers. Instead she was happy to be in Charlotte.

"Sleep on the plane?" Patrick asked.

"No." She'd been thinking of Meredith, and biting her lip, and writing a letter.

"Where's Hollingsworth?"

"Staying in Tarpley for now," Natalie said.

"Oh, Nat."

"Holly took to the kids. There was a whole cat thing. You wouldn't understand."

"Okay. You'll miss him."

The golf cart dumped them at the baggage claim and he called for his driver.

"Something happened while you were on the plane," he said.

"What?"

"They found Roland guilty." He grinned.

"On a Sunday?"

"You're back in the city now."

Her heart twisted. "That's wonderful."

"It is. Congratulations, Natalie."

"I'm going back," she said.

"What?"

She produced her letter. "This is my two month notice. I'll need that much time to get things together. Job hunt. Pack. Sell my condo."

She'd bought it two years ago after a promotion. Charlotte was so cheap she could have bought two. She'd pretended to love the space. She'd tried. But it never felt like a home.

"You're going down there without a job?"

"I'll find one. There are a thousand things I can do."

"Like what?" He swung to face her, to meet her eyes, to give her the death stare that got so many confessions--so many people to stop acting in their own self-interest and act in his.

"Nat, you'll get another case like Roland. Don't make it about that. Your career--"

"My career? I'll find another."

"This is more and you know it. You can have anything you want. A.D.A. Hell, D.A., if you showed one ounce of ambition."

"Patrick. God."

"Sorry." He ran his hand along the back of his head. "Natalie, you don't know this woman."

"Pat--"

"Listen to me. Hear me out. She's going to go to jail for a long time. A very long time. And you're going to be, what, stuck with the kids? Do you want that? Them?"

"Yes."

"She's going to use you. She's going to hit you up for money and--"

"Patrick!" she took his arms, shaking him. The crutches clattered to the floor. People glanced at them.

She took his arms more gently. "I don't care about any of that stuff."

"Nat. I don't want you to get hurt."

"Just help me." She let him go, hanging her hands at her sides. "Okay? Help me screw up my life."

"Okay. Okay. Get your apartment on the market as soon as you can. You can live with us. Maybe we can get you severance, or disability, or you can telework, just until you're settled in down there. I'll call my contacts and see if anyone's heard of Tarpley."

He rambled on, picking up her crutches for her and then taking her bags. She followed him to the car, glad he was on her side. Glad to follow his plans once again, glad he would help her even if he couldn't use her as his pawn. Maybe it had never been about that. Maybe she'd just been a good attorney.

His friend. She smiled at him as they settled into the backseat of the town car. He winked and patted her hand.

"Thanks for all this, Patrick."

"Sure, kid," he said. "How far are you from Hilton Head, anyway?"

Her apartment was cold and smelled of dust and neglect. The power was still on. There was a note from her neighbor about Patrick picking up her cat. She turned on the lights and sat down on the couch. There was no edible food left in the fridge, but there were six messages on her answering machine. Two from Patrick, one from the neighbor, two from the police, and one from Meredith.

She played Meredith's message twice, shocked at how foreign Meredith's accent sounded already after three hours back in Charlotte. The boys were noisy in the background, chaotic and frightening. Her eyes welled up.

"Hey, Nat, just wanted you to hear a friendly voice when you got home. The boys say hello~"

"Hi, Natty!" they chimed.

"Anyway, welcome home." Meredith paused. Natalie counted the seconds. Then, "Take care, Natalie."

Natalie couldn't listen to it, not with the lump rising in her throat and the tears stinging in her eyes. She ordered Chinese, and then realized she didn't have any cash. She used the emergency supply in the shoebox in her closet. While eating, she went over her finances.

Not good.

She found herself surrounded by Chinese containers and paperwork, depressed and tired and in pain. Her cat was gone and she was alone with the hum of the refrigerator. She picked up the television remote.

She set it down.

She knew she'd succumb eventually to the need for money, to the need for the fantasy of other people's lives filling her home, to the path of least resistance.

She glanced at the phone. She remembered all the nights she'd waited for it to ring.

She picked up the receiver and dialed.

Chapter Twenty-Nine

Two Months Later

Meredith sat in the uncomfortable, too-small chair across from her lawyer. They were in a holding office, waiting for the judge to arrive. In fifteen minutes, they would all herd into the courtroom and her life--the sliver of life she held onto between Vincent's death and today--would be gone. She'd been crying more and more.

The boys caught her last night. They'd piled into bed with her and said "What's wrong, mommy?" and "We'll be good, don't cry," which made her cry more.

"Call Natty, she'll help," Merritt said.

That had been even worse.

She put her head in her hand.

Her lawyer coughed.

Samson Okoru had worked his way through law school with the state's help, in return for a defense attorney post in a small town. On behalf of North Carolina, and not on behalf of her, he did this work. He was completely professional, but she was pretty sure he thought she was guilty.

A knock came on the glass of the open door. She glanced up.

Natalie grinned.

"Took you long enough," Meredith said and stood.

"I started driving as soon as I hung up the phone. It's a long drive."

"Do you have to go back?"

"This weekend, to put the rest of my stuff into storage and sign the final paperwork. I can't believe those turkeys are taking my condo."

"I'm sure it's a nice condo."

"I'm sure."

Samson said, "You have five minutes," and then left, heading for the water fountain.

"I'm sorry it took so long," Natalie said.

"Don't be." Meredith felt her eyes filling with tears. She hastily wiped them away. All that time lost~all those weeks~she'd be damned if she was going to lose this time, too, by crying.

"The preliminary background check is done. I can take the boys if~while~" Natalie stopped talking and swallowed.

"Good."

Natalie reached out and pulled Meredith against her.

Meredith bit her lip until it hurt. "Good."

Natalie's hand cupped her head. Meredith was amazed at how right the embrace felt~how much she remembered Natalie's body from before, when she'd spent weeks convincing herself she'd imagined it. Here was Natalie~ real and holding her. Meredith reached up and cupped Natalie's face. She pulled back far enough to see Natalie and laughed.

"What?"

"I never saw you in a suit before. I guess I never figured~you look so powerful."

"You've got the idea."

"Nat."

"I promise, I'm just muscle. The press are out there."

"I know."

Samson tapped on the glass. "The judge is here. The bailiff is calling us."

Meredith swallowed.

Natalie took Meredith's hand from her cheek and kissed her palm. "I'm right here."

"Thanks." Meredith held Natalie's gaze, trying to express all she felt, all the thudding in her heart.

Natalie gave her a faint smile.

Samson held out his hand. Meredith took it, brushing past Natalie. The door to the courtroom opened in front of her. She dropped her lawyer's hand. Natalie's hand touched her back.

"Vincent's parents are already inside," Samson said.

Meredith took a deep breath. "I'm ready."

The trial was an exhausting recitation of charges and details. They'd broken for lunch before opening statements. Meredith struggled to stay awake as the judge droned on.

Natalie furiously scribbled notes.

At lunch, the lawyer tucked them into a dark van. Meredith just buried her face in Natalie's neck while Samson practiced his opening statement.

Natalie gave him tips.

"Why didn't you do this before? If you were going to do it at all?" Natalie bit her lip.

Samson coughed and took a sip of water.

"What?" Meredith asked, lifting her head.

"We did," Natalie said.

"We talk on the phone a few times a week. She's good."

"I could have been a D.A., they told me," Natalie said.

"Nat."

"Don't worry. I won't be writing wills for old people. I'm consulting for a firm in Charlotte. We'll see. I might get out of criminal law."

Samson snorted.

Natalie touched Meredith's cheek. "My heart's not in it."

"The military wants a plea arranged. They don't want PTSD or homosexuals or war atrocities all over the news. Tomorrow we may have an offer," Samson said.

"I can't go to jail," Meredith said.

"It's the parents driving it, then?" Natalie asked.

"The whole town. Merry, you really should have considered Charlotte. Death has turned Vincent into a hero," Samson said.

"He was always a hero," Meredith said.

"Your freedom isn't going to change anyone's minds."

"What are they going to do? Them and their minds? They'll be too damn polite to shun the boys, and too damn greedy to shun my money at the market. And wait until I deliver one of their babies or patch up a bloody knee."

Samson sipped water.

Natalie grinned. "And to think she's staying because she likes these people."

"I'm not raising my boys in some strange city with strangers."

Natalie nodded.

"You've got more friends than you think, Merry," Samson said.

"I have enough."

"They've risked shunning too."

"It's hard to do the right thing," Natalie said.

"Real easy to do the wrong thing," Meredith said.

Natalie pulled her back into a hug.

Meredith cried when the prosecution called her a murderer.

She promised Natalie and Samson and herself she wouldn't, but she did, in the face of the lies about money, about promiscuity, about selfish greed and her cold-heartedness. She made herself look at the crime scene photo. Vincent, lying on her kitchen floor, blood soaking his shirt. She remembered the fear inside her--the picture transported her back to fear, sharp and painful. She'd believed he could stand back up and come after her. Calling 911 had been about calling for backup.

Vincent looked like an angel in the picture. At peace.

When her lawyer spoke, she only stared at her hands, feeling nauseous and ashamed at his gentleness. He made a rational, calm argument for forgiveness.

She knew didn't deserve forgiveness.

Chapter Thirty

Natalie came home with her. She walked with a slight, almost imperceptible limp. The boys knew who she was when she stepped over the threshold. They hugged her. They squealed.

Natalie winced at the sound. "I've been away too long."

Meredith took her hand.

After pizza, they put the boys to bed together. Meredith handled reading stories, snuggled against Beau, while Natalie sat with Merritt and closed her eyes and listened. The boys seemed mostly asleep when Meredith and Natalie left, but Meredith made Natalie stand outside their door, listening. A minute in, they brought Merritt water. Two minutes in, Meredith shushed them.

"They must think you're a god," Natalie said.

Meredith grinned. She took Natalie's hand. They stood another minute. Meredith shushed the boys again. Natalie and Meredith giggled together. Then Natalie's hands were running up and down Meredith's arms and Meredith was holding her waist and the boys could have lit their room on fire and Meredith wouldn't have noticed.

Natalie bent her head and barely brushed her mouth against Meredith's. Meredith held herself still, simply returning the pressure and then increasing it until there was a solid, affirming kiss.

Meredith pulled away. "Hungry?"

Natalie grinned and shook her head.

"Want to watch television?"

"No."

"I think I hear the boys."

"No you don't."

Meredith tugged Natalie closer, slipping an arm around her waist. "I don't know what to do with you."

"You've got to put up with me. We're a family now," Natalie said. She smoothed Meredith's hair back from her face and kissed the corner of her mouth.

Meredith kissed Natalie's cheek. She sighed as Natalie kissed her jaw.

"Are you going to be old-fashioned?" Meredith asked.

"Kátit," Natalie said.

Meredith tilted her head. "Bless you."

"The only phrase I know in Russian. Well, that I can use effectively. I learned it from the gangs at my high school, long before I learned the English equivalent from my defendants."

Meredith snorted, and said, "Fine, brat. Tell me."

"In the colloquial it means, 'Word.'"

Meredith slapped Natalie's stomach. Natalie laughed and pulled Meredith into a hug. Meredith tucked her head against Natalie's neck. Natalie stroked her hair.

"Kátit," Meredith said.

"There, now you're as bilingual as I am."

"Good." Meredith kissed her neck.

Natalie trembling, said, "I'm not sure who's supposed to take care of who."

"I've been thinking. We have complementary strengths."

Natalie pressed her cheek to the boys' door.

"Hear anything?" Meredith asked.

Natalie shook her head.

Meredith pulled back from the hug. She took Natalie's hand and led her upstairs to the bedroom. Natalie swallowed. Her hand was sweaty in Meredith's. Meredith held Natalie's fingers between both of her hands.

"Are you ready?" Meredith asked.

"Your bedroom."

Meredith nodded.

"Our bedroom."

"Yes."

"For the rest of our lives."

"Probably," Meredith said.

"I'm ready."

"You are old-fashioned," Meredith said.

"Maybe we should have waited. For this."

Meredith shook her head. "There were no guarantees."

Natalie lifted her hand to guide Meredith's fingers up to her lips. She kissed each one and said, "There are now."

"I love you," Meredith said.

She never said it in their epic phone conversations over the last two months, afraid her dream wouldn't come true, afraid to spoil it.

"I love you, too."

"Come inside." Meredith pushed open the bedroom door.

They walked in together. Natalie pulled away and went to the bed. She smoothed her hand over the pillow. Meredith was proud of the quilt on her bed, of the drapes she'd chosen, of the furniture matching, but her things weren't very modern. Maybe it wasn't the bedroom Natalie wanted to spend the rest of her life in.

"Hey," she said.

Natalie glanced up.

"Now, don't think I'm going to be sleeping naked every night. I have nightgowns and flannel pajamas and slippers."

"Slippers?"

"Bunny slippers from the boys~well, from Vince, through the boys, when they were two~kind of morbid, I suppose. Real fur."

Natalie raised her eyebrows, walking back to Meredith.

"And crocodile slippers. Those are fake."

Natalie settled her hands on Meredith's hips.

Meredith swallowed. "And my dad's old leather slippers. His feet are too big, though."

"What about tonight?" Natalie asked, slipping one hand around Meredith's waist to bring her closer.

"Tonight~" Meredith started, her words cut short by Natalie's kiss. She lost her breath when Natalie touched her. First her breast and then her side and then her hip. She guided Natalie's hand back to her breast. Natalie squeezed. Meredith squirmed. She wrapped her arms around Natalie's neck, afraid she would swoon.

Natalie worked her fingers under Meredith's top. Meredith clung to Natalie, unable to keep a gasp from escaping her lips. Natalie's kiss touched her neck. Wherever Natalie touched her, she felt answering fire inside of her. She pushed back against Natalie's hands.

She was startled by her own urgency. Natalie was touching her before she had a chance to breathe. She hadn't caught up to Natalie being there in her arms. Already making love to her.

They hadn't been sexual during their separation. Nor loving, nor tender. As practically as possible they made plans, rooted in realism, within their limitations. Flights of fantasy had no place between them. Romanticism was the enemy of anyone facing prison.

Natalie's lips touched her ear. She hissed, pulling herself more tightly against Natalie until she was pressed against Natalie's thigh. Her hands gripped Natalie's shoulders as hard as she could. Her shoulders ached.

The touch of Natalie's lips made her feel as if she were falling.

"Natalie, the bed."

"Right," Natalie said. She pulled back, breathing hard. She disentangled herself enough to pull them both to the bed. She turned down the sheets. She fluffed the pillows.

Meredith rubbed Natalie's back, feeling the muscles flex and extend.

"I'm sorry," Natalie said, sitting on the edge of the bed to take off her socks. "I've been thinking about this a lot."

"Me too." Meredith kissed the top of her head.

Natalie dropped her socks on the floor.

"We'll have to talk about that, too."

Natalie settled her hands on Meredith's hips.

"Later," Meredith said.

Natalie stood. She took Meredith's face in her hands to kiss her. Hard. Deepening. Meredith tangled her fingers in Natalie's hair. She tugged her closer. Natalie bit at Meredith's lip. Meredith seized. Natalie broke the kiss and showered smaller, damp kisses on her cheeks and neck.

"I've never wanted to do that to anyone," Meredith said.

"Not even Sharon Stone?"

Natalie turned them so Meredith's back was to the bed. She gently urged Meredith down. Meredith sank onto the mattress. Natalie worked up Meredith's shirt and pulled it over her head.

Meredith folded her arms around her torso, blushing and feeling cold. "Maybe when she was a cowboy," she said.

"I didn't see her as a cowboy."

"What were you thinking of?"

"*Basic Instinct?*"

Meredith poked Natalie in the stomach. Natalie sat beside her on the bed. Meredith shifted toward her. Then they were kissing. Natalie's hands were on Meredith's bare skin. Meredith found herself lying back on the bed with Natalie over her, her mouth following the slope of Meredith's breast to the cup of the bra.

"Natalie," she said.

Natalie worked her hands under Meredith's back, against the mattress, and unclasped her bra. She drew it back and Meredith freed her arms.

"Not on the floor," Meredith said.

Natalie snorted and got off the bed. "Where?"

"The closet--there's a hamper."

"A hamper?" Natalie glanced at the bra.

"Don't argue." She worked herself up on the bed to lie back on the pillows.

"I can see how this is going to go." Natalie tossed the bra in the hamper and turned around.

"Will you miss the bachelor lifestyle?"

Natalie knelt on the bed. She met Meredith's eyes with an expression of lust that made Meredith's chest ache. She thought she should be scared, but all she felt was an answering call inside her.

"Not as much as I would miss this," Natalie said.

Meredith reached for her, but Natalie ducked away. She opened the top button of Meredith's jeans.

"Hurry," Meredith said.

Natalie unzipped the fly and worked the jeans over Meredith's legs. Meredith blushed, feeling each inch of her exposed. Natalie tugged her panties down with the jeans. She didn't ask Meredith before dumping them on the floor.

Meredith, naked, sat up and cupped Natalie's chin and drew her forward. She leaned back and gazed into Natalie's eyes, dark and wide, gazing into hers. In the moment before Natalie's lips touched hers, Meredith whimpered. The light brush of Natalie's mouth was a relief.

Meredith pulled Natalie close, holding Natalie's head so their kiss became more intense. She arched up, rubbing herself against Natalie's clothed body. She hooked one leg over Natalie's calf.

They had been so careful at the beach house, so unsure. But now, no thinking. Just touching. Groping. Natalie's lips burning and Meredith tugging up the back of Natalie's shirt, stroking her back, wanting her closer. Natalie's thigh moved between her legs. She groaned. Natalie shivered against their kiss.

She groaned again at Natalie's hand on her breast. "Don't stop," she said.

Natalie kissed her shoulder. Natalie's lips were so soft they felt like cotton against her skin. Meredith wanted to lie back and feel each touch of Natalie's lips, but desire was building within her making the passivity impossible. She found the seam of Natalie's pants and pressed. Natalie shifted, bringing herself to Meredith's fingers.

"Yes," Natalie said. "Make love to me."

Natalie was on top of her, pressing down on her, and fully clothed against Meredith's nudity, but Meredith felt powerful when she pressed her fingers and Natalie trembled.

"You'll have to~" she tried to say. She pulled Natalie's shirt up her back.

Natalie stopped kissing her neck only when the shirt bunched over her head, interfering, and then she lifted her head long enough for Meredith to get the fabric off. Meredith reached for the bra.

"Wait," Natalie said.

Meredith didn't wait. She unclasped the bra and moved her hands underneath the loose cups. She stroked and Natalie shuddered.

"God," Natalie said.

Meredith lifted up to kiss Natalie's collarbone. Natalie made a strangled sound. It sent a charge through Meredith, ending between her legs. She clutched Natalie's shoulders, kissing her skin.

Natalie pushed her back to the bed, gently but firmly. She met Meredith's eyes.

Meredith grinned.

Natalie grinned back.

Meredith trembled, impressed with Natalie's strength, decisiveness, her own body's response to it. Natalie lowered herself. Their breasts touched. Natalie's weight on top of her, her nipples against her, was almost enough to make Meredith orgasm.

If Natalie's hand had been there~

"Please," Meredith said, sliding her hand down Natalie's abdomen, under the waistband of her slacks. The fabric accommodated her hand just enough she could curl her fingers into Natalie's panties and press to show what she meant.

"Please."

Natalie kissed her and then rolled off of her, Meredith's hand sliding free. Natalie sprawled onto her back, panting, gazing at the ceiling. Her chest rose and fell with great heaves.

Meredith watched her, propping herself on one elbow.

Natalie turned her head and said, "If you do that I'm going to~And I want to at least be naked, with you, in our bed. The first time." The speech seemed to take away her breath. She held Meredith's gaze, slightly open-mouthed.

Meredith reached for Natalie's fly.

Natalie twitched. "I won't make it if you~"

Meredith grinned.

Natalie closed her eyes, gritted her teeth, and then unzipped her slacks.

Meredith pulled the sheets over them. She saw relief in Natalie's exhale. The slacks went somewhere to the bottom of the bed, under the covers. Natalie turned and took Meredith in her arms.

They kissed.

In Natalie's arms, with nothing between them, Meredith's lips twitched against Natalie's kisses. Natalie held her loosely. She hugged Natalie back, nipping at her lips, opening herself up to Natalie's tongue, which was darting and playful rather than urgently forceful like before. Meredith's breasts tingled, but did not burn, against Natalie's. Only when Natalie rubbed her back, with long, sensual strokes, lightly using her nails, did Meredith lay back.

Beckoning.

Natalie kissed her, only kissed her, until Meredith took Natalie's hand in hers and brought it between her legs. "Now," she said, and let go of Natalie's hand and instead mirrored the action against Natalie, reveling in Natalie's surprised, urgent cry.

"Now," Natalie said.

Natalie breathed heavily against Meredith's ear. Meredith couldn't stop herself from shaking against Natalie's fingers, so eager to please her. Tears stung her eyes. Natalie's hips moved against her, first deliberately, and then erratically.

When she thought she'd have to stop touching Natalie because the orgasm was coming, shatteringly, Natalie froze and let out a choked sob. Meredith pressed. She forgot about herself and concentrated on Natalie's pleasure.

Meredith held her, reveling in the sweat of their bodies and the spasms against her hand. Natalie relaxed on top of her, slipping slightly to her side, and planted one sloppy, wet kiss on her cheek.

"Oh," Meredith said.

Natalie's body shuddered, like she was laughing but didn't have the breath for sound. Her hand moved, dragging across Meredith's skin, igniting her so completely, her skin flushed, her breath gone, and she came, lifting her hips up to Natalie's hand, shameless. She saw spots.

"Breathe," Natalie whispered in her ear.

She took a deep breath and her senses came rushing back to her body.

In the aftermath she felt sweaty and cold, and Natalie moved to hug her, half-spooning her until Meredith rolled over, her back to Natalie, breathing in and out, blinking as her bedroom took focus. Trying to recover herself. She tried to speak, and licked her lips and wetted her mouth before getting out, "Closer."

Natalie's grip tightened, and she felt Natalie's chin against her hair. She rolled back, crowding into Natalie's embrace, lifting her face so Natalie could kiss her. Then she settled back.

Natalie smoothed Meredith's damp hair off her forehead.

Meredith swallowed. "I think this will work out."

"As long as we don't have to get out of bed."

Meredith pulled her down into a long hug. She allowed herself a moment where the kids didn't knock on the door, and the cat didn't meow, and no one came to rob her or take her away or call her names. She heard nothing but Natalie's breathing. Her eyes drifted shut.

Natalie squirmed, getting comfortable. She left one arm splayed across Meredith's stomach, below her breasts. Meredith breathed deeply. She never slept on her back.

She'd learn.

"Don't fall asleep," Meredith said.

"I won't."

"I want to talk to you all night, and know you, and~"

"You're going to tell me to put my clothes back on, aren't you?"

"For the children's sake. Not mine."

Natalie nuzzled her shoulder. "Later?"

"Later."

Meredith yawned. She rubbed Natalie's wrist, feeling bones, tracing curves, enjoying the weight of Natalie's arm and how it secured her, anchored her to Natalie.

"So, what's your favorite color?" Natalie asked.

Meredith laughed. She turned toward Natalie to remind herself of the color of Natalie's eyes and make her choice from there.

The phone rang.

Meredith sat at the defense table. Samson sat next to her, his hand over hers.

Natalie was behind them, leaning over the barrier. Meredith's in-laws crowded the other side of the courtroom, a flock of angry people, staring at Meredith, not at the judge. The courtroom was filled with locals--Meredith's co-workers, curiosity seekers, senior citizens, the unemployed and reporters from all over the state. Two men in uniform stood in the back.

The judge took the paper from bailiff and then nodded at Samson.

Samson rose and Meredith stood beside him. The room went quiet.

The judge read, "We, the jury, find the defendant guilty--"

The blood rushed from Natalie's face. Not the comforting sound of "Not guilty," the first word breaking the dam, letting everyone tune out the rest.

Guilty. Intractable no matter what followed.

Meredith gasped.

"--of voluntary manslaughter. Thank you, jury. Sentencing will be carried out--" The judge studied his calendar. "Monday at 11 o'clock. Defendant released on her own recognizance until then. Those wishing to make a victim impact statement should file with the clerk. Court dismissed."

Meredith sank back down into her chair.

Natalie touched her shoulder, but directed her attention to Samson. "Thanks a lot, asshole."

Samson ignored her and squeezed Meredith's hand. "It'll be all right, Merry."

Meredith took a deep breath and released it as a sob. She didn't look up as the courtroom emptied.

Natalie stroked her hair. "I'll take you home."

"The kids--"

"We'll handle the paperwork."

"They'll fight you. They'll win."

"Probably. Don't think about it right now."

Meredith nodded. Samson helped her to her feet and held the gate open. Natalie pulled Meredith into her arms and held her, helpless to stop the sobs, only able to buffer them with her body and hold Meredith up.

The press waited just outside the courthouse. Meredith held Natalie's elbow, despite Natalie's limp, despite the fact that if Meredith leaned on Natalie too hard, Natalie might collapse.

"Ms. Jameison, do you have a statement?"

"Ms. Jameison, are you going to appeal?"

"Merry, do you think justice was served, when a family has lost their son?"

"What are you going to tell your children?"

Meredith was wan as Natalie pushed through the crowd toward the waiting car.

Samson waved at the press, trying to get their attention turned toward him. "I'll make a brief statement."

People took pictures and followed Natalie and Meredith until they were in the backseat of the car.

"We will not be appealing. We've stated all along Ms. Jameison has taken responsibility for her actions. We will focus our efforts on sentencing..." Samson began.

Meredith went into her bedroom.

Natalie talked to the babysitter. She didn't tell Merritt or Beau about the conviction, she just fed them dinner and played with them and helped them feed the cat. She took dinner to Meredith, who sat, tear-stained and pale and unfocused in bed, while the boys washed up. Then Natalie read the boys stories and stayed with them until she was sure they would sleep and not interrupt her later.

She crept into Meredith's bedroom. Her chest constricted.

Meredith sat in the same position, hugging her knees. She'd at least attempted to eat, though. The plate had lost a third of its food.

Natalie sat on the bed. She took Meredith's hands.

Meredith trembled. "I'm a murderer."

"You're not a murderer."

Meredith's voice was thick with tears. "I expected absolution. I don't know. I thought this would all go away."

Natalie squeezed her fingers.

Meredith swallowed. "What's going to happen next?"

"We can worry about—"

"No, tell me. In legal terms. What do I do?"

"We'll hope for lenient sentencing, and we'll file for a temporary guardianship if you want the same day. Grandparents don't have many legal rights in North Carolina."

"I know. But you do?"

"If we'd been together longer..." Natalie lowered her head.

Meredith leaned forward, pressing her forehead to Natalie's shoulder. Natalie let go of her hands and moved closer, embracing her instead.

"It's going to be okay," Natalie said.

"I'm going to be punished for this forever."

"I know. But I'm not going anywhere. And neither are your children."

Meredith turned her head, tucking against Natalie's neck. "I feel awful. Dirty. I..."

"What?"

"I don't want you to touch me. It disgusts me. I want to curl up in a ball and have you far away, where it's safe. I'm toxic."

"Merry," Natalie cupped Meredith's cheek and tilted her face up.

"Don't."

Natalie kissed her anyway, the warm lips she kissed so many times before pliant to her touch, unresisting as she brushed across them, as she stroked Meredith's jaw. Only when Meredith closed her eyes did Natalie hold her close and let her cry.

Meredith glanced at no one as her father-in-law took the stand. He spoke about Vincent, but he was not describing the boy she had loved, the boy whose secrets had been hers, not his father's. She tried not to hate him, but the terror inside her needed focus. Natalie sat on her left side, Samson on her right. The courtroom was as full as it had been at the verdict.

Someone sketched a picture of her children's grandfather, crying on the stand. Then the judge spoke. Samson squeezed her hand and she gazed up, and met the judge's eyes, and tried to be open to a future decided by others.

"With mitigating circumstances and your status as a first time offender, the sentence imposed is three years in prison."

Meredith held her breath. Her ears pounded. Her vision swam and she thought she might go blind.

"Taking into account time already served, I sentence you to a minimum of six months and a maximum of two years at Conrad Correctional Center for Women."

Natalie's hand settled onto her shoulder.

"Guardian ad litem will continue under the previous agreement, and temporary guardianship of Merritt and Beau Jameison will remain at the Jameison residence and pass to Natalie Ivans, am I correct?"

Meredith swallowed and nodded.

Vincent's father stood. "We object."

"You've filed your objection here and while I'm not a family court judge, I suspect you have a case. Supervised visitation will continue under the previous agreement while that proceeds. Is Natalie Ivans here?"

"Here, Your Honor," Natalie said, standing up.

"I understand the boys will be staying at their current residence and entering kindergarten on schedule in the fall?"

Meredith bit back a choked sound.

"Yes, Your Honor," Natalie said.

"And you will respect the visitation schedule and guidelines put forth by the county-appointed guardian?"

"Yes, Your Honor."

"Your occupation, Ms. Ivans?"

"I'm an attorney, Your Honor."

The judge rolled his eyes. "And your relationship to Meredith Jameison? I assume this domestic partnership filing from Raleigh indicates other contractual commitments as well?"

"Yes, Your Honor."

The judge nodded and wrote something on his form. "Ms. Jameison, you have three days to get your affairs in order before presenting yourself at this court house for transportation to Rocky Mount. Court is adjourned."

Meredith buried her face in her hands.

"I'll file for a commuted sentence with the governor," Samson said.

Natalie nodded.

"And I'll talk to the press. Why don't you two go out the back way?"

"Thank you, Samson."

Meredith took a deep breath. She uncoiled herself long enough to hug Samson and then stood, reaching for Natalie's hand.

Natalie and Meredith settled onto a bench at Clement Park, where they could watch Merritt and Beau on the playground. Other parents were there, and those who didn't recognize Meredith were quickly informed by those who did, so Natalie and Meredith sat alone, isolated but unmolested.

"We should have gone up to Rose Hill," Natalie said.

"I don't want to leave home. Not until I have to. Three days."

"I'll bring the kids up every week. It'll pass by before you know it."

"I don't know. When I get out, will I be better, then? Will those women over there stop looking at me like that? Will I be able to enjoy a day like this without wanting to throw up?"

Natalie wrapped an arm around Meredith's shoulders. She gazed past the playground at the tree line. The sky was a pale blue with white clouds.

There was just enough heat to feel warm. Perfect weather for running. But she couldn't run anymore.

Meredith took a deep breath. "I should pray."

Natalie squeezed her.

"I can't."

"We'll pray together."

Meredith settled her hand onto Natalie's leg, but didn't speak.

"Merry?"

"I just can't. Will you?"

"Sure. God likes your voice better, though."

Meredith grinned, but her eyes were squeezed shut.

Natalie kissed Meredith's hair. "Let me convey your sentiments."

Meredith nodded.

"And His," Natalie said.

Meredith's grip tightened.

Natalie turned, so she was whispering close to Meredith's ear. "This is what I remember saying over and over as a child. I never knew it in Russian, but that probably doesn't matter. God speaks English, right?"

"I sure hope so," Meredith said.

"Our Father, Who art in heaven, hallowed be Thy Name; Thy Kingdom come; Thy will be done, on earth as it is in heaven."

Meredith breathed in and out with slow, measured breaths.

"Stop me if you know this one."

Meredith shook her head.

"Give us this day our daily bread." Natalie hesitated.

Meredith shifted, turning to face her on the bench.

"Forgive us our trespasses as we forgive those who trespass against us."

"You have someone in mind?" Meredith asked.

"And lead us not into temptation."

"But deliver us from evil." Meredith mouthed the words along with Natalie.

Natalie cupped Meredith's cheek. "They're all staring at us, you know."

"I know. I don't blame them. I would be staring, too."

Natalie shifted, tucking herself against Meredith's side.

"I want to just cry and cry until I fall apart, until I disintegrate right here in the park, in the sunlight."

Natalie nodded.

"But I want to stay here with you. Is that selfish?"

Natalie shrugged, with Meredith's hair brushing her cheek and Meredith's warmth radiating up her side. "No, I think the other way is selfish. The people who love you don't want you to go away. You have to stay with us. Even if it hurts."

"It does." Meredith tilted her chin. "You have no idea how much."

Natalie knew she couldn't really conceive of Meredith's pain. Her own agony at the impending separation seemed like a wispy, tangential ache. She didn't know how she was going to take care of four-year-olds and make American cheese sandwiches or find money to support them or get to Rocky Mount or deal with the neighbors or supervise non-custodial visits without punching anyone in the face.

She couldn't even bear the thought of going to sleep alone next week. The week after that, and the week after that, might wear her down, might make her give up.

"I love you," she said.

Meredith put her head on Natalie's shoulder. "I know you don't think it's enough, not with everything else, but that's what's going to get us through. It's the only thing."

Natalie reached for Meredith's hand, tangling their fingers.

"I love you, too."

The words made Natalie feel lighter. Merritt waved at them before he threw himself down the slide. She felt something like rejoice in her chest, watching him. "Maybe you're right."

Meredith lifted their linked hands and kissed Natalie's fingers. "Sometimes I am."

"I think everything might actually turn out to be easy."

Chapter Thirty-One

Four Months Later

"I want to stay," Beau said, crying.

Natalie ignored him. His crying turned to kicks and piercing shrieks hurting her ears and making her hands tremble as she tried to buckle him into the booster seat.

"Beau~"

"Why do we have to go back? You're horrible."

Merritt sat calmly in the other booster seat, waiting to be strapped in. Tears streamed down his face as he peered through the car window. His grandparents, Anthony and Irene, stood on the porch watching the display.

"Beau, you know why we have to go back." Natalie said.

She'd attempted this argument before. Reason, bribery, threats, nothing could match tearing a just-turned-five year old away from doting grandparents and toward a near-stranger. The supervised visits hadn't been this bad, except for giving her heartburn. Natalie wasn't enough. Not without Meredith. The kids needed family. Whatever family they had.

Anthony walked toward the car.

Merritt's face lit up.

"Let me help," Anthony said.

"It's fine." Natalie gave a final tug on Beau's strap.

He was still crying, but not screaming, more interested in what Anthony might do. Natalie walked around the car and opened the door. Anthony took a step back. Merritt submitted to the seatbelt, but kept his eyes on Anthony.

"Natalie," Anthony said.

Ms. Ivans, she wanted to correct him. Just to be petty.

"Is there anything you need?"

She needed money. She needed a job. She could do with a bag of groceries, or a kind smile. But she shook her head. No weakness he could put on a form to declare her unfit for custody. It would be so easy, and they were so willing. All four of them.

Meredith would never forgive her. The universe would probably never forgive her.

She closed the door on Merritt's yearning face and got in the driver's seat. "See you next week, Mr. and Mrs. Jameison."

Merritt finally let out a wail.

Beau kicked the back of Natalie's chair. "I hate you!"

Natalie put the car in gear and waited for the blur of her own tears to recede before pulling out of the driveway. Beau didn't mean it. His grandparents bribed him, or stuffed him with candy, or slandered her. The voodoo magic would wear off by the time they got home. Beau would have his own toys, and Hollingsworth.

Not Natalie. She would never be enough enticement to stay.

"Wait until you find out what we're having for dinner," she said.

When Natalie put the boys to bed, she wanted to ask them if they really hated her. She wanted them to apologize. She wanted them to feel guilty for breaking her heart, for making her feel bad. But she made them read to her, trying to be at ease with Beau comfortably in her arms, pointing at the pictures. Dog. Balloon. Girl.

Merritt fell asleep quickly, his stomach filled with ramen and turkey. Beau lingered, warm and squirmy. When Natalie closed the book and lowered the light, he blinked at her.

"Love you, Beau," she said, kissing his hair.

He nodded. He hesitated.

She waited. If she didn't give him his space, he would react defensively and close up before she got to know the secrets causing ripples in his cheeks, fluttering in his eyelids.

"You know," he said, a phrase that made him sound so much like his mother Natalie's heart lurched, "There are worse places I could be."

She smiled.

The television was on mute, showing an eleven o'clock sitcom Natalie was glad she didn't have to pay for. She'd cleaned the kitchen after dinner, but the small family room was in disarray. Toys were underfoot. The blanket over her lap smelled like applesauce. The big screen television she'd brought with her from Charlotte took up too much room, crowding out books and puzzles.

The television. The legal briefs spread out around her. Bad food on the coffee table. Despite uprooting her entire life, despite finding love, and family, despite losing the job that defined her, Natalie's nights were exactly the same as they were a year ago.

She didn't know how long she'd have to wait for change. She wanted to be patient. But she didn't want this.

The thought of cleaning depressed her. The laptop was in her lap. If she stared at Quicken long enough, maybe more money would appear. And everything else she might need. She'd already checked her email a dozen times. She'd only gotten a message on Facebook from Melanie, a paralegal at the state prosecutor's office, inviting her back for a weekend.

As if she could afford the gas.

Food stamps got her pretty far. Her court-assigned social worker, Rebecca, had looked askance at her when she explained she'd quit a $60,000 a year job to come to Tarpley with no job prospects. But with two boys and no assets–not even a car anymore, just Meredith's station wagon, she'd qualified.

"You just sold your condo," Rebecca said.

"In the Charlotte market."

Rebecca winced sympathetically.

"I have some savings, but I have medical bills, too."

Rebecca read her form. "And Meredith Jameison isn't receiving income?"

"Not in prison."

"You never know. Are the children on Medicaid?"

Natalie shook her head. "Blue Cross."

Rebecca ran the numbers. Natalie's life, reduced to a federal equation. Reduced to her ability to hold off bill collectors long enough to pay the power bill. Court costs hadn't helped, either. But she'd left with $50 per child per month, which she supplemented, despite feeling guilty, by buying cards from junkies at sixty cents on the dollar outside the Food Lion.

They wouldn't starve. At least not until Meredith came back and could starve with them. Maybe they could move. Charlotte, or California, or Moscow.

Anywhere but here.

Rebecca took her hand. "Natalie, there's other things you can do."

"I'm listening."

She'd left with a promise of hope. The church that had abandoned

Meredith would deliver groceries the first of each month. She could get free school supplies, free clothes.

"What I really need," she'd said to Rebecca, "Is a job."

Rebecca squeezed her hand, but offered no hope.

Beau and Merritt didn't complain about the food. Fresh eggs and good cereal and juice and vitamins in the morning, and whatever came out of a box at night.

In four months, she'd done two wills. One for Jake's father and one for another Laotian immigrant long past retirement age. She'd contested four speeding tickets and she'd helped Mrs. Cranston's friend Ida, whose neighbor's dog kept crapping in her yard.

It all amounted to less than $1000 in legal fees. The first time she'd gotten a gig, she'd taken the boys to MacDonalds to celebrate. The second time, she'd just taken them to the library.

There had also been her Big Case, coming from the public defender's rotation, two meth heads who'd been caught selling from their truck. She wasn't able to get them into rehab, which was non-existent except for a facility three counties away and the A.A. and N.A. meetings around. She wasn't able to get the sentence reduced. Five days in county jail.

But she got paid a hundred bucks.

She'd met a couple other public defenders in Duplin County doing the same beat as her. Family law practice, on call public defenders. Patrick tried to get her a transfer to the fourth district court, but the few positions were all held by lifers.

She'd make do.

Quicken suggested she sell her soul. Or maybe one of the kids. She knew immediately which one it would be. She'd have to live with the guilt of a quick, impure, unloving thought all night. She turned up the volume on the television. Maybe something mindless would distract her. She closed Quicken. Behind it was her letterhead. Natalie Ivans, Attorney at Law. Sad and empty. A blank slate.

The hospital was hiring. The meth heads she'd defended worked there in laundry services. No longer. They, too, would be going to see Rebecca. Natalie might see them outside Food Lion. Maybe they'd offer her a deal on food stamp cards for representing them. Maybe they'd firebomb her house for not getting them off.

The sitcom faded to a commercial, loud and jolting. She grabbed the remote and turned it down again, then listened for reaction upstairs.

Silence.

Her phone rang, equally jarring. She scooped it up from the coffee table, glancing at the caller ID. Her heart raced, hoping it was Meredith.

"Natalie Ivans," she said into the receiver.

"Ms. Ivans, this is Sherriff Duarte."

"Sheriff? Is everything all right?"

They'd do a notification at the front door. They wouldn't call her~

"I got your name from the public defender's list."

She nodded. They'd met, in passing. He would know her name already.

"I was looking for it," he said.

"What can I do for you, Sheriff?"

"Can you come up to Route 40? Up by River Landing, Northbound. There's been an accident. A~An accident."

"Of course." She slid the laptop off her lap. "Someone need a lawyer?"

"Yes. Someone needs a lawyer, Ms. Ivans. My son."

"I'm on my way."

He hung up before she lowered the phone. She glanced at the staircase. She didn't know if she should change into her suit. Certainly she couldn't go in her jeans. The September heat would be stifling, even at night.

And the boys. She could take them, leave them in their booster seats, safe in the car, locked away. Screaming. Demanding attention. She couldn't call a sitter this late at night, on no notice. She crept upstairs, first to her bedroom, changing into khakis and a sweater. Checking her briefcase. Delaying the inevitable. But Sheriff Duarte' voice held urgency and River Landing was a good 20 minute drive, even this late at night.

The boys were asleep, and only shifted slightly when she slipped into the room. She set Meredith's cell phone on the table between them, with a note.

Call Natalie.

Do not pass go. Do not collect $200.

All they had to do was hit send.

Hollingsworth meowed from Merritt's bed. She patted his head. She wished he were a dog. A big, protective, parental dog.

"I'll be back," she said.

Chapter Thirty-Two

Natalie parked along the shoulder, behind squad cars and an unmarked Toyota. She got out, nervous of the trucks lumbering past. The squad cars' blue lights were blinding in the night. The accident scene was wrapping up. Ambulances were gone. A car was being lifted onto a flatbed tow truck. Natalie could tell it was totaled.

A policeman stepped away from the sheriff and approached her.

"Natalie Ivans," she said.

He nodded and they walked together toward the sheriff. Her hand was sweaty as she gripped her briefcase. Beyond the tow truck was a state trooper's car. Natalie blinked, water-eyed from its lights, and turned to the sheriff, who held a blue pallor.

"Thank you for coming," he said, offering his hand.

"Of course, Sheriff."

The sheriff glanced at the policeman, who nodded and went toward the state trooper car.

Natalie cleared her throat. "Is your son in trouble, sheriff?"

Duarte gestured toward the state trooper car. "Luis. This is his fifth DWI. He..."

Natalie waited. The way she waited for Beau. The way she waited for her leg to heal, for Meredith to come home, for a jury to come back with a verdict.

"This time, he killed someone."

She nodded.

"Two girls driving down to see their parents at River Landing. They were so close to getting there." Duarte coughed hoarsely and gazed up. Stars glittered overhead.

Natalie put her hand on his elbow.

"They weren't intoxicated, that we could tell. Just..."

Just dead.

"I don't know what to do with him," Duarte said.

I know."

"He killed somebody."

"I'll help."

"I thought you could. I remembered you. Because." He met her eyes but didn't finish his thought.

Because Meredith killed somebody.

Natalie hadn't been her attorney.

She glanced at the state trooper's car. She thought about her kids.

"Go on over. We're almost done here. Deputy Fasan will be handling the case," Duarte said.

Natalie nodded and went to the squad car. The state trooper opened the back door for her. Crouched against the window on the other side was Luis Duarte, crying. He gazed at her with wild, sorrowful eyes, and then his expression tightened. Toward anger.

"Luis, I'm Natalie. I'm your attorney."

He swallowed and nodded. "Yes, ma'am. Dad~"

"Yes. Luis, I'm going to need you not to talk to anyone else."

"It was their fault," he said, his nail-polish-vomit breath washing over her, loud enough for the state trooper outside the door to hear. "They swerved right in front of me. If they hadn't~I was fine."

"Luis~"

"I know I could have made it home. It was their fault."

He bent over, shuddering with sobs, gripping his thighs. He was handcuffed. He'd wet his pants. The smells and his attitude made Natalie want to retch, want to flee.

She sat, trying not to think of him as a worthless human being. The kind she'd held no sympathy for as a prosecutor. "Get them off the streets," she once told juries. "Before they kill somebody."

Luis raised his head. "What did you say your name was, ma'am?" He inhaled, fighting more tears.

"Natalie."

"Natalie. I've been through these. I appreciate the help, but I know the procedure better than you do. I know what they're going to do to me."

"Probably."

"Then what are you doing here?"

"Someone died. Changes things."

"They swerved right in front of me."

"Are you injured?"

Luis shook his head. "No, ma'am."

Two girls died and he was scratch-free. Natalie's stomach twisted. She pictured the girls' parents, not grieving and broken, but angry, unforgiving, wearing the faces of Anthony and Irene Jameison.

The state trooper knocked on the window.

"I've got to talk to your father, all right? Luis?"

Luis glanced at her. "Don't say anything to anyone."

"I'll see you at the jail in the morning, okay?"

"What about bond?"

She put her hand on his shoulder. "There's not going to be any bond."

He nodded.

The door opened. She slid out. The trooper handed her a card. "Tarpley's city jail."

"I know where it is. Thank you."

He got into the driver's seat. Natalie walked toward Duarte.

"How is he?" Duarte asked.

"He's not hurt. I'll meet with him in the morning."

Duarte nodded. "I just can't~I can't believe it." He was a more composed version of his son, the tears and fury and recrimination hiding behind a lifetime of police work.

The state trooper's car pulled out, and the tow truck left, leaving only the two squad cars and her own car. Broken glass littered the nearest lane and the shoulder. Chalk marks marred the road, though everything had been cleaned up. The pictures had been taken.

"I'll need the police report," she said.

"Everything will go through Fasan." He gave her a card. Fasan's name, cell phone number, and the case number were written on the back.

"Thanks," she said.

"What are his chances?"

"For what?"

Duarte gazed at the accident scene. "For not being~For getting better."

"I don't know." She set up an appointment to talk to him tomorrow afternoon, and then got back in her car. She checked her phone, even though it hadn't rung. No calls. She prayed the boys were still asleep.

Then, because it was habit every time she prayed, she sent a good thought to Meredith.

And then for Luis Duarte, and the parents getting a knock on the door in the middle of the night in River Landing. Fasan would have to go there.

Not Duarte. That was too much for any man.

She remembered the same flash of horror when her phone had rung with the city number. But it was someone else's tragedy tonight. She drove carefully and slowly home, staying away from the other cars on the road, her knuckles white on the steering wheel.

The boys hovered in Mrs. Cranston's foyer, glancing nervously at Natalie. She'd told them she had a job, but they'd never really experienced her with one. To them, her days in court were with Meredith, and that had not turned out well.

"There's lunch." Mrs. Cranston shooed them.

Natalie smiled.

"A case, huh?"

"I'm going to be Luis Duarte' public defender."

Mrs. Cranston's eyes narrowed. "The sheriff's son."

Natalie knew what was coming.

"On the news this morning they said he killed two kids."

Natalie nodded.

"Driving drunk."

"Someone's got to be his lawyer, right? Not the best job in the county."

Mrs. Cranston gazed at her steadily. "Just when I thought you couldn't get any worse. Sink any lower."

"Yeah." Natalie headed for the door. "You've got to be careful who your neighbors are."

Luis sat across from Natalie in the interrogation room. Sober and showered, he still looked angry, and more menacing without the bags under his eyes. Without the pathetic stench.

"They're listening," he said, nodding at the mirrored wall.

"It's illegal."

Luis snorted.

Natalie glanced at her notebook so she wouldn't have to look at him. "Why don't you tell me what happened?"

"You know what happened."

"Come on, Mr. Duarte."

"Don't start with that shit. Ma'am, sir. It doesn't mean anything."

"Luis." Natalie leaned forward. "What the fuck happened last night?"

He scowled. "I was driving along. Slow, man. Like 50 miles an hour. I was buzzed, the song was good. Something came out right in front of me. I thought it was a deer."

"You hit it?"

"The impact was like, like, I don't know. So hard. Everything just stopped, and then got really fast again. I spun and then I was in the ditch."

Natalie had fragments of memory from her own accident. The deer, soft and brown and alive, looking right into her eyes with its own black ones. She shivered.

"What next?" she asked.

"I got out of the car. Their car was all smashed up. They~" He glanced at the mirror.

"You stayed."

"Of course I stayed. What kind of asshole do you think I am?"

"Did you call 911?"

"No. No, I didn't even think of it. I was stunned. I just... Someone passed by. And then pulled over. They must have." Luis put his head in his hands.

"What is it?"

"There was screaming."

Natalie wanted to reach out to him.

He rubbed his face, scrubbing hard, and glanced up. "I didn't ask for this to happen."

She nodded.

"It just happened. God, if those assholes hadn't~"

Natalie flinched.

"When do I get out of here?" he asked.

"Your bail hearing's at three."

"And then I can go home?"

Natalie took a deep breath. She'd hardly ever done this~given bad news to a suspect. To a murderer. This wasn't her field. She could break a victim's heart all day long. Justice wasn't coming.

But for Luis, justice was coming.

"Luis, look~"

"What?" He hit the table.

"Bail's going to be high. I don't know we can pay."

"Of course. Of course he wouldn't pay. He's against me. He just wants me to go the fuck away. Go rot somewhere."

"Who?"

"Who? The guy who hired you."

"Why do you think he~"

"He hired a prosecutor. I asked around. If he wanted to help me he would have hired Tim Hoyle."

"That what your buddies in lockup tell you?"

Luis sneered. "Why are you here?"

Natalie ran her fingers through her hair. She had no idea why she was here, getting a splitting headache, dealing with a client who hated her on sight. She'd been at the accident scene less than ten hours ago.

"I came to see you first. I haven't talked to your father yet."

"He's paying you."

"He's paying me to defend you."

Which wasn't quite true. She'd go on the public defender dole, based on Luis's income. He could have another attorney if he wanted. Despite already being on the log sheet for the pubilc defender's office, maybe Tim Hoyle was the one up to catch the case.

"Why do you think he wanted me, Luis? I'm not local. He wants someone who doesn't have to pick sides. Someone who doesn't know the police or your friends or the victims. I can be~"

"Impartial? It's always about him, isn't it? His reputation. First sheriff from El Salvador. Like it matters. They just thought he was Lumbee. Did you vote for him?"

"I wasn't here. Luis, where does this anger come from?"

He leaned back and folded his arms. "Middle child?"

She chuckled.

"You?"

"Only child."

"Yeah. What a surprise. You don't understand anything."

Natalie considered while he gave her space, tense and exhausted like a bull, flush with anger but unwilling to charge. Not yet. Not again. He wore too many wounds already.

"You think I don't understand family, Luis?"

"I don't think you'll ever understand mine."

She got up, gathering her things. "Well, if the truth is on your side, you won't need me at all."

Luis glanced away.

"But if it's not... you're going to have to tell me all about your family. And how it's all their fault."

"It is," he said as she left. "It is!"

Chapter Thirty-Three

"The police report won't be finished for a few days," Duarte said

"What will it show?"

Duarte sighed and shook his head.

"Sheriff, accident reconstruction isn't my forte."

"I can tell you it looks like Luis was going about ninety miles an hour."

"So he was lying."

"He always lies." Duarte looked sharply at her. "You can't tell?"

"I would have assumed, if I was...in court. But I'm trying to give him the benefit of the doubt."

"You don't need to give him the benefit of the doubt to defend him."

"Does anyone?"

"He killed two people!"

Natalie was silent as Duarte got half-out of his chair, his face flushed red. He leaned on his hands on the desk. She counted breaths with him. At four, he sat back down. "I keep forgetting he's not just some guy we arrested last night. He's my son."

"What will he be charged with?" she asked.

"There are different charges we could pursue but..."

"But you always start with the biggest."

"Felony death by vehicle in the first degree."

A jolt went through Natalie. She rubbed her arms as goose bumps appeared. "You can't believe he actually planned to kill someone last night?"

"He was going to sooner or later."

"He's your son."

"Vehicular manslaughter is a cakewalk if you can plea it down."

"You didn't hire some slick personal injury lawyer from the phone book."

"I have before. What good did it do?" Duarte cleared his throat. "What am I going to do?"

"I promise you, he'll get the best defense in the state."

Duarte nodded. "Thank you."

"Will you be at the bail hearing?"

"No, no I don't think I should be. Fasan will be there, though."

Natalie got up.

"Stop at the clerk's office on your way out and give Fasan your email address. He'll forward you everything you need. I told him to cooperate fully."

"Thank you."

He leaned across the desk, offering his hand. "No, thank you."

Natalie felt a bit uneasy, sitting in the park on a warm September day, eating the peanut butter and jelly sandwich she'd packed for lunch. She should be with the boys, but between the meeting with Luis and the hearing, she wanted focus.

Her phone rang, as if to remind her she had responsibilities.

But when she saw the caller ID, it wasn't Mrs. Cranston or the jail or the prison, but a reporter she knew from Rocky Mount.

"Natalie Ivans, attorney-at-law," she answered the phone.

"Hi, Natalie, Erica Mendes. Do you remember me?"

"Of course. I haven't thanked you enough for the article you did on Meredith's conviction."

"That my editor fought me tooth and nail on. But then we looked good, didn't we? Being the only paper covering that side of the story. Thanks for the full access. I didn't get a Pulitzer, but I swear it helped."

"I'm glad you could exploit my family in the hopes of a trophy, Erica."

Erica laughed. "Now I'm calling to exploit someone else's."

"This isn't a social call?"

"Does it feel like a coincidence?"

"I just didn't know news traveled so quickly."

"The court has Luis Duarte on the docket for murder. Come on."

"Felony death by vehicle."

"Who's the victim?"

Natalie shivered, thinking of the two girls. "I can't tell you, Erica."

"Is it the same Duarte as the sheriff?"

"Yes."

"It's all over Twitter already anyway. But if I can get Rocky Mount News as the confirmation re-tweet~"

"Erica."

"Sorry. That's not why I called you. Just daydreaming. I want to do a story."

"How did you know to call me?"

Erica was silent.

"You didn't know to call me?"

"I called Tim Hoyle. Then I called Deputy Fasan. He gave me your name."

"Makes sense."

"I already had your number. So what do you think?"

"Of what?"

"Let's meet for lunch. I haven't seen you in a couple of months, anyway."

"Not much happens in Tarpley to write about."

"One more pig roasting and I swear I'll kill myself."

"What about the Top Ten Toys That Will Kill You For Back to School?"

"That's the kind of stuff junior editors write. Come on, lunch? You owe me a favor."

Natalie did. The article on Meredith had been a godsend in a dark time. Luis could use that kind of help. Natalie liked Erica's company. Her intelligence and wit and the scary cutthroat work she did. Natalie missed having that in her life.

"You're buying," Natalie said.

"I'm buying. But isn't it unethical? Last time we went Dutch."

Two months ago Natalie had looked at her savings, her medical bills, and her mortgage. The car insurance money was gone to bills as soon as her company cut the check. No more wine brunches with Erica Mendes.

"I don't care," she said.

Erica whistled. "This is going to be a good case."

Beau scribbled furiously on a piece of blank paper. He thought purple was a great color.

Natalie sat next to him at the kitchen table, Merritt in her lap. The sun was still high but she knew she should start dinner. She didn't want to move. Merritt squirmed against her.

"Hot dogs for dinner?" Merritt asked.

Natalie winced. "Don't say that."

Merritt grinned. He liked the face she made when he said it.

Beau glanced up from his grape artwork. "Can I have two?"

"Yes, but you know the rule."

"Wait five minutes between eating them. Mommy's rule. But she's not here."

"Mommy's rules are my rules." Natalie gave Merritt a squeeze.

He beamed.

"Guys," she said.

They loved to be called guys. Not boys, like everyone called them. Or kids, which was so much worse. They both turned to her.

"Are you excited about school?"

Merritt nodded.

Beau resumed coloring.

"Now, when you get there, guys, there are going to be little kids there. They're not going to know as much as you. They might not know their ABCs, or how to spell their name. You have to be patient with them, all right? No making fun of them."

Beau nodded solemnly.

Natalie kissed Merritt's hair. "And, there will be guys there who know more than you."

Merritt frowned.

"I know, right? But they will. You can't get jealous. Just see if they'll teach you, and if they won't, teach the other kids instead, okay? No use in getting angry."

"There are worse things," Beau said.

Natalie nodded.

Merritt grabbed a white sheet of paper from the stack and, after considering Natalie's face, chose a forest green crayon. He carefully spelled out, "Natalie."

"That's me. Perfect."

Soon, she'd fix hot dogs and Merritt would spend 20 minutes putting little red and yellow dots of ketchup and mustard along the bun and then complain his food was cold.

Beau would stuff half a hot dog into his mouth and then spend long minutes trying to chew it into submission. Natalie would get to witness the glory of his open mouth.

For now, she just got her own sheet of paper and chose Merritt's favorite color, red, and wrote "Merritt" in scrawl as large as his.

"We can tape them to the door," Merritt said.

Beau nodded.

"What color, Beau?"

He handed his purple crayon over.

Chapter Thirty-Four

Meredith rolled onto her side. She kept everything of value in bed with her. Her Bible lay at her elbow. By her hip were *The Black Stallion* and a *People* magazine.

Natalie's big idea was Meredith could read what the kids were reading. For two months, Meredith read Harry Potter with trepidation, waiting for the report her children were frightened, that they'd become occultists, that they would hate reading forever. Natalie brought her a picture of the boys in witch hats, and then confessed she bribed them to put them on for the camera. Magic, they could take or leave.

Her toiletries were in a bolted-to-the-floor locker on the other side of the room, under the sink. She could drown herself, or strategically slip and fall. But it wasn't that kind of place.

It was almost a nice place.

She had the room to herself, dormitory style. Convent style. She could go down the hall to the bathroom at night without asking permission. She had a radio. Not that Rocky Mount aired any decent radio stations. She strayed from sports to country to contemporary, but the music echoed shallowly in her and failed to move her.

Opening the Bible, she gazed again at the photographs. Her boys, posing for their yearly portrait at the mall, dressed for Easter, smiling in little suits. Her boys in the witch hats. A snapshot Natalie took in the car right before driving to the court house to drop her off for prison transport. Their last moments together. Natalie was grinning goofily. Meredith, behind her shoulder, was terrified.

For four months, Natalie brought the boys up every Saturday, and came up by herself every Wednesday. For the first month, Meredith would sit with Natalie at the picnic table outside, curled up in her arms, unmoving, not speaking, her eyes closed so she wouldn't see the guards. Natalie would always kiss her goodbye and the giddiness would last until Saturday.

The last night, the waiting, was always the hardest.

She carefully tucked the pictures back into the Bible pages. It hurt to see them. Her children marked the crease of Matthew 11. "John the Baptist, who was in prison..."

Guiltily, she closed the Book and put it beside her pillow. She picked up *The Black Stallion.*

Burdette stared disdainfully at Meredith's cereal. Meredith opened her milk carton without comment. Burdette had potato wedges and eggs on her plate and hard biscuits. Even the look of them made Meredith nauseous.

"That what your kids eat, Merry?" Burdette asked.

Every morning.

"I don't let them have the cereal. Just milk. They lap it like kittens."

Burdette's first smile of the day.

Meredith smiled back and began to eat her cereal.

Burdette stabbed a potato wedge with her plastic spork. It split into two. She scooped up a half. "Could use some ketchup."

Meredith glanced at the ketchup bottle two seats down. The rest of the table was empty. "Why don't we just sit there?"

Burdette stared at her as if she were crazy.

Meredith shrugged.

Burdette ate the other half and asked, her mouth full, "What's on the agenda for today?"

Meredith's morning would consist of lying in bed, staring at the ceiling, listening to the radio. The thought depressed her. Her afternoon was her shift at the infirmary. Then dinner, then staring at the ceiling.

Maybe she could call Natalie, but she felt weak, yearning to do that. If she felt weak, she should turn to the Lord, who was better suited. Natalie had so much on her plate. Meredith felt selfish for missing her.

Burdette waited patiently for her answer. She didn't have anything else to do.

"Better not to ask. You?"

Burdette slumped. "Group therapy. I hate that shit. Why aren't you going?"

"Infirmary shift."

Burdette scowled.

"Let me know what everyone says, okay?" Meredith asked, hoping to diffuse Burdette's jealousy, her anger at feeling so exposed, flayed open, day after day.

Burdette pushed at her food. The nausea set in. Meredith could see the greenish tint of her face. "I need a drink," Burdette said.

"Well, thank God you're here with me."

Burdette rolled her eyes and glanced away, at the other tables where sleepy women ate breakfast. But she stayed, patient and blank, as Meredith ate.

Meredith gazed at the ceiling and, for a lack of anything else to do, thought about Burdette. Burdette had no other friends. She was aggressive in group therapy, but the rest of the time she was passive. Limp. Unattentive. Meredith had no other friends either. People were happy to see her in the infirmary, but out on the grounds she kept to herself.

She wasn't a junkie like over half the women here. She hadn't been caught up in any crime with her boyfriend. She'd been willing, and she felt different, separate from them. She tried not to judge.

Burdette was, she reasoned, the most like her.

"What are you in for?" Burdette asked the first morning, in a calm, dead tone Meredith would eventually get used to.

"Voluntary manslaughter. Of my husband." She didn't know if she was supposed to lie, if she was supposed to claim to be a cop killer, or make sure no one thought of her as a molester. She didn't want to say shoplifting at Macy's. Not when it was Vincent's death.

Burdette nodded, dissected her breakfast burrito. "I shot my old man. While he was asleep."

Revulsion bubbled up in Meredith. She swallowed hard to keep it in her throat. And with it, shame. This was how people saw her.

Burdette saw her.

"I stabbed mine," she said.

"So we're murderers," Burdette said, and politely looked away while Meredith cried all over breakfast.

Burdette was an alcoholic, and absent alcohol in prison, she'd tried to take up smoking, but her hands shook too much and the smoke made her cough. So, a dry drunk, she waited. At her prison A.A. meetings, she regaled the potency of alcohol. Life was better on the other side, all else was mean-ingless.

Meredith attended a few meetings. She found them more painful than the regular group sessions. She couldn't really understand why Burdette felt nothing.

Mail call went out over the loudspeakers. Meredith rolled out of bed.

Meredith carried three envelopes on her tray as she settled in at lunch. Burdette carried no envelopes and eyed Meredith's with interest. Most people opened their mail at lunch, wanting camaraderie to protect them from the emotional turbulence of news. Dear John letters were common. As were pictures from kids and the occasional angry screed from a lover or a parent.

Meredith got a letter from her cousin Hank once a week and had received two cards from the hospital. The prison gave her stamps to write back. The depression would sink and she'd have half-formed thoughts on paper.

"Dear, Natalie, you're all I think about, and it terrifies me."

She knew Natalie was exercising similar caution. She saved her affection for when they were face to face, and let her letters be full of frivolity and business.

The children's letters, by contrast, nearly killed her.

"I'm afraid to open them," she told Burdette.

"Afraid one of the kids has lost a tooth?"

Meredith studied at her hands. Missing such an event would break her heart.

Burdette plucked the largest envelope, surely a square greeting card, from Meredith's pile. Then she glanced at Meredith.

Decorum mattered.

"Go ahead," Meredith said. She picked up her fork. The meatloaf stared up at her.

Burdette tore the envelope and pulled out a card with a puppy on it. "They never search your mail."

"I think they steam it."

Burdette snorted. She'd had a pen pal for a while, through the state program, but things got so racy she'd read the letters to the lunch crowds and the letters stopped coming. Burdette blamed the guards.

"Dear, Mommy," Burdette read. "So close to Merry. I can't believe that's your name. I would never let anyone call me Bernie."

Meredith tilted her head.

"Except my grandpa."

"Go on. You have responsibilities."

"Dear Merry. We went to grandma's yesterday."

Meredith pushed her plate away.

"The penmanship is astounding. And it's not even in crayon. Your girl-friend must have transcribed."

Not all of the children's letters came in childish scrawl. Natalie would work with them on important messages. Meredith imagined them at the kitchen table together. Her eyes stung.

The smell of meatloaf was becoming overpowering. She pushed her tray toward the empty seat beside her.

"We didn't want to leave. But Natalie made us. Can we live with grandma? She's nice. We're going to get school supplies soon. All together. Even Natalie."

Meredith covered her face with her hands.

"But not... Hollingsworth. He has to stay home." Burdette glanced up. "Hollingsworth? Really?"

As if the answer would change if she asked it enough times. As if there was some super secret, exotic story behind the cat's name only the privileged knew, and Meredith would someday let her in. Or slip up.

"It's Natalie's cat," Meredith said.

Satisfied with the standard response, Burdette read on. "Don't worry, I told Natalie it was better than nothing at our house, but I miss you. Prison sucks–You let your kid use 'sucks'?"

"Prison sucks."

Burdette glanced around the dining hall, shrugged, and finished read-ing. "Love, Beau Jameison. So formal, that kid."

"Natalie's a lawyer, remember?"

"Right. Anyway, the 'Love Beau Jameison' is in his handwriting." Bur-dette passed the letter back.

Meredith cradled it to her chest.

"Want me to read Merritt's? Maybe he's on Team Natalie."

Meredith shook her head. "Let me ride this one for a while. Otherwise I won't be able to eat."

"You and your feelings."

"I bet you're more fun when you're drunk."

Burdette smiled.

"Fuck you. Fuck you! Can't you see I'm in pain?"

The shouting echoed from the doctor's office into the main room of the infirmary, where Meredith was inventorying bandages, feeling useless. She couldn't see patient records, she couldn't inventory medications or syringes or haz-mat. She couldn't even order office supplies. She could only listen to the screaming, like clockwork, every Monday at 3:13 p.m.

Patricia strode into the main room after slamming Doctor Canard's door. She was trembling from head to toe, sweating, but she still caught herself up short when she saw Meredith.

"Sorry about the shouting."

"I know you're hurting."

"Canard says I'm not. How can he know? God, wouldn't I be a fucking model prisoner if I didn't feel this? All the goddamn time?"

"I know."

"Give me something, Merry."

"You know I don't have access."

"You have a key." Patricia glanced at the bolted door. Behind it, another bolted door, behind it, a combination safe. Inside the safe, nothing but adrenaline and insulin. The antipsychotics were in a different room.

Patricia wanted oxycontin.

"I don't have a key." Meredith held up her empty hands.

"Fuck."

"I'm a prisoner, just like you."

Patricia leaned against the counter holding Meredith's perfect line of gauze. Meredith met her gaze.

"I forget," Patricia said. "I mean, you don't look like a murderer. And I--I look like a junkie."

"Patricia--"

Patricia was serving three years for helping her boyfriend break into a CVS. The sentence was longer than Meredith's two year maximum, and she felt guilty.

Patricia pushed herself off the counter. "Remember, Merry... You help us... We'll share."

Meredith didn't say anything as Patricia left. Her bravado stolen by the knowledge there were more of them than her. Their need to dull the pain was so much stronger than her loyalty to an infirmary. No wonder Burdette was her only friend.

Canard pushed her to take a different job. He'd told her to study for her Physician's Assistant license. Natalie agreed with him. Playing secretary when she should be working on restoring her Registered Nurse license was a waste of her time. But this was all she knew how to do. The infirmary was the only place in the hospital where she felt normal. The library or the prison wash or the cafeteria would only remind her of where she was.

"I'm taking her down to three ibuprofen every six hours. Only twelve pills a day." Canard said as he came out of his office.

"Why?"

"It's not helping."

"What would help?"

"Eating right. Exercising. Get some sunlight. She needs to change the way her body does things."

"She'd say it hurts too much."

Canard nodded. "I've got eight more patients. Two drug-seekers, heart palpitations, cancer follow-up..." He studied his chart. "Can you take the splinter, the boil, and a preliminary on the rash? I think it's going to be bug bites, but see if it's something we'll need prednisone on."

"I'll need~"

He tossed her the key.

Meredith passed Burdette the letter from Merritt at dinner.

"I can't believe these people write you every day."

"I'm lucky," she said.

"Blessed."

Meredith shook her head. She began to eat. Merritt's letters, she could handle. Beef and rice stew, she could devour.

"Hi, Mom!" Burdette showed her the card. "The kid wrote this one. Orange magic marker."

"He likes orange," Meredith said.

Burdette flipped the card and read on. "I don't want to go to school. Beau does and I hate him. We're going shopping for school supplies but you're not here. It's unfair. Why can't you be here for school?"

Meredith sighed.

"I'd like to point out every word is spelled correctly. Your girlfriend is a control freak."

"Maybe my kids are perfect."

Burdette grinned and read, "'I can't take Holly'~Okay, that's cheating, '~Either. GOSH.' All caps."

"And he's the sweet one," Meredith said.

"It says, 'We're going to read *The Black Stallion*. I love you so much I wish you were here. Your letters are not the same. My letters are not the same!' There's like, six exclamation points. And he loves you. But not as formally as Beau. He just says, 'Love Merry.' Does he mean you or him?"

"That's our joke," Meredith said.

Burdette tucked the letter back in the envelope. "These things are the only good thing happening around here."

"That's not true."

Burdette frowned.

"It's stew day. Don't speak ill of stew day."

"Right." Burdette pushed around some rice.

"Do you think we should invite Robin to sit with us?"

"Do you think we should--" A dangerous spark appeared in Burdette's eyes, a reminder Meredith was among prisoners, she wasn't discussing the office luncheon or her neighbor's surprise party.

Robin Turner sat two tables away, by herself, staring at her stew with the same disinterest as Burdette. Burdette followed her gaze. "You just want her stew."

Meredith grinned.

She didn't say she wanted intelligent conversation. A change of pace. She'd trade her *People* for a good talk or a newspaper. She knew she wasn't as smart as Natalie. Nursing school had been a struggle, had been concentration and study and memorization. Repeat, repeat, repeat.

But for the chance not to have the same conversation tomorrow she'd had today, she'd learn particle physics.

"She doesn't want her stew."

"She doesn't want any part of this. Fucking white collar bitch," Burdette said.

Robin Turner was the only woman at Conrad Correctional convicted of fraud. Passing bad checks was common, and Meredith heard stories of women convicted of insurance schemes. But a true financial theft was so rare everyone called Robin "Martha Stewart," and stayed away.

Even a murderer was better company.

"What do you think she'll do when her time's up?" Meredith asked.

"She'll write a book."

"Probably."

Burdette pushed her plate toward Meredith. "Eat this and stop looking so pathetic."

"Come to the chapel with me later?"

Burdette shook her head. "*Jeopardy!* is on. *Jeopardy!* is on every day, Merrybelle. When are you going to stop asking?"

"When I leave."

Siba was in the chapel when Meredith arrived, eyes closed, forehead to prayer mat. The chapel was in a separate building from the dormitory Meredith lived in~but not quite a church. Still storage and administration. She was sure the armory was nearby. But the chapel was bigger than the hospital's. There was a prayer room for Muslims down the hall, and a meditation room, but Siba was claustrophobic. She preferred space to face Mecca.

She didn't mind Meredith. Most people went to the chapel for morning or afternoon services and it closed at eight, just as *Jeopardy!* ended. Meredith liked the quiet.

She slipped into a pew and sat.

And waited.

Despite the posters of Jesus on the wall, despite the polished wood altar and cross, donated by the local Presbyterians, Meredith didn't feel His presence.

She didn't feel anything.

Siba got up and nodded in her direction without making eye contact, and left.

Meredith took a deep breath.

She didn't bring her own Bible here, but there was one in front of her, tucked into the pew. She could open it up, seek comfort, read at random, or distract herself with stories or metaphors. But she knew the words already.

"Where has your beloved gone, most beautiful of women? Which way did your beloved turn?"

There was no comfort in the words. Only in the way she used to be able to close her eyes and feel His arms around her. His love would pour into her and she would gather her strength and pour it back out onto her children.

He wasn't here.

Meredith shut her door, wishing she could lock it. Burdette might come in, ranting about nightmares. Or the guards might come in to search her stuff for drugs. Or searching for something worth more than what they had.

Most nights were uninterrupted, but she never slept deeply. Lying in bed, fresh from her shower, in her last clean prison jumpsuit, she pulled out the envelope from Natalie.

"I'm sorry~" it started. Meredith hated when Natalie opened with apologies. Lately every letter came like with self-recrimination. Her chest hurt. Her fingers shook as she held the sheet of elegant stationary~Natalie's, from her home in Charlotte.

"~I didn't want to censor the boys. I don't want them to not tell us things. Beau's okay. Really. By tomorrow he'll have forgotten. We all miss you and are counting the days."

Meredith glanced at the calendar. She marked Xs for each day's passing. Four months of Xs. But her release date was fluid. They could deny her release. They could judge her a menace.

Nevermind she had a job and a family waiting on the outside.

"Don't give up, Merry. Wednesdays are the best days of my life."

Meredith grinned.

"Is spending time with your in-laws like being in prison? Probably not. But if you want to switch places for a week, I'm willing. New pictures as soon as the kids buy their backpacks and lunch boxes. How do you feel about *Terminator* school supplies?"

Heat rose in Meredith's cheeks.

The letter was signed, "All my love." No name. Meredith read the letter again. Then she folded it up and stuck it in her Bible and turned out the lights.

In the dark she could pretend she was just home alone. Except for the smell.

She closed her eyes.

Tomorrow would be exactly the same.

Chapter Thirty-Five

Unless Natalie hit traffic in Goldsboro, the drive to Rocky Mount took two hours. In two hours, she could be in Raleigh, arguing a state petition for a commuted sentence. In one hour, she could be at the beach, remembering the best time of her life.

But the prison was in Rocky Mount and she burned a full tank of gas going there and back each Wednesday. Thirty precious dollars. Hitting the highway with her station wagon made her long for her BMW.

The prison reminded her of army barracks, all stately brick buildings and cultivated lawns surrounded by a fence she fantasized she could climb. She parked under an elm and locked her purse in the trunk and carried in her ID, keys, quarters, 5x7 photographs, two drawings of Hollingsworth and the backyard, and twenty dollars in ones.

At the prison gate, she handed over everything and let herself be patted down.

"Good to see you, Ms. Ivans," the guard said.

"Ida."

She locked everything but the pictures and the cash in a locker, got a three minute lecture on rules and regulations, and then was led into the prison courtyard.

Meredith was waiting for her.

Natalie broke into a smile and Meredith stepped toward her. Natalie glanced at the guard, who nodded, and then she took Meredith into her arms and held her close. Meredith was warm and strong and gripped her tightly, smelling of cherries and soap, her hair clean, her elbows bony.

They couldn't kiss. Kissing was banned. They stole one for goodbye, each time. Natalie knew the routine by now. But if she buried her face in Meredith's hair, maybe she could—

Meredith laughed and held her even tighter.

"Hi," Natalie said.

"Hey," Meredith said, rocking her back and forth, until the guard coughed.

Meredith stepped back. Natalie took her hand.

"She times us. We get thirty seconds," Meredith said.

"I wish you hadn't told me."

"Will you be counting next time?"

Natalie nodded.

"You wouldn't believe the things I count. Steps. Bites. Bars."

Natalie squeezed her hand.

They sat at the picnic table. Meredith's straw-colored hair captivated Natalie's attention. She wanted to run her fingers through it. Their short time together before Meredith had to go away had been sweet and passionate. Natalie craved her. Being so close tempted her.

Meredith tilted her head toward Natalie, smiling. She smiled so much when they were together.

Meredith slid her hand over Natalie's knee. "Pictures. Give me the pictures."

"These pictures?" Natalie held them up.

"Those." Meredith didn't reach for them. She was too dignified.

Natalie used both hands, leaving her leg unguarded for Meredith's wandering hand. She flipped over the first picture. Merritt, leaning over his spotted hot dog creation, mugging at the camera.

Meredith giggled. "You let them eat that?"

"Turkey dogs."

"Do they know?"

"Nope."

"Natalie."

"What?" Natalie leaned into her shoulder. "Are you going to tell me not to lie to the children?"

"Use your best judgment."

Natalie grinned and turned over another picture.

Meredith snatched at it. Natalie lifted her hand.

"Natalie," Meredith said warningly.

"Hm?"

Meredith settled her hand onto Natalie's stomach, sending heat through her shirt, streaking up her chest. Streaking down.

The guard coughed.

Natalie handed over the picture. "I let the kids take it. They were jealous of the camera."

"They knew you were coming to see me."

Natalie nodded.

"And they knew what I wanted. Good boys."

"Whatever."

Meredith bumped shoulders with Natalie, studying the picture. Natalie, sprawled on the couch, beaming with Hollingsworth in her lap.

"You look so relaxed," Meredith said.

"For the picture."

Meredith glanced up.

"And because the boys were happy."

Meredith chuckled.

"And because I'd get to see your face when you saw it. I tried extra hard."

Meredith met her gaze. They didn't dare move. The guard was watching, and probably inmates, too, from the windows. Cars were passing by on the road outside. Nothing was private. Nothing was theirs.

Natalie swallowed. "There's more."

"I don't need anything more."

"Okay." Natalie lowered the last picture.

"Well, if you brought it all the way here."

Natalie raised her eyebrows.

Meredith tilted her head.

"Fine." Natalie offered the picture. The boys standing on their heads against the living room wall, and Natalie between them, sitting like a Buddha.

"Let me guess...Jake took this."

Natalie shook her head, grinning.

"Hank?"

"Yeah."

Meredith turned the picture upside down and laughed. "Look at you all."

Natalie checked her watch. They'd used up nearly a third of their time.

"What is it?" Meredith asked.

"I got a case."

"Good!"

"It's bad. It's a bad case, Merry."

When Meredith wrapped her arms around Natalie, neither Natalie nor the guard begrudged her, and Natalie told her about the scene out on I-40 two nights ago, and how Luis Duarte was uncooperative, and how River

Landing was devastated.

"You have to do it," Meredith said.

"I know."

Meredith kissed Natalie's shoulder.

"The money~" Natalie started.

"Not for the money."

Natalie exhaled.

"Defense of the indefensible."

"His father just wants his son, like, what? Whole? Safe? I don't know."

Meredith straightened, thumbing through her pictures.

"I'm sure your friends wanted you to just stay around. Hank and Theresa. They didn't want change."

Meredith nodded. "Change comes brutally. What I don't get is all these people in here. Some who altered lives, like I did. Some who had their lives altered for them, by getting arrested, or sent away. And they don't see it."

"They want to go back."

"Even if before was awful."

"But not you?"

"I have something completely different to go back for."

"Kind of. But your home, your boys, your job... those things haven't changed." Natalie hesitated.

"It's okay."

"Maybe there was an aberration, and that was the change, and now it's back to~" She couldn't quite say 'normal.' "~What it was before."

"So I'm just like them."

Natalie patted her back. "Just like them."

Meredith leaned back, gazing at the sky, and then turning to see at Natalie's smile. "You're cheerful for someone who has to say goodbye in five minutes."

"That's when~" Natalie lowered her voice. "I get to kiss you."

"And flirting, too?"

"I can't help it. I'm giddy. This is my favorite place in the world."

"Prison."

"You're here. It's a beautiful day. Warm." Natalie inhaled. "I think... God is here. Isn't He? I come here and there's so much more light. I think this is where He hangs out. Prisons. And with you."

Meredith glanced away.

"Here." Natalie dug in her pockets for the twenty dollars. "For snacks."

"Snacks," Meredith said.

"You should eat more."

Meredith didn't accept the money. "You should eat better."

"How do you know the ministry isn't giving me organic vegetables and grass-raised beef and brown rice?"

"You've got a pimple right here." Meredith touched her cheek.

Natalie snorted.

"And you shouldn't drive four hours to see me for such a short time," Meredith said.

"Oh, stop."

Meredith chuckled.

"Our thirty minutes are almost up."

"Yeah."

"Thirty seconds, thirty minutes... is she always like that?" Natalie nodded to the guard.

"Yes. We call her Treinta."

Natalie glanced at the guard and then kissed Meredith, a quick, stolen press of lips to make her heart flutter and her palms sweat and everything right with the world.

"I will do anything," she said as they separated, "to do that once a week."

"How about twice?" Meredith kissed her, curling her arm around Natalie's neck to pull her close.

Howls erupted from the walls.

The guard's hand landed on Natalie's shoulder. "I'm gonna toss you out on your ear, Ivans."

Natalie grinned and got up. "See you Saturday."

"I'll be counting the days."

Natalie followed Ida into the prison offices, temporarily blinded after the sunlight. Ida went to the file cabinet. "Got your mail, Ms. Ivans."

"Great."

"You really do case work for all these people?"

"I see what's there. Sometimes it's just drafting a letter or whatever. But I know all of these women have their own lawyers. Why me?"

"Because you're not another lawyer. You're family."

Natalie smiled.

Ida handed her a packet of letters.

"How's Merry doing?"

Ida pursed her lips.

"Ms. Johon."

"Still the same, Ivans. She doesn't talk to anyone, doesn't leave her room much. Really eats only on stew day. People like her but she doesn't really have any friends, you know? They know her from therapy, where she's compassionate, or from the infirmary, where she takes care of them. But it's not like, a friend."

Natalie nodded.

"I couldn't help overhearing..."

"Of course." Natalie leaned against the doorway.

"That stuff about light. Meredith doesn't to go to the chapel services here. You know, ministers come from all over. Even got a Buddhist guy once a week, and these other freaks from Raleigh who—anyway. Meredith avoids them like the plague."

Natalie frowned.

"She goes to the chapel every night to sit, though. I guess to pray. It's her routine. While Siba's all up in there praying to Mohammed or whatever, planning to bomb us all."

Natalie raised her eyebrows.

"They don't talk either. Siba's worse off than Merry. But still, on Saturday, you should encourage her to play Monopoly with the girls. Watch *Project Runway*. Something."

"I'll bring it up. Thanks, Ms. Johon."

"Enjoy your letters from the wrongly incarcerated."

"Injustice is everywhere."

Ida led her out, where she got her keys and her ID, and she felt a pang as she left the prison. Now a chain-link fence separated her from Meredith. She wanted to throw herself against it, make Meredith clutch her fingers through the holes. But instead she got into her car. Ten minutes away, she'd sit in a nice restaurant with a nice woman and talk about the outside world as if Conrad didn't even exist.

She couldn't shake the feeling her whole life was there in the little courtyard, and the rest was just some gray mist she wandered through until she could get back inside the garden again. She'd mention this in the letter she wrote Meredith tonight. No matter how wistful it sounded. No matter it made them both hurt just a little more.

"The eggplant is divine," Erica said, tapping the menu in front of Natalie.

"I haven't eaten eggplant in ages."

"And never like this."

Natalie glanced around the Italian place around the corner from the *Rocky Mount Telegram* offices. "Is everyone in here a reporter?"

"The water and sewer offices are across the street. They're in here too. But yeah."

"Afraid you're going to get scooped?"

"About as much as they are. So, Natalie Ivans, what brings you to Rocky Mount?"

"Wednesday mornings I drive up to Conrad Correctional Facility to visit Meredith Jameison."

"Ah." Erica hissed through pursed lips. "How does that go?"

"Wonderful."

"I see."

"But if you're going to quote me, you should go with something neutral like 'adequate.'"

"Adequate. Conjugal?"

Natalie blushed. "Of course not."

"Every baby reporter on the beat does a Conrad story. But I haven't been there in years."

"It's all right. For a prison."

"And you don't think Ms. Jameison should be locked up?"

"I think she did what she had to do, and we'd hope our loved ones~our sisters, our mothers~would do the same thing."

Erica nodded. "But we're not here to talk about Meredith."

Natalie sighed.

The waiter came and she ordered the eggplant and the mozzarella and tomato salad and declined wine, though Erica ordered the house red.

"Really, have some," Erica said.

"I have to drive."

Erica shook her head. "One glass. We used to have wine. Have you ever drunk wine except with me?"

"A while ago. But still because of you, actually."

Erica pursed her lips charmingly. Then frowned and straightened. "When I told you about Meredith."

"Yes. Wine, it goes so good with confession, doesn't it?"

"I'm sorry, Nat."

Natalie shook her head. "Don't be. It's probably the kindest way I could learn the truth."

"But still, as your friend, let me tell you. This chaste, pure living is not the way to God. Good deeds matter. Whether or not you dance, or drink, or cut your hair not so much."

"You can tell them, Erica. The world. Or the good people of Rocky Mount, Raleigh, and Wilmington. I'm only taking this case for the money."

"Don't be so cynical. Tell me about Luis Duarte."

"He's a fucking shit heal drunken asshole and~" She paused for breath.

"If he died instead of those girls, we wouldn't be here? Couple of white college girls from the right side of town kill the Mexican with the criminal record? They wouldn't have even been charged."

"Hoyle would take his easy money for the plea." Natalie couldn't think about it without her chest constricting. Luis had a father who loved him. He was a human being. She'd gazed into his eyes, made jokes with him, felt his curses, his breath, on her. She closed her eyes.

Erica waited, as wine came, as salad came.

Natalie speared a mozzarella slice, but couldn't bring herself to eat it until she said, "Victim advocacy and advocacy for the accused are not so different. We'd like to believe evil exists, but..."

Erica leaned forward.

"What does the police report say?" Erica asked when their plates were clean.

"They've only released the preliminaries. They're working out models, or somesuch."

"Trying to find a loophole for the boss's kid."

Natalie raised her eyebrows. "Trying to be thorough."

"Mm." Erica took a sip of wine. She was on her second glass.

"Anyway, I brought you a photocopy."

Erica took it. "Redacted up the ass."

"But signed by Deputy Fasan."

Erica sighed but scanned the paper. Natalie waited, letting her draw her own conclusions. They both knew how to read primary evidence.

"Ninty miles an hour?"

"The cop's son had a black box in his car, of course."

"And it was a nice car. Nicer than mine."

"And mine. But I'm not a young man."

Erica nodded. "And he was drunk?"

"Are we getting dessert?"

"Want to split a tiramisu?" Erica leaned forward, elbow on the table.

"Sure. Means..." Natalie pulled the blood test sheet out of her briefcase. "Station alcohol level test, and breathalyzer."

"0.10? Barely above the legal limit."

"Cops will testify he was disoriented at the scene."

"But he'd just killed two people. He was probably freaked out."

"This was his fifth DUI."

Erica nodded. "I'm having those records sent to me. But still. You'd want stronger evidence."

"He was going ninety miles an hour. Whose side are you on when you write this?"

"The side of the truth, Natalie."

Natalie nodded. "I'm on his side."

"He's lucky to have you."

Natalie shook her head.

The waitress came back. Erica ordered tiramisu and two forks. The waitress gave them an odd look.

"Surely people share dessert here like, every single day," Natalie said.

"Never people so attractive." Erica grinned.

Natalie pointed at her.

"Having a good day, Nat? Got to see your girlfriend, got a new case, get to have the best lunch in town."

"And I get to go home to my sweet boys."

"I'm envious."

"You'll find a special, uh, someone."

"I think we all know who I'll find."

"Hey, Erica, you ever wanted to be on the TV news instead?"

"Heck, no. I want to write. Words are immortal."

Natalie raised her eyebrows.

"These looks are not," Erica said.

"I hope when you're in your 80s you'll be the next Liz Smith."

"Me too, Nat. Me too. Especially if it's all the way in New York City."

The tiramisu came and they were quiet as they ate. Their forks clanged in the middle, chasing the last bite.

"You. You're paying."

"I should have ordered two. Or three. Remind me next time."

Natalie nodded.

Erica paid the check with her credit card, but then held out two folded twenty-dollar bills to Natalie.

"I don't--"

"Promise me," Erica said, cutting her off. "You'll only spend this on a manicure."

Natalie glanced at her nails.

"A real manicure given by real Vietnamese girls. Not at Walmart."

"I promise."

"Not on gas," Erica said.

"Not on gas."

Erica narrowed her gaze.

"There's a charity for family of the incarcerated sending me gas cards."

"Oh, really?"

"And stamps."

Erica grinned.

"Not so much gas, but lots of stamps."

"Well, look at it this way. Five or six more felony death by motor vehicle cases and you can buy your own stamps."

"And pedicures. You have no idea."

"I don't want to have any idea," Erica said.

Natalie nodded.

"As much as I like you."

"Let's talk about something else. You know," Natalie held up the two bills. "If you really cared, you'd send me a subscription to your paper. I even cancelled the local one."

Erica pulled out her iPhone. "I'm going to make a note."

Natalie nodded.

"What's your address?"

Natalie got out her business card and laid it on the table.

"Right. I have one of those somewhere. Probably on my fridge where it can be especially useless. Let's order coffee."

"Let's talk about something besides crime," Natalie said.

"Okay. The paper's been all aflutter about the 24th district race for State Senate."

Natalie was glad caffeine was coming.

Erica gestured. "Though, I guess that's still technically a crime, at least in my book."

Chapter Thirty-Six

Natalie would never clean if it weren't for the Thursday night babysitters. Daniel and Jake came over to take care of the boys and give her a little time to herself. Often they took the boys to the movies, to the park, for ice cream. Whatever there was to do in Tarpley. Beau loved the soda shoppe. A devoted little extrovert, he'd watch the other kids with glee and beg Jake to let him play KC and the Sunshine Band on the jukebox while Merrit shyly tried to strike up adult conversations with Daniel about childish things.

Thursday afternoons, therefore, were devoted to cleaning. Beau soft-scrubbed the upstairs bathroom—bathtub, toilet rim and outside, and counters. Merritt did the downstairs bathroom, no tub, so he also scrubbed the kitchen counters, standing on a chair, carefully moving it from place to place.

Natalie knew Meredith would wring her neck once she found out.

She took care of picking up and vacuuming. Laundry, they left until Saturday mornings.

"All done," Beau said.

Natalie went into the bathroom, which smelled mildly of cleanser and glistened white. "It's beautiful in here, Beau."

Beau nodded. She squirted toilet bowl cleaner then handed the bottle to Beau. "Take this to your brother."

He scurried out.

The soaking gave her just enough time to clean the counter.

The toilet flushed downstairs. She rolled her eyes. Playing with the toilet was why she didn't let them scrub the bowl unsupervised.

"Guys," she yelled.

Giggling echoed.

She finished the counter and then the toilet and went downstairs. In the hallway outside the guest bathroom, Merritt clutched Beau in a headlock.

"Natalie, help," Beau said.

"He messed. Up. My. Cleaning!"

Beau squirmed.

Merritt punched his head.

"Stop it!" Beau shouted.

"It's not fair," Merritt said.

"Unhand him."

They both cringed away from Natalie.

She clawed her left hand together. Merritt slowly released Beau. He didn't want the claw, where Natalie would lift him up by his shirt collar, like a lioness carrying her young. She thought it was adorable, but it made him feel powerless.

"He hurt me." Beau said.

"Beau, in the kitchen. I've got a surprise for you."

Beau slithered down the hall.

Natalie knelt next to Merritt, who was still red with rage, and whispered in his ear. "If you clean up your brother's mess this time, I'll make sure he doesn't get to clean either bathroom next week. He's lost his privileges."

Merritt nodded.

She pushed him at the bathroom and then went into the kitchen.

Beau stared at her. "I don't see a surprise. Are we going to the soda shoppe tonight?"

"No. Game night."

"I hate game night." Beau flushed nearly purple.

Natalie opened the junk drawer and pulled out a brush. "The surprise is, I need you to do the most important job. You get to brush Hollingsworth."

Beau lit up.

"If you can find him."

Beau snatched the brush and ran upstairs.

Natalie sighed. Anything to burn off their energy. She glanced into the family room.

"We have a social worker, guys," she said. "I don't want us to get accused of hoarding. And half-eaten candy attracts bugs. And rats."

Every Thursday they cleaned. Every Friday the house looked like this again. She fought the temptation to throw herself onto the couch and watch Oprah. Instead, she turned on the radio. Meredith's favorite Christian Talk station began to play. Natalie missed Meredith more and less at the same time. She braced herself, wondering if she'd get a missionary morality tale or an hour long sermon on one line in the Bible. At this rate, she'd never be able to learn all the lines. But it was a parenting call-in show.

She gazed at the ceiling. "Very funny."

A soothing, family doctor voice followed her into the kitchen, where she pulled stationary from the stack and sat down.

"Dear, Merry," she wrote. "Today I have bribed and lied to your children. Hope it's all right..."

"Best two out of three," Jake said, watching as Daniel slammed his game piece into the rainbow square.

"How many games will it take to convince you I'm the Candy Land champion?" Daniel asked.

"It's a game of chance. And if the kids aren't playing, do we have to?"

Jake glanced over his shoulder to where Beau, Merritt, and Suriya were intensely discussing Hollingsworth, who lay within their triangle, being petted.

"Good point," Daniel said.

Jake nodded. "Let's do something adult."

"Here?" I think my house is going to be lacking," Natalie said.

"Wine?"

Jake pushed Daniel's arm. "Why does adult have to mean drinking? Should we smoke and watch porn and eat junk food, too?"

Daniel smirked.

"Thank you again for the beautiful barbecue," Natalie said to Daniel.

"Pshaw. Just crock pot magic."

"Do you have a crock pot, Natalie?" Jake asked.

"I think so. This is North Carolina, right?"

"Well, if you don't find it, we're leaving ours here."

"It has a programmable timer," Daniel said with glee.

"Fabulous."

"Have you been following the 10th district race, Nat?" Daniel asked.

Jake groaned and put his head in his hands.

"I have."

Being unemployed meant she could read the paper's website each morning, over cheap instant coffee. Or, on Sundays, the Coffee of the Month Patrick had given her. Either way, she knew more than she wanted about the three morons running for the 10th district against the incumbent; who she was voting for because everything seemed fine.

"Democratic leadership has been sucking North Carolina dry. That's why our Hispanic population has quintupled in the last twenty years."

Jake closed his eyes.

"We're the perfect welfare state. Overqualified people are getting food stamps like they're handouts~"

"Food stamps are a federal program," Natalie said.

"~And they're still using them to buy booze."

Natalie glanced at the children.

"Daniel, please."

"We need to do something before we're all equal with the wealth distribution. All of us, living out of our car."

Suriya began to scream.

All three adults turned, but Merritt and Beau were nowhere near her, and seemed horrified. Hollingsworth darted into the kitchen.

"Oh, just her 'I need to be changed' sound. Charming, isn't it? Two years of sign language and baby chatter."

"I'll~" Jake started.

"No, I will." Daniel went and scooped Suriya up with one arm, grabbed the diaper bag, and pounded upstairs.

Beau and Merritt glanced at Natalie.

"Okay, yes. You can turn the T.V. on. Mute, okay? Only subtitles."

Jake frowned at Natalie.

"They watch *Law & Order* on TNT that way. It's a little scarring, but I think it's helping their reading."

Jake shook his head. "I'm sorry about Daniel. We're having some problems."

Natalie put her hand on Jake's. "Serious?"

"Republicans are okay in good times. Even cute. But now the economy's tanked~Daniel's bank has had the feds going through the papers for a month. They might seize it. Daniel doesn't like the feds much. And now they're talking about raising taxes on the places we might not be able to afford anymore. Daniel's investments have not done well, Nat. We might sell the beach house. At a loss."

"Oh, Jake."

"We're doing okay. I mean." He gestured at her living room. "But my income is the steadiest right now, and it just pisses off Daniel more. He thinks I'm driving up health care costs. All on my own. Exploiting one of the only avenues for revenue. Like I even know what it means. Every discussion is a fight about the state of the universe these days."

She rubbed his fingers.

Daniel came back and found them morose at the kitchen table. "Being an adult is fun."

Natalie got up. "The boys baked cookies for dessert. We'll have some milk and turn on the sound, okay?"

"Bread and circuses," Daniel said, and gazed at the television.

The cell phone's third ring pierced Natalie's dream. Meredith disappeared. Natalie groaned. She answered on the fifth, unsure if her mouth would work.

"Ivans."

"Natalie Ivans?"

"Mm."

"I'm calling from Tarpley City Jail, ma'am. This is a courtesy call to let you know Luis Duarte has been placed on a 24 hour suicide watch."

"I'll be right there."

"You don't have to~"

"Put me in the visitor's log." Natalie hung up the phone.

Chapter Thirty-Seven

Natalie walked with Fasan to the infirmary, hesitating when Sheriff Duarte' voice boomed from the exam room.

"What the hell were you thinking?"

The response was inaudible. Natalie took another step forward. Fasan put his hand on her arm. She frowned.

"We have the labs, Luis. You weren't incapacitated. You were just stupid. You cared more about driving your car fast and listening to your music than you did anything else, even your surroundings? Was the speed worth it? Was it another rush? How could you be so callous? You're worthless."

Silence.

Natalie crept forward. Fasan followed.

"Don't you have anything to say for yourself?"

The silence continued.

"Well, you'd better think of something. Or you're going to be in prison for a very long time." Duarte stormed out, his eyes widening as he saw Natalie and Fasan. He moved past them without comment.

"You've been briefed?" Fasan asked.

She nodded.

"Need me to stay?"

Natalie shook her head.

"I'm going to leave the door cracked, so speak quietly. He's tied up. He won't be hurting you."

"Thank you, Deputy."

He nodded, glanced at the doorway, and then waved her inside.

"Hey, get me out of here. This is ridiculous."

Luis yanked at his wrist restraints. He was on his back in a bed, though it was tilted up so he was almost sitting.

Natalie didn't say anything, just came and sat down in the chair by the bed. The seat was warm. The sheriff must have sat, too.

"I didn't try to kill myself." The right side of his face was bruised.

"What did you do?"

Luis glanced away, his face hard.

Natalie leaned back. The only other thing on her agenda today was a manicure.

"I was crying. And I... I guess I was banging my head on the wall."

"Hence the bruises?"

"And the blood. It wasn't like~There wasn't enough~I wanted~"

Natalie kept silent. The sheriff stole all her complaints from her. Hearing them from his mouth showed how ineffective they sounded. The boy had been shamed and cajoled his whole life. She wouldn't be able to get through if his father couldn't. Robbed of a game plan, she just listened.

"I didn't want to kill myself," he said.

"Well, you succeeded."

Luis rolled his head back, gazing at the ceiling. Natalie studied his face. The bruises. Red marked his wrists where he pulled against the restraints. His orange jumpsuit. He'd been denied bail but his hearing for pre-trial detention wasn't for another week. The holding cells weren't going to be enough. Maybe another city jail would take him.

"I'm so angry all the time," Luis said.

"At who?"

"At me, who do you think? And at my father. At those girls. At my friends, who wouldn't let me crash on their couch because they wanted to have sex. At my car, which~You know how many DUIs I have?"

"Five, counting this one."

Luis snorted. "Right. You're the lawyer. Every time I got one, I thought, it's just the Man, my dad, you know. Gotta set an example. Gotta hold me to a higher standard while turds who blow .16s go free. I wasn't doing anything worse than anyone else. I wasn't~"

She leaned forward, not touching him, but was gratified when he turned to meet her gaze.

"Why couldn't he go after real criminals? I wasn't a killer."

She nodded.

"I'm not a killer."

"I know," she said.

"Can you make him stop visiting me? Make him stop pissing me off."

"I will."

"Really?"

"I can do anything you want, Luis," she said, reaching for his hand. "Except free you."

He nodded.

She squeezed his fingers. "Can I have the doc give you something? Calm you down?"

He shook his head. "You can't."

"Why not?"

He gripped her hand. "I'm a junkie."

"Luis."

"I'm twenty-four. Don't tell me I'm just a kid."

She glanced away. At twenty-four, Meredith was married with two children. Vincent had gone to war. She'd graduated from law school.

"I won't tell you, Luis. Your life is already over."

He nodded.

"We'll just see what you do with the rest of it, okay?"

"Yeah."

She got up. "I'll go talk to your father."

"Hey," he asked, when she was at the door.

"Yeah?"

"I've been asking around. Are you really a lesbian?"

She hesitated. She would always hesitate for that question. Her whole life she would wonder if protecting herself was better. If it was really true at all. If the person asking would hit her, or shun her, or confess secrets, too.

"Yes," she said.

"I've never met a lesbian before. Well, like. People at the supermarket, sure. But I've never known one."

"Here I am."

He nodded.

"Nobody is going to tell me who I can and cannot speak to," Eduardo said.

"Sheriff~"

"My own son doesn't want to see me? Maybe if he wasn't such a screwup I wouldn't have to be on his case all the time. If I could leave him alone without him~"

"Sheriff?"

He slumped into his chair and frowned. "Ms. Ivans, what you're asking for is idiotic."

She said nothing.

"He's in jail here. I work here. I see him all the time."

"I've just filed the paperwork to get him transferred to Burgaw."

"You what?"

"They've got a better facility, and~"

"I will not see my son in prison!"

"I know what you're going through," she said.

He closed his fist, but nodded, meeting her eyes.

"You can't see him," she said.

"Why not?"

"You make him feel bad."

"He should feel bad."

"He should, and he does. But it has to be his feeling, not yours."

Eduardo gazed at the ceiling. His shoulders slumped.

"You saw his head," she said.

"I did. The moron."

"And you put your trust in me. Let me take care of him. I know the system."

"I know the system, too. I want to see him."

"Because you love him."

He nodded. "I do."

"Please. I'm making an official request."

"I'll respect your request, Ms. Ivans."

"Thank you." She got up. "I was thinking I'd take him to church on Sunday, if you don't mind. And if he's off his hold."

"He stopped going to church when he was ten. He bit his mother."

Natalie nodded.

"I don't want him out there where they could hurt him."

"I promise. It's not that kind of church." She picked up her briefcase and went to the office door.

Eduardo nodded, but he seemed lost in thought.

Outside, Fasan tapped her arm. "We're done with the accident scene analysis."

"You are?"

"Even the fire department's secondary evaluation and the Charlotte PD's scene reconstruction people had a look. Just to be sure. And three different insurance companies."

"Do they have good detectives, too?"

He rolled his eyes. "I made copies for you. Can I take you to lunch and talk them over?"

"You're buying."

He stopped short. "You're the attorney, Ms. Ivans."

"I'm a public defender, remember?"

He sighed. "All right."

"You can even take me somewhere halal."

He laughed. "I wish. What about Dosa? They've got a vegetarian lunch buffet."

"All right. You know, even with the hospital, they're the only Indian restaurant in town."

"There's only a couple of Indian doctors on staff. Not enough to sustain more than one restaurant, or something. I know the owner's brother is a surgeon. They totally got lost on the way to Cary."

She grinned, but he seemed lost in thought. "They get vandalized sometimes, and bring us free food when we catch the nutjobs."

"Why?"

Fasan shrugged. "Some people around here think they're Muslim."

"Despite the elephant in the window? Not that it matters."

Fasan nodded. "Not that it matters."

Chapter Thirty-Eight

Natalie pulled into Conrad's parking lot Saturday morning with a splitting headache. The kids had screamed for the entire last hour. If they were going anywhere but Rocky Mount, she'd have turned around and driven home. But they knew it. She'd tried separating them, putting Beau in the front seat and Merritt in the back.

Merritt kicked Beau's chair for ten minutes before Beau tried to climb into the backseat and she nearly veered off the road. She'd let them run around in a field until she was afraid they'd be late. At the exit for Conrad, the screaming contest began. She was supposed to be judging. Merritt's shrill shriek was more potent than Beau's bellow.

"I'm hungry," Merritt said.

"There's a peanut butter sandwich right next to you."

"I want MacDonalds."

I want Meredith not to be in prison. I want you to shut up. I want to go as far away as possible.

Natalie turned around and peered into the back seat. "You have two choices."

The voice on the parenting radio said always give them two choices. Empower them. But no more than two. Rookie mistake.

Beau and Merritt sat quietly in the backseat, trying to kill her with their hateful gazes.

"We can sit here, and have peanut butter sandwiches, and play cards, maybe listen to the radio. Or we can go inside and see your mom. But remember, when we go inside, they'll frisk you. And you'll have to be on your best behavior. Now, I want to see mommy more than anything else in the world, but I love you guys and I want to hang out with you, too."

Beau leaned sideways to gaze at the fence. The first month, Meredith would wait on the picnic table for them. But then the boys got too excited and would fight their way through security. So Beau was just imagining her there on the table.

"I hate it here. Why do we have to see her here?" Merritt asked.

Natalie closed her eyes.

"Mommy did something bad, so they locked her in jail. Remember, dummy?" Beau said.

"Don't call–" Natalie started, opening her eyes.

"I don't remember," Merritt said.

"Mommy made daddy go away, so she went away. It's an eye for an eye."

Natalie glanced at Beau. She didn't want to see Merritt. If he said he didn't remember again, her heart would break.

Merritt opened the sandwich bag and stuffed a quarter of the sandwich into his mouth.

Natalie opened her door. "Bring that with you. Beau?"

Beau lifted his present.

Natalie checked her pockets. Keys, ID, cash.

She took a boy's hand in each of hers and they walked inside the prison. She availed herself of a locker, putting Merritt's half-eaten sandwich inside. He'd want it later. Beau cried when the guard opened his package, delicately lifting off the lid to reveal the travel shampoo and body wash. Then he laughed when Joanne smelled them.

Then Joanne checked the clock, tsked, and ushered them into the visitor's room.

Two other families were already at tables, each in corners, seeking as much privacy as possible. Meredity sat at a table, alone.

"Mommy!" The boys ran for her as she knelt, taking them in her arms.

Natalie walked over more slowly.

Meredith kissed Beau, and then Merritt, and then straightened. "Hi."

"Hi." Natalie extended her hands and Meredith took them.

Beau tugged at Meredith's arm. "I brought you something!"

Meredith let go of one of Natalie's hands in order to tap Beau's shoulder. "What?" She sat back in her chair, closer to Beau's eye-level.

Beau set the present on the table. Meredith worked open the lid and then beamed.

"I picked them out at Walmart," Beau said.

"Thank you, Beau. Next time you come I'll smell like these."

Beau laughed so hard he collapsed in a heap on the floor. Merritt went to kick him. Meredith grabbed his arm.

"What's so funny?" Meredith asked.

Beau giggled and pulled himself up.

"She...she sniffed them," Merritt said.

Beau pushed Merritt, breaking into laughter again.

Meredith glanced at Natalie.

"The guard sniffed them. I'm happy to see you."

Meredith pressed her forehead to Natalie's. "Me too."

Beau settled, panting, gazing up at the ceiling.

Merritt wrapped himself around Meredith's free arm.

Natalie met Meredith's eyes. She would have been perfectly content to stay in this position forever. It didn't matter she was in a prison visitor's room, or lunch was a half-eaten sandwich getting warm in the locker. Meredith was here.

"This is all I need," Natalie said.

Meredith tilted her head so her lips were closer to Natalie's ear, and whispered, "You make me into such a sinner, Natalie Ivans, because I need just a little more."

Meredith brought her Bible to group therapy. Carol and Juanita brought New Testaments with them, and Siba brought her Qu'ran. They were all ornamental books in the concrete and steel class room.

Meredith hated the room, and the folding chairs, covered in graffiti and stained from years of use, sagging and leaving her with back pain after an hour of emotional anguish. Quite the hair shirt. Posters hung uninspiringly from the walls. Don't do drugs. Get help with pregnancy. Earn a G.E.D.

Believe.

Burdette loved group therapy. Here, under the counselor's watchful gaze, people had to confess. Burdette soaked up the information, studying each person.

The upheaval disturbed Meredith. Just when she learned to trust someone, the person was gone, free or moved into a different group. Replaced by a stranger, just come to town.

She didn't like telling her story over and over again. Each time, under each stranger's gaze, it felt raw and new. She wanted it to saturate into the prison's presence. Like outing herself, there came the fear of judgment and the residual shame of who she was.

Burdette didn't care how many times she repeated her story. She used to tell it in different ways, using funny voices, dramatic effects. Now she let other people tell it if they were willing.

"Burdette, she shot her husband."

"Merry, she knifed hers."

Today, the photograph of Natalie sprawled on the couch with her cat, tucked into the Book of John, was what Meredith focued on. She kept her head down. She listened.

Unkindly, she judged.

Jolene, new to Conrad this week, shorter and skinnier and smaller than the rest of them, covered in tattooes, told her story for the first time. "They said I was shoplifting, right? But what they didn't get was I had a kid to feed. And the store owed me. They knew it. They should have been paying me, but they fired me. I got what was mine. But no one listened."

Burdette knew all the words by now. "Do you feel you're here unjustly?"

"I'm innocent."

People nodded.

"It's the system. Just because they got me on camera with the Blu Ray, they think it's the whole story." She laughed. "They didn't even check my shoes. No one listens."

"We're listening, Jolene. We're all with you."

"I figured everyone in here got screwed, too," Jolene said.

"You know who else listens?" Burdette asked, jerking her head toward Meredith.

"Burdette~" Charlotte, the group leader, warned.

"No. Tell her, Merry. Who's going to make it right, since the cops are corrupt, the system's corrupt, and we~we don't really give a shit."

"Burdette," Meredith said.

"Shoot. We don't give a shoot."

Jolene laughed.

Meredith knew if she didn't participate, if she kept her head down and thought about Natalie, thought about the world outside, first Burdette would hound her, and then Charlotte. It was unfair, like Jolene said, to be in this position. To do this duty she didn't care about.

Jolene gazed at her attentively, probably wondering if she was some new prison toy to play with.

"God listens," Meredith said.

"God listens?" Jolene said. She glanced around at the other faces in the assembled circle. "Did she just say, 'God listens'?"

"It's true," Burdette said. "If He can listen to me calling His name every night when I'm getting off, He can listen to you."

"Where's your kid now?" Meredith asked.

Jolene snorted. "With my mom."

Charlotte smiled pleasantly. "We're glad you're with us, Jolene, even if these circumstances aren't ideal."

Jolene slouched back against her broken chair.

Charlotte turned to Robin. "You've been quiet, Robin."

"I think I'm the only one here who, though I didn't do anything illegal~" Robin said.

A wave of protest rippled through the circle.

"~I did something wrong," Robin said.

Jolene rolled her eyes.

Burdette grunted.

"And when I'm done serving my time, I'll go back to my life, like I never left it. And I have to wonder," Robin glanced from Meredith to Charlotte, "What's the point of it all?"

"Do you want to make a change?" Charlotte asked.

"Why should she?" Burdette asked.

"I don't know," Robin said.

"Why are you here? Not at Conrad, but here, in therapy?" Charlotte asked.

"It's a good way to learn about the world."

Meredith's grip tightened on her Bible. She caught Robin's gaze, and asked, "Do you have love?"

"I have a husband," Robin said. She considered, and then added, "I think so."

"Good, so she won't tell you to love God," Burdette said.

Meredith wrinkled her nose.

Siba leaned forward. "Do you do good things?"

"I don't do bad things."

Jolene scoffed.

Siba tilted her head.

Robin glanced at her hands. "Oh."

"Robin, I'd like to continue this conversation next week to see what conclusions you've drawn. Or what new questions have arisen," Charlotte said.

Robin nodded, not looking up.

"Siba~" Now that Siba dared to speak, Charlotte would pounce.

Siba folded her arms, smoothing her shawl, trying to withdraw. But she gave Charlotte her attention.

"Last week we were talking about your children's education. What thoughts have you had?"

"Are you kidding me? How is this theraputic?" Jolene asked.

Burdette tapped Jolene's chair with her foot, illiciting a stern glare from Charlotte. Burdette ignored it and said, "Remember how God listens?"

Jolene nodded.

"You gotta listen, too. So shut the fu~" Burdette glanced at Meredith. "Shut~Oh, hell, just be quiet."

Jolene looked Burdette up and down. And then she bit her lip and turned her whole body toward Siba.

Siba swallowed and began to speak.

Chapter Thirty-Nine

Wheeler's dog rested his head in Natalie's lap. She petted.

"He just wants steak," Wheeler said.

"I've heard that about dogs."

Wheeler put a plate of steak and mashed potatoes in front of Natalie.

"Thank you."

He nodded and brought over the decanter, pouring red wine into her glass. "Ksara's Shiraz Cabernet. From Lebanon. You'll find it's very forgiving with steak."

"I'm sure."

He chuckled and sat down.

The dog settled for lying down underneath the table. Natalie rubbed his stomach with her foot.

"Dr. Hank?" she asked.

"Hm?"

"Am I the only one you ever have over?"

He glanced around the condo. "Mostly."

"Thank you, then."

"It's my pleasure. You can tell me all about Meredith and the boys and your work."

"Don't you want to hang out with the other doctors?"

"I see them all day long. Honestly, Nat, I'm a member of the Elks, I go down there a couple times of month. It's all good."

She nodded. "Merry's good. In fact, I have news."

"Yes?" He took a sip of wine.

"She's got a probation hearing in two months."

"Really. Seems sudden."

"It feels eternally far away to me. But she's nearly off intake probation at Conrad. Which means she can join a work detail. She won't, but~"

"Outside the prison, you mean?"

"Yeah. Like picking up trash."

"Sounds like it would be a good way to get fresh air. See the beautiful highways of North Carolina."

"I agree. But she wants to stay in the infirmary."

"Nat. Her prison job is not going to be taken into consideration with the review board or any job application~"

"I know, I know. I think she honestly likes the work."

Wheeler shrugged. "She's crazy. I mean, who wouldn't want to pick up trash?"

Natalie took a sip of wine. Not too sweet, but thin, when she wanted something substantial. She cut into her steak. Bright, wounded red in the middle, charred on the outside.

"Beautiful, isn't it?"

"The best steak I've ever seen, Dr. Hank."

She took a bite. The crust, salty and meaty, crunched and the flesh underneath was warm and smooth. Almost like butter.

"Mine don't taste like this," she said, taking a sip of wine. The Ksara didn't challenge the steak, just ran around her mouth, refreshing it for the next bite.

"It took years to perfect the technique of the sear. And decades for us to start growing our own Kobe cattle in the US, close enough to be shipped by mail."

Natalie stopped mid-bite. "How much is this beef?"

Wheeler pushed the fork toward her mouth. "I'm a doctor, remember?"

Natalie swallowed. "Well, I'm a lawyer and I've never had the pleasure of this before. To answer your question, no, no steak for the boys. They don't chew enough. They like fried chicken, though."

"I'll send you home with a recipe."

"Thank you?"

"And some Panko. Crust won't set right otherwise."

Natalie ate more steak.

Wheeler asked, "All right, what is it?"

"What do you mean?"

"You seem more cheerful than I've seen you since the day you moved to Tarpley. What gives? I know it's not Luis Duarte. I treated the guy once for poison ivy. You'd have thought I was torturing him instead of writing a prescription."

"I've been working my old friends in the prosecutor's office. Pulling some strings with the attorney general."

"Early release?"

"No." Natalie exhaled. "Small favors. All we can trade for these days."

Wheeler nodded.

"I feel bad enough, doing it. It's unethical. Do you know how many women are incarcerated in the state of North Carolina?"

"Only know there are 300 up with Meredith, which, incidentally, is the staff of the hospital."

Natalie shook her head. "She gets a 24 hour release."

Wheeler smiled. "Wonderful. When?"

"Thursday, when Jake takes the kids."

"You scheduled it around babysitting?"

"What else do I have to schedule around?"

"Good point," Wheeler said.

"Is there more steak?" Natalie asked.

The dog lifted his head.

"Better. There's dessert."

Luis wore a suit and paced outside the court room with Natalie, holding the cotton tie in his hands. Natalie wanted to ask him if he needed help, wanted to wrap the thing around his neck and be done, but she just watched. She counted his steps. She checked her watch. They were running out of time.

"Luis~"

"Why do I have to wear this? I look fine without it. Like, I wouldn't even wear this to a wedding."

Natalie frowned.

"It's so old-fashioned."

"Luis, you've got to seem like you're willing to play the game. You have to humble yourself before them. Appearing clean-cut~like them~will go a long way."

"What?"

"If you want the judge's sympathy, you're going to have to make yourself meek." She took a deep breath. "Submissive, even. If you show even a hint of anger, or apathy, they're going to~"

"I don't care what the judge thinks."

"Luis, hey."

He stopped his pacing and turned in her general direction.

"They're going to think you're a monster," she said.

"I'm not~"

"I know. You have to act sorry, even if you aren't. Even if it's not your fault. Pretend."

"Fake it 'til I make it?"

"Exactly. The tie?"

"I know how to put on a tie." He slung the tie around his neck and popped his collar. Then frowned. "Do you have a mirror?"

She pulled a compact out of her purse and held it up for him.

A portly white man carrying a briefcase passed them, paused, looked them up and down, and went inside the court room.

Luis snorted.

"Who's that?" Natalie asked.

"I guess he's the other lawyer." Luis straightened his tie.

Natalie nodded. "There's another thing you have to do, Luis."

He raised his eyebrows. In a suit and tie, with his hair washed and the bruises on his face healing, he looked almost... sweet. Like a boy about to enroll in business school. A Young Republican.

"You have to ignore everything they say," Natalie said. "Everything."

"Okay."

"Even if they lie."

"Okay."

"It's going to get bad in there, Luis. Believe me."

"Okay, already. Geez."

"See? You failed the first test."

Luis squared his shoulders and made his face into stone. "I'm ready. Test me again."

"Now you look defiant. What did I say?"

Luis' expression flashed with anger.

"Second test."

Luis exhaled. "This is going to be a huge failure."

"I know."

"It's okay, though." Luis glanced at the door. "I don't know if I want to go to Burgaw."

"Why not?"

"I know I told you I didn't want to see my family, but, my dad's here, and all my friends are here. I'll miss my dad. This is everything I know. I think I've been to Burgaw like, once in my life. The only time I've left Tarpley is when I went to the beach. Or Raleigh on school trips."

"You've never been to Charlotte?"

Luis shook his head. "Seen the skyline in postcards. It's nice."

"It is. Luis, I know there are pluses and minuses to this. But trust me. This is why I'm your lawyer, Luis."

"But you're not my mother."

"Would your mother send you away to Burgaw?" The subject of his mother hadn't come up before. Eduardo had not mentioned her, either.

"Not that far. She's just smack me and lock me out of the house."

Natalie raised her eyebrows.

Luis didn't meet her gaze. "Until I calmed down."

"Ah."

"I'm calmed down, now."

"Remember what I said."

"Don't call them on their bullshit lies. Got it."

"Right. Remember, I used to be a prosecutor. I know exactly what they're thinking. And I know exactly what they're thinking of you. We can use my skills to our advantage."

Natalie pushed open the door for him. He went through and she followed, up to the defendant's table. The first time she'd ever sat on this side of the table had been at Meredith's trial. Meredith needed no coaching on humility. But the lies made her white and paralyzed with rage. "Ignore them, ignore them, ignore them." She directed the thought at Luis' head.

Then she turned and offered her hand to the portly prosecutor.

"Jacob Weinstead," he said, shaking her hand. "I'm the district attorney for one third of everything southeast of Fayetteville. Usually do traffic cases, though. I guess this is a traffic case." He glanced past her shoulder at Luis.

She nodded. "Natalie Ivans."

"I Googled you." He lowered his voice. "If I may ask, what in the hell are you doing?"

"I moved for love."

"So what's in the papers, all true?"

She nodded.

He grinned. "I never like to assume. Take the facts in evidence as they are. Life seems smoother that way."

"I agree."

"Is there anything I need to know before we get started?"

"No."

He nodded.

She sat down next to Luis.

"You two seem chummy," he said.

"One more piece of advice, Luis," she said.

"I'm not sure I can do three things at once, ma'am."

"This one's easy. Don't trust anyone in this room. Not the judge, not him, not the court reporter. No one is your friend."

He nodded. "Then that~?"

"Was just civil discourse."

He studied the empty judge's chair.

"You know, Luis, speaking of civil discourse. A lot of people just call me 'Nat.'"

Luis looked horrified.

She grinned.

The bailiff came in, and then the judge. She set her nameplate out. The Honorable Fran McCoy. The court room filled with defendants awaiting other cases. Mostly traffic infractions, some shoplifting. Natalie had seen the docket. Twelve speeding tickets, four petty thefts, one vandalism, six drug charges~four pot, two meth~and a man suing his neighbor. Weinstead was working them all for the county's side.

McCoy said, "I have before me a petition for transfer to Burgaw Correctional Facility, pending trial. Is this correct?"

Natalie stood. "Yes, Your Honor."

Fran glanced at Weinstead, and then flipped her paper over. "No filing for bail?"

"No, Your Honor."

"Alcohol treatment?"

"No, Your Honor."

Luis twitched.

Fran gestured to Weinstead. "Any objections?"

Weistead stood. Natalie sat.

"My only question is why, Your Honor? Transport will be a considerable expense, and then Burgaw will have to cover his incarceration. Duplin County Jail is just fine. Why the special treatment for the accused?"

Fran glanced at Natalie. She stood. Weinstead sat.

"We're willing to reimburse the city for transportation expense, your Honor. As Luis' father is Sheriff Eduardo Duarte, we feel there could be implications of bias or favoritism at Duplin."

"And you don't want that?"

"Not in this case, Your Honor. We're not asking for any bail or mandated treatment~" she glanced at Weinstead. "But this small thing would benefit my client immensely, and also separate him from the fabric of Tarpley, so healing could continue."

"Mr. Weinstead?" Fran asked.

He shrugged.

"Transfer will take place as soon as Burgaw is ready to receive. County clerk will notify you of your trial date."

Weinstead shook hands with Natalie again, and then she and Luis headed for the court room exit.

"The police are waiting?" Luis asked, when they were in the lobby.

"They'll take you back to your cell."

He nodded.

"You did good in there."

"That guy was an asshole. I thought the judge was going to say no."

"All part of the fun."

"How come you didn't ask for bail?"

"So I could bargain for Burgaw. Not good to ask for two conflicting things at once."

"Then why am I being charged with felony death and involuntary manslaughter?"

"If you're a defendant, I mean. Prosecutors like to be conflicting."

"Why didn't you ask for drug treatment? Don't you think I need it?"

"Would you want to go?"

"Heck, no." He shook his head. "I've been. It doesn't work."

She tilted her head.

"I'm not an alcoholic. I don't have the problem. They do."

"I'm not going to put you through it for nothing, Luis."

"Thanks. I'm so tired of it. 'Oh, send him off to rehab, he'll come back fine.' You know what rehab's like?"

"No idea."

"It's full of whiny morons hunting for a fix. I'm not like them."

Natalie shook her head.

Luis exhaled. "I think I'm actually looking forward to Burgaw."

"Yeah," Natalie said, rolling her eyes. "Think of it like a vacation."

Chapter Forty

On Thursday Meredith's one-on-one therapist pulled her in for an appointment. Breaking routine.

"How are you, Merry?" Dr. Embry asked. She appeared to be about twelve-years-old, doing her civic duty, getting prison rotation on her resume and out of the way, before moving onto something better by the time she turned 30. Maybe she'd have babies. Maybe she'd publish articles. Meredith didn't much like her. Dr. Embry made her feel like a science project.

"I'm good," she said.

"How was yesterday?" Embry persisted. "The visit?"

"She didn't come."

Embry smiled.

Meredith felt her cheeks grow hot. She sat on her hands.

"And how do you feel?" Embry asked.

"How do I feel?" No pictures, no chance to hold someone in her arms who was from the outside, who smelled of the outside, who smelled like her children. "Pretty rotten."

"Merry, we've talked about work release before."

Meredith shook her head.

"It's time to start thinking about your future."

"My future? Doctor, I've been thinking about my future plenty."

Dr. Embry nodded.

Embry had grown up in North Carolina, which was the only thing that made her bearable, but being from Cary, she didn't have an accent. Not to native ears, at least. Her inflection made Meredith self-conscious.

"I know what you mean. You've got your future. But I'm talking about getting from point A to point B. Reintegration."

A shiver went through Meredith. "I'm not~"

She wanted to say "Not ready." She wanted to say, "I don't want to."

"We need to talk about it. It's going to be uncomfortable."

Meredith sighed.

"Your first probation hearing is in two months. Do you feel ready for it?"

"No."

"Maybe when you first got here you thought six months was going to be nothing. Twice a week with your family was going to be enough. Therapy might kick-start some things for you, you might, with a hint of arrogance, actually do some good in the infirmary."

Meredith's eyes stung.

"I've seen you get more depressed, Merry, as time goes on."

"Don't~"

"I won't give you anything, I promise. But it worries me."

Meredith nodded.

"It worries you, too?"

"Yeah."

"Merry, I know you don't like me, but try and trust me."

"I don't need~"

"Anyone's help?"

Meredith glanced away.

"You don't want anyone's help because you think you're undeserving."

Meredith set her jaw.

"But it's not the same as not needing it."

Meredith found herself not breathing, and forced it out in a gust.

"Do you know why Natalie didn't come yesterday?"

Meredith shook her head. "She just called and said she wasn't."

"Not why?"

"No."

"Or that she couldn't?"

Meredith replayed the conversation in her mind. "No."

"Because she didn't want to lie to you. Not even for your own good. Or to be nice. That's rare, Merry."

"I know it's rare~" Meredith stopped.

Embry leaned forward. "Tell me."

Meredith shook her head.

"The words are all there. Just let them out."

"I know it's rare. I've seen hundreds of patients, cared about dozens of them, fallen in love with a handful. Do you know how many looked back? Do you know how many even saw me? One. Just one. Of course she's trying so hard to be good. It's just~"

"You think there's a point where people stop trying? Effort is finite?"

"She made a mistake. One in a hundred is an anomaly. A fluke. An outlier. And those get discarded."

"And she'll go back to being normal."

"To her own life."

"If I may," Isle said, with Meredith red-faced, breathing hard, gazing away from her, out the window. "Go another level deeper."

Meredith closed her eyes.

"You hate yourself for not letting her go, am I right? For still needing her to come up, despite the burden it places on her. It makes you feel selfish."

"I feel selfish all the time."

"You didn't used to feel this way."

"Selfish?"

"Alone."

Meredith tried to think of a time when she didn't feel alone. When Vincent was sending her letters from overseas. Just like she and Natalie were sending letters now. Words forming crazy dreams for the future. She had seen it manifest. Vincent's friend killed in war, his hopes crashing down. His home life, his children, his town, suddenly and irrevocably fake.

"This isn't the life she wants," Meredith said.

"Where is God in all of this, Merry?"

Meredith gave a short laugh. "Yeah. Where is He?"

Embry offered Meredith a sheet of paper. "I know why Natalie wasn't here yesterday."

"Why?"

"She's coming today. You've been granted 24 hour family leave, for good behavior as part of your pre-parole program."

"What?"

"You'll be released at three o'clock. Go, get ready."

"How do I get ready?"

"How do you feel like getting ready?"

"I feel like throwing up."

"Well, that's a start. And then maybe a shower?"

"Yeah, okay." She'd have to shave her legs. And brush her teeth like never before. And~She gave Embry a panicked look.

Embry waved her off. "Go, go."

Meredith changed into jeans and a white blouse. Her own clothes, which they had on file for her at the prison, but she wasn't allowed to wear unless leaving. The guard handed over her wallet. She opened it to study her driver's license. She nearly cried. There she was, free and granted the right to operate motor vehicles by the state of North Carolina.

The wallet still held twenty-five dollars and a picture of Vincent and the boys. She closed it and put it into her pocket.

"I'm ready," she said.

But she wasn't, not for the blinding sunlight of the September day. Not for the gates sliding open. The guard walked her to the entrance and then let her go.

"Really?" Meredith asked.

"Really, Merry. Go on. Get out of here."

Meredith scanned the parking lot and the row of trees beyond the gate. Her own car was there, the old station wagon under an oak tree. Natalie leaned against the hood, smiling. Not moving. Just smiling.

Meredith resisted the urge to run toward her. She didn't know what she'd do once she got there. Natalie kept smiling and when Meredith neared, opened her arms. Meredith flung herself at Natalie, hugging her.

"How did you~" she asked against Natalie's shoulder.

Natalie rubbed her back with firm circles. Meredith had missed those hands.

"I pulled some strings," Natalie said.

"You..."

Natalie only held her.

"I don't deserve this," Meredith said.

Natalie cupped her head and gently drew her back, to smile into her face.

Meredith felt her heart opening, easing.

"I don't care," Natalie said, and kissed her.

Meredith sighed into the kiss, reveling in the feel of Natalie's lips sliding against hers. Her heart pounded, first in fear~but as seconds passed and no one stopped her, no one condemned her, she parted her lips, straining to deepen the kiss. Natalie responded, and then Natalie's tongue moved against hers and her heart pounded.

Natalie's fingers were in her hair, scratching lightly. Meredith broke the kiss. She laughed.

Natalie raised her eyebrows.

Meredith reached up to trace them. "I thought I'd be nervous."

"Me, too."

"I have to go back in there tomorrow."

"Don't think about it."

"The boys?"

Natalie squirmed away from the car, creating distance between them. "I didn't bring them. They're with Jake."

"Of course. It's Thursday." Meredith felt a pang of regret. Twenty four hours with her children would have been a treasure. She missed them so much it hurt.

Natalie pulled her back into a hug. "If I kiss you again, we're never leaving this parking lot."

"And people are watching us, anyway."

"Don't you hate that?"

Meredith shook her head. "They're my friends. My family, I guess. I don't mind it in there."

Natalie squeezed her shoulder.

"So, we're not going home?"

"No. Wilson."

"What's in Wilson?"

"Do you want to be surprised?"

"No. No, I'm~" Meredith tucked her cheek against Natalie. "I'm so used to routine I don't know how much shock my system can take."

"Patrick's sister's cousin's boyfriend has a house at Silver Lake."

"We know a lot of people with great houses."

Natalie stiffened. "Yeah."

"What is it?"

"Just Jake..."

"Oh yeah, you told me in your letter. And he sent one, too."

"He did?"

"Once a week," Meredith said.

Natalie hugged her closer. "You're unforgettable."

"Take me away from all this."

Natalie actually blushed, stepping back to open the passenger side door. "You don't like it here?"

"I don't want to spend another minute here if I don't have to."

Yet Meredith lingered, standing at the door, glancing back at Conrad. Now she was breathing free air, she felt like a different person. She was scared.

Natalie asked, "What is it?" as she opened her own car door.

"I hate my therapist," Meredith said.

"I know."

"But she was right."

Meredith sat with her bare feet on the dashboard, studying Natalie. She'd tried gazing out the window, but Natalie was too distracting. They'd driven in silence for nearly forty-five minutes. No music. No talking beyond directions. Left here. Straight forever. Meredith supposed they should talk. About bills and the kids and their future. Their plans. She didn't want to, though.

She just wanted to stare.

Natalie rolled her neck and let go of the steering wheel with her right hand. She reached for Meredith.

Meredith took her hand. She studied the fingers. She bent the knuckles and made them straighten again. She wanted to feel that hand against her cheek. She settled for squeezing gently.

"Are we supposed to be talking? About the kids, or my case, or whatever?" Natalie asked.

"I may be getting out, soon."

The hand stilled, but Natalie didn't draw away. "I know."

"I don't know what's going to happen. Are we just going to pick up where we left off? Will I have a job? Will you resent me?"

"We've lived together before."

"Kids are cute for a day, but. Come on, Natalie. You don't have to be grateful forever."

Natalie swallowed. Her voice sounded choked when she said, "You're thinking too much, Merry. Whatever's right will just happen. It'll settle into place."

"I don't have any faith."

Natalie glanced at her.

"I thought everything was going to be all right. I got through the trial. I got through the bus ride to prison and then I walked into that place. They took away my clothes. They locked me in a room all by myself."

Natalie squeezed her hand.

Meredith laughed. "Isn't this ironic, or something?"

"It's something. Give and take. I've been reading my way through the library."

Meredith rubbed her knuckles.

"I have a lot of time."

"You're getting adjusted."

"Settling in." Natalie glanced at Meredith again. "Meredith, have faith in me, if no one else. I can do this."

Meredith lifted Natalie's hand to her lips. "You know just what to say."

Natalie chuckled.

"Oh, don't tell me that's in a book, too."

"Made it up myself."

"Fancy lawyah speak, I'm sure."

"Want me to say something in Latin?"

Meredith kissed her hand. "Yes."

"Oh, shoot. Let's see." Natalie hesitated. "Essentiala negotii."

"What does that mean?"

"Basic terms."

Meredith smirked.

Natalie let go of Meredith's hand to point at a sign. "We're almost there."

Chapter Forty-One

They were almost at the cabin before Meredith more closely examined the hand she'd been caresssing. She bent Natalie's arm back at the elbow, until her fingers were at eye-height. Natalie drove slowly with her free hand, glancing at her.

"You got your nails done."

"Took you long enough."

"When?"

The nail polish was chipped in a few places, but Natalie's nails and hands were smooth and seemed well-looked after.

"Friday."

"You can't afford~"

"It was a gift."

"Someone gave you a manicure as a gift?"

"Well, someone paid for it." Natalie didn't want Meredith imagining some woman bent over her, intimately caressing her fingers. The way Meredith was doing now.

"Who? You don't know anyone~like. Women."

"Why don't we have more women friends?"

"Children ruin everything."

"I haven't been to a good happy hour in a year. We've got to go to Wilmington more often."

"I agree. So, who?"

"Oh, Erica."

Meredith's hand tightened on hers.

Natalie raised her eyebrows. "Oops? She interviewed me for the Luis Duarte case."

"You told that woman all that boy's business?"

"Strictly professional."

"Except your hands are like this." Meredith pressed Natalie's palm between hers.

"I promise you, she hasn't seen them."

"No, I understand. I'm in prison. She's gorgeous. She's intelligent. If you want to spend your time with a soulless, amoral~" She hesitated.

"Harlot?" Natalie asked.

"I was going to say strumpet."

Natalie freed her hand to put the car in park. Then she shifted in the seat to see Meredith. "My only thought was of how you'd like it."

"I do. How did you not get snatched up before me?"

"I just didn't date. I didn't bother."

"Why not?"

"Who was out there?"

"You didn't want~"

"Two five year old boys and a girlfriend in prison? I had no idea. Or I would have looked a lot more closely at my case load."

"You just knew what you didn't want."

"I didn't want anyone sharing the life I was living."

Meredith cupped Natalie's chin, cautiously moving her fingers across the skin. "You seem happy."

"I am. When you're not around, I'm not as happy." Meredith dropped her hand but Natalie caught it, and held it. "You're here."

"I'm here. I'm~" Meredith's throat caught. She wanted to say, "I'm all yours." But she wasn't sure. She only knew she wanted to stay right where she was, gazing into Natalie's eyes.

So she did. Natalie gazed back.

Meredith's stomach growled. Her face got hot. "I'm sorry. I'm used to eating at six o'clock every day. Routine."

"Let's see what I brought, then."

"You brought stuff?" Meredith asked as Natalie got out of the car.

"Have I ever."

Meredith came around the car as Natalie opened the trunk. Inside, there were blankets and sheets and a cooler of groceries. Meredith pulled the bag closer. Hamburger meat, buns, eggs, her salt and pepper shakers from home, apples, oranges. She glanced back at Natalie.

"And two presents," Natalie said.

"Presents?"

"Let's get this stuff inside."

Meredith gazed around the area. The water line was past a grove of trees.

She didn't see a dock. Just the green lake. The cabin itself was a ranch, small and unexciting, except the side facing the water was all glass. "This is nice."

"I thought it would be better than a hotel."

Meredith blushed.

"Yeah. Exactly." Natalie picked up the cooler and wrapped a plastic bag around her wrist, too.

"Let me."

"Nope. Get the blankets."

Meredith carried them to the door, following Natalie, who put her groceries on the ledge to unlock the door. Meredith took a last glance around. There was the flat wildness of Eastern Carolina all around them, and a few other wooden cabins peeking out from between the vibrant green. She found it hard to believe there was anyone else within fifty miles.

"Nat?" She called, as they went inside.

"Yeah." Natalie settled her groceries onto a kitchen island.

Meredith dumped the blankets on the couch and came toward her. "When this is all over."

Natalie folded her arms, giving her full attention. Meredith grinned and pulled her arms apart to take her hands.

"Yes?"

"I want you to take me somewhere out of state."

"Like where?"

"California, maybe. To see the beach."

"We have a beach."

"To ride the trolley."

Natalie grinned. She let go of Meredith to encircle her waist. "I'll take you to California."

Meredith chuckled.

"And to Paris."

Meredith shivered.

Natalie kissed her cheek. "And to Rome." Her lips brushed the side of Meredith's neck. "Madrid. Shanghai."

Meredith hugged her tightly. "I was thinking Atlanta?"

"Atlanta."

"To the Coca-Cola museum."

Natalie chuckled. "I counter with Charleston."

"I've been to Charleston."

"But have you ever gotten on a boat there, and gone to the Bahamas?"

Meredith shook her head, smiling. "My parents and Vincey's tried to send us on a cruise for a honeymoon."

Natalie tried to pull back, but Meredith kept her embrace secure. "We talked them into the downpayment for the house, instead."

"So practical."

"But a real~" She couldn't quite bring herself to say it. A real honeymoon. She and Natalie on the deck of a boat, the wind in their hair, the smell of the sea. She just said, "I'm so lucky."

"Me too."

Meredith let Natalie kiss her, and rubbed her back in return. "I thought," she said, when Natalie's lips moved to her ear.

"Hm?"

"I'd be more worried."

"About what?"

"About going back. About being here. About my routine."

"And you're not?" Natalie's nose nuzzled into her shoulder.

"I'm only thinking about you."

Natalie gave her a squeeze.

"Let's skip~" Meredith said, but her stomach rumbled, vibrating against Natalie's. And she knew her blood sugar was dropping. Without a boost, she'd lose her good humor.

"Cook dinner for me," Natalie said.

"My presents~"

Natalie slapped her hip, and then went to get the blankets. "I'll just be making the bed."

Meredith found herself alone in the kitchen. Free, and completely alone. She could go anywhere. Do anything. She gazed at the ceiling, considered crying as emotion welled up in her chest. She gave into the urge to spin around in a circle, her arms outstretched. "For this I don't even mind going back."

Then she realized she was talking to God and stopped, her heart pounding.

Chapter Forty-Two

Hamburgers sizzled in the frying pan and plates were out when Natalie returned. She sat on a stool at the counter and leaned on one elbow.

Meredith offered Natalie a potato chip dipped in onion dip.

"Thank you." Natalie ate it from her fingers.

"I want to cook for you every night," Meredith said.

Natalie looked her up and down. "I would love that."

"Good." Meredith fed her another potato chip.

"What do I do?"

"You do everything." Meredith put down the chip and gazed at Natalie, who was smiling with a bemused look, perfectly calm. Her dark eyes followed Meredith's face as Meredith took in her cotton shirt, the expanse of throat revealed by the neckline. The hands with their short, perfect, pink nails.

Meredith wanted to see if Natalie's toes matched.

She had known her entire life she wanted to be with a woman, but never expected to be, not something real, beyond a night, or a stolen look. Only Vincent shared her secret.

Now she had this woman right in front of her, radiating such peace Meredith wanted to be still, too. As still as the water outside.

She said, "I owe you~"

"Nothing. You owe me nothing."

"But~"

"No buts."

"Natalie Ivans, you mean to tell me you did all this for me, and you don't want sex?"

Natalie grinned, her eyes bright. She took Meredith's hand. Meredith dipped closer to kiss her.

The microwave timer went off.

"Argh," Natalie said.

"Ain't you hungry?"

"Yes."

"As hungry as I am?"

"More," Natalie said.

"Not possible."

"Let's find out."

Meredith assembled burgers and Natalie poured apple cider and they ate together on the couch, side by side.

"There's dessert," Natalie said.

Meredith brightened.

"But let's go for a walk."

"A walk?"

"By the lake?"

"But I haven't walked anywhere in a really long time."

"Agoraphobic?" Natalie asked, getting to her feet.

"Let's find out, I guess." Meredith glanced past Natalie to the bedroom door, feeling a tug. Natalie took plates to the kitchen. Meredith got up. She was afraid of the strange area, the wide sky, but the fear was exhilarating. Something new. Even if it was a new rock, a new tree.

And Natalie. "Wither thou goest." She shook her head. No. God could not be with her here, if he had not been with her in prison. If that empty space, those cold cement walls, where people needed him most~

"Merry?"

Meredith blinked, and found Natalie peering at her with a concerned expression.

"I'm all right. I was just thinking."

"Okay. Ready?"

Meredith offered her hand. "Ready."

Outside, the lowering sun turned everything gold and orange. Meredith inhaled deeply. The day was warm. They'd sweat if they stayed out too long. She didn't want to sweat. Not yet. Natalie squeezed her fingers.

"Where to?"

Natalie glanced around. "There's a dock." A quarter around their inlet, a dock with a gazebo jutted into the water.

"Public access?" Meredith asked.

"I don't see a mansion. I guess so." She tugged Meredith's hand.

Meredith walked with her, trading her hand for her elbow to lean into her shoulder. At the gate onto the dock, Natalie glanced around nervously, but no one appeared to chase them away. No creature stirred.

In the gazebo, Meredith could take in the sight of their cabin, diagonal and close by. And the sky sending orange light to the water's surface, and the trees, and the grasslands. She inhaled, and just as she reached for Natalie, Natalie was there, wrapping herself around Meredith from behind. Meredith covered her hands, feeling secure. She tried to take in the whole universe.

"Merry," Natalie said, close to her ear.

Meredith leaned back.

"I love you."

"I love you, too."

Meredith turned in Natalie's arms and hugged her again, kissing her, letting it linger, opening her mouth and when Natalie's tongue didn't enter right away, she sought it out, invading, tasting. This is where she wanted to be.

"I want to feel like everything will go wrong," Meredith said, drawing back. "But I can't."

"I don't care if I have to wait two months or two years."

"What if we don't get along?"

"We already know we get along."

"Only when you're crippled."

"Hobble me all you want."

Meredith just pulled her close, tucking her head against Natalie's shoulder. She waited to see if she would cry. She didn't.

Natalie sniffled. Meredith stroked her back. Natalie sniffled again. Then she shook with full-blown sobs, quaking in Meredith's arms, sagging until they sat together on the bench, Meredith rocking her, trying to figure out what to say to her besides, "Hey, hey, it's okay, honey."

Natalie squeezed her eyes shut, breathing hard, but the shaking subsided. "I don't think I'm as strong as you."

"Why?"

"I don't want to let you go. I don't want to wait. I hate all the empty spaces where you should be. I hate them."

Meredith shivered, but she cupped Natalie's cheek. "It's going to be all right."

Natalie nodded.

Meredith stroked her cheek.

"I'm glad you're here," Natalie said.

"You are?"

"Of course."

"Show me."

Natalie kissed Meredith, then brushed away her tears, and tried to get up. "Ow."

"Stiff?"

"Yeah. My butt hasn't been on anything that wooden in a long time."

Meredith chuckled as she slipped an arm around Natalie's waist. Natalie leaned heavily into her. Natalie's leg and side had nearly been crushed, and despite the pins and the surgeries, she would never be the same again. Always misshapen, always close to pain. Meredith was glad Natalie was a lawyer, and not anything else. If she deteriorated, she could still be that.

If Natalie--who Meredith knew, was supposed to be using a cane, but wouldn't, who trained herself not to walk with a limp even though it hurt-- had to use a wheelchair, had to let the kids take care of her, hand and foot, Meredith would want to spend every minute with her.

"Nat. I'm not afraid."

"Of what?"

"Of anything."

"Yeah, well, you've been to prison. It hardens a woman."

Meredith laughed. "But you have it worse. I remember what Tarpley was like, alone. Having everyone know what I did. All those people staring."

"Every time I leave the house."

"People in prison are, uh."

"Please don't tell me 'nice.'"

"Not nice, but no one casts the first stone."

Natalie nodded.

They went onto the porch and into the cabin together. Natalie freed herself and hobbled to the bedroom. "Time for your presents."

"Should I wait here?"

"No. Come on in."

Meredith went into the bedroom. Natalie sat on the bed. She held out two child-sized tee shirts. "The boys wore these today, until I left the house. And slept in them."

Meredith took them and pressed them to her face. Her boys. She inhaled deeply. Their smell consumed her. It was all she sensed for long moments. She breathed in.

"They'll be so happy. I told them mommy would be cradling them close tonight."

Meredith held the shirts to her chest. "I wish I could have these on the inside."

"I know. Stupid regulations."

"They just don't want to deal with all the clutter." Meredith rubbed her cheek against soft fabric. "So are these my two presents?"

"No." Natalie scooted back on the bed until she was against the headboard. She picked up a box from the beside table.

"Are those what I think they are?"

Natalie beckoned with the box.

Meredith kicked off her shoes, then leaned over and took off her socks, before crawling up on the bed. "Give me."

Natalie opened the box, revealing six chocolate bonbons.

"Chocolate." Meredith moaned.

"Speaking of things it sucks not to have in prison."

"Whoever enacted that 'public health' law, you have a duty to vote against him."

Natalie groaned. "Please don't talk about the local elections."

Meredith picked up a chocolate, her eyes widening.

"Sorry. It's just Daniel. And Erica. All they care about."

"They're such boring people," Meredith said.

"At least Daniel's watching the kids."

"Can we call later?"

"Absolutely. It's on my itinerary."

"After chocolate?"

"And..."

Meredith grinned. She bit off half and then offered the rest to Natalie. Gooey, dark chocolate filled her mouth. She chewed, letting it coat her mouth, and swallowed, barely noticing Natalie licking her fingers.

Chocolate.

She took another piece. "You brought me chocolate."

Natalie grinned.

"Because you love me."

"Very much."

She bit into the chocolate. Peanuts, this time. She pressed it to Natalie's lips, moving closer. Natalie accepted.

"Thank you," Meredith said.

"Another?"

"One more."

"And then what?"

Meredith rubbed Natalie's stomach. "Then."

Natalie tensed.

"You take some Advil for your leg."

"All right."

Meredith picked a chocolate and nibbled. "Should we take showers?"

"No."

"No?"

Natalie turned, careful not to dislodge Meredith's chocolate, and wrapped herself around Meredith. "Not on your life."

Meredith popped the bonbon into her mouth.

"Hey. Where's my half?"

Meredith chewed, then slid lower on the bed, beckoning.

Natalie leaned over her and kissed her, then let Meredith finish chewing, and swallowing, before pulling her down for another kiss. Natalie settled against her. And winced.

"Advil," Meredith said.

"It takes a long time to kick in."

"Then you'd better get started."

Natalie grumbled and got off the bed, going to her bag. Meredith pulled down the sheets and arranged pillows. Outside, it was gray. Early. But they'd wasted too much time already. She was not willing to be anywhere else.

Natalie kicked off her shoes, and then took off her watch.

"How do you feel?" Meredith asked.

"All right."

"Does driving hurt?"

Natalie glanced away.

"Natalie, I won't make you stop coming."

"I have a process. Going up there I can't wait to see you. And coming back, well, I'm driving on air."

Meredith chuckled.

Natalie stretched back, settling onto the pillows. "Is this where you want me?"

"Yes."

Natalie lowered her eyelashes. "So you can do what to me?"

"What are my choices?"

"Anything you want."

Meredith slouched down onto her elbow, settling her hand on Natalie's stomach for balance. "I could think of a few things."

"Do share."

"When we're home, maybe."

Natalie raised her eyebrows.

"When I've drunk a little more wine."

Natalie grinned.

Meredith kissed her, and it felt so good she moved over Natalie, keeping contact with Natalie's lips, which tugged at hers, opened to her, inviting her into the heat. And then Natalie's arms were around her, holding her close. Meredith wriggled, reveling in the feeling. She found Natalie's tongue and stayed, tracing and tasting, drawn by scent and touch and desire.

She moved to Natalie's jaw, and then to her neck. Her leg moved between Natalie's until her knee found the bed, anchoring her. Linking them together, almost completely, as Natalie took hold of her hips, shifting until they slid together.

"Natalie," Meredith said, as Natalie's hand traced her hip.

"This feels really good."

"Don't stop."

"I don't intend to."

Natalie raised her knees, pressing firmly into Meredith. They moved together, slowly but with purpose. Hips grinding. Arms reaching. Meredith knelt and kissed Natalie again. This kiss was hungry and Natalie cupped the back of her head, intensifying it. Meredith rocked down. And then she was so close. She twisted, sliding to the side, onto the bed again.

"Whoa," Natalie said.

"I just need a minute to catch my breath." Meredith held herself still until she was sure she wasn't going to explode on contact, and then covered Natalie's heart with her hand. "I don't want it to be over too soon."

"You know, we can do it again."

"Oh, we will."

"Merry."

"I'm here." Meredith traced her breast.

"I have an idea."

"Yeah?"

Natalie captured Meredith's hand, stilling it. "Maybe we should get undressed."

"That's a great idea." Meredith sat up. "I'll go first."

"All right."

"And then I'll help."

Natalie grinned. "Whatever you say."

Meredith pulled her shirt over her head.

Natalie's bravado fled. She stared, open-mouthed, as Meredith reached behind her for the bra.

"Let me," Natalie said.

"You're supposed to be lying right there."

"Just turn around."

Meredith turned around and leaned back. Natalie stroked her shoulders before unfastening her bra, and then letting Meredith pull it off. Natalie urged her back, so Meredith was lying face-up across Natalie's torso, with Natalie's arms around her.

"This is nice," Natalie murmured.

"Yeah."

Natalie's hands moved over her stomach, down her sides, and then over her chest, stroking and circling, until Meredith groaned. Natalie's hand hovered against the side of a breast. "Merry?"

"Please."

"Please what?"

Meredith took her hands and placed them against her breasts. "Please don't torture me anymore."

Natalie squeezed.

Meredith groaned again, consumed with the sensations going all the way through her.

"Is this all right?" Natalie asked.

"If it's with you."

Natalie tugged on her nipples, bringing them more prominently into the room, before covering them with her hands and squeezing.

"This is a good position," Natalie said.

"It is?"

"Because if I could really reach." Natalie's fingers danced down Meredith's stomach to the button of her jeans. "We'd be done by now."

"That'd be no fun."

Natalie kissed her shoulder. "No. Is it my turn?"

Meredith turned over, until her bare breasts pressed Natalie's clothed ones as she leaned down for a kiss. Natalie sighed, lifting herself against Meredith's mouth. Meredith pressed closer. "I can do anything?"

"Yes."

"Any requests?"

"Take off my shirt. Please."

Meredith untucked it from Natalie's pants and helped push it over Natalie's head. Then she plucked at a bra strop.

"I can~" Natalie started.

"No, let me."

Natalie stilled as Meredith drew the straps down and then pressed kisses along Natalie's bare shoulder.

"I thought we promised no torture."

"I made you promise." Meredith kissed the hollow between her breasts.

"Merry."

Meredith worked her hands under Natalie's back, undid the clasp, and sat up, pulling the fabric.

"Thank you," Natalie said, closing her eyes.

"Mmhm. My pleasure," Meredith said.

Natalie arched her back. Meredith took that as an invitation. She kissed Natalie's chest, following the slope of a breast to its point, kissing lightly before moving to the next one. Up and down. She wanted to get used to the taste again. She swiped with her tongue. Natalie's responses encouraged her. The hardening of her nipple, the shivering of her torso, the redness of her neck. She spread wet, wide-mouthed kisses across bare skin. She felt powerful, calling forth this energy in Natalie.

Her own nipples, grazing Natalie's side, echoed her own desire and Natalie's. She kissed Natalie's side, and then encountered jeans.

"Wait." Natalie said as Meredith touched her fly.

Meredith paused.

"The place you were in a while ago," Natalie said, panting.

"I remember."

"I'm, uh, there now."

Meredith knelt, moving back, until she could stand by the bed.

"What are you doing?" Natalie asked.

Meredith undid her own pants. "Nothing."

Natalie swallowed.

Meredith looped her fingers in the waistline. "If this is too much, I could turn around."

"You're fine."

"You sure?"

Natalie nodded, not moving any other part of her but her chin.

Meredith pushed her pants and panties down and then stepped out of them. She stood naked before Natalie, who was still immobile but looked serene. Meredith wanted to be in her arms. She didn't want to cover up. She wanted to see Natalie, too.

Natalie reached down and unzipped her own fly. That was almost enough to send Meredith into convulsions. She bit her lip. Natalie saw her expression.

"Help me," Natalie said.

Meredith took hold of the jeans, tugging as Natalie lifted, and they slid off her like a sheath. Natalie was as naked as she was, and there was no reason not to go to her, to slide along an expanse of skin, of heat, of love, while Natalie laughed and pulled the blankets over them. Meredith pressed her nose to Natalie's neck, smelling the faint oil in her hair, the sweat clinging to her arms. She wanted to follow the sheen under Natalie's breasts, and lower, to where the earthiness of the lake walk gave way to something muskier, something only for her. She kissed Natalie's chest, over her heart, and then her belly button.

"Please don't stop me," she said.

"Who's stopping you?" Natalie touched her temple. "We're just beginning."

Meredith lifted her head and met Natalie's intense, passionate gaze. "Our whole loves."

Joy came to Natalie's face. "Our whole lives."

Meredith lowered her mouth. She resisted consuming Natalie with one taste, to give instead of take, to love. She wanted to love with more than with her tongue. Her heart ached. Her loins ached.

Natalie's grip tightened in her hair, so deliciously Meredith could barely catch the warning.

"We have time," Natalie said.

But Meredith had not tasted this in so long. She traveled along folds, sought heat. Found places to made Natalie scream and let go. Or hold on tighter. She remembered. Prison was a woman's sea of offers, of loneliness and lust. And pictures of Natalie in her Bible.

"I need you," she said, breathing in, kissing Natalie's thighs.

"I need you, too."

An affirmation. The frenzy receded. Meredith settled into the moment. She lapped, instead of strafed. Natalie writhed underneath her.

Meredith circled once more around Natalie's clit, and then moved lower to the source. She circled again, tentative, until Natalie whimpered.

"Please."

Meredith slipped inside, pressing with her tongue, with her whole face, and she touched the pulse with her fingertip. Natalie's hips rose. She froze and Meredith felt only what moved inside. Blood rushing, muscles vibrating.

"Oh God," Natalie cried, shuddering against Meredith.

Only when she twisted away, panting, limp, did Meredith let her go.

"That felt so good. I haven't felt that way in a long time."

Meredith rested her chin on Natalie's stomach, gazing at her with wide eyes.

Natalie blushed. "Come here."

Meredith slid up Natalie's body, stopping to kiss each breast, and then her heart. Natalie caught her in a hug and they rolled onto their sides.

"Really?" Meredith asked.

"Geez, Meredith. I got two kids. All I want to do is go to sleep."

Meredith grinned.

Natalie propped herself up on an elbow. "You mean you, uh."

"Sometimes. Usually, um, after you visit."

Natalie brushed hair from Meredith's face, and then leaned in to kiss her, tasting herself, nuzzling Meredith's cheeks until Meredith giggled and pushed her away.

"I love you," Natalie said.

"I love you, too."

Meredith was restless. After making love to Natalie, what she'd obsessed about, and almost feared for so long, the goal achieved, other things began to slip into her mind. Stir her body. She had focused on one thing, and had let that obliterate everything else. But now Natalie was tracing her arm and she squirmed.

Natalie's touch left her. "Are you~"

"Earlier, um."

Natalie grinned. "I remember earlier."

"You said, 'Oh God,' when you, uh."

"Came like an earthquake?"

"Oh, was that what it was like?"

Natalie reached for Meredith's hand. "It was amazing," Natalie said.

"But when you~was that, you know, just a saying? Or were you~"

"It was definitely a prayer. From my lips to His ears."

Meredith rolled onto her back.

Natalie tugged on her hand. When Meredith didn't respond, she rolled onto Meredith, half-covering her torso, and met her eyes.

"It's just--" Meredith said.

"Should I?"

"Stay. I want you. I want." Meredith's hands settled onto Natalie's shoulders.

"Meredith. Tell me what's going on?"

Meredith shook her head, closing her eyes. She'd had to ask. She'd had to know the answer. But she didn't know what to do with it. She didn't talk about this in her letters, not about God, not about what Natalie was doing. She realized, with Natalie's dark eyes above her, curious and open, Natalie had tried.

"Dear Merry, the sermon today..."

"Dear Merry, Angel took the boys to Sunday school..."

"Dear Merry, I read this passage and..."

"Oh, God," Meredith said.

"That was rhetorical."

"I just want to be with you. Only with you." Meredith opened her eyes in time to see Natalie's narrow. "I talk about this stuff in group therapy, in regular therapy, in the chapel, in the yard. I can't talk about it with you."

"But you--"

"I was just surprised."

"You make me happy." Natalie kissed her neck. "And He's a part of you."

"He makes you happy?"

"The whole package." Natalie kissed along Meredith's collarbone. When she tried to move lower, Meredith tugged her back, eye-to-eye.

"I need you here," Meredith said.

"Like this?"

Natalie slid her hand between them, finding Meredith, who spread her legs wider, linking her ankles around Natalie's calves, locking her in and moving with her, body against body like they'd been in this rhythm their whole lives, and not only a few times.

"Yes," Meredith said.

"You like this?"

A hopeful expression spread across Meredith's face. "Maybe a little more."

Natalie pushed two fingers into Meredith. "Like this?"

"Like that. Natalie." Meredith urged her closer. She grabbed Natalie's hips, rocking in tandem, meeting each thrust of Natalie's fingers. "I want you inside me," she said. She wanted Natalie to block out the rest of the world.

Natalie was moving too fast, her fingers were too hard, overwhelming Meredith, who could only jerk against her, trying to keep up, losing the battle of the pace. "Natalie," she said, a plea, but she was being swept away, being separated from her sense of control, and then her fears, and then her entire body.

She met Natalie's eyes but the gaze broke as Natalie bent to kiss her, consuming her breath just like the rest of her body and Meredith fell apart beneath her and Natalie~Natalie remembered~sinking down on Meredith just as Meredith came, adding weight, a sense of being crushed, so she could crest, and cry out, and be filled one more time. Everything became Natalie.

She coughed, almost a choked sound, and Natalie eased up, just enough for her to breathe. She could see Natalie's face again. She wet her lips. "Yes. Just like that."

"You're so easy."

Meredith hugged her close and then let her go.

Natalie rolled onto her back. "When do we do that again?"

"Having sex with you for twelve hours straight is not going to solve any of our problems," Meredith said.

"What problems?"

Natalie stumbled out onto the porch, wrapped in a robe. Inside, with the sun streaming in through the windows, it was almost warm enough for the air conditioner. Outside, there were hints of fall's arrival. The air was crisp. The lake shimmered, inviting her closer.

Natalie's leg complained, missing the warmth. Limping to the stairs to retrieve something from her car caused a greater protest and she hesitated, hand on the banister. If it was just the leg, she wouldn't care. But it was her side~the pain moving through her reconstructed hip, radiating up her ribcage. Her whole life, they'd told her. This would be her whole life.

She turned away from the stairs and hobbled back inside. Meredith still slept. Curled up in the comforter, half in Natalie's vacated space already, seeking warmth, she appeared young and at peace. This girl, who was free now, could have anything.

"Hi, I'm unemployed," Natalie muttered as she went to her purse. "And I can't walk. And I'm over thirty. My mother told me that means I'll never get married. And I hate kids." She swallowed two Advil, considered, swallowed a third. She had a big day ahead of her. Her heating pad, her comfortable couch~ they were far away.

She kept the pills with her. Percocet, even, if she didn't want to drive, or move, and just lie there in the bliss of being pain-free.

Like Meredith was doing now, stirring, no taint of prison on her, washed away by making love, by walking outside.

Natalie moved closer.

"Hi," Meredith said.

Her smile was so radiant Natalie leaned down to kiss her. A hand clamped down on her arm and pulled. Heart pounding, leg aching, she settled onto Meredith, lifting only high enough to see her face.

"Hi."

Meredith's hands moved to her hair, threading, drawing her into a hungry kiss. Natalie responded as Meredith's leg rose between hers, bending at the knee, bringing Natalie closer by virtue of desire quickly turning to desperation.

"God," Natalie said. "You're gorgeous."

"I need you." Meredith scrambled for Natalie's hand, yanking it between their bodies.

"Wrong hand." Pain radiated through her bad side.

Meredith let her go, faintly grinning, eyes closed. Natalie righted herself, sliding her hand to Meredith's center, finding her wet.

"What do you need?" Natalie asked.

"I need you. Inside me. Take me." Meredith's eyes stayed closed, but she babbled, searching for the phase to make Natalie's fingers thrust into her, strong and sure. "Natalie."

Natalie rocked her hips, leveraging herself against Meredith, seeking to go deeper. Her own urges brought her against Meredith's leg, seeking relief, but she couldn't be bothered to adjust the awkward angle. All her focus was on Meredith. Feeling Meredith's nails dig into her arm in response.

"More," she said. Meredith thrust up to meet her.

"Don't stop," Meredith said in return, moving with her, stroke for stroke, moan for moan. "Don't ever stop."

At home again, but not feeling so empty, Natalie mulled how to update her Facebook status. Sometimes this took hours of her day. She swapped stories and videos with her former co-workers, casual acquaintances, envious of their work, wishing she could give advice on their briefs, but she was rarely asked. She was an outsider and was treated like one. A diversion.

Patrick would only send her pictures of the kids. He wouldn't talk about the law.

Clarice, though, would ask her to proof things, and send her emails, and asked her to the movies, though they never hung out when Natalie was in Charlotte.

"It's like you're in prison, not the other girl," Clarice wrote. "I have her on Google alerts."

Natalie's friend Melanie, whom she met at the art museum on a lunch break two years ago, had started having lunch with Clarice once a month after Natalie quit her job. To consult on Meredith's case, at first. Now they were planning a dinner party.

"Bring your kids," Melanie wrote.

Impossible.

Natalie wrote as her status update, "Things are getting better."

Chapter Forty-Three

"Dear, Merry," Angel wrote. "I'm sorry my letter is late. I've been writing it between shifts, on paper in my locker, or in my glove compartment, or at home, but it's hardest there. The noise, you know. I let the kids draw you a picture. It's included. If you were here, querida, this would be like reading my blog."

Meredith hung the drawing on her wall, a mass of purple scribble and orange streaks. There were four other pieces of paper enclosed, and one post card of the state capitol. In the back, everyone in Angel's family signed in different colors. She hung the post card up, too, signatures forward.

She started with the piece of paper stained with coffee.

"There's a new patient on your ward no one likes. Mr. Cranston. Your neighbor's father. She comes sometimes. Once she even brought your boys and let us play with them while she talked to her father. They don't get along. He doesn't get along with anyone. He needs you, Merry. They're going to take part of his liver out. But it won't be enough."

She flipped the paper over and found numbers for a football pool, and Angel's annotation. "I lost. Gambling is a sin, *si*? And cursing is on the rise. It's Mr. Cranston's fault, but still, it's on the rise. We're the animals, Merry. Not you. It's like *Othello*."

"We don't talk about you much at the hospital, even though your picture is still there. We don't want to jinx anything. If we don't fill your absence ourselves, maybe you'll come back and do it."

She folded the paper and took a deep breath. Most people were at Sunday morning services while she sat on the picnic table. There were perks to being at services. There were fewer perks to sitting outside on a chilly morning. But Robin was out here, jogging from fence to fence and back again. Meredith counted her steps.

Robin noticed her. "Want to join me?"

Fifty-six steps, from fence to fence. Meredith shook her head. "I'm not big into that, I have to say."

"Not big into exercising?"

"Yeah."

"And not big into eating."

"Depends on what they're serving."

"Tell me about it." Robin hovered beside the bench, standing. She wouldn't sit down unless invited. Personal space was all they had left in prison. "And you're not into church."

"Well, not this church." Meredith patted the bench.

Robin sat. She was out of breath.

"You either?"

"The only God I worship is money."

"Seems more like Satan."

Robin gazed at her, wide-eyed.

"I mean, it got you here, didn't it?"

Robin pursed her lips. "What got me here... It's bullshit. It's all bullshit. Maybe it's Satanic bullshit. How would I know?"

Meredith shuffled her papers.

"Good letter?"

"They're all good letters."

"Even the painful ones?"

"Especially the painful ones."

Robin nodded. "I don't get letters. Husband calls once a week but I can't hold onto him with my hands."

"This one's from a co-worker. He's telling me about an obnoxious patient at the hospital. Violating HIPAA, I guess. The patient's related to my neighbor."

"You're from a small town, right?"

"Yeah."

"So everyone knows everyone."

"Like you wouldn't believe. Well, like prison, actually."

"I wouldn't. I don't even know my neighbor. Much less the relatives. Or the medical status."

"The worst part of being here. Being separated from everything I know. From everyone."

"Yeah. I feel the same way. I want to go back to doing what I was doing and I can't."

Meredith nodded.

"Come on, walk with me. Let's see how many steps it takes to do the whole thing."

"I don't know."

"Are you busy?"

"I don't want the letter to be over too quickly." Meredith got up.

They walked, without speaking, around the entire perimeter of the fence, tracing buildings, darting through alcoves. When they returned to the bench, Meredith took a look around, 360 degrees.

"I lost track somewhere in the 300s," Robin said.

"Counting is about repetition."

"So, it's not just a lark?"

Meredith shook her head. "Nothing's ever just a lark."

Robin snorted.

Services let out and they watched the crowd of women walk out of one warehouse-shaped building toward another.

"Lunch," Meredith said.

"Let's join them."

They fell into step with the crowd, and were for moments anonymous women, herded through institution doors. Then they were settled at Burdette's table.

Burdette grunted.

Meredith forced herself to eat three bites of scrambled eggs and one bite of biscuit before she pulled out her letter.

Robin had been trying to engage Burdette in conversation. Burdette was about to toy with her, as a spider might its prey, but she reached for the letters.

"Pictures."

"Angel said he forgot he couldn't just email them to me. Not to prison. So he went to Walmart and printed them out. They're from the last party they held with the swear jar money."

"You kept a swear jar?" Robin asked.

"Doesn't everyone?"

"No." Burdette shook her head. She considered the picture and then passed it to Robin. "So, this is how other people live."

"They look happy." Robin took another picture. "They got 'Thank you, Merry' on the cake. Did you swear the most?"

Meredith laughed.

"Did she swear the most? Have you met her?" Burdette asked.

"This morning I sweared more than she did."

"She's a fucking saint," Burdette said.

"They don't have to thank me for anything." Meredith smiled, though, as her eyes filled with tears, and she took another bite of biscuit.

"Think there's a correlation between people who admit to their crimes, and good people?" Robin asked.

"No," Burdette said. "And I don't like you."

Robin grinned.

Meredith swallowed. "I don't think people are good or bad."

Burdette rolled her eyes.

"And I don't think prison will change a thing about us."

"Hear hear," Robin said.

"She doesn't even curse. She clearly has no idea what she's talking about."

"I don't care what she says," Robin said, jerking her head toward Burdette. "I like her."

"Great. Don't pay attention to Merry. She just got laid."

Meredith blushed and opened her milk carton.

"It makes anyone insufferable," Burdette said.

"Funny. I thought the glow was holy light."

"I'm getting new friends," Meredith said.

"You go ahead. Because we sure ain't getting you a cake, Merry," Burdette said.

Robin watched them thoughtfully, and then tried the eggs.

A mistake.

Merritt ran up to Natalie and held aloft a *Transformers* backpack.

"No," she said.

"Why not?"

"First of all, you know how your mother feels about violence."

Anthony Jameison, standing beside her at the cart, snorted.

"Second of all," she gave him a warning glare, "*Transformers?* I know you think they're a little passe. I mean, I watched them when I was a kid. Don't you want to be cool?"

Merritt scowled.

"*Pokemon?*" Natalie suggested.

Merritt's scowl got bigger. He slunk back to where Beau and Irene were at the backpacks.

"What's the difference between *Transformers* and *Pokemon*?" Anthony asked.

"Guns, mostly. And realism."

"I don't know if it matters."

"Probably not. But Merry made her feelings clear."

An awkward silence fell between them. Beau showed Irene a plain brown backpack covered in pockets and buckles. Natalie crossed her fingers.

"Thanks for doing this," Natalie said, for the fourth time.

"Our grandkids will only get one first day of school. We want it to be special."

Natalie nodded.

Merritt ran up with a red backpack.

"What's the logo?" Natalie asked.

"*Digimon.*"

"Maybe," Natalie said.

Merritt pouted.

"Have you seen them all yet?" Natalie asked.

Merritt shook his head.

"What if the perfect one is buried? What if there's something better and you haven't seen it yet?"

Merritt ran back to the backpacks.

"Do you often trick the children?"

"Often," Natalie said.

"They seem happy."

"I guess."

"We thought this transition would be more difficult."

"Would it have been, if they weren't in the same house, surrounded by their things, their neighbors, reminders of their mom?" Natalie asked.

"If there weren't reminders, maybe they would miss them less."

"They would just be confused, having feelings and no place to anchor them."

"What do you know about child psychology?"

"I've been reading. What do you know?"

"I raised a good man. He made beautiful children."

Natalie squeezed the bridge of her nose.

"We probed them, you know," Anthony said.

"You did what to those boys?"

"I mean, we questioned them. About what goes on at your place. About food, playtime. Arguments. Nothing about when they lived with Meredith--we can use our own imagination--but how exactly they're being treated. Are they hurt? Or, on the flip side, are they spoiled?"

Natalie wondered if all of Walmart could feel her rage.

Anthony went on. "They weren't evasive. They were confused. They bragged about, 'Getting to write mommy.' They don't like it when you have to go to work. Beau says he can write his name because you're a lawyer."

"Merry taught them." Natalie massaged her forehead.

"They seem to be doing okay. I don't know we would have done a better job," Anthony said.

Natalie nodded, squeezing her eyes shut.

"But we love them more. We're family."

"We're a family. We want to be a family."

"Why?"

Natalie opened her eyes. "Why?"

"You seem like a decent woman, Ms. Ivans."

"Thanks."

"Why Meredith?"

Natalie watched Beau and Merritt traipse up and down the aisles, backpacks on their backs. Next would be lunchboxes. Another battle. Natalie and Anthony were supposed to be tackling the less glamorous stuff on the kindergarden list. Crayons. Paper. Kleenex. Glue sticks. She tried to imagine why they needed so many glue sticks.

"Why Meredith? Because I love her?"

"That's not an answer."

"It was good enough for you. What do you want me to say? She's smart, she's funny, she's solid. She's faithful. She's generous."

"She's not perfect. She--"

"I know. She gets depressed. More easily than she'd ever admit. She eats horrible things. She's not intellectually curious. She feels way too much. She lives in her own world despite what the rest of us say."

Anthony said nothing.

"Do you want a list of my faults, too?" Natalie asked. Her anger wasn't fading, but radiating through her, even as Irene waved at them and they loyally pushed the cart after her to the next section.

"She married our boy. She made a family. And then when she found out he was--he was." Anthony hesitated and took a deep breath. "She got jealous and took him away from us. Rather than divorcing him or even making it a public scandal. She had options. Even if he betrayed her. We would have helped him."

"Wait," Natalie said. She put her hand on the cart to stop their momentum.

Anthony turned to her.

Natalie closed her eyes briefly. This was going to be hard. This was so not her responsibility. She met his gaze and said, "Meredith knew Vincent was gay before she married him."

"She what?"

"She did. Those boys are not~They got help. With the conception. They wanted a family."

"To be a facade?"

"No. A real family."

"But Meredith found out about Vincent's friend in the war. He was going to take his boys and leave her."

"You know, Mr. Jameison, I just thought you didn't actually believe that. I thought you were just punishing her."

"And I think you're a moron for believing they lived some fairy tale," he said.

Her grip tightened on the cart.

"Ms. Ivans," he said.

"You have noticed who Meredith's with now, haven't you? Did you ever consider Meredith and Vincent had an arrangement?"

Anthony's eyes widened. Natalie could see he never, in fact, considered what she and Meredith did together. And he was imagining it now, in vivid color. She winced, but was still furious enough to ask, "What, you thought we were sisters?"

"Or you were after the boys."

Revulsion hit her like the roof collapsing. She leaned on the cart.

Anthony tried to change the subject. "Meredith just seemed so happy. You know. With Vince."

"She was." Natalie gasped, trying to take in air.

"I'm sorry. We did ask the boys. Obliquely, of course. This explains why Beau said, 'No, she's mommy's friend.'"

"I didn't ask to come to Tarpley. I just ended up here."

"So you have no personal responsibility at all."

"To Beau and Merritt. To Merry. Not to anyone or anything else, Mr. Jameison."

Anthony shook his head. "I got no problem with how people live their lives. As long as it doesn't affect the kids. And they seem all right."

"If you knew, why did you let it go on?"

He frowned.

"About Vincent, I mean." Saying his name felt sacrilegious, but he was a part of her life now.

"I guess Merry was a distraction. We thought if she weren't around so much, he could meet someone else. He always had such good buddies. Like Jake. I know he babysits sometimes. I mean, he was popular. We thought the guys would set him straight." He chuckled bitterly.

Natalie opened her mouth.

"Why didn't he just tell us?"

She closed her mouth.

"Why not just come out? Both of them? We didn't raise him in a hateful environment. We didn't tell him to go hating gay people or anything like that. But he went and joined the army. For God's sake, why would he do that if he was--That confused us so much."

"Meredith said--" But she stopped herself. She wouldn't do that. Those were Vincent's most private feelings. The kind of man he was--only Meredith knew. And Jake. Now her. Maybe one day, the kids. But not his parents. Vincent's feelings were none of their business. So instead of telling them truths about the war, she made guesses about his sexuality.

"It's hard enough in the city. Where meeting someone is just going down to the 'arts' district and finding a coffee shop. Maybe going to a film festival. Or going to a school where there are two thousand students, so a good twenty of them are in the Gay Straight Alliance. Growing up in Tarpley? Vince probably only knew one or two people like him. Even in the Army, the way it is, I'm sure there were more."

"Obviously," Anthony said, snorting.

"Maybe settling with Meredith meant he didn't have to leave home. She's--"

"She's poor white trash," Anthony said.

Natalie hadn't expected those words to come out of his mouth, but the hard expression told her he was serious.

"She went to college," she said, lamely, unprepared to defend Meredith's reputation this way. Murder, religion, sexuality, sure. But the rural ways of North Carolina were still a mystery. Like learning a foreign language, she felt like she needed to go to the bathroom and could only remember the word for "bus station."

"Yeah, who do you think paid for it?"

Natalie didn't know much about Meredith's parents. They were still alive, somewhere in western North Carolina, which might have been another continent. Meredith didn't talk about them much but she seemed to like them all right, and Natalie assumed they were marginally better than the Jameisons.

"And look who's paying now," Anthony said. "She upgraded."

The hate, Natalie realized, was something she would never be able to relieve or talk them out of. The boys could go to Harvard, Meredith could save their lives at the hospital, she could bake cookies or fix parking tickets or pray for them, but their hatred of Meredith would remain absolute. It was a fact of Natalie's life, like air and water. And love.

Beau came up to them, proudly holding aloft his box of 64 Crayolas. Natalie knelt and asked him what his favorite color was and watched him pry open the box until the crayon smell, waxy and rubbery and childhood, filled her senses. She put her hand on Beau's back, listening to him talk, resisting the urge to take Beau in her arms and shelter him from the world swirling around them.

Chapter Forty-Four

The alarm woke Natalie early. Sunlight taunted from outside her window. She'd been getting the boys up at seven every morning for the week before school started, timing breakfast and dressing before the bus was due to arrive at 7:45. She wanted to drive them to school. She saw no good reason not to. But Meredith insisted they embrace their independence.

Natalie took them on a couple of dry runs to their classroom, met their teacher, pointed out repeatedly which bus number to ride. The alarm clock read 6:02 before she finally moved enough to turn it off. The bed was too big—a sea of empty space to traverse. She rolled onto her back. "You should be here," she thought to Meredith.

Next to the clock was a picture of Meredith and Vincent, arm in arm, taken on the porch the day they'd moved in. The boys were already two years old by then, and Meredith was working at the hospital. The newest nurse on the block.

"You should be here, too," Natalie said to Vincent.

Natalie wasn't quite sure when she'd started praying with Vincent in her thoughts. She still felt like an interloper in this house, with the boys, while their parents were absent. But she felt inside their realm, invader or not.

She got up at 6:15 and wrapped a robe around herself. She could take a shower when the boys were gone.

When the boys were gone. No more cloying attention all day long when she was trying to file briefs or do research. No more begging Mrs. Cranston for help. No more sounds. No more cries. No more lunch around the kitchen island, with Merritt throwing cereal at Beau. No more Hide and Seek Hollingsworth.

Maybe she should homeschool them.

Meredith's voice echoed in her head, telling her they needed a chance. They needed to try. If it was a mistake, she could homeschool them to be perfect, faithful, shut-in lawyers later. But the mistake had to be made.

Natalie slunk downstairs. In the kitchen, she made peanut butter and jelly sandwiches. Two each, cut in half.

"Too much food," she heard Meredith's voice in her head.

"One to eat and one to trade."

"I don't want them trading."

"Let's just see what happens? If it's a mistake..."

"I should never give you a good argument."

Natalie chuckled and spread peanut butter. The bread and the peanut butter came from WIC, the raspberry and apricot preserves from Jake's father's farm. She was still grinning as she tucked the sandwiches into plastic bags and added an apple, chips, cheese slices, and filled their thermoses with half orange juice, half water.

She made coffee.

At 6:45, the alarm clock upstairs began to blare.

She listened.

The sound went off. But no other sounds were heard. She'd set out their clothes last night, hoping they would serve as a reminder of what today was. No shuffling. No yelling.

She frowned and took the first step. The door flew open at the top of the stairs.

Merritt, dressed, hair uncombed, rushed down the stairs. "Hungry," he said.

"Make yourself some cereal."

Beau was still in his pajamas. He carried his first-day-of-scool jeans and looked tousled and confused.

Natalie called to the kitchen, "Make me and Beau some, too."

"Aw," Merritt said.

Natalie ascended the stairs. "Mornin', Beau."

He nodded.

She herded him back into his room and picked up his shirt. "Drop the pants," she said.

He dropped his bundle and raised his arms. She draped the shirt over his hands first and he giggled as she pulled it down.

"Pants, Beau," she said.

He nodded.

She went to the door.

"Hey, Nat," he said.

She glanced back.

He grinned. "It's the first day of school!"

"How was school?" Natalie asked. She'd been pacing in front of their block, but now the bus came and disgorged ten children, including hers, with their fingers and toes intact.

"Fun. Katie was there. And Josh. And Patricia." Beau rolled the pronunciation. "Patreeceea."

Natalie laughed.

Merritt took her hand. "I don't want to go back."

"Why not, Merry?"

"It was boring."

"Merry knew everything. Every time the teacher did something, he knew it," Beau said.

Merritt ducked his head.

"Do you have homework?" Natalie asked.

"You have to read us a poem," Beau said.

Natalie nodded.

"Do I have to go back?" Merritt asked.

"Do you think you'll be able to keep our deal?"

Merritt considered as they walked into the house and into the kitchen, where she'd set out crackers, apples, and peanut butter. She sat down across from him at the table.

"I can," Merritt said.

"Good. I promise when mommy's home we'll talk, okay?" Homeschooling would only be an option with two parents, but she believed in it as much as Meredith did. In theory.

"When's mommy coming home?" Beau asked.

"Soon."

That night, she chose from Meredith's side of the poetry shelf, a ratty second-hand book marked from years of school use. Her own book collection, moved down from Charlotte in a U-Haul, augmented Meredith's—nearly tripled it—But she wanted the boys to experience their mother's tastes. She took the book upstairs to where the boys were already in bed. She checked their teeth. Both minty fresh. She sat on Beau's bed.

"This is your mother's book," she said.

Merritt beamed.

"Have you heard of Langston Hughes?"

They shook their heads.

"Well, here's the poem. The first of many, okay?"

She should have done this earlier, when they'd watched cartoons before starting dinner, before baking cookies for their lunch boxes. She should have made copies for them, and wrote down how they felt after she read it, and put it in their book bags to talk about tomorrow.

Homework. She'd learn.

"Ready?"

They nodded.

"It's called 'Daybreak in Alabama'..."

Chapter Forty-Five

The sign was posted prominently at the front gate of the prison, but Natalie parked anyway, willing it not to be true.

"Stay in the car," she told Beau and Merritt.

"But~"

"Stay in the car."

Merritt began to tear up.

Beau scowled as she crossed the parking lot, toward the gate. Ida was at the top of the steps. "Visitation's cancelled."

"What? Why?"

"No leave today. All I can tell you."

"What happened?"

Ida's expression tightened.

"Ida, please. I drove a long way."

"So did we," said a man leaning against the fence. "I'm not leaving here until I get in."

Ida said to him, "It won't be today. Please, go home."

But Natalie couldn't go home, not yet. Her body ached. The thought of another two hour drive made her sweat. "Can I call her?"

"No."

Natalie glanced back at her car. "The kids..."

"You're not the only family who came a long way."

"Damn straight," the man said.

"It'll be better if you just go."

"Is Merry~" she didn't know how to ask the unthinkable. "Do I have to worry about Merry?"

Ida softened. "You never have to worry about Merry."

Natalie nodded. She gazed at the buildings beyond the gate. She searched for Meredith in the windows and didn't see her.

"What do I tell my children?" she asked.

Ida shrugged. "The truth."

"Why~"

"There's no visitation today, Ms. Ivans."

Natalie strode across the parking lot, despite her knee about to buckle. Beau and Merritt got out of the car.

"Boys, what did I say?"

"Can we see mommy now?"

"No. We're not going to her today."

"Why not?"

Natalie knelt and held them at arm's length. She considered telling them someone had been bad at the prison, and it had been locked down. They understood lockdown. During their first week of school, they practiced. In case of a bomb or a shooter. Would they accept the explanation? But the prison wasn't locked down. There were no alerts, no armed guard posts. Just no visitation.

She considered telling them Meredith was with a patient who needed her. An emergency. They would be jealous, though, that Meredith would choose a stranger over them. Natalie would have to explain sometimes people had to make sacrifices to help other people~it wasn't easy~Merry was a hero.

They wouldn't like it.

"I don't know," she said, and hugged them.

"Are you going to cry, Natalie?" Merritt asked.

"I might. I miss your mother."

"Me too," Merritt said.

Beau was silent. He lifted his chin off Natalie's shoulder and gazed at the prison.

"So, we can't spend our morning here at prison," Natalie said, stressing 'prison' like it was an icky, ironic thing. "Let's do something else in Rocky Mount instead."

"What can we do in Rocky Mount?"

"Well, we can go to McDonalds." She felt guilty when their faces lit up. Teaching them to gorge on bad food when times got tough was not a positive life lesson. But she wanted to defy all the rules of the universe, if they were going to change arbitrarily on her anyway.

"You have to have apple slices," she said.

Merritt looked confused.

"And after that, we'll go to the children's museum, okay?"

"Okay. Can I pet the snakes?" Beau asked.

Merritt shrieked. "I don't want to see any snakes."

"Beau can pet the snakes. And Merritt, you and I will go watch the tide machine, okay?"

Merritt nodded against her arm.

"But first, I'm getting an apple pie," she said.

She herded the boys back into their booster seats and strapped them in, and then got in the driver's seat. The prison loomed in front of her. She blinked away tears.

"Just a little setback. Nothing to worry about. Nothing at all."

Jolene frothed at the mouth. Her legs were strapped down to the infirmary bed but her arms were free and she held Meredith's hand in a tight grip.

"You have to give me something. You have to."

"I'm giving you all I can," Meredith said. She tried to speak in a soothing voice, tried to keep a calming touch on Jolene's sweat-soaked forehead. But Jolene was burning up, and Jolene was hurting her. She wanted to run away.

The clock was ticking. Natalie was outside, waiting for her.

"Drugs. Oh my God, how much pain do I have to be in before you give me drugs?"

"The doctor will be here any minute."

"You said that before. He's not here. It's just you and me, Meredith."

And the guard outside. Just the three of them. The rest of the guards were restoring order, double-checking, after Jolene, overly pissy for days, finally punched Burdette.

And had not stopped punching her.

"Why didn't you tell anyone you were sick?" Meredith asked.

"I just had a headache. They won't even give you advil around here."

Meredith stroked Jolene's forehead.

Jolene groaned.

"The doctor's got to come up from the Rocky Mount hospital. But then he'll give you something for the pain, all right?"

"Give me what."

"Whatever you want. Oxycontin. Morphine. Percocet."

Jolene smirked, her teeth clenched. "What do you think I have?"

"You got bit by any animals lately? Dog? Cat? Possum?"

"No. The heck?"

"Bats?"

"Yeah. I found a bat a few days ago. Just tossed it over the fence. It didn't bite me or anything. Oh, God, is this what becoming a vampire feels like?"

Meredith smiled.

Jolene glanced at her, shaking with pain. "Let me tell you, it sucks."

"I believe you."

"I know this ain't Anne Rice. Tell me what I got, Merry."

"I'm not a doctor."

"You know, don't you. You know. Merry, please."

"I don't know. Probably just a bad flu. An infection. Some mold from the shower."

Jolene shuddered and Meredith gripped her hand.

When the doctor came, Meredith would tell him. Then she'd demand the vaccination shots. Then the whole place would go into lockdown. It wouldn't matter for Jolene. The rabies would kill her.

"Let me call Natalie," Meredith said.

Ida walked her back to the ward. "Can't."

"Please. She drove up here, didn't she?"

Ida was silent.

"Ida. Please just tell me."

"She came. With your kids. Leave was cancelled."

"Let me call her. Let me explain."

"I can't."

"Ida~"

"Stop asking, Jameison."

Meredith cringed. Whatever she said next would mean a loss of privileges.

Ida opened the gate. "Maybe tomorrow."

Meredith nodded and went through.

"Merry?"

Meredith turned back, peering at Ida through the bars.

"What about Jolene?"

Meredith shook her head.

Ida turned away.

Meredith made her way to the chapel and curled up in a pew, her back against the wall. She wanted to cry. She wanted to heave.

She didn't want to pray, but she did, for Jolene's body and soul. There would be no more chances for Jolene's redemption, no more time for her to get a clue, to change, to find joy or love or children. Meredith pressed her cheek to her knees. She didn't glance up when Siba came in. She closed her eyes against the faint sound of prayers. Mecca was that way. She didn't look.

Then Siba slid into the pew beside her.

Meredith exhaled.

"What's wrong with Jolene?" Siba asked.

"She's sick. Real sick."

"She going to get better?"

"No."

"We going to get sick?"

The fear went through Meredith's heart, paralyzing her. She thought of Natalie. She closed her eyes.

"Merry?"

"No. We're not going to get sick."

"But Jolene."

"Yeah."

"We should include Jolene in our prayers."

"Yeah."

"How long she have?"

"A few days. They're going to move her to Rocky Mount Hospital. Pump her full of painkillers. Watch her go."

"I always thought Jolene was a bitch. But now." Siba's voice trailed off.

"Yeah. She'll die that way."

"Instead of as someone else. So sad."

Meredith nodded. She kept her eyes shut. Otherwise tears would rush out.

"Ladies?"

"It's Ida," Siba said. "And a stranger. Dressed up like you."

Meredith sat up and rubbed her eyes.

A nurse standing next to Ida held up a syringe box. "I'm going to have to give you these, okay? Mandatory."

Siba turned to Meredith.

Meredith nodded.

Siba swallowed. "Where?"

"In your arm. What are your names?"

"That's Merry and Siba. I'll check them off." Ida studied her clipboard.

Siba slid out of the pew and into the next one. She winced as the nurse injected her. Then the nurse moved to Meredith.

Meredith offered her arm.

"You've been exposed? You're Merry?"

Meredith nodded.

"You touched the patient."

Meredith had her hands all over Jolene. There'd been sweat and foam and finger-crushing grips. She remembered the heat under her hand, and Jolene's rapid heartbeat. She nodded.

"Did you have gloves?"

"Didn't have time. Jolene was insistent. I wasn't stationed in the infirmary at the time. I just saw her punch Burdette."

"Burdette tagged, too?"

Ida nodded.

"Okay. We'll monitor you both. And a couple of Jolene's other friends."

Siba snorted.

Ida raised her eyebrows.

"Jolene didn't have many friends. She'd only been here a few weeks," Ida said.

"Must be hard. If she'd been on the outside—"

"She would have picked up a damn, cute, fuzzy little bat in her backyard," Ida said.

"Or called animal control," Siba said.

Meredith sighed, barely jerking when the needle went into her arm.

"You didn't hesitate?" the nurse asked.

"I'm a nurse."

"Seen worse?"

"I've seen bad."

People dying of cancer, so gaunt and wracked with pain their own families could barely stay with them, lingering, inevitably toward death. And Natalie, half-dead raw meat scraped off the highway, barely even human.

"Rabies is really bad," Meredith said.

"I've never seen a case. But we always expect one," the nurse said.

Meredith nodded. "I'd better go with you. Help people understand." She got up.

"I'll put it in your file," Ida said.

"Thanks."

Maybe it would buy her enough cooperation to call Natalie.

She couldn't think of tomorrow, not when today Burdette was still in the dining hall, with an ice pack on her cheek, covering up bruises and dried blood.

Chapter Forty-Six

Luis leaned against the car window. Trees went by. Grasses. More trees. A tobacco field. He glanced back at his driver. "So, you get me sent all the way down to Burgaw, and now you're dragging me all the way back to Tarpley?"

"You're implying I'm in charge of your life," Natalie said.

"Aren't you?" He scowled and tapped his head against the window. Tap, tap, tap. She tried to ignore it. She wished for music to blast it away. No music. That would lead to arguing. So just driving.

Tap.

"When the choice is getting burned by holy water or rotting in that place, I'll do whatever. Hell, I'll dig ditches."

"Is it that bad?"

"It's jail. I mean, even if it wasn't that bad, it'd still be bad. I'm used to doing whatever I want. I can't do anything now."

Natalie nodded, gripping the steering wheel tighter.

Tap. "Where are you taking me?"

"My church," she said.

"What, like where faggots and fairies go to pray for rainbows?"

She glanced at him.

He coughed. "Sorry. Um. What, some Orthodox thing?"

"Come on, Luis."

"Sorry, you don't know what kind of conversations I have every day in jail."

"I can imagine."

"Because of your~"

"Right." She gave him another warning look.

He grinned. "I'm not going to call her any names, I swear."

"How's your family, Luis?"

"Dad drives down like, every other day. Doesn't he have stuff to do in Duplin? Serve and protect?" Luis shook his head. "My brother, lots. My sister, she couldn't be fucking bothered. In fact, she's pissed I wasn't bringing her money every week like I used to. So now I'm worthless. She doesn't even have to pretend to be nice."

"But with the people who do come?"

"Yeah, it's better. Dad has to be nicer. After making all that effort, he doesn't want to waste it."

"And you?"

Luis slouched in his seat.

She glanced at him.

"Whatever, I miss my family."

She glanced back at the road.

"I'm sure they miss their family too. This is so messed up."

She nodded, and drove in silence.

He let out a heavy sigh.

"Guess again?"

"Where we're going?"

"Yes."

"I'm going to Hell," he said.

"Luis."

"Okay, okay. Lighten up, man."

She glanced over, taking in his gray skin, his slightly trembling hands, and his washed but tousled hair. She tried to lighten up.

He shifted, facing her. "You're going to take me to one of those crazy foreign churches, right? Orthodox?"

"Not Orthodox."

'But you're Orthodox."

"I was."

"You can never not be something you were."

"Deep, Luis."

"It's not fair."

"What's not?"

"Life."

"Right."

He stared at her as if she were stupid.

When the car pulled into the parking lot, he frowned at the tiny church. "Catholic? Look, not all Hispanics are Catholic, *chica*."

"I told you, this is the church I attend."

"*Y por que?*"

"Because~Just because." She didn't want to go into it. Why Meredith re-fused to go back to the little Baptist Community church was her business, not Natalie's. Natalie would have preferred something else~anything else~but Meredith was gone, and Angel was here, and he was looking out for them.

"Are your kids coming?" he asked.

"Yeah. Angel's bringing them. They wouldn't have enjoyed a trip down to Burgaw."

"What, an hour in the car with you?"

"It's four hours round trip every Saturday morning. They just love in-carceration."

Luis scowled, but didn't say anything as they got out of the car. He tugged at his suit. He'd changed in the car. No fashion in prison. But it was his own, and the tie his father bought him when he turned sixteen. He glanced around.

Natalie took his elbow.

"Does everyone know who I am?" he asked.

"Yup."

"You probably won't be able to come back to church here."

"Whatever."

Natalie guided him toward the doors. A woman greeted them and handed them programs. Luis craned his neck as they passed into the cool, dusky atrium. "Who's that?"

"No idea."

He frowned.

"I don't volunteer here, Luis. I just show up with my kids and sit in the back."

"What kind of church is that?"

"What kind of church did you go to?"

He shrugged. "I haven't been since Sunday School. But we went to As-sembly of God. We could like, walk from here." He pointed at the church across the street.

"Well, we're here now."

"I could make a break for it."

"What would you do?" Natalie asked, as they slid into a pew.

"Go out into the woods and cry about what I've done? Why bother? I can do that in jail."

"Aloha, *chica*," Angel said, appearing at their pew.

Natalie got up to kiss him.

Beau slithered past him to hug her waist. She patted his hair. "Thanks for bringing them."

"No problem." He glanced past her at Luis.

"Angel, this is Luis. Luis, Angel."

Luis nodded.

Angel nodded. "We'll just~" He took Merritt's hand and walked around to the other side of the pew, so Merritt sat next to Luis, and then Angel. Natalie sat on Luis' left side, and then Beau. She put an arm around Beau's shoulders.

"When we go find a new church with mommy, can it meet later?" Beau asked.

Natalie nodded.

Angel scoffed. "Morning has broken."

"Like the first morning," Luis said.

Angel punched his arm.

Merritt reached for a Bible and opened it at random and began to read.

Luis raised his eyebrows.

"He gets bored. But~"

"It's Corinthians. And it's in Spanish. And he's five."

"Siempre doy gracias a Dios por ustedes, pues él, en Cristo Jesús, les ha dado su gracia," Merritt read.

Angel shuddered.

"Dude, that's like, the worst pronunciation I ever heard," Luis said.

"I don't know what it means, either," Merritt said.

Beau leaned into Natalie's shoulder.

"I don't get it," Luis said.

"I grew up going to Russian services. I had no idea what was going on. This is kind of like home."

"And the boys are learning, right?" Angel asked.

Merritt grinned and read another sentence.

"That's right. It's the future. Listen up," Luis said.

"Are you sure I should be in your secret club, Angel?" Natalie asked.

"Yeah, I second that," Luis said.

"Everybody's welcome in the House of the Lord."

Luis sat down as the hymn ended. He hadn't known the words, and he'd been subjected to Natalie's terrible pronunciations as she read alongside him. Beau mimicked Angel's sounds on the chorus and sounded pretty good. Luis had been able to follow along the text, but he didn't read Spanish well.

He had no use for reading it~he spoke it because everyone around him spoke it~but he'd eschewed his peers in high school and learned German in-stead, which worked out well. He'd gotten Bs in German while his compadres got Cs and Ds in Spanish. He'd mocked them in German, and had only got-ten punched once.

He got called a Nazi a bunch of times, though.

The priest went up to the podium. Before today, Luis wasn't sure when he'd seen an actual live priest. Collar and all. He was like in a TV show.

"Weekly prayer requests..." Luis translated in his head, half-paying at-tention.

Merritt was kicking him, his foot swinging sideways. Making light, not-icable impact with his calf. He didn't know how to try and make the kid stop without making a scene, but it was annoying, and the more it went on, the more it hurt. Merritt was carving a bruise into his skin.

Kick.

"...Roger and Erin Garden, whose daughters Sarah annd Laurie, surely watch over them..."

"Stop, dude," Luis said.

Merritt ignored him.

Angel glanced over.

"And let us pray for those incarcerated... Jose Lupone... Juan Cansada... "

Merritt kicked harder.

"Jerk," Luis said a little louder.

Merritt smirked.

"...Meredith Jameison..."

Beau glanced up. Angel put his hand on Merritt's shoulder.

"...And Luis Duarte."

Luis clamped his hand down on Merritt's leg. Merritt let out a howl. Angel moved his hand from Merritt's shoulder to his mouth, covering it, and leaned over to whisper something to him.

Merritt squirmed.

Luis glared at Natalie. "They're praying for me?"

She didn't look at him. "It's time to pass the peace."

He automatically stood with the rest of them and offered his hand. *"La paz sea..."* he said. Strangers touched him. He wanted to run, to get some air, but Natalie and Angel had him boxed in. He couldn't push past him. Angel could take him down. And Natalie~

He raged silently, because the only other choice was more humiliation. He didn't sing the last hymn. He just stared stonily ahead.

The priest met his eyes.

Luis followed Natalie, who held a boy's hand in each of hers, and stepped from the atrium into the sunlight. He blinked and shivered. Late September. At least he'd be warm this winter. He wouldn't have to drive all over the county in the cold. He wouldn't have to spend Thanksgiving with his sister, or babysit her kids, or try and pick out the perfect Christmas present for his father.

Feliz Navidad, he thought.

Natalie stopped by Angel's car. "We're going to have lunch, on the lawn. Just us. I thought you might want to talk to the priest, when the crowds have left?"

"No," Luis said.

Natalie pulled a cooler out of the trunk.

"Yeah."

Natalie nodded.

Angel smacked Luis on the back. "Nice meeting you."

"You too."

Angel got into his car. Natalie handed the cooler to Merritt, who struggled but moved toward the lawn.

"He's leaving?" Luis asked.

"Yup. It's just you and me."

"What if I bolt?"

"The cops'll hunt you and shoot you like a dog," Natalie said.

"Uh."

"Not really. But I'll probably never get hired again."

"You trust me?"

"Sure. You haven't been drinking, have you?"

He rubbed the back of his neck, waiting out the pinprick of defensive anger. She spread out a blanket on the lawn and the kids hopped onto it.

"I didn't even take communion," he said.

"Because of the alcohol?"

"Yeah." He turned away. His cheeks burned.

She opened the cooler.

"You didn't take communion, either," he pointed out.

"I'm not Catholic."

"Me either." He sat down on the blanket.

Beau took a peanut butter sandwich and glared at Luis, as if Luis would take his food.

"You don't believe in God?" Luis asked.

"I do. I think. I have faith. But this whole 'this is my body' stuff? It doesn't make any sense."

"I don't think you can have one without the other, Ms. Ivans."

"I think we can do whatever we want."

"Then I want a sandwich."

Luis and the priest sat in the first pew together. Luis gazed at the cross, at the table, at the Bibles.

"Do I have to do this in Spanish?" he asked.

The priest smiled. "No. I'm Father Zato."

"Luis. Luis Duarte."

"I know your father."

"You do?"

"He brings me out on calls affecting our community. When there is a need for a priest, or a Spanish-speaking clergy member, or Hillary from the Methodist church isn't available."

"Like what?"

"Mostly suicides. Some accidents."

"Like~"

"I didn't go to River Landing."

Luis nodded.

"Do you have something you wish to confess?"

"I'm not Catholic, Father."

"I understand. But maybe it will ease your soul."

"Purify me?"

Zato said nothing. His hands were folded and resting in his lap. Luis mimicked the action.

"You know what I did," Luis said.

"I know a little bit about what happened. I don't know what you did."

"I killed~Father, I confess~Bless me, Father, for I have sinned? Scratch that. Two people I don't even know~I never even met them~they're dead because of me."

Zato nodded. "What else?"

"I hate~" Luis hesitated. He hated so much.

"I've heard it all. Even this."

Luis nodded. He gripped his knees with his hands and stared down, away from the church and everything else, and he spoke.

Chapter Forty-Seven

Natalie leaned on the shopping cart. Beau sat inside, but Merritt was circling her. "What do we get next?"

"Uh. " Merritt frowned at the cart. "Milk?"

Natalie turned to Beau. "And where is the milk?"

Beau pointed toward the back of the store.

"Let's go." She pushed the cart.

Merritt followed her.

She studied her WIC checks. After milk, they'd get juice. Beau built himself a fort of cereal boxes and tuna cans. Natalie had to keep the carrots away from him, in the actual child seat.

"Milk." Beau pointed.

Merritt got some.

"The bigger one, Merry."

"Which color?"

"Blue."

"They have red at school."

"I know. Blue."

Merritt sighed, but brought her the gallon container.

She stuck it next to Beau.

"Now juice."

Merritt frowned. "I don't know where juice is."

Natalie swung the cart to the left. Juice and eggs were given entrance into the fort.

"What else?" Merritt asked.

"Toilet paper."

Beau giggled. "We always buy toilet paper." He whispered it, as if the words 'toilet paper' were forbidden."

"What else do we always buy?" Natalie asked.

"Peanut butter."

"Right." She pushed the cart.

With macaroni and cheese, roast chicken, frozen peas, hot dogs and buns, cookies and crackers and juice packs for lunches, she settled her cart in the checkout aisle. "Boys, go sit on the bench."

Merritt regarded the bench warily.

Beau rushed to it.

"Do not move from that spot. If you do, no hot dogs."

Merritt paled and ran after his brother.

Natalie grinned at the cashier. "Okay, I have WIC, food stamps, and cash items. How do you want to start?"

She was over the shame long ago, but her cheeks still tinted pink as she spoke, trying to maintain eye contact. The cashier, she knew, was dead to the process. But other people could hear. She resisted the urge to glance around.

Merritt shrieked.

She glanced over. They were already anticipating her glare, and sat on the bench, legs swinging, trying to look innocent. She turned back to the cashier.

"WIC first," the cashier said. "It's usually the most pain in the ass."

Natalie nodded and handed over the checks. The cashier took a pen and began to scan the items.

"Hi, Mrs. Cranston!" The boys leapt off the bench and ran over to hug her as she rolled past them toward the exit.

Natalie groaned. So much for anonymity. She smiled politely. "How's your father?"

"He's all right. He's recovering from surgery. The medications make him, well, nicer."

Natalie nodded.

Mrs. Cranston turned away, patted the boys, and left the store.

Natalie exhaled.

"Food stamps?"

Natalie put the divider down between the items she thought qualified and the paper goods. The rotisserie chicken was an extravagance. But even in line, it smelled good. She went to bag and cart the WIC items while the cashier scanned food stamp items, setting aside ones that wouldn't go through.

Two other registers were open~one was express, too far away for anyone to notice or care about her. The other was right next to hers, and the woman waiting for her husband to bag their groceries was staring at her.

Natalie blinked. The woman smiled faintly, and then glanced away. The name came to Natalie before the face registered. Maria Sandoval. From church. She put her head down and kept bagging.

"We're doing cash now," the cashier said.

Natalie nodded.

"Is there a limit?"

Natalie wanted to say no. The urge to be haughty was nearly overwhelming. But she only had $25 in her pocket. "20 bucks," she said, "And whatever the tax is I can cover it."

The cashier nodded.

A hand touched her arm. Natalie glanced sideways.

Maria's lips were pursed. "Can I help with anything?"

"No, Mrs. Sandoval. Thank you." Natalie's lips felt numb.

Maria nodded. "I'll see you on Sunday."

"See you then," Natalie said.

She went to the register and paid $17.30 for her cash items, finished bagging, and made the boys push the cart out of the store. The relief at being in the cold air again was enormous, until she saw Meredith's station wagon waiting for her. The kids were pushing each other. She chased after the cart to keep it from crashing and gingerly leaned it against the car.

"Get in," she said.

"We can unload."

"I've got it. In you go."

Beau pouted.

Merritt slithered into his booster seat.

"Can we push the cart back to the store?" Beau asked.

"Not on your life."

Natalie loaded the groceries into the back, returned the cart, and settled into the driver's seat. She checked the receipt. The cashier hadn't charged for the chicken. She leaned back and closed her eyes. Something poked her shoulder. She had forgotten to buckle in the boys. She would have to do that before they could go home. But first, she waited for her sight to unblur from the sudden onslaught of tears.

Chapter Forty-Eight

"You're so stiff, Natalie," Jake said, as she did squats, her body screaming in agony.

"Gee, wonder why."

"Let me give you a massage."

"What?"

"I'm working toward my certification. I want to make a little extra money."

"I"m not paying you enough?"

"It's just hard right now."

"Daniel?"

He tsked. "I don't want to talk about Daniel." He guided her to the couch. "Take off your clothes and lie down."

She scowled, but did as he asked.

He began to rub her shoulders. "So, seriously, a vacation. Take the kids. Go away. Anywhere but Tarpley."

"You just said things were so hard."

"My point, my friend. We all need a break. We need to re-center."

"Find our peace?"

His hands moved to her back. "Yes. Doesn't this feel good?"

"Don't stop."

"Where would you go?" he asked.

"Charlotte."

She'd accepted her first paycheck from the Luis case. The income wouldn't last. But it was more than she'd earned in a while, and too little to really matter.

"Come on, Natalie. Listen to your therapist. Go home."

"I'll see what my case worker says."

He chuckled, moving down on the couch. "And now, the gluteus maximus."

"Yeah, Jake. Rub my butt."

She'd gotten the kids up early enough so they slept in the car on the way to Charlotte. She got to listen to NPR, which kept the kids sleeping and her happy. Telling the teacher she was pulling them out of school hasn't gone as splendidly.

"They won't learn discipline, they won't learn routine, and responsibility~"

"I promise, I'll teach them the letter C, okay?"

"I may need to report it to your case worker."

"Go ahead. Need her number?"

Rebecca said, "I agree with their teacher. It doesn't seem like a good idea. Want twenty bucks for gas?"

Beau made a groaning sound and sat up straighter. Natalie met his sleepy gaze in the rearview mirror.

"Are we there~" he started, and then his eyes widened. "Whoa." The skyline had come into view. Beau had never seen buildings so tall.

"They're skyscrapers," she said.

"Who lives there?"

"They're banks."

Beau squinted. Then he poked his brother. "Merry, wake up. Skyscrapers!"

Merritt squirmed.

"Look how high we are above the ground," she said, as she took the ramp up over the city.

Beau covered his eyes. "Let me know when we land."

Merritt giggled. "We're flying."

Natalie took her exit and then they were street-level again, driving through buildings. "There you go."

Merritt and Beau glued themselves to their respective windows.

"Where are we going?" Merritt asked.

"The science museum."

"Like last week?"

"A different one."

If she just drove around the city, letting them stare at buildings and parks and fountains, they might have the same experience. She was tempted. They could drive past her old condo.

"And we're meeting friends, right? The friends you had before Mommy and Uncle Hank?"

"Yes. They're still my friends. I just don't get to see them much." She pulled into the museum's parking deck.

"It's dark," Beau said.

"Your eyes will adjust. They're coming here for lunch."

"To the museum?"

"Yes."

Beau gaped. "Are they kids?"

She parked, unbuckled her seatbelt, and turned around to grin at him. "They were once."

"My God," Melanie said, looking Natalie up and down.

"What?" Natalie and Melanie sat on the wooden slats of the touching pool. Natalie was making sure Beau didn't splash anyone.

Merritt was gazing at the tide generation machine.

"You seem..." Melanie hesitated. She was tall and lean with dark hair and pale skin, as Irish as they came in Charlotte, and wore a power suit.

Their friend, Clarice, said, "You look like a redneck, Nat. Are those capris?"

Natalie glanced at her legs.

"The cane makes you seem eccentric, though," Melanie said.

"Melanie," Clarice said. She wore slacks and a blouse, though looked as formal and thin as Melanie. Just shorter and with much redder hair.

"I'm trying to help," Melanie said.

"I'm normal." Natalie said.

"Do you wear those things to work?"

"I wear suits to work."

Clarice raised her eyebrows.

"Okay, I wear business casual. Remember Fridays?"

Clarice folded her arms.

"Okay, okay, jeans."

Melanie gasped.

"I can't believe you," Clarice said.

"What?"

"We haven't seen you in like, six months. Not since you sold everything and moved away, like a~cultist, or something~and now here you are. With kids!"

Beau glanced up.

Natalie waved to him.

He went back to daring himself to touch a sea anemone.

"They're cute kids, though," Natalie said.

"Did you borrow them for this occasion?" Clarice asked.

Melanie nudged her.

"Come back to the office. Or get a job in a firm here. It's not too late."

Merritt came over, apparently bored of the waves, and wrapped himself around Natalie's hand.

"I'm never coming back," Natalie said.

Chapter Forty-Nine

The Charlotte traffic going east was unforgiving as rush hour neared. Between watching out for SUVs and watching out for carjackers, she had no concentration for anything in the backseat, beyond checking once or twice to make sure the boys were still alive.

Only when they pulled into a gas station off 74, did Beau speak up.

"Natalie, I don't feel well."

"Are you going to throw up?" she quickly got out of the car and opened his passenger door.

Beau shook his head. "Not that kind."

Natalie examined him. He seemed redder than usual, and puffy. He was breathing with his mouth open.

"Are you having trouble breathing?" she asked.

He nodded.

"Are you itchy?"

He considered. He nodded.

"Jesus, Beau, what did you eat?"

His eyes filled with tears.

"Okay, we're going to get gas, and then we're going to drive to the hospital, okay? Where mommy works?"

Merritt lit up. "Will she be there?"

"No, honey. But maybe Uncle Hank will, okay?"

Merritt looked noncommittal.

Beau scratched at his throat.

"Shit," Natalie muttered. "Shit, shit."

Merritt giggled.

She filled the car with gas, and then she walked into the store, and peered out the window at the boys, and called Hank's cell phone number.

"You've reached Dr. Wheeler at..."

"Shit," she said.

The man behind the counter frowned at her.

"Sorry. Hank, Beau is sick. I think he's having a reaction to something--or maybe the flu--but he doesn't have a fever and he doesn't feel queasy. But he's kind of raspy. I don't know. Maybe it's meningitis." She stopped. "I've become one of those hysterical parents. Please call me back and tell me what to do. Otherwise I'll be in Tarpley in two hours. Or maybe I should go back to Charlotte. There's lots of hospitals there and we're only an hour outside of town, or maybe--"

The voice mail cut off.

"Shit," she mouthed, where the cashier couldn't see her.

Maybe she should await further instructions. Being in the middle of nowhere had to be worse, though, than the cities at either end. Or the city at one end, and the one-horse town with the "regional" hospital thriving on Medicare and chronic outpatient treatment.

She went back to the car and got in. "How you doing, Beau?" she asked, glancing at the rearview mirror.

He shrugged.

"Did you touch one of those fish?"

"I touched lots," he said.

"Gross," Merritt said.

"And frogs. And a snake. And a tarantula."

So he could have been poisoned by some exotic animal and there would be no antidote in Tarpley. Or maybe anywhere. Maybe she should drive to Atlanta, where the CDC was.

"Okay, Natalie, get a grip. When you start talking about the CDC, it's time to check yourself," she said.

She started the car and cautiously pulled out onto Highway 74.

An hour outside of Tarpley, the phone rang.

She hit speaker. "Hank?"

"Hi, Natalie. Can I talk to Beau?"

"Sure." She passed the phone back. "Don't drop it."

"Hi, Uncle Hank."

"Hi, Beau. Natalie says you're not feeling well."

Beau shrugged.

"Hey now, I'm going to need verbal answers, okay? Yes or no if you can't think of anything else."

"Yes," Beau said.

Natalie smiled.
"Does your head hurt?"
"No."
"Does your stomach hurt?"
"Kind of."
"What's the last thing you ate?"
"Ice cream."
"At lunch," Natalie said.
"You guys haven't eaten dinner? McDonalds or anything?"
Merritt brightened.
"No, we're just driving home," Natalie said.
"Beau, does your back hurt?"
"A little."
"What about your skin?"
"Yeah."
"Repeat after me, Beau. 'The rain in Spain falls mainly on the plain.'"
Beau laughed.
"Come on, try it."
"The rain in Spain something on the plane?"
"Good."
Natalie could hear the wheezing and the hesitation between words as he got more breath. She sped up, focusing on the road in front of her.
"Merry?" Hank asked.
"I'm here," Merritt said.
"Do you notice anything odd about your brother?"
Merritt giggled.
"For serious now," Hank said.
Merritt studied Beau. "He's like purpley. Magenta."
"Great," Natalie said. "Beau is magenta."
"I am not. Shut up." Beau lunged for Merritt.
Merritt squawked.
"Natalie?" Hank asked.
"Yes, Hank."
"Still heading to Tarpley?"
"Yes."
"I think it'll be fine. I'll meet you at the emergency room, okay?"
"Yes."
"Natalie, pry your fingers off the steering wheel. Just a little bit."

"I'm all right."

"Do either of the boys have an inhaler?"

"No. Don't think so?" She felt guilty for not knowing for sure, but neither kid had asthma, or any kind of attack in the four months she'd been responsible for their little lives.

She didn't know what the judge had been thinking.

"Either of them have regular allergies?"

"Merry's allergic to the cat, but he doesn't take anything for it."

"No Claritin? Benedryl?"

"No."

"You said Beau didn't have a fever?"

"Not one I could feel."

"Okay. See you there."

She hung up and drove, and thinking of Luis, slowed down.

By the time they were ten minutes outside of Tarpley, Beau's gasping was audible and constant. Merritt was scribbling. Natalie tried to dissuade him, knowing he would get carsick, but he couldn't sleep with Beau beside him like that, and Natalie stopped playing music. She didn't want to miss any changes in Beau's breathing.

Beau squirmed.

"We're almost there," Natalie said.

"It hurts," Beau said.

"What does?"

"Everything."

A shudder went through her. She would have preferred to pull over to the side of the road and cry, or maybe pass out. She glanced at Beau in the rearview mirror.

He pulled up his shirt. His stomach was covered in hives.

"Well, that sucks," she said.

Hank paced by the nurse's station, his cell phone against his ear. "We've got a medical emergency with Meredith Jameison's son. It would be helpful if she were here."

"Can I get authorization from someone who isn't her cousin?" said the voice on the other side of the line. Monica-something.

He handed the phone to Dr. Singh.

"Yes, I'm Dr. Singh." He paused. "The exact diagnosis is still being assessed. Dire? Possibly life-threatening. He's been exposed~Meningitis? Why does everyone think it's meningitis?" Singh handed the phone back to Hank.

"Even if we authorized medical leave, we don't have transport."

"Do you need an armed guard?"

"Let me check the file." Another pause. "Not with Jameison. But we can't just throw her out the gate and have her walk to Tarpley."

"I'll take care of it."

"We won't authorize anything until you call back with a diagnosis."

"It'll take you two hours to get her down here as it is."

"These procedures are in place for a reason, Dr. Wheeler. These women are criminals."

"And almost all of them have children, am I right?"

A sigh came through the phone. "Call me back."

Hank hung up and then called Natalie. "Hey. Do you know anyone in Rocky Mount?"

Chapter Fifty

Natalie pulled the car into parking strip just beyond the emergency entrance. Her heart had been pounding since the gas station and she finally allowed herself a moment of relief.

"Are we going inside?" Beau asked.

"Yes. Merry, I want you to stay in the car."

"But~" Merritt said.

"No buts. Stay. I promise I'll be right out to get you."

Merritt screamed.

Natalie sighed. She unstrapped Beau and took his hand and they walked together toward the entrance.

Merritt banged the window with his fists. But he didn't get out of the car. Natalie didn't dare glance back and provoke him.

Beau concentrated on breathing.

Hank met them inside the door, a syringe case in his hand. "Hi, Nat. Hi, Beau."

"Hi, Uncle Hank," Beau said, raspily.

"It is anaphylaxis?" Natalie asked.

"Sort of. Not what you're thinking. He would have presented while you were still in Charlotte."

"Thank God." Natalie nearly sagged to the floor. Her pressure on Beau's shoulder kept her up. He squirmed.

Hank knelt.

"Is meningitis? Staph? Swine flu? Frog poisoning?"

"Natalie, please."

Natalie clenched her jaw.

Hank knelt and lifted a flashlight with his free hand. "Say ah."

"Ah," Beau said, and then coughed.

"Lift your shirt."

Beau lifted his shirt.

"Okay. We cleared an exam room for you guys. Let's go."

"Wait, Merritt's in the car."

"I'll have Theresa get him."

Natalie nodded and squeezed Beau's hand and they followed Hank through the emergency room to the offices beyond, and into an exam room.

"Beau, I'm going to need you to turn around and take off your pants."

"No." Beau shook his head.

"Stranger danger," Natalie said.

"I'm not a~"

"Well, of course not. Most kidnappings and molestations are by immediate or close family members."

"He's five, for crying out loud. I'm a doctor, not a~"

"Hey, Beau? How about if Uncle Hank leaves, and you and I get you undressed, okay? Just us."

Beau nodded.

"How does he know you're not a~" Hank asked.

"Life is about minimizing risk, not eliminating it. You'll just have to trust me. Out."

"There's a paper gown in the drawer there." Hank stepped outside.

Natalie helped Beau take off his clothes, wincing at the sight of the red bumps all over his body. She helped him with the gown, apologizing when he braced himself against the sting of the scratchy fabric against his raw skin.

"Hank," she called.

Hank came back in. He took out a syringe. "I'm going to give you this."

Beau shook his head.

"And then I'm going to give you good news."

"He'll live?" Natalie said.

"The best news ever."

"How about you give him five bucks?"

Beau nodded. "Give me your lunch money."

"We are going to have to have a talk," Natalie said.

"I'll give you one dollar, and good news, if you turn around for ten seconds. Can you count down from ten?"

"Ten... nine..."

"You can't start until you turn around."

Beau turned around.

"Let's count together," Natalie said. "Ten... nine..."

"Eight..." Beau said.

Hank injected him. "When you get to one, your butt is going to hurt. A lot. And I'll be over there." He dropped the syringe in a hazmat box.

"One. Ow! I hate you, I hate you." Beau pounded at Natalie.

"Oh, sure. And when the rash goes away, he won't even remember this?"

"Why can't he breathe?" Natalie asked. Even Beau's choked sobs were cut off by long, coughing, gasping sessions.

"He's got hives in his throat. And he's swelled up some. That's closing up his throat. And probably making it hurt."

Natalie held Beau's fists down and tried not to cry.

"We'll keep him overnight. Just in case something goes wrong."

"Just in case something goes wrong and he dies?"

"Natalie. Natalie, sit." Hank pointed to a chair.

Natalie sat.

Theresa knocked. "Everyone decent?"

"My butt hurts." Beau said.

Merritt slipped into the room. "You look like a leopard."

"What's the good news?" Natalie asked.

Beau glanced up.

Hank sat down in the chair next to Natalie and put his arm around her shoulders. "The good news is, boys, your mommy is coming to see you."

Natalie and Beau burst into tears.

Meredith apprehensively followed Ida out to the gate. She'd changed into slacks, and heard only Beau was sick. A car was waiting, but she couldn't see who was inside. "Police escort?"

"You're minimum security. Report back within 24 hours."

"Okay..."

She'd been watching *Cash Cab* with fifty of the other inmates, crowded in the mess hall, waiting for dinner to be served. Robin and Burdette knew most of the answers between them. She hadn't known a thing.

Since the rabies scare she'd become more involved in prison life. The inmates came to her when they wouldn't go to the doctors. People had been seeking her out in the chapel, so she avoided the chapel, leaving Siba to pray alone. She missed those nights of quiet.

But God hadn't been so absent. Things had gotten easier lately. Warmer.

She got into the passenger side.

Erica smiled at her. "Hi, Merry."

"Erica? You're~" she tried to come up with an explanation.

"Driving you to Tarpley. Yup. Right on down 95."

"For a story?"

"Just as a favor."

Meredith nodded. A favor to Natalie. Erica was gorgeous~even now in the fading light~and sophisticated. Smart. And she liked Natalie, and Natalie liked her. Meredith leaned back. "Thank you," she said.

"No problem."

"Your chance to see Natalie again?" She held her breath.

"I love that woman," Erica said, laughing. "But don't you worry, Merry. I can't give her what she wants."

"What's that?"

"You to come home to every night."

Meredith closed her eyes.

Erica put the car in drive. Only when the smooth, constant speed of the highway reverberated did Meredith say, "I can't give her that either."

Erica put the car in park. Meredith tried to leap out of the car, nearly suffocating herself with her seat belt. She unclasped it.

Erica laughed at her.

"Why don't you stay at my place tonight? It's too late to drive home."

"Are you kidding me? No way. I'll be fine."

Meredith gazed at the sky.

"I want to go home and sleep in my own bed, Merry. Have Natalie drive you back tomorrow."

Meredith quivered. "Yeah, all right."

Erica gave a little wave.

Meredith marched toward the hospital. The doors slid open, then closed behind her. She was free again. And alone. Her hands shook. But this was territory she knew. She headed to the nurse's station.

"Merry!"

She turned and Colleen rushed toward her. "How's Beau?" she asked as Colleen hugged her.

"He's all right. He's on the third floor. Let me take you." Colleen took her hand. "How the hell are you, Merry? You look good. I didn't think~" she blushed as they got onto the elevator.

"Want to see my prison tats?"

Colleen's eyes widened.

"I'm just kidding."

Colleen exhaled.

"You can't see them."

"Who you been talking to, girl?"

Meredith felt pinpricks of heat on her cheeks. The elevator opened. Colleen pulled her to the fourth room on the left. The children's ward. And there was her boy, small and covered in angry red welts. She cried out.

Merritt, who'd been curled up on Natalie's lap, scrambled up. "Mommy!"

Meredith hugged him, shuddering with the sensation of having him in her arms again, out where they were free. No prison reception room. She kept her gaze on Beau.

"He's all right," Natalie said.

"That's what Colleen said."

Colleen winked at them and then left, closing the door.

Natalie reached to hug her, but Meredith moved toward the bed.

"It's just an allergic reaction. Probably to something he ate, since it was in his throat," Natalie said.

"How did it happen?"

"We were at Discovery Place. I don't know. There's some freeze-dried ice cream."

"It was gross," Merritt said.

"You don't know? You were supposed to be watching them."

"I was." Natalie took a step back. "I was watching them."

"And you let Beau poison himself?"

"Where were you?"

"You know where I was."

"I was doing the best I can."

"Taking them all the way to another city? What were you thinking?"

"Merry."

"And then driving them back here? Why didn't you take them to the hospital there? You're irresponsible, Nat, and~"

Merritt's fingers dug into Meredith's hip. "Don't yell at Natalie, Mommy."

Meredith exhaled.

Natalie, tears in her eyes, brushed past them. "I'll leave you some time to be alone with your boys."

"Where are you going? We're not finished."

"I'm finished. I'm going to my car."

Merritt began to cry.

Natalie slammed the door.

Beau woke up. "Mommy?"

Meredith took the last step to the bed and wrapped herself around Beau. "How do you feel?"

"I'm okay."

Meredith hugged him close. "I love you so much."

"I love you too, Mommy. Where's Nat?"

Meredith glanced over her shoulder.

"Where's Merritt?" Beau asked.

Chapter Fifty-One

Natalie curled into herself in the passenger seat of the station wagon, convulsing with sobs. She couldn't even get into the back seat with the booster seats there. She had two lives in her hands, and she had almost lost one of them.

A knock came at the window.

She glanced up. Merritt peered over the sill. She opened the door.

"Are you by yourself?" she asked.

Merritt nodded.

"Go to the driver's side."

He grinned and walked around the car and got in, nearly short enough to stand in the seat.

She brushed at her cheeks. Having him there was calming. "You okay, Merry?"

He nodded. "Are you?"

"I think so." She offered her hand.

He took it. "Is Beau going to be okay?"

"Yes."

"Will I get it?"

"What?"

"The spots. Will I have those?"

"No, I don't think so. That's a special Beau disease."

Merritt grinned.

"Merry, tell me how Beau's been doing at school."

Meredith hesitated before knocking on the window. Natalie and Merritt were dozing with the seats back. She went around to the driver's side and knocked, and then opened the door. Merritt groggily sat up.

"Hi, Merry. Colleen's going to take you back to Beau's room, all right? And stay with you."

Merritt turned to Natalie.

"I'm going to talk to Natalie for a while, okay?"

"She was crying."

"I know."

"She cries a lot."

Natalie had her eyes closed, but she was still and tense. Listening. Meredith helped Merritt out of the car. Colleen took his hand. Meredith slipped into the car and shut the door.

Natalie rolled onto her side and opened one eye. Her cheeks were puffy. Her nose ran.

"I'm so sorry. I shouldn't have said those things," Meredith said.

"You were right." Natalie rolled back onto her back, just when Meredith wanted to touch her.

"No, I wasn't. I was wrong. I was just so scared. When they came and got me and said there was an emergency, I had to get down to the hospital or~I didn't know what was going on. I only knew I was really far away, and I felt so helpless. Natalie, I was terrified."

"When you feel that way you should come to me, not yell at me."

"I'm coming to you now. Natalie, please. I'm still scared."

Natalie shifted, meeting her gaze. "How do you think I feel?"

Meredith closed her eyes. She wrung her hands. She didn't want to know how Natalie felt, how awful it must be, day in and day out. "Natalie~"

"Every time they turn us away from the prison on visiting day. Every time I don't get a letter. You could be in there, hurt, or, I don't know. I hate not knowing."

Tears dripped onto Meredith's hands. "I'm sorry."

Since they were in this raw place, their defenses weakened, their pain already exposed, Natalie offered up the rest. "I don't know how much longer I can do this."

"Are you unhappy?"

"It's not~I just don't know why I'm doing this. It's endless. It feels, I don't know."

"You don't love my children."

Natalie met her eyes. "I don't mind taking them to school, or helping them with their homework, or putting them to bed, or staying all night at the hospital holding their hands. I do love them, Merry. As much as I love you. But everything is a reminder of what I don't have, instead of what I do. It's just so empty. Even loving them is empty."

Meredith cupped her cheek, gratified when Natalie didn't flinch away.
"I need you," Meredith said.

"I'm not doing a very good job."

"Yes, you are. Natalie, I'm scared of everything. You're the only thing I'm not scared of."

"Even if I-"

"Even if you leave. If you want to. I trust you, Natalie."

Natalie covered Meredith's hand. "You're only saying that because you don't have any other options."

"I have plenty. Foster care. Uncle Hank. Vince's parents. I choose you."

"I choose you. I wish you were here to choose."

"It won't be long, my love," Meredith said.

Natalie closed her eyes with Meredith's fingers stroking her face.

Despite the hospital noises, the family managed to sleep until six. Meredith curled around Beau and Natalie and Merritt slept in the second bed. Then the morning shift came through and everyone wanted to see Meredith. She was dragged out into the main lobby and hugged and pawed while Natalie tried to get the cranky children moving.

Theresa brought Doctor Radoni in. Beau was less pink. "Took the liberty," he said to Natalie, "Of filling your prednisone prescription. The pills are pretty big. Can he swallow them?"

"Can we cut them in half?"

"Sure. Three times a day, so you'll have to talk to the school nurse."

"I will."

"We can leave?" Beau asked.

"We sure can. We have to take Merritt to school."

Merritt frowned.

"I want to go to school too," Beau said.

"Oh, Beau."

"He'll be all right," Radoni said.

"Don't you want to spend time with your mommy?"

"I want to do both."

Radoni handed Natalie the prescription bag and slipped out. He paused at the doorway. "Oh, one more thing. Dr. Wheeler asked Theresa to set up an appointment for all three of you in about three weeks, when the prednisone's worn off. For a meningitis vaccination. Said he was tired of hearing about it."

Natalie grinned.

"More shots," Beau said.

"That's right. Come on. Let's get Merry and go."

Meredith slid into the booth at Hardee's. Beau followed. She slung an arm around his shoulder. "What time is it?"

"Nearly seven. The boys have to be at school by eight. We should really go home and pack their lunches."

"Just this once, can't we go to the cafeteria?" Merritt asked.

"You want to eat that food?"

"It's what all the other kids eat."

"Square pizza and unspeakable vegetables?"

Beau nodded.

"Merritt?" Natalie asked.

"I like my own lunch. But just this once."

"Just this once," Meredith said.

"And Hardee's for breakfast? It's your lucky day."

"Mommy's back," Merritt said.

"Good point."

Meredith glanced around. She saw faces she recognized from PTA meetings or shopping or neighbors. Some folks were just eating their breakfasts. Others stared. At her, at Natalie, at her and Natalie. "Nat," she said. "I've been thinking."

"About what?"

"Once I'm out, really out, maybe we don't have to stay in Tarpley after all."

"I tried getting you to leave."

"I know. But this was all I knew." Meredith stared hard enough that some people glanced away. "But now that I've been up at Conrad, I've been like, desensitized. I know I can survive someplace else."

"This is your home."

Meredith took Natalie's hand over the table. "You're my home."

"Sweet, but~"

"I know. We'll talk about it later. I just wanted you to know how I feel."

Natalie squeezed her hand.

Natalie left Meredith to paw at her stuff while she went to shower. Meredith had been in the living room, gazing around at toys and mementos.

When she got out of the shower, wrapped in a robe, Meredith had made it to the upstairs bedroom. She held a picture of Vincent.

"How're you doing? Is it weird? Being here?"

"It's really weird." Meredith turned around. "Mind if I take a shower?"

"It's your house."

Meredith made a face.

"It's a free country?"

"Now I know you're just messing with me."

"Yes, ma'am."

Meredith went into the bathroom. "I'm sorry. It must be a major disruption to have me here so unexpectedly. And the hospital and all."

"Everything else is a major disruption. This is fine. I just don't want to get used to it."

The water went on.

They hadn't really touched other than some hand-holding in the car. Natalie felt the trepidation, the distance between them. She craved Meredith but she still stung from the rebuke. She was still worried about the kids.

The hollowness threatened to explode if she touched Meredith and Meredith didn't want it. And yet, she craved it. She sat on the bed and glanced at the clock. 10:14 a.m. Only two days ago she'd been complaining to Jake. She'd concocted a getaway plan. Now here she was with Meredith in her shower. She scooted up on the bed, lying back on the pillows. Maybe if she took a nap, she could wake up without the sinking feeling of ennui.

The water shut off.

Meredith came out, hair wet. Naked. "That felt so great. I missed my shower. I almost cried."

"Because you missed your shower?"

"I miss everything." Meredith sat on the bed.

"Even me?"

Meredith twisted, tucking her cheek against Natalie's arm. "Especially you. Don't make me cry."

"I won't."

"Good."

"How's prison?"

Meredith laughed. "How's the case?"

"Same."

"Same."

Natalie turned on her side and pulled Meredith closer. "I can't believe you're really here."

"Did you secretly get Beau stung by a bee to spring me?"

"I would never."

Meredith nuzzled her neck.

"I wish I was clever."

"Oh, you are. You just save it for someone else's kid."

"He pays me."

Meredith snorted.

Natalie rubbed Meredith's back, marveling at how good it felt. Marveling at how her mood could change so swiftly.

"Before you ask," Meredith said.

"Yes?"

"I'm not sleepy."

"All right."

"I don't want anything to eat."

"Okay."

"I think the house is perfectly clean."

Natalie rolled onto her back, bringing Meredith with her. Meredith dug her elbows into Natalie's shoulders, enough to rise up and see Natalie's face.

"It's the middle of the morning," Natalie said. "What do you want to do?"

"I want to, hm. I want to pretend nothing else exists."

"Not even~?"

Meredith touched her lips. "Not even."

Natalie tried to keep the doubts to herself. The expectation that a few stolen moments with Meredith could combat the days and months without her, or their arguments wouldn't intensify, the boys would get older and less cute and more independent and it would be harder to protect them. She might never have a case that would make her rich and famous, not after hobbling away from the last one.

That the sadness in her life could be cleared away by a few kisses was laughable. She should have known at the start. She'd been such a romantic when she'd had money and no attachments.

She stared at the ceiling as Meredith kissed along her collarbone.

Meredith shifted, and soon Natalie felt her robe parted, and then there was bare skin pressing against her, breast to breast, leg to leg. She groaned. Meredith freed her arms from the fabric. Laid her bare.

"I'm doing better in prison," Meredith said, between kisses against Natalie's jaw. "Settling in. But you're doing so much worse, aren't you?"

"I'm okay."

"I should be here." Meredith slid down, kissing her chest, and then her stomach. "Taking care of you." Her fingertips traced Natalie's bad side.

"Merry." Natalie reached for her head.

"I love you."

"I love you, too. Come back."

Meredith lifted her head.

Natalie met her eyes and tugged at her hair. "Here?"

Meredith knelt and hovered until her lips were just over Natalie's.

"I wonder what normal life will be like," Natalie said, as Meredith settled against her. Her hips rose of their own accord, scissoring their legs. The shifting to readjust, to position, became light rocking. A comfortable, warm heat grew in her belly as she kept her hands in Meredith's hair.

"This is normal," Meredith said.

"Come on. This is not normal." Natalie touched Meredith's nose with hers.

"What do you want? Something like Jake and Daniel have?"

"Something like you and Vincent."

Meredith didn't slow her grinding, though consternation came into her expression. "This is nothing like Vincent and I."

"But~"

Meredith kissed the corner of her mouth. "This is so much better." She kissed Natalie's lips fully. Natalie arched into the kiss, using her hands to hold Meredith's head close, so she could nip and explore. Her tongue found Meredith's and the kiss deepened. They moved together, still slowly, but with longer, harder thrusts.

Natalie sighed and broke the kiss. "I love being naked with you."

Meredith grinned.

"I feel like it gives my life purpose."

"What purpose?"

"To be naked with you."

Meredith laughed. Natalie rolled them over so she was on top. Meredith pulled her down for a kiss.

"We have hours," Natalie said.

"When I come back, we'll do other things besides make love."

Natalie pushed into her. "Oh?"

Meredith's eyes closed. "Like chores."

"This isn't a chore?"

Meredith slapped her ass. "You just said it was your purpose in life."

"Hm, but I lied."

Meredith grabbed her hips, arching up. "Oh yeah?"

"My purpose in life is to make you come."

"You're going to have to wait," Meredith said, as she rolled her head against the pillow, panting when Natalie kissed her face.

"I don't think so."

"No? You feel too good for a wham, bam, thank you, ma'am."

Natalie grinned, but settled herself more snuggly against Meredith underneath her. "My leg might disagree."

"That's okay. Put all your weight on me. I can take it."

Natalie kissed Meredith, closing her eyes. They slid together, mouth to mouth, body to body. Meredith's hands moved along Natalie's back, over her ass, up to her neck and shoulders, wherever she could reach. Soon they were moving together more forcefully. Meredith twisted in frustration, trying to make more contact with Natalie's center. Their kisses were light, sloppy brushes of lips between gasps. Natalie rolled, putting more of her weight on her good side.

"Are you ready to concede?"

"To what?" Meredith asked, trying to pull her back.

"To my purpose in life."

Meredith's eyes opened. She met Natalie's. Their movements stilled. Then Meredith turned on her side, facing Natalie, and threw a leg over her hip.

"I'll take that as a yes."

"Please. Hurry."

Natalie moved her hand between Meredith's legs. Meredith pulled her closer, kissing her hard. Natalie groaned, and then lost her breath entirely when Meredith's hand touched her. They moved together, Natalie feeling clumsy but Meredith's cries and kisses showing she didn't seem to mind.

"Natalie."

"I'm right here. With you. Serving the universe."

Meredith kissed her again, and then shuddered, sending vibrations through them both. She slipped away from Natalie to press Natalie's hand against her, jerking. When she finally stilled, gasping for breath, Natalie rolled leisurely onto her. Meredith wrapped her limbs around Natalie. "Thank you."

Natalie kissed her cheek.

"There was something you stopped me from doing earlier."

"Now's good," Natalie said.

"You have to get off me, then." Meredith pushed at her.

"But you feel amazing."

Meredith grinned.

Natalie slid to the side, letting Meredith touch her shoulder and guide her onto her back.

"I love you. I am so sorry about everything."

"Merry."

"I love you so much."

Natalie brought her close for a kiss, and thought she could kiss Meredith forever. Meredith touched her again. Natalie was grateful for Meredith's lips on her breasts. Then her abdomen. Then lower. Natalie groaned and offered herself.

If she was good, if she sacrificed, if she managed to keep everyone she loved alive, she would be rewarded.

Chapter Fifty-Two

"Dear Mommy" was in Beau's blocky lettering. The rest of the letter was Natalie's penmanship. "School is nice. I don't have many friends yet, because people think I'm mean. Natalie says smile more. Smile smile smile."

Meredith studied the smilie faces drawn all over the letter. She showed it to Burdette.

Burdette smiled.

"She says laugh, too, but not at anyone. It's hard. Merry doesn't have many friends either, but he likes his. He's like, cool."

"The like is crossed out," Meredith said.

"Good luck."

Meredith folded the letter and put it in her pocket. The green beans and mashed potatoes on her plate hardly seemed like a good compliment to her letters. Nor did just Burdette. Since Robin had joined them at meals, things were livelier. But Robin was at an appeal hearing.

People came, people went. She couldn't keep track anymore. If a face became familiar, she'd try and remember their name, too.

"Want my roll?" Burdette said.

"Yes."

Burdette held it up. "For your milk."

"Fine."

They swapped.

"Your mind seems elsewhere, girl," Burdette said.

"I'm thinking of home."

"You ain't homesick."

Meredith shook her head. "Just thinking." She ate the roll. "I have to get to the infirmary."

"Can I have the good drugs, Doc?"

Meredith was so used to the question she didn't even acknowledge it. She took her tray to the counter. She'd gotten past her fear of the infirmary and of the demanding patients and the lines between what she could do off-the-books and what she should never do.

Jolene's death hit her hard. There'd been other deaths. Other transports. New rashes and old conditions, HIV shots and pre-natal vitamins.

"It's almost like the outside," she'd told the doctor. "Once I remember they're patients and not~"

"Peers?"

"Yeah." She was glad he'd said peers. Criminals were the furthest thing from her mind.

"I'm sure you have your share of drug-seeking, indigent behavior in the hospital, too, amongst the real emergencies."

"And the thousandth person with the common cold," Meredith said.

"Feeling like death isn't dying. You'd know. So you'll be all ready to go back. When's the parole hearing?"

Meredith hugged herself. "Thursday."

"Natalie coming up?"

"With the kids. She's taking them out of school. I wish she wouldn't."

"Stuff in life more important than school. Almost anything, in fact."

"Says the doctor."

"I blew off a few classes."

"That's reassuring."

"We can't all be perfect, Merry." He squeezed her shoulder. "Your hearing is more important than school. Believe me."

She didn't know what to believe.

Ida let them sit on the picnic table, shoulder to shoulder, trying to keep warm in the unreasonably cold early October, as long as they faced her. She sat at a desk doing paperwork. In her warm concrete room.

Meredith squeezed Natalie's hand. "You didn't have to come. I'm seeing you tomorrow."

"Miss the chance to see you?"

Meredith's cheeks were red from the wind.

"I know routine is important," Natalie said.

"In my life. Not in yours."

"Tell me about it. No two days are the same. Heck, no two visits to Burgaw are the same. That place is definitely not like this place. And every day it's something different with the kids. The bus doesn't come. One of them has an earache. Playdates~they have playdates now~with people who have never heard of you."

"Who are these people?"

"New staff at the hospital moved in with their kids, Beau and Merritt's age. They're brown."

Meredith snorted.

"They're teaching Beau manners. He takes off his shoes at the door now."

"All the better not to kick Hollingsworth so hard."

Natalie nodded. She brought Meredith's bare, chapped hand between hers, rubbing to create friction. She glanced at Ida.

Ida wasn't watching.

She pressed.

Meredith bumped her shoulder.

"Want to go over what you're going to say?" Natalie asked.

"I have no idea what I'm going to say."

"Samson will be there. And me."

"Thank you."

"They'll want to know everything. All the stuff you never thought you'd have to say again. That you thought was private. For your therapist."

Meredith closed her eyes.

"I'll be bringing a letter from the hospital."

"For what?"

"For your future gainful employment."

"Right. What will I make? Minimum wage?"

"Well, not as much as a WalMart worker, but more than KFC."

Meredith put her head on Natalie's shoulder. She opened her eyes. Ida was staring right at her. She straightened.

"So, they'll write down everything you say, and Samson says, and the letter, and whatever questions they ask me, and they'll FedEx it to the Commission."

"What questions will they ask you?"

"What kind of home life you'll have. If you'll have a bed, if there's enough to eat. The basics."

"I hope they don't ask you if you're obnoxious."

Natalie grinned. "There are other options."

"Like what?"

"You could go to a halfway house. Or a group home situation. Or go to Wheeler's or a friend's. Or even live on your own."

"You mean, in an apartment? Or I could kick you out?"

"You might not want to kick me out until you transfer back guardianship of your children, but yes."

"I don't want any other options."

"No?"

Meredith curled her fingers around Natalie's. "I want what I've been dreaming of."

"Okay."

"Okay?"

"We'll do it."

Chapter Fifty-Three

"Dearest Meredith," Natalie's letter started. Meredith had waited until she was in bed to read. "I can't help but see you everywhere. When I'm arguing with the principal~twice already!~when I'm with Luis, or when I'm just in the kitchen, or when I'm alone at night, as I know you are now, reading this, I can't get you out of my mind. You're my imaginary friend. I realize when you come back it won't be the same. But this is better than your absence. It's like I'm one step closer to you. Hurry home soon, or I'm going to rob a bank and get myself thrown in Conrad.

All my love, Natalie."

His suit made him itch. The unfamiliar wool chafed him. Luis shifted in his seat, hoping to pull the fabric away from his skin.

Natalie glanced at him.

He frowned, trying to hold still. The court room was mostly empty. No spectators bothered to come this time. Not even his father. Just the judge, the prosecutor, and the victim's family.

The victims. He scoffed.

"Ants in your pants?"

Luis wondered if a male attorney would be even more of a jerk.

The judge tapped his gavel, signaling the end of a speeding ticket case, and flipped through his day planner. He glanced at the defendant's table. Luis folded his arms.

"The People v. Luis Duarte?" the judge asked.

"Yes, Your Honor." Natalie stood.

"The entered plea is not guilty. Do you wish to change your plea?"

"No, Your Honor."

"Are we hearing on bail?"

"No, Your Honor."

"Change of venue?" He glanced at Jacob Weinstead first.

"I think we're fine, Your Honor."

"Okay. Opening statements are set for three weeks from Tuesday. Ten o'clock. Any discovery?"

"I think we have everything, your Honor."

"Very well." He reached for his gavel.

"Wait, wait," Luis said. He tugged on Natalie's sleeve. Everything was happening so fast.

"Your Honor, can I have a minute to confer with my client?"

"You can."

Natalie sat down.

"I don't want a trial," Luis said.

"You don't?"

"Why aren't they just letting me go? Isn't that what this hearing is for?"

"That's what the last one was for. Luis, they're not going to let you go."

"It was an accident!"

A murmur went through the courtroom. Probably at the parents. Luis was breathing hard. He thought everyone was on the same page with this. At least, him and Natalie.

"Everyone knows it was an accident," Natalie said. Her voice was calm. She put her hand on his shoulder.

But the exchange he just witnessed belied that. "But~"

"It's just whether or not the accident could have been prevented. That's what the trial sorts out."

Luis rubbed his jaw. "Of course it was. If those bitches hadn't cut me off, then~" He couldn't help his voice from rising.

Natalie clamped down on his arm. "Luis. What's rule number one?"

"Don't speak."

She nodded and squeezed his arm. "Of course it was an accident."

He shrugged.

She glanced at the judge, and then stood. "We're ready, Your Honor. Three weeks on Tuesday is good for us."

The judge banged his gavel.

Despite the weeks in jail, the police reports Natalie showed him, the photographs of the two girls, his car~Despite his days being cotton trousers and card games with gangbangers in for pot and coke~he only now, with the sound of wood slamming into wood, felt his life crashing down around him.

"I don't want a trial," he said, knowing he was almost begging.

Natalie stood at his side, holding onto his shoulder until the spots began to recede from his vision.

Meredith woke to pounding at her door, and then it flung open and a horde came through into the tiny cell. She reached for a weapon but of course she had none. She held up *The Boxcar Children* to defend herself from the blows landing on her. Her worst nightmare, every time she was alone in this room, finally realized.

Blows landed. Like rain. Like pillows. And then kisses on her face. Her shoulders. The light was too dim to make out faces but she smelled Siba. And then Robin's distinctive leafiness. Burdette's bleached bone aspects.

Then another nightmare came to her. Maybe this was an orgy. She pushed at them, starting to pray.

"It's your last day," Burdette said against her ear.

She'd been so close. The parole granted, strings pulled, all set.

Jacqui, standing near the doorway, laughed. "So we got you a cake."

Meredith lowered the book. She tried a small smile.

In the dimness, five women smiled back.

"A cake?"

"What are you going to do when you get out of here, Merry?"

"She's going to buy a better Bible."

"I'm never going to turn back," she said.

Burdette snorted. "Good for you."

Chapter Fifty-Four

Meredith did look back, peering at the prison buildings rising above the fence. Natalie leaned against the station wagon, waiting for her. Meredith took a moment. She needed this space and distance from prison to car. She gazed up at the sky.

The sun beat down.

Natalie was the destination. She took another step. She felt lighter. She suddenly wanted to run. She wanted to cry.

She shifted her bundle in her arms and walked swiftly, grinning so much her face hurt. Natalie opened the backseat and Meredith tossed in her stuff, and then turned to Natalie. A foot separated them.

"Do you want to drive?" Natalie held up the car keys.

"Do I want?"

"Do you want to drive?"

Meredith smiled. "Yes. Yes, I do." She hugged Natalie. "I want everything," she said, as Natalie encircled her waist.

"Okay."

"Natalie." Meredith squeezed her tighter. "You smell good."

"It's cinnamon."

Meredith buried her nose in Natalie's neck.

"I stopped and got cider. And stuff. On the way up."

"Natalie." Meredith loosened her grip. "I want to drive."

"Yup."

Meredith stepped back and Natalie opened the driver's side door and then leaned over the door as Meredith settled in. "And," Meredith said.

Natalie raised her eyebrows.

"I'm never kissing you in front of a prison again."

Meredith pulled into her own driveway. She stared at her house. Natalie didn't move. She'd been quiet and tense most of the drive and Meredith didn't question her. She'd had a lot to process and was glad to be left alone with her thoughts.

Remembering how to drive took up her first half hour of concentration. Then it was autumn leaves and open highway all the way down until Goldsboro. Then it was shaded groves and stoplights.

Meredith stared.

A red late-model Camry was in the driveway. "Whose car?"

"Daniel's. He picked the kids up from school today. They're inside. He won't be staying."

"He can."

"But he's not."

Meredith turned off the car. "I'm nervous."

"I understand."

Meredith unbuckled her seatbelt and turned to face Natalie. "Can you, uh."

Natalie met her eyes, unbuckling her seatbelt, too.

"Can you...closer..."

Natalie leaned closer.

"Kiss me?" Meredith asked.

Natalie nodded.

Meredith covered the remaining distance and kissed waiting lips. She closed her eyes. Natalie's mouth dragged across hers, and then puckered to kiss the corner of her mouth.

"Thank you," Meredith said.

"Want to go inside?"

Meredith considered.

"Or, want to kiss me again?"

"Definitely."

Natalie leaned in.

"But inside." Meredith got out of the car.

Natalie rolled back against the seat, smiling.

"Mommy!" Beau ran from the front door. Merritt lingered with Daniel, shy. Natalie got out of the car and went the porch and took his hand.

"Is she here?" Merritt asked.

"She is. She isn't leaving again."

Meredith knelt, hugging Beau to her, and waved Merritt over. He went.

Daniel kissed Natalie's cheek, picked up Suriya's carrier, and went to his car.

"Wait~" Meredith started.

Daniel waved. "Later."

Meredith kissed her children, tears streaming down her face. Their near~ness and warmth contrasted with the cold day, with the cement under her knees~her driveway, her house~and she clung to them, fearing only that she might squeeze them too tightly. She wanted Natalie closer and she didn't want to move.

"Natalie."

"I'll wait."

"Boys, can we go inside?"

They each took one of her hands and pulled her toward the door. Inside she smelled pizza.

"It just came!" Beau said. "We waited until Natalie called us from the road and then Daniel got it." They ran into the kitchen. Plates scraped. The refrigerator slammed.

"You got pizza?" Meredith asked as Natalie closed the door.

"It's a special occasion."

"We can't afford pizza."

"We don't have it every night."

"Is Daniel buying dinners? Because~"

"Merry, can we not fight about money your first night home? Just for tonight? Tomorrow you can yell at me all you want."

"I'm sorry. I'm sorry, it's just~"

"Weird?"

Meredith nodded and went into the kitchen. The kids laid out four plates, each with an identical portion of pizza. Two slices, cut narrowly. Four glasses of water were arranged in the vague vicinity of the plates. The smell of mozzarella was intoxicating. Her mouth watered. She glanced into the liv~ing room.

Too clean. The coffee table had moved and the TV tilted just slightly. She frowned.

"Tomorrow?" Natalie asked.

Meredith closed her eyes. "It's going to be a big adjustment."

"For all of us."

"Sit down, Mommy," Beau said. He looked triumphant as he waved her into the chair at the head of the table.

She sat and glanced up at Natalie.

Natalie squeezed her shoulders.

"Are you going to sit down, Nat?" Merritt asked.

"In a minute. Go ahead."

Merritt bowed his head.

Meredith bowed hers, peeking at Beau out of the corner of her eye. She covered Natalie's hand on her shoulder.

"Thank you, God, for mommy. Thank you so much!" Merritt said. "And thank you for the pizza. And Natalie. And... Beau."

Beau didn't bow his head, but he watched Merritt, and mouthed "Amen" when Merritt said it.

"Amen," Meredith said.

Natalie kissed her hair.

Meredith tugged her lower and said in her ear, "All right, all right. Some things might have changed for the better."

Natalie kissed her temple. "Eat your pizza."

Meredith dozed on the couch. The boys were on the floor, wrapped in blankets, watching Cinderella. Merritt said he liked the mice, but she knew he liked the ball scenes, too. Beau liked the witch. Meredith held Natalie's hand, leaning against her shoulder. The pizza had been exquisitely warm and rich and full of flavors she hadn't tasted in months. So unlike the pizza at prison it was criminal.

Criminal.

She smiled. Then yawned. "We should go to bed."

The thought scared her. She felt like she was in this bubble of love and pizza and Disney, and if she left it, she might end up back in prison. "I don't know if I can sleep."

"No?"

"The noises are all different. The people are all different."

The kitchen behind them was where she killed Vincent. She didn't want to think about it, wasn't trying to, but after so long away the house felt foreign. She was trying to reattach herself.

Natalie shifted, putting her feet up on the coffee table, pulling Meredith back into her arms.

"Natalie."

"Shssh. You get the inside."

Meredith glanced at the boys. Beau leaned back against the couch, his eyes drooping. Merritt was still riveted by the screen.

"When I first moved here," Natalie said, her voice low and calm.

Meredith squirmed, settling on her side, her head on Natalie's chest.

"You told me the boys often slept out here. They liked it best."

Meredith nodded.

Natalie stroked her hair. "This is the family room."

Meredith closed her eyes. She couldn't sleep, but if she listened to Natalie's heartbeat and felt Natalie's arms around her, she could almost be happy.

"Natalie," she said.

"Hm?" Natalie stroked her back, then along her side.

"I love you."

"I love you, too."

"Tomorrow, we need to talk about how much TV the boys are watching."

"Tomorrow. We have all the time in the world to negotiate a settlement."

Meredith slapped Natalie's stomach.

Beau crawled onto the couch and sandwiched himself along Meredith's legs. "Can I stay here?"

"Yes, Beau," Meredith said.

"We've got you trapped. Is this like prison?" Natalie asked.

Meredith tilted her head to kiss Natalie. "No."

Chapter Fifty-Five

Meredith changed into scrubs and pinned her hair back. She wore her old scrubs, the ones that didn't fit anymore. She had a new locker, along the bottom row, eight across from her old one. She'd gone right to her regular spot, hesitating only when she noticed the masking tape reading "Rachel."

Masking tape on her new locker read "Merry" in Magic Marker so fresh she could smell the ink.

Inside she'd found a single cupcake in a small bakery box. Otherwise, there was no special party, no hooplah, just the hospital as normal, with a few of her letters posted to the staff bulletin boards along with advertisements for cheesecake and free kittens and warnings about hand washing.

She stuck her picture in the locker liner. Natalie and the boys in the kitchen. Natalie was leaning against the sink and the boys sitting on the counter on either side of her. If Meredith had been there, she would never have allowed it. She would have been too afraid the boys would fall. But Jake had been there to take the picture and to put them back together.

Natalie wanted real portraits. Real department store, formal suit, fake background portraits. But Meredith had done those with Vincent to send around on the annual Christmas cards to show they were a real family. She preferred the snapshots.

"Hey, you made it," Angel said, coming into the locker room in his street clothes.

"I couldn't wait."

Angel grinned as he dumped his stuff in the locker and took out his scrubs. "I'll show you the ropes. We'll work the same shift for a few days, until you get the hang of it. And then you get the nights."

"Woohoo."

"Do you have a schedule?"

"We'll work it out." She hoped. Underemployment was better than no job at all, and this job, hours or not, was better than Wal-Mart. In Tarpley, she'd be unhireable as a home care nurse, even if it was what she wanted to do. For now, seeing her children a few hours a day would feel like a blessing for a long time. She didn't need more.

Angel pulled on his shirt and made sure his crucifix wasn't showing. "Okay, *chica*, I know you know where most things are, but let me show you the dark recesses where the nurses fear to tread."

"I'm ready."

"To clean up shit? And other hazardous bodily fluids? To take crap from doctors, patients, and nurses? Oh, you ain't ready. But you will be."

"Can't touch the drugs, can't heal the patients. It'll be just like prison." She spoke with bravado, because it wasn't actually true, and Angel nodded in response, but there was a glint in his eyes like he didn't believe her. People probably wouldn't believe her about anything for a while.

"You'll have to tell me what's worse, Merry. Being a convict or an ex-convict."

"So far, no comparison"

Angel showed her the bed rotation, gave her the patient list, and offered to supervise her first sheets and gown changeout.

"I think I've got it," she said.

"Okay. You're starting with the worst patient on the block. I mean~"

"You don't have to change your lingo for me, Angel."

He nodded. "Anyway. It's all downhill from here."

She pushed open the door. "Hi, Mr. Cranston, ready for your bath?"

A string of curses greeted her.

Angel gave her the thumbs up.

She grinned. She was back.

Meredith ate lunch with Wheeler on her second day back at work, when things were starting to feel normal. The tiny cafeteria~a break room with a register~served them whatever the patients were eating, so they settled in for fried eggs and toast and marmalade.

"How's everything, Merry?" Wheeler asked.

"Fine."

He rubbed his jaw and frowned. "How's Natalie?"

"Fine?"

Wheeler took another bite of toast.

Meredith ate in silence, trying to figure out why he'd asked. "You spent a lot of time with her, right?" she asked.

"Dinner once a week. Technically you saw her more."

She nodded. "What was she like?"

"What was she like? Natalie-ish. You know."

Meredith pushed at her plate. "I'm not sure."

"You're not sure? She's the same girl who's been visiting you for months. Things don't change just because~"

"Of course they do. Of course they do. It's tense. It's wonderful, but it's tense. I don't know what to do."

Wheeler tilted his head.

"So why don't you tell me what you invited me to lunch to tell me," Meredith asked.

"Since when are you so perceptive, Merrycakes?"

"I've been in therapy for half a year. People have tells."

"I don't have a tell."

She took his hand. "It's written all over your face."

"I like Nat," he said.

"But?"

"No buts. Don't screw it up, Merry."

Meredith exhaled.

"You trusted her with your children. Don't you trust her with the easy part too?"

"I don't know if~"

"She was strong for you. She took care of you. Every day she held it together. She kept everyone fed and distracted and she walked when it hurt to walk and didn't run back to Charlotte. She had faith, Merry. Not in that part, she hated that part. In this part."

"And I'm grateful. Hank, I don't know what to say to her. I don't know how to say thank you. It feels inadequate, and overwhelming, and like, trite. I can't think of a way to repay her."

He squeezed her hand. "Take care of her. That's all. The way she took care of you."

"She's been running everything without me. She doesn't need me to take care of things."

"Maybe she doesn't need you to. But she wants you to. I'm sure there are some things she wants to give up. Not everything. But you have to share."

Meredith gazed sadly at her eggs.

Wheeler shook her hand. "Merry, remember who you are. Be nurturing, for crying out loud."

"What if she~"

"She's not that complicated a woman. Hug her."

Meredith paced. She didn't want to pace, but she couldn't keep still, not with that woman sitting on her couch, eating cookies Beau and Merritt baked for her. Like she belonged. That~

That social worker.

Natalie shifted pensively and unhappily, sitting on the couch.

Rebecca introduced herself, had been friendly, obviously used to a warmer reception. Meredith tried, but her skin crawled. And now Rebecca had her job information, and her prison records, and she felt utterly exposed.

"Will we lose the food stamps?" Natalie asked.

Meredith froze.

"Don't think so. Not until the guardianship transfers back, which is in process, but it'll take a few months to sort out, since you're still living here and all."

"I'm back. We don't need the food stamps anymore," Meredith said.

Natalie winced.

"I'm sure it's been helping~" Rebecca started.

"We don't need them."

Natalie beckoned and Meredith sat down next to her. Not touching.

"I want them," Natalie said.

Meredith pursed her lips.

"Even with your combined incomes, you're below the threshold. For now. And they're not really combined. Raleigh may recognize your parternship and the local judge may be humoring it, but the federal government doesn't. In fact, it may be easier once you've got custody, since Natalie had... more income."

The words were a punch in the gut. Meredith managed not to scream. She wanted to scream until this woman left her home.

Natalie was nodding along. "Thanks, Rebecca."

Meredith felt light-headed. Nauseous. She forced herself to breathe.

Rebecca tapped at her laptop. "Okay. That's all the information we have on hand. I'm here to help you both take this information and make a budget. Make a plan."

"We don't need~"

Natalie's hand settled onto her leg. "We can't talk about this on our own?" Natalie asked.

"No. We're going to do it today. The three of us. No matter how long it takes. Then when I come back in a month we're going to see how it's progressing. If you're off track. What tweaks need to be made."

"I'm not in prison anymore," Meredith said.

"Meredith. You've never done this before. I've done this a hundred times. I know what will work. It's the easiest path for you," Rebecca said.

"To get where?"

"To get your life back."

Meredith bit her lip until it hurt.

"It'll be good to talk about this. To get everything out in the open," Natalie said.

Meredith hated her a little bit.

"I know something that will make it better," Natalie said. "Rebecca?"

Rebecca nodded.

Natalie shifted until she faced Meredith. "Hey."

Meredith stared at her, trying not to yell.

"I want to adopt the children."

Meredith teetered forward, burying her face in Natalie's chest. Natalie held her. When she could breathe again, she said, "All right. I'll trade food stamps for that."

Rebecca chuckled. "The next hour is going to be terrible, Meredith. But I promise you, you get through that hour, and every one after will be just a little bit easier. Instead of the other way around."

That was the fear deep inside of Meredith. She nodded.

"We're not going to talk about maybes. If you get a promotion, if Natalie gets a full time job again. If the custody arrangement with the Jameisons changes. No expectations. We're going to talk about what you have, right now. And what you can do with it."

"Can we get cable?" Natalie asked.

Meredith shifted closer, holding Natalie close, squeezing her eyes shut, as a stranger dissected her life.

The diner was in the heart of Tarpley, and though Natalie didn't know everyone else sitting in the dim dining room at lunchtime, she suspected they knew her.

"Do you really want to put the county through the expense of a trial? We're poor people here," Weinstead said.

"Really? You're going to appeal to my morality? I used to be a prosecutor too."

Weinstead nodded. "But surely you know you could never win."

"Maybe it's not about winning. Maybe it's about making money throughout a trial, rather than having the well dry up so fast."

"There will be plenty of other cases."

"Not if I don't get anything out of this one. Who would want to hire the woman who got the sheriff's son sent to jail? Shouldn't she have been able to pull strings? Something?"

"Not my problem."

She took a sip of iced tea and glared at him.

He didn't quake. "And the way I see it, it's not really your problem, either. Luis, he's your problem. You can't take this to trial, Ms. Ivans. Even he doesn't want it."

"It's Natalie, and what are you offering?"

"Aggravated felony death, ten years."

"The max? I could go to court and get the max."

"And ask the jury to split hairs? If we went to court I'd go for first degree murder."

Natalie leaned back and gave him an incredulous stare.

"Concurrent?" He asked.

"Darn right it'll be concurrent."

"I'm not letting him go with community service. I have to answer to the families."

"I have to answer to the sheriff."

"We all have to answer to the sheriff. I don't want to get a speeding ticket every time I go through Tarpley."

Natalie shook her head.

"What does Luis say?"

"Luis says he's innocent."

"Maybe in a karmic sense, but not according to the North Carolina General Assembly. Who do you think a jury will side with?"

"I know who a jury will side with." Natalie sighed.

"So, what do you want?"

To go home to my family and hold them close and shut out the world. All the charity in the world was better than this job. "Drop the aggravated, five years, concurrent."

"Okay."

"Okay?"

"It's in line with sentencing guidelines. Maybe a part of me believes in the fluke theory. Every day millions of drunks drive home and arrive safely."

"And every day millions of girls make it to their families unscathed."

"So, we have an unfortunate intersection of fate. Luis Duarte was barely drunk~probably not drastically incapacitated~and those girls were speeding."

Natalie thought of her own police report. She couldn't remember the accident, she would never know if reality reflected the white-washed sheet going to her insurance company, or the demonizing tale the victims were concocting for Luis. "This isn't statistics. A family is ruined forever. Shouldn't Luis be, too?"

"That's not the way justice works."

Victims didn't control the process for a reason. Her own children's grandparents would never stop grieving. A family lost a lifetime of weddings, grandchildren, joking around at holidays and smiling and hugging. They wouldn't have more children. No grandchildren. Irreplaceable. Gone. She couldn't ever see it as meant to be.

"You're right," she said.

"About what, Ms. Ivans?"

"I don't like my job."

Chapter Fifty-Six

"I can do that," Meredith said, as Natalie carried her dishes to the sink. She'd changed after the hospital into jeans and a Wolfpack sweatshirt. Natalie was still dressed in slacks and a blouse from her client meeting and Meredith hated the idea of her splashing the clothes.

"I've got it."

Meredith glanced at the boys, who were in the family room, playing checkers. She got up and went to Natalie. "You cooked."

"What did you think?"

"You're a taco master."

Natalie turned on the sink.

"Really," Meredith said, putting her hands on Natalie's shoulders. "I can do chores."

"You worked all day."

"I won't break."

Natalie stiffened against her.

Meredith bumped Natalie's shoulder with her chin. "Let me take care of this."

"It's~"

"Let me take care of you."

Natalie didn't say anything. She turned off the sink.

Meredith nuzzled her back. "I'm sure readjustment will take a while. But I've got help. I'm dealing."

"I'm dealing, too."

"You're waiting," Meredith said. She risked Natalie's anger. Natalie was tense and unmoving. She kissed Natalie's shoulder.

"I'm being patient," Natalie said.

Meredith attempted to slide her arms around Natalie's waist, but Natalie turned around, facing her.

"Everything's great." Meredith said.

"Impossible."

Meredith cupped Natalie's face in her hands.

Natalie leaned forward until her forehead touched Meredith's.

"Stop waiting," Meredith said.

She tilted her head up, just slightly, and Natalie's lips found hers. The kiss was chaste and sweet and they drew back to glance at the children.

Beau was thinking hard about his next move.

Merritt idly petted Hollingsworth while he waited, posing like a super villain.

Natalie pulled Meredith into the hallway, toward the foyer. Out of sight. She kissed Meredith again, and guided her until Meredith's back was against the wall. Meredith closed her eyes as Natalie kissed her again and again. She wanted this unrestrained passion waking her up, making her want to grind into Natalie's hips already. They'd made love before bed, intense and serious and somewhat tired, avowing their connection, and they'd had playful romps in the afternoon, between shifts, between reality's crashes. But she wanted something to blot out the universe, to make her feel like a sinner, like the first time she'd taken Natalie, against all odds and all common sense.

She worked her way under Natalie's shirt, stroking her back. Natalie's tongue invaded her mouth. Meredith groaned, wanting more. She sucked on Natalie's tongue, hungering for deeper kisses, demanding them. Her hands moved from Natalie's back to her ass, pulling her closer, until her thigh was between Natalie's and she was pinned between her lover and the door. Natalie pushed against her, breaking the kiss and panting deliriously in her ear.

"We should~" Meredith tried to say.

Natalie moved back, taking her wrist and pulling her toward the bedroom at the front of the house.

"The boys."

"We'll listen. We won't go too far."

She shut the bedroom door and resumed her position against Meredith's thigh. Different wall, same shuddering movements. Meredith rubbed Natalie's hips, urging her closer, urging hot kisses against her lips, her cheeks, her neck. When Natalie's teeth found her earlobe, Meredith escalated, pulling Natalie's shirt upward. Natalie complied, lifting her arms, and the shirt fell to the floor and Meredith was unclasping Natalie's bra and slipping her hands underneath. Natalie's lips worried her shoulder. Meredith found the tip of a breast. Natalie pressed the front of her jeans.

A thud sounded in the living room.

"They knocked over the board," Natalie said.

"They have to learn to fight their own battles."

Merritt let out a shrill scream.

Hollingsworth yowled.

"They might break something," Natalie said.

"The precious furniture." Meredith gave Natalie a little push, reaching down to get Natalie's shirt.

Natalie reluctantly opened the door. "Boys?"

"See?" Beau said. "Nat's gonna be pissed at you."

"At you!"

"You let them say 'pissed'?" Meredith asked.

"They think we can't hear them." Natalie pulled on her shirt.

"My children are not very bright." Meredith went into the living room.

Merritt pointed. "Beau cheated."

Beau folded his arms. "You destroyed the proof."

"Well, since checkers is over, let's take a walk while it's still light outside," Natalie said, behind Meredith.

Beau scowled. "I want to play again."

"Are there fireflies?" Merritt asked.

"And frogs."

"And neighbors," Meredith said.

Natalie offered her hand to Beau. He took it.

"A walk, really?" Meredith asked.

"The world awaits."

By the time they made it outside, it was fully dark. They stuck to the sidewalk under the streetlamps. The boys were excited to be out past dark. They strolled to the main road and back, passing dog-walkers who nodded politely and ignored Meredith and Natalie hand-in-hand.

"Did you~" Natalie wasn't sure what she wanted to ask. She didn't know how much of this life was hers, and how much was Meredith's alone.

"Did I do this with Vince?" Meredith shook her head. "The boys were practically babies, Natalie. Everything's new."

Natalie winked.

Meredith pulled her closer. "It's cold out here. You're warm."

Natalie hugged her shoulders and brought her against her chest.

Beau tried to climb a street sign pole.

"We'll never get them to bed," Meredith said.

"Benedryl?"

"Not on your life."

Natalie kissed Meredith, rewarded when Meredith squeezed her waist.

"Let's go back," Merritt said.

Natalie nodded.

"Okay, boys, whoever gets there first gets to pick which book we read tonight."

Beau took off running.

Merritt threaded his fingers through Natalie's.

Meredith took her other hand and they walked leisurely back toward the house. "What do you think he's going to pick?"

Merritt shrugged.

"*Jack and the Beanstalk*. He likes triumph," Natalie said.

When they got to the house, Beau was already in bed under the covers, grinning smugly.

Natalie sat on his bed. "Breath test."

He breathed on her, showing white teeth.

"Minty. Did you pee?"

"I wanted to be first."

"You were. Go pee and then pick your story."

Beau climbed out of bed.

Meredith got Merritt ready, and then tapped the top of Natalie's head. "I'm starting to like the way you do things."

Natalie grinned.

Beau came back and rifled through his books and produced *Jack and the Beanstalk*.

"What do I win?" Natalie asked.

"You'll find out later."

As soon as they closed the door to the boys' room, Natalie wanted to push Meredith against a wall again. The rush of arousal reawakening made her see spots. She leaned against the door and asked, "Should I take a shower?"

"No." Meredith shook her head.

"I'm sweaty."

Meredith walked toward their bedroom, glancing over her shoulder. "You've been wearing that blouse ever since I got home. Almost."

Natalie nodded.

"I want to take it off you."

Meredith shut the door of their bedroom, and then locked it.

Natalie took her by the arms and pulled her into a kiss. Meredith stumbled, clutching her sides, trying to hold onto the touch of her lips. Instead of the wall they landed on the bed, Natalie over Meredith. She took kiss after kiss as her weight held Meredith down. Meredith squirmed until her leg was between Natalie's. She groaned and then pursued the kiss. Natalie's arms were by her head, holding her up, and she couldn't last for long.

"Sit up," Meredith said.

Natalie pushed herself up with her arms, glad of the relief straightening brought her muscles. She straddled Meredith's hips, ignoring the twinge in her thigh.

"Is this okay?" Meredith asked.

"I'm fine."

"Maybe you should take some ibuprofen before~"

"Before we have sex? Merry."

"I'm a nurse."

"I'm not waiting," Natalie said.

"You're impatient?" Meredith asked, reaching for the hem of Natalie's blouse.

"What do you think?"

Meredith slid her hands underneath the blouse. "We could make this go faster."

Natalie twisted her hips, pressing down on Meredith.

Meredith closed her eyes. Her hands stilled.

"Who's impatient now?"

"You can't do that."

Natalie kept moving. "Why not?"

"I want to~"

"What?"

Meredith pressed her fingers into Natalie's sides. "I want to focus."

Natalie stilled, but when Meredith's eyes fluttered open, offered a mock pout. "You told me I didn't have to be patient."

"Please?"

The word was so sweetly and simply offered Natalie didn't move. Meredith cupped Natalie's breasts, squeezing, feeling their weight, before drawing back to lift Natalie's blouse.

"Help."

Natalie pulled the blouse off. Sitting over Meredith gave her a strange sense of power. She felt almost weightless, but it was Meredith's hands, back on her breasts, Meredith's heat under her, holding her imprisoned. Meredith unclasped her bra and pulled the straps down her arms. Naked from the waist up, facing Meredith's intense gaze of lust and scrutiny, Natalie was paralyzed.

Meredith cupped her cheek. "Natalie."

"Like what you see?"

"You're all I'll ever see. For the rest of our lives." Meredith traced Natalie's lips.

Lightness overcame Natalie, even as the ache in her leg intensified. "I think we should switch positions," she said, just as Meredith's free hand settled on her pants.

"You do?"

Natalie rolled off, sprawling onto her back. "I do."

Meredith snorted, but got to her knees. "Can I?" She tugged at the waistband of Natalie's pants.

"Yes."

Then Natalie was naked and Meredith reached for the fly of her own jeans.

"Let me."

"You're over there."

"Come closer."

Meredith knelt over Natalie, kissing her lightly, nipping and laughing despite Natalie's hand on the back of her head. Natalie shivered as Meredith's cotton shirt brushed against her nipples. But it wasn't exactly what she wanted. She reached for Meredith's jeans and undid the top button. Meredith's lips grazed her temple. Natalie pulled down the zipper and the lips stilled. Natalie worked her hand inside. Meredith would be wet, she would be warm—

"Natalie."

Meredith fell to her side, kicking off her jeans, taking her panties off. Then she reached for Natalie, kissing her. Gone was the teasing, replaced by the heat stoked in the early evening. Natalie pulled Meredith on top of her. Meredith moved up, so they were closer together, heat echoing heat, but it wasn't enough.

They were suspended in their desire, kissing, moving together, but no closer to the edge. A part of Natalie wanted to stay, to feel Meredith against her, where they were linked.

But a bigger part of her wanted to jump off the cliff. She urged Meredith's hips higher, just as Meredith's mouth moved from her lips to her cheek to her throat, preparing a descent.

"Nat~"

"I can't wait anymore."

"Whatever you want." Meredith pulled off her shirt. The words were mumbled, distracted, as Meredith kissed the side of her breast, but a surge went through Natalie. "Higher," she said, pulling at Meredith's hips.

"What?"

"Above me."

Without a word, Meredith moved up, kneeling above Natalie so her hips were over Natalie's head and her hands were steadied in the pillow. Natalie grabbed her and brought her to her mouth before Meredith changed her mind.

"God," Meredith said, nearly collapsing.

Natalie stroked, hungry for the taste, for more of it, for more of Meredith. Each pass of her tongue consumed her. She spent time thrusting her tongue into Meredith to see how far she could go. Walls squeezed at her, even as heat and pressure beckoned. But she was neglecting the rest of Meredith, and Meredith's frustrated cries reached her ears. She shifted, bringing Meredith into her mouth, not using her tongue, just breathing and sucking. Meredith bucked.

Natalie squeezed her ass.

Meredith bucked again, trying to grind down, finding only softness when she needed friction.

Natalie stroked a lightning path all the way along her, flicking into the curve of her ass before dipping once more into her, and then along folds, through neatly trimmed curls.

"Natalie," Meredith said, pleading.

At the first firm brush of Natalie's tongue, Meredith jerked up. Natalie held her hips until she settled again, shifting until the stroking was just where she needed it. She rolled her hips and they found a rhythm together, pushing Meredith steadily higher until she sat back, her hand pulling Natalie's hair, her feet digging into Natalie's arms.

She cried out. Natalie tasted the orgasm as Meredith shuddered over her. She wished she could see Meredith's face, and the flush of her skin.

Meredith gasped, kneeling on her hands and knees.

Natalie closed her eyes, smiling, until Meredith slid down and kissed her, cleaning her cheeks, tickling her chin.

"Whatever you want?" Meredith asked, and then kissed her ear.

"I can't get enough of you."

Meredith settled with her head on Natalie's chest. Her breathing was still harsh, but she was still, except for her hand moving up and down Natalie's side. Over her arm. Along her breast. Natalie savored the taste left. Though her senses were on fire and the light stroking of Meredith's hand almost painful, she was content to lie with Meredith wrapped around her and contemplate the rest of her life. She had no thoughts beyond their bed and the things they could do.

"You're burning," Meredith said.

"I want you."

"You want me to do what?" Meredith asked. She pressed a kiss between Natalie's breasts, over her heart.

Natalie shivered. "I want you to... anything."

"I can do anything." Meredith rolled into a crouch. She blew across Natalie's nipple.

"Anything's good."

"No requests?" Meredith hovered above her breast.

"Don't make me~"

Meredith gave a lick, and then met her gaze expectantly.

"~Move," Natalie said.

Meredith chuckled.

Natalie gathered her strength and arched upward. Meredith captured her nipple, sucking with firm but not painful pressure. A steady response after a teasing one was such a relief, so graciously arousing, that Natalie only cradled her head. For a while there was only the suckling, the intent exploration by Meredith to see what kinds of pressure and friction did what, to explore how hard her nipple could get before her groans became constant. She switched nipples. The second one already stiffened in anticipation, in kinship, and Natalie yelped at the first touch of Meredith's mouth.

Meredith kissed her way down Natalie's stomach, leaving Natalie's chest exposed again. "Merry," she called. The desire intensified in every moment. Being kissed became a form of torture.

Meredith reached her hip. She glanced up.

"Come kiss me."

"I was going to~"

"Here." Natalie touched her lips. She puckered.

Meredith made a show of sighing and crawling back up to kiss Natalie's mouth. "This can't possibly be~"

"I love your kisses."

"But~"

"Closer." Natalie rolled her head so Meredith's ear was near her lips. "Fuck me."

"Natalie Ivans."

"Hurry."

Meredith's fingers crept over Natalie's thigh. Natalie arched, wanting to offer all of herself to the touch, feeling flayed open. Meredith's fingers stilled.

"Stay with me, Nat."

"Oh, I'm here."

"Here." Meredith waited until Natalie's eyes met hers, with Meredith on her side, propped up on an elbow while her other hand pressed into Natalie's thigh. At Natalie's focused attention, Meredith kissed her and slipped her fingers in at the same time.

Natalie seized and deepened the kiss. She thrust her tongue into Meredith's mouth as Meredith's fingers penetrated her, not soothing the ache but increasing it, until Natalie felt like she was boiling. She sought a more comfortable niche rather than release and then it was there, Meredith sliding into her and the kisses raining down on her.

"This," she said.

"Yeah?"

"Just for a moment."

This was bliss. Natalie turned her head. The kisses became nuzzles against her neck. She wasn't still~She trembled with arousal, must have been flushed~She just existed.

Then she pulled Meredith closer. Meredith responded, swiping her thumb across Natalie, precisely. She just knew.

Fireworks. Swimming dark spots. Coming apart must have seemed like a guttural convulsion from Meredith's point of view but Natalie shattered into light. As the orgasm subsided Meredith's fingers, strong inside her, chafed, bringing her back to reality with the slight discomfort of pain, of the cold room, of smelling sex.

She chuckled.

"Hey, Nat."

Natalie reached down and guided Meredith's fingers from her, and then rolled over into her arms. She adjusted, Meredith, ever the nurse, helping her until her limbs were correctly arranged for minimal aggravation.

"Now we should shower," Meredith said, rubbing her back with damp fingers.

"Nope."

"Change the sheets?"

Natalie shook her head.

"Go again?"

"In a minute."

"Okay." Meredith kissed her temple.

"You're not going to call me lazy?"

"Natalie, what you just did~"

"What you just did to me."

"Mm. It was beautiful. Absolutely beautiful. You can get away with so much if that's how you respond to me."

"Some of us saved ourselves. Didn't go willy nilly in prison."

"Thank you," Meredith said, close to her ear. "For saving yourself."

Natalie grinned, eyes closed, and kissed her collarbone.

"By the way," Meredith said, as Natalie drifted off.

"Mm?"

"We're changing churches."

Chapter Fifty-Seven

Natalie settled into the empty house, glad to be back from Burgaw. She'd explained to Luis he'd have one more hearing, and he'd have to listen to the victims speak, and he would have to give an elocution. She offered to draft it for him--she'd brought down a brief paragraph--and he'd seemed to listen. No motivations, no feelings. Just facts. This is what happened, not what does it mean. Neither she nor Luis nor anyone knew what it meant, anyway. He'd fought her about the five years, but not hard. Just for show. A part of him wanted to go away, to escape this life.

Meredith was at the hospital for training, but soon she would start the night shift. The lowest on the orderly totem pole. She had as much prestige as a janitor, and though she didn't complain, it depressed Natalie. Meredith's reinstatement could come quickly, within a couple of months, or it might drag out six or more. She had to pay $25, which the hospital was covering, and get twenty hours of re-training, which was going to be more complicated.

The orderly position was open at the hospital. A nurse's position wasn't.

So much was uncertain. But Natalie had a new case. Another DUI, two counties away where they lacked an attorney. Weinstead recommended her over calling up an ambulance chaser from Wilmington or Goldsboro, since Hoyle was on a cruise.

Clarice was on Facebook, posting pictures of Patrick and the office staff at the Halloween party. Natalie shook her head, bringing the laptop into her lap. The heat eased the soreness in her leg and hip.

Just as she was typing up a comment to Patrick's pirate hat, her cell phone rang.

She opened it, remembering to say, "Natalie Ivans, Attorney-at-Law."

"Howdy, Ms. Ivans," came a friendly, if tense male voice. "My name is Fred Jerrad. Sheriff Duarte gave us your name."

"You need a lawyer, sir?"

"My boy. They brought him in tonight. Say he, uh."

"Yes, sir?" She'd pushed the laptop off her lap and was digging around for her briefcase.

"He attacked a girl. Now no one got hurt, but they're saying, I don't know."

"He at the jail now?"

"Yes, ma'am."

"I'll head over. Is this through the public defender's office?"

"No, ma'am. We do all right for ourselves. I don't understand."

"Understand what?"

"They're saying he attacked her, uh, sexually. Some high school student. He doesn't get close to many girls, it's not his way, but we would have– We don't even know how he even met her."

Her heart sank. She clutched the phone.

"They even took her to the hospital. They came and found him this morning at the house and put those cuffs on him. The Arab said we could see him as soon as you got here."

She tried to swallow the lump in her throat. She'd been intending to cook dinner for her family. Pot roast. She was going to help the boys with their homework, as kindergarten and cute as it was. She was going to make love to Meredith and read children's stories and write snarky comments on walls.

"I'll be there soon, all right, Mr. Jerrad?"

"Thank you. Please clear this mess up for us."

She closed the phone.

The church Meredith chose was the Eternal Light Assembly, which didn't even have "Church" in the name.

"It's the black church," Natalie said.

"Don't even."

"I only mean they may not want us here. I mean, it could be private. I know the Orthodox Church didn't want anyone just wandering in. I mean, not to worship. If they were hungry, sure."

Meredith folded her arms.

"We can try it," Natalie said, submitting, getting the children dressed in suits. She'd been tempted to complain that it wasn't her fault Meredith had been run out of every other Protestant church in town, even the Methodists, and the Catholic Church was perfectly fine.

"Everything's in Spanish," Meredith said.

"Works for me."

"I want to get something out of it."

"So learn Spanish."

"I want to take Communion. And I'm not converting. Or confessing. And no, we're not driving down to Wilmington for Jake's church. I don't care if Buddhist leaders are called Reverends, too."

"Talk about a girl who needs to find some Zen."

"One more quip and no ice cream for you."

Natalie sulked, but went where Meredith wanted her to go. She'd been guiltily relieved to see a diverse crowd. Some were in interracial couples. But no couples, that she could tell, were gay. Many of the churchgoers didn't seem to be from Tarpley proper, like the Jameisons, but from the outlying farms and even smaller towns. Natalie resisted clinging to Meredith's hand as they followed the crowd through the door.

Merritt pointed. "There's Joseph, from school. Can I go say hi?"

"Yes, Merritt. Stay in sight."

Merritt nearly bolted off, and then reached back and poked Beau. "Coming?"

Beau followed.

"Aw," Natalie said.

"Maybe they have a day care."

"I can take care of our children."

"I mean, for the service."

"Oh."

Meredith smiled. Natalie took her hand.

They went back the next Sunday. Despite Angel's and Natalie's protestations the Catholic Church offered better offender support services.

"Because they're the Catholic Church. And this is just some guy and his wife who've been called to preach," Meredith said.

"Well, exactly," Natalie said.

"I'm not going anywhere I don't fit in. And my children don't fit in."

The service started after the first hymn and the pastor, George Waters, instead of walking to the pulpit, came between the pews.

"Brothers and sisters. We have a murderer in our midst." He gazed right at Meredith.

Natalie tensed.

He pointed right at Meredith. "A murderer!"

Beau squeaked. Natalie pulled him into her lap and put her arm around Merritt's shoulders.

Meredith had gone completely white. If she told Natalie to bolt, she'd bolt. If she told the kids to scream, they'd scream.

"She reminds us evil is in all of us. Not in 'them.' Not some bad neighbor. Or some bad driver. In us. In her. In all of us."

A tear appeared at the corner of Meredith's eye. Natalie wanted to reach for her but she couldn't move. If she reacted, the boys would react. Merritt shivered beside her.

"She is a mother, and she has helped many of us in this town. We all know her. And she is a murderer."

If he said that word one more time, Natalie was going to choke.

"We are all her victims. Her children, growing up without their father. His friends and family. Those who would have benefited from his labors. Our very country, for he was a soldier."

Natalie hung her head.

"But there is another part to the equation," Waters said. "There is God's part. And I don't presume to speak for God, but I can guess." He was at the entrance to Meredith's pew. Only the wooden railing separated them. "I can guess," he said, his voice bellowing in the tiny chapel.

Meredith met his eyes.

"God forgives you," he said.

"Did you hear that?" He looked around, making eye contact with a dozen people before going back to Meredith. "God forgives you."

Meredith trembled.

He touched her cheek. "Sister. God forgives you."

Meredith's tears trickled over his fingers.

"Let no one accost this woman! God has forgiven her. And if God can forgive her for the most heinous of crimes~Then God can forgive you, too. God loves you just as much as he loves this woman. If you open your hearts to him. If you have a personal relationship with God, He will forgive you." He let go of Meredith. "Will you stand with me?"

She swallowed and gave a tiny nod. He guided her up, holding her elbow, and then embraced her. She cried in his arms. Beau cried, too, his head buried in Natalie's shoulder. Merritt watched, wide-eyed.

Waters addressed his audience. "God forgives her. Do we forgive her?"

"I forgive her," voices murmured in the crowd. "I forgive her." The sound got louder and hands touched Meredith's back, and Natalie's shoulder, and Merritt's head.

"I forgive her."

About the Author

C. E. Case lives in Northern Virginia. *The Riches of Mercy* is her second novel. Her first, *Little Disquietude*, came out in 2011 and is available worldwide.